As if he had willed it, she tilted her head toward the sky. The moonlight seeped into the folds of the hood, and finally he saw her clearly.

Her eyes were pale. Green? Blue? He could not be sure. Perchance they were a shade of tarnished silver, exotic, unusual. In any case they were pale and intriguing.

There was a deep, pervading sorrow in her expression. She was not old by any measure, but a single tear on her soft cheek made him think she no longer believed the poet's version of her life.

Did she follow the dictates of courtly love? Had her heart had been given to a man who was not her husband? A dozen such questions hammered at Desmond's mind as he studied her pale face. And as he memorized her features, it hit him that *this* was the maiden of his dreams. She was young; she was beautiful. An innocent sorrow filled her face. Here was the kind of woman he had aspired to wed. Here was a virginal maiden he could teach the pleasures of bed sport while she came to love him. She would be devoted, submissive . . . she would be perfect.

"Are you wed?" Desmond heard himself ask.

Long, wispy lashes swept down over those fascinating pale eyes. "I am not wed now and shall never be. . . ."

Dear Readers,

In July of 1999, we launched the Ballad line with four new series, and each month since then we've presented both new and continuing stories set everywhere from medieval England to the American West—the kind of passionate, romantic stories you love best, written by the most gifted authors. At the back of each book, we'll tell you when you can find subsequent books in the series that have captured your heart.

This month, the fabulous Willa Hix returns to historical romance with her new series, *The Golden Door,* which follows the adventures of a pair of half siblings new to America during its lush Gilded Age. In **Cheek to Cheek,** a young woman fleeing an arranged marriage finds herself faced with the possibility of real love—with the man who has hired her as his aging mother's companion. Next up, ever-talented Linda Lea Castle continues the triumphant saga of *The Vaudrys* with **Surrender the Stars,** as King Henry III commands a loyal subject to wed a mysterious woman who may be his doom—or his heart's destiny.

Reader favorite Kathryn Hockett sweeps us back to the turbulent era of *The Vikings* with the **Conqueror,** a warrior sworn to vengeance . . . but tempted by desire. Finally, Cherie Claire concludes the lushly atmospheric story of *The Acadians* with **Delphine,** as fate reunites a dashing smuggler with the girl who once professed to love him—but who has become a woman with wealth, obligations—and desires—of her own. Enjoy!

Kate Duffy
Editorial Director

The Vaundrys

SURRENDER THE STARS

Linda Lea Castle

ZEBRA BOOKS
Kensington Publishing Corp.
http://www.kensingtonbooks.com

To readers and writers and dreamers so bright,
A tale of lords, ladies, lovers and knights . . .

And for the people in my life who give me love acceptance, and forgiveness on a daily basis, you all know who you are. I love and appreciate and thank God for you.

The Vaudrys—Orphaned as infants, Rowanne was raised as a hostage, Desmond as a pampered lord, and Lochlyn as a Scottish border reiver. The ogham stone prophecy says the Vaudrys rise from the dead and are destined to love only once. . . .

Prologue

Sevenoaks Castle,
Kent, England

Aislinn unplaited her hair and pulled the carved ivory comb through the softly crimped tresses. Firelight winked on a tangle, turning her red hair the hue of flame as she worked the teeth of the comb through the snarl. Once she had not minded her hair; now she hated it. It was sinful hair, Satan's favorite according to the wagging tongues of Sevenoaks. She had never been accused of being a minion of Satan or of being cursed by her hair until she came to Sevenoaks as a virgin bride of fourteen. Now she longed to cover her head to hide it, but tonight was her wedding night—again.

Her new husband would expect her to come to the marriage bed with her hair unbound and her ardor high. She knew well what was expected of her on this night. After all, she had performed this ritual four times in five years. Three other times she had bathed and perfumed her body, combed out her hair, and waited inside the bed curtains in her private solar for her lord husband to take his rights upon her body and consummate their union.

But that had never happened.

Aislinn at nineteen was still an untouched virgin, much wedded but never bedded. Now, at her advanced age she was soon approaching the time when she would not be desirable as a wife or a woman.

The Poison Flower, the castle harpies called her. The village drabs, the miller, the castle folk, they acted as though she didn't know about the hateful name. They thought she didn't know, or mayhap they believed Aislinn did not bleed and grieve like other women.

But she did know about the name and the rumors because Giles told her all. He was her only friend.

When her first husband succumbed to brain fever on the very night of their wedding, Aislinn believed it was only the old battle wound on his temple, as Giles had told her. He prayed with her, comforted her and explained how such an old wound could kill slowly. After all, Giles was well skilled in healing arts, and Theron was a battle-scarred warrior.

When her second husband died of a bloody flux, Aislinn tried to believe it was just coincidence. Mayhap there had been some ill humor in the food. Mayhap the honey mead had soured as Giles suggested, yet no other man or woman of Sevenoaks sickened after eating and drinking that eve. Only her new husband had died on his wedding night, like Theron before him.

The rumors had grown like mushrooms after a rain. But Giles had managed to convince her 'twas some weakness of the man's own bowels, or some brush with ill humors on his way to meet Aislinn at Sevenoaks.

Giles told her about the terrible stories and the name she had been given. *Poison Flower . . .*

But when her third husband clutched at his throat and collapsed across their marriage bed with his eyes bulging and his tongue swelling within his mouth, Aislinn no longer believed Giles. She did not argue with her dear cousin—he was a man of God, he had his faith to cling to—but she no longer scoffed at the whispered chants and secret talismans he said her people used to ward off evil. She was chatelaine of the keep, but the people feared and hated her.

Though never openly challenged, Giles kept her informed of the gossip. She had wicked hair, the color of hell's flames. To wed her was to invite death. On and on went the litany of her sins. She was accursed; all the castle folk believed it.

Now she readied herself for her latest husband. He would be here anon. The fourth righteous man, Bartholomew.

"Prithee, Lord, let him be hale and hearty," Aislinn beseeched. "He is not an unpleasant man to look upon, and though not young, Bartholomew is vigorous and strong. His body is still hard with muscle. There was a glint of youthful anticipation and lust in his eyes as we said prayers on the steps of the chapel. If it be your will, oh Lord, let Bartholomew of Lewes bed me and live."

She turned to the outer door of her chamber after a light knock of warning. But 'twas not Bartholomew of Lewes who stood pale and shaken in the archway. It was her best loved cousin, Giles, the abbot of Tunbridge Wells. He fingered the heavy jeweled crucifix that hung about his neck.

"Dear Aislinn, it grieves me to be the one to tell you: it has happened again. While having a last cup of mead with his men, your husband, Bartholomew of Lewes, gasped and went to God."

Aislinn heard her own scream of denial, and then the world around her collapsed into a sea of black.

One

" 'Tis said Lackland's heir is a dullard who has no liking for sport," Coy remarked. "I know not why he would sponsor such as this tourney."

"But his own son, Edward, is a shrewd tactician. Either he persuaded his sire to host the games, or the reports of Henry's soft nature are much exaggerated." Desmond shifted his weight on the back of his destrier, Brume.

Baron Desmond Vaudry du Luc sat near the field of honor and waited his turn in the lists. He and Coy of Brambourg had been together through years of Crusade and the strange occurrences that brought their former leader, Brandt le Revenant, to marry Desmond's long-lost sister, Rowanne Vaudry. After Desmond inherited the du Luc fortune and titles, Coy traveled with him, dividing their time between tourneys and the responsibilities of Mereworth Keep in the south. 'Struth, they did much wenching and hawking on the way.

"Perchance the king thought a tourney would cool the hot-blooded barons who grumble and plot against the throne," Desmond said.

"Aye, 'tis true there is much discontent. I have seen many being swayed by the younger de Montfort's wily charms. I am well pleased to be here on the field and far from court. I have heard it rumored that the king will soon raise taxes to support his son Edmond's claim to Sicily's crown."

" 'Twill not help the king to venture so much on a second son," Desmond warned.

"Aye, but 'twill aid de Montfort if the plan angers the barons."

Desmond nodded and lapsed into silence. He would have had little to say on the matter of the fractious barons even if the dust had not become a thick choking cloud that made talking difficult. The bright red and purple of the king's pavilion had succumbed to the grit. The rich, bold colors proclaiming his exalted station were now the same dusty brown as the plain tunics of the peasants gathered beyond the green to watch the spectacle of combat and savor a glimpse of their king.

A pair of mounted knights, their horses brightly caparisoned, thundered toward each other. The destriers' hooves churned up the dusty field, tossing dirt into the breeze. Lances met with a crash. One knight fell with a metallic clatter as wood splintered against metal armor. With the breaking of that lance, the contest was won. A loud cheer went up through the royal pavilion and the crowd of villeins.

"Your turn to win another horse and armor, Desmond. None are your equal among any of the challengers, so I will not waste my breath to wish you good fortune." Coy patted the flank of Desmond's gray stallion. Brume answered the kindly gesture by trying to kick Coy's mount.

"Foul-tempered beast," Coy declared with a half-hearted snarl. "And me the one who makes sure you have the cleanest quarters, the clearest water."

Desmond laughed. "He means naught by it. 'Tis only that his blood is up for the joust. And if you are seeing to Brume, then what, pray tell, is my new squire doing?"

"I but helped the lad so he could turn your armor in a barrel of sand." Coy winked. "And a fine job he did; your glorious reflection is like to blind your opponent."

"Then if I am victorious, 'twill be Gwillem I thank for it." Desmond chuckled and dropped his chin. The top plate of his helm slid smoothly down to cover his eyes and the bottom of his face. Now he viewed the field through metal louvers.

A trumpet's blast rent the calm air. Desmond did not have to put his spurs to Brume's sides. The stallion reared and thundered toward the green. He ran fast and true, at precisely the correct time changing his lead to shift his direction ever so slightly to the right. Years of practice and schooling made the move second nature to the great warhorse. Now the opponent's lance would slide down the armor plate and lose its strength. Desmond positioned his own lance above his hip and braced himself for the impact.

A roar went up, echoing inside Desmond's hot, airless helm, when his opponent was unhorsed with an explosion of wood against metal. He reined Brume around and came to a prancing stop before the king's pavilion. Coy was waiting nearby, the stubble of his dark beard split by a wide grin. Gwillem ran up to take the jousting lance from Desmond's gauntleted hands.

"Well done," King Henry bellowed. "Victorious in three out of five runs. You are truly the best knight of this tourney, du Luc. By my beard, your winnings will be two mounts with full armor and a bag of coin, but know 'twould not be so if Prince Edward were here. The prince is the best horseman and warrior in all of England and France."

"I have heard his praises sung far and wide, sire. I consider myself fortunate not to have faced him this day," Desmond agreed.

"Well spoken, du Luc, and true. You are as sharp of

wit as you are skilled at combat. Come, join us for a cooling draft of wine." The king waved his hand and ewers of wine appeared. "Ah, here is my jester. Sit, refresh yourself, and enjoy my fool's wit."

Desmond's armor creaked from his sollertes to his helm as he stepped down off Brume. He tugged the helm up, relishing the cool draft of dusty air. Metal clanged with each tread up the wooden steps to the king's dais. It was cooler beneath the covering of woven cloth. Desmond took the goblet of wine and watched the monarch's favorite jester, Pounce, hop and gambol before the pavilion.

While the king was being entertained, a bevy of peasants flooded onto the field of honor. The rope dividing the jousting field was taken down and the debris of broken armor and shattered lances cleared away. Padded targets painted with bull's-eyes were wheeled onto the field. Archers strung their longbows and tossed pinches of dirt into the air to test the direction of the wind. Near the kitchens of Combwell Priory, folk gathered to witness the next challenge of skill.

Barrows and stalls had been hastily assembled. Merchants and craftsmen hawked beer, ale, meat pies, and sharp-honed blades between contests. The thrill of competition had lifted spirits among high and lowborn. Lordlings dug coin from their purses and wagered on their favorites. Ladies flirted and gave bright bits of cloth as tokens to the competitors they admired.

Desmond quaffed deeply of the fine wine the king offered, glad his part in the tourney was over, content with his winnings of two fine destriers, stout armor, and gold. He and Coy would set off for Mereworth on the morrow with his riches in tow.

"Pounce is the kingdom's greatest fool." The king tossed a coin into the air. The jester neatly snatched it without missing a single step of his exuberant dance.

"My son has no liking for his humor. Prince Edward is a fine warrior, but he has little affection for jests and entertainment. He is driven and determined to restore much of what my father lost."

Desmond was saved from having to reply to that remark when the wiry jester tumbled and strutted before the pavilion. His voice was loud when he said, "Our good liege Henry the Third was as wise on the day he was born as he is today." Pounce juggled balls and trilled on a whistle carved from a reed as he did an airborne flip, letting the impact of his words settle over the crowd of nobles.

Desmond frowned at the jester. It was obvious Henry took the remark to mean he had been born with uncanny wisdom, but 'twas well known throughout the land that Pounce meant Henry was as simple today as a newborn infant. The sarcasm was oft repeated over jackmugs of ale and beer in common tapping rooms from Essex to Chester. Desmond could well imagine hot-blooded Prince Edward taking offense at the fool's words. It was a wonder that Pounce's head was still firmly attached to his neck, for Edward was quick to defend his father and the crown he would someday wear.

"Do you tarry awhile yet here at Combwell, du Luc?" the king asked Desmond when Pounce scampered away. "Or are you off to another tourney?"

"On the morrow Coy of Brambourg and I depart for Mereworth. I have been much gone of late, and though my steward, Galen, is more than capable, I have a yearning to be home for a time."

"Then you must sit with me at high table tonight, du Luc. As the champion of the day, you have earned the right to sit above the salt."

"You do me great honor, sire." Desmond nodded.

"Tell me, du Luc, do you favor spiced fowl? Even now my cook prepares a dish of sweetened blackbirds for my pleasure." The king spoke with childlike delight and smacked his lips in anticipation.

"Ah, I see they will be starting the archery anon. In the meantime, I must have a word with the good abbot I see coming our way." Henry gestured toward Giles, the abbot of Tunbridge Wells, striding toward the pavilion. The churchman's brow was deeply furrowed.

Desmond had heard much about the man who had risen from humble beginnings to become a major power within the Church. He was rumored to be so rich that he now made loans rivaling the Jewish merchants of London. Gossip had the abbot personally financing several Crusades to retake Jerusalem.

"Abbot, you look much troubled, and rightfully so if my advisors are to be believed. Tell me, what shall we do about your much-wedded cousin?" King Henry waved the churchman toward an empty seat. "The woman vexes me sorely."

The abbot of Tunbridge Wells bowed his head and swept the edges of his cloak away as he sat down. "Alas, sire, she is blameless, I swear upon my soul. She wants only to marry and breed worthy subjects."

"But she is neither wedded or breeding, is she?" The gaze of the king was sharp and intent as a falcon's.

"Nay, sire, she is without husband or issue. But has any woman ever endured so much sorrow?"

"Or so much good fortune, one might ask." The king's aristocratic brows rose. "With each wedding her portion grows. My advisors marvel at her ability to be widowed. Some suggest she has a hand in the mysterious deaths."

"The rumors are thick as fleas on a hound, sire, but 'struth, Aislinn has benefited little. Since each good man has gone to God without issue and left no other heir, the greater portion of their estates have been forfeited to the crown. Indeed, sire, one might say *England* has benefitted most by her tragic sorrows."

Silence hung as thick as the dust from the tourney. The king smiled coldly.

His voice was low and brittle as flint. "Except for those bequests which went to the Church?"

The abbot extended his gloved hands, palms up in a gesture of supplication. "Small tokens meant to ease the poor souls into heaven. They were no more than trifling amounts of little consequence. My poor cousin is distraught. 'Tis God's will that the aging men she wedded were destined to die."

"Perchance the maid herself is the victim of dark forces."

"Sire, I swear as a man of God—"

The king lifted his hand to silence the churchman. "Do not grow nettles, Abbot. I am inclined to believe your assurances that your cousin is not using some skill to rid herself of a troublesome lord. After all, you are a devout man, and if the king of England cannot put his faith into the abbot of Tunbridge Wells, then what will become of us all?"

"As you say, sire." Giles fingered the thick, ornate gold crucifix hanging on his neck. Desmond's curiosity about the mysterious events was aroused.

The king heaved a great, dramatic sigh. He was slouched in his chair with his fine furs padding the wood and making him resemble a drowsy lion.

"She needs must have a husband. I have done my best by betrothing her to goodly men of character, and yet none have lasted beyond the bedding. Is she such a rough ride? Is bedding the wench such a loathsome task that none survive the ordeal? Or is it a mortal chore that only one in the bloom of youth can withstand?"

The abbot's face colored hotly. Desmond wondered if the churchman was so devout a man, so chaste and pure that he should be mortified to hear Henry's ribald remark, or was there some truth to the tale? Was she an insatiable minx that sucked life from the men she wedded and bedded? Who was this harpy that killed husbands and so vexed the king?

"Mayhap I have erred by sending her milksops and old men. I need to send her a vigorous stallion of England, a man so hale, hearty, and randy that he will ride her well, plow her deep, and plant his seed. Aye, that would quiet the wagging tongues who call your cousin Poison Flower, eh?"

"Poison Flower, indeed!" The abbot snorted indignantly. "Cruel jibes and rumors."

"I see the name doth offend you," Henry said, casting a sly glance at the abbot from under his thick lashes.

"My cousin Aislinn has done her duty, sire. It wounds me to see her slandered."

"She will not have done her duty until she breeds—often. The crown needs heirs, knights, and warriors, not corpses." Henry's eyes narrowed.

"As you say, sire; forgive my hasty tongue. It is only that it grieves me to see her tormented by the venomous tongues of uncharitable trulls."

"This broth of rumors and death will not do. I will send her a man that will survive the rigors of her bedchamber. I will send a true flower of English manhood—a man reputed to be a great lover, a worthy champion to do his duty and beget an heir."

"Do you speak of Prince Edward?" the abbot asked, his eyes widening.

King Henry studied the abbot for a moment. "Nay, though my son could no doubt tame the vixen. I speak of another man who is known to be a gallant knight with the heart of a troubadour. He has forfeited the fines owing to him from his rebellious villeins for marrying without his permission. He has been known to pay the tax himself when a serf begs permission to leave the boundaries of his land and journey elsewhere to ply a trade."

The king looked straight at Desmond. "Tales of his largesse have reached the royal chamber and caused some grumbling in the households of other barons who are not so generous or willing to see peasants wedded for love."

Desmond felt the crawl of flesh at the nape of his neck. During the last year at Mereworth, he had listened to tearful declarations of love and had been swayed to pay a handful of fines in the name of true passion. Surely the king had not heard of such quidding amounts. It was not Desmond's own fate that was suddenly hanging by a gossamer thread.

Or was it?

"What say you, Desmond Vaudry du Luc? As a man who believes in the whims of the heart, what say you about a poor maid who cannot keep a man alive long enough to get her with child?"

"Sire?" Desmond swallowed hard. An invisible noose tightened around his bachelor's neck. "I have no opinion since I do not know the maid."

"Ah, I see. Then tell me your thoughts on taking a wife, du Luc. Surely you have an opinion on that matter."

"Sire, I fear I am not the stuff of which a good husband is crafted. I like hawking, wenching, and drinking ale with my fellows. I enjoy riding my horse at breakneck speed, sharing my bedchamber with willing wenches, and stag hunting with my favorite hounds. I am by nature too reckless and selfish to be a proper mate to any woman."

King Henry narrowed his Plantagenet gaze on Desmond. People might say he was dim of wit, but Desmond saw a keen intelligence and a flash of arrogant annoyance in those eyes that were said to be much like his shrewd grandmother's, the famous Eleanor of Aquitaine.

"Then as your king it is my responsibility to settle you and keep you safe from your own reckless nature. What say you to taking a wife of my choosing?"

"Sire, I am your man in all things," Desmond said weakly.

"You have heard our converse just now. What say you about a maid that goes through husbands quicker than a sheep through the stile? How many at last count, Giles?" Henry asked.

"Four."

Henry made a fist and slapped it into his other palm. "Four stouthearted knights of the realm have not lasted the bedding of that wench. I would have it otherwise, good Desmond. I shall send her a man proven to be strong of limb and brave of heart."

Desmond opened his mouth at the very moment a royal herald blew his trumpet. The king's attention was momentarily shifted to the archers below.

"Ah, the archers are assembling on the north green," King Henry said. "There are no finer bowmen in the world."

The abbot of Tunbridge Wells leaned over the cloth-draped edge of the pavilion to get a better view. His tonsure was covered with a patina of dust, making his brown hair look grizzled. Afternoon sun played on the crucifix.

"I fancy putting up a wager on the best archer in the land—that yeoman in green, I think." The king rose, gathering his robes about him. He gave a royal wave to the assembled nobles. "Who among you will take my wager?"

When none responded, he glared at the nobles. "Come, are you all milksops? Who will take my wager?"

"I will, sire," the abbot said.

"Ah, good, good—gaming sweetens the outcome. Now, what keeps my blackbird pie? Does my favorite cook not know I am hungered?" Henry's question required no reply. A page scurried off toward the priory kitchens. The lad skirted the targets smoothly and disappeared into a stone building where plumes of smoke belched from the stone chimney caps.

"They are loosing their first arrows, sire," the abbot said. "I will take the bearded man on the end. He has the arms of an archer."

"So ho, that one is a true shooter. He hit the bull's eye three out of five at Nottinghamshire. But I believe my green lad will best him." The king stood up to get a better view.

Desmond watched volley after volley of black-fletched arrows fly toward the straw-filled targets at the far end of the green. The King's attention was focused solely on the competition of archery. Perchance the question of Desmond's unmarried state would be forgotten. He prayed he could slip away to the serenity of Mereworth before the monarch's sharp, aristocratic gaze fell upon him again.

"Desmond Vaudry du Luc, are you familiar with Sevenoaks Keep? 'Tis near to your own barony of Mereworth, is it not?" Henry asked mildly.

Too late. Desmond felt like a mouse beneath the gaze of a falcon.

"Aye, Sevenoaks is but a few leagues away—though I have never been there. I know it by reputation only."

"Then you will journey to Sevenoaks and learn of it intimately. Study the lay of the land; see to the harvests and upkeep of the holding. Do your utmost to see all is as it should be, for 'twill now be your responsibility. You will take to wife the wench Aislinn, known as the Poison Flower. What say you, Vaudry Du Luc?"

Desmond had it on his tongue to claim some malady of mind or weakness of limb that would make him unfit for such a boon. But at the moment the words were forming, the door of the priory kitchen swung open. A herald blew his horn. Liveried pages carrying trays of steaming pies appeared. Bringing up the rear of the procession was the king's cook, carrying a huge covered pie. Steam drifted from slots cut into the crust.

"Ah, my favorite cook appears with my sweet black-bird pie," King Henry said with a hearty laugh. "And about time. I trow I am hungered greatly."

Another volley of arrows sliced the sky, a few landing here and there. A stray arrow hit the cook. The fletched shaft protruded from his chest. Wide-eyed, slack-mouthed, he went to his knees like a heart-wounded stag. For a moment, he remained on his knees; then he toppled forward. His face went straight into the steaming pie.

"By the Holy Rood!" King Henry stamped his feet. His eyes went round with shock and rage. "Who loosed that arrow?" His roar caused men to tremble and wring their hands.

" 'Tis impossible to say, sire, all the arrows are fletched in the same manner with black feathers today. 'Tis the way of doing things at competitions to ensure all have an even chance at victory," a frantic herald explained.

Servants swarmed to the cook. He and the pie were both declared beyond help.

"By my beard, someone will pay. My pie is ruined, my favorite cook lies dead." The king glowered toward the archers, his lips curling into a snarl of rage. "One man among them is guilty. I will have him now. Bring him."

"But sire—"

"Bring him."

"But we cannot know who among them is guilty, sire," a royal advisor reasoned. "Only one among them loosed the fatal arrow, but we have no way to know the hand that nocked it."

Henry's eyes narrowed down to slits. "Then round up every archer. If you cannot say who is guilty or innocent then behead them all." Henry sat down in his chair, the picture of abject misery and total power.

"But sire, there are three hundred and fifteen archers listed for today—"

"Three hundred and fifteen, you say?" He rubbed his jaw thoughtfully.

"Aye, sire." The advisor let out a sigh of relief.

"Then I suggest you find more axmen to see the task done quickly." The king turned to Desmond, his eyes hard as quarry stone. Behind Henry's back, archers were beginning to be herded up like dogs. Then a makeshift block, a large tree stump, was found. Two hooded axmen stood ready, their rippled, sinewy arms gleaming in the bright sunshine. Desmond wondered if they were part of the royal cortege, brought along in case of such an emergency.

"I will have your answer, du Luc. Will you do your king's bidding and wed the lady Aislinn of Sevenoaks, known as the Poison Flower?"

Two dull thunks echoed across the green. A pair of heads rolled onto the bloody earth. Within minutes, another thunk of ax blade sounded. A second pair of heads rolled away.

The bile rose in Desmond's throat at the sight of the butchery. "I say 'tis better wed than dead, sire. I will leave for Sevenoaks Castle anon."

Two

Aislinn paced the tiled floor of her well-peopled solar and tried to calm herself. She had sent Giles to speak with the king on her behalf. She hoped that with Giles's aid, the king would be persuaded to let her remain unwed. She had instructed Giles to offer Henry a heavy tax, or even a fine if necessary, for her to avoid another wedding. A messenger had come to tell her that Giles was on his way back to Sevenoaks, but the courier gave no hint of success or failure—if he even knew the king's decision.

Now she walked and prayed and hoped that the king had been swayed by her cousin's pleas and offer of coin.

"I shall not wed again. No matter if the king's mind is changed or nay, I shall not wed," Aislinn said aloud, realizing too late that her words had drawn the attention of the castle women working with needle and distaff in her warm, bright solar. One woman's eyes and hands were busy, but her ears were as pricked as those of any woodland fox. Aislinn had banished all her personal maids and tiring women to the lower hall for sleeping many fortnights ago, but by day they seemed to gather around her like gadflies.

Was that disapproval she saw puckering the woman's lips? Did she share a look of conspiracy with another woman spinning brown wool into yarn? Aislinn was convinced they were there to gather fodder for the gossip mill below stairs. By speaking aloud she had provided them with a plum: she openly spoke of defying the king. The malicious drabs could add treason to her long list of sins. In clutches of two they leaned their heads together and whispered.

Poison Flower. Did she hear it or imagine it? Aislinn's shredded patience and tolerance snapped like a dry twig.

"Why do you look at me thus?" Aislinn blinked back the hot burn of tears. She recognized the cruel and knowing glint in their eyes. "Think you I do not hear what is whispered outside my door? Think you I do not know you brand me wicked and call me unnatural? Do you imagine I am not stung by your ridicule? Or do you think my hateful red hair shields me from the venom of your words?"

One of the drabs' cheeks flamed red, and Aislinn took a small measure of satisfaction at having hit the mark squarely with at least one among the group. If only she could find a way to permanently silence all the sharp, wagging tongues. . . . With a meow, her pet untangled himself from the thick furs within the curtained bed, momentarily drawing her eyes and her attention.

"Ah, Pointisbright." Aislinn picked up the ginger tomcat, stroking his soft fur. The spinner's eyes were round with fear. At any moment, Aislinn expected her to begin uttering prayers of protection from evil.

"Go. Leave me. I do not wish to look upon your faces again this day or any other. Find another place to spin and sew and spread your vile lies. You are all banished from my sight—forever."

The women gathered their wool and scuttled to the doorway, murmuring prayers and apologies in their wake. Only when the thick studded oak door was shut tight and barred did Aislinn release the breath she had been holding.

"Oh, Pointisbright, I know I should have held my

tongue. By nooning there will be a story that I caused fire to dance and you to speak. Would that you were a wizard's wicked minion so that I might pour out my heart to you and have you work your magic. But there is no pleasant ending to my woes. Each day I see the castle folk look at me with greater fear and loathing. I have no other friend in all the world but you and Giles."

She walked to the deep-chiseled window casing. Expensive pieces of cut glass were held within an intricate web of lead. The window glass had been a gift from Theron, her first husband, upon their betrothal. At fourteen Theron had seemed bigger than life, a fearless warrior who had gone on Crusade and furnished his home with mementos of battles won and the rich trappings of acquired wealth. She had been mesmerized by his daring and the life he offered her as chatelaine of his keep.

He had shown her intriguing secret passages built into the walls of Sevenoaks, secrets that only they shared. For a fortnight before their wedding, he had happily revealed sliding panels and hinted that after the bedding he would reveal a most wondrous treasure to her. But the treasure of becoming a woman and wife had never been hers.

"Oh, Theron, I miss your kindness. The castle folk did not fear me when you yet lived. I looked forward to learning the secrets you held, but now I care not."

Her zest for discovery had been buried with him. Three more dead husbands had truly siphoned off her enthusiasm for life. Now her days were endless hours of loneliness. The only peace she found came in the night, under the stars.

Aislinn ran the tip of her finger over the smooth, cold surface of the window. The lovely glass Theron had installed in their private solars, fragile though it was, had lasted longer than the man and his promises of protection. Her own reflection stared back at her now, pale and thin, with the hated cloud of red curls.

"Oh, Lord, what can I do to live as other women live? What atonement can I make? What prayers can I say?"

But the Lord did not answer; instead the grind of wood and rope announced the raising of the portcullis. Giles entered the bailey, with twenty armored guards from Sevenoaks as his tail. Their mounts were lathered and wet from hard riding. Giles glanced up, their gazes locked through the clear glass of the window. Without being told, Aislinn knew why he had ridden to Sevenoaks as if the hounds of hell followed.

The king has condemned another man to wed me. Another man must forfeit his life.

"The day is bright and fair, Desmond. You are richer since the tourney. How can you wear such a dark scowl?" Coy inquired cheerfully as they trotted their mounts side by side on the king's road with the remainder of their group trailing behind. Gillyflowers and ox-eye daisies sprouted with wild abandon. It was a perfect spring, the kind that troubadours admired and all good Englishmen treasure.

"Enjoy the spring if you can, but do not ask me to do the same. You are not journeying to be shackled to some old crone, four times widowed, an insatiable harpy that sucks the marrow and life from her husbands' bones," Desmond said sullenly.

"Is this true, Desmond? You have said little about the king's choice for you. Is she old and ugly?" Coy lifted his brows. "Did the king say she is long past the bloom of youth?"

Desmond shrugged within his armor. The heavy gambeson and padded tunic were hot, but lawlessness plagued the kingdom, and no traveler with his wits would go about the countryside unarmed or unescorted.

"I dared not interrupt the king while he was tallying

heads on the green. I had no desire to add my own blood to the archers' by being foolhardy enough to inquire about the woman's looks. A woman four times widowed must be old enough to be my own mother."

Coy laughed heartily. "Many men have made a fine life with a handsome older woman. What truly vexes you?"

Desmond shot him a quelling gaze. "It has been in my mind to have a union like my adoptive parents. Lady Alys was younger than Basil. She doted on him, adored and pampered him. I have hoped to avoid wedding for a time and then take a young, fertile maid to wife—not a widow who has been soured by other husbands."

"Ah, so you want an infant that you may train to spoil you." Coy shook his head. "You are a vainglorious creature."

"How can you make merry over my misery?"

"Desmond, I hardly think—" Coy began.

"Nay. Speak to me no more on this subject since you offer only cruel jests. Make yourself useful and ride back to see how my squire fares."

Coy raised his brows but he did not leave. He rode silently beside Desmond with an expression of bemusement on his swarthy face.

Desmond was too much in ill humors to banter with his friend. Whether Coy agreed or not, Desmond had neatly avoided marriage for good reason. It was a fine plan he had. Many of the most agreeable households he knew of were made up of settled knights and submissive, cooperative young wives. It was well known that as a woman aged she became less inclined to see reason. Desmond had hoped to breed a castle full of strong sons and die before his wife reached that stage of stubbornness. But Henry had killed his hope, ruined his plans.

He had no choice. He was honor-bound by his monarch's will, so he would take to wife a sharp-tongued shrew who had buried four men.

But he would not like it.

The king's will was final and, if disobeyed, fatal. Desmond was powerless to change his fate, and with the death of his favorite cook, Henry's fine Plantagenet temper was roused. Only a fool would gainsay Henry on any matter for at least twelve months, and only then if the king's favorite cook had been replaced and his cooking skills included spicing blackbirds.

"I am doomed, and all because of a dead cook and a thrice-damned blackbird pie. Has any knight's fate ever been soured by so foolish a reason? Would that I had never attended the tourney. Go, Coy. Make yourself useful," Desmond said with a weary sigh. "See if Gwillem fares well with the new mounts. That big black has a wild eye."

Coy turned his head and glanced at the entourage following. "The lad looks well enough."

Desmond glared at his friend-in-arms. "I could have done as much as that, Coy. Gwillem is new and green. I would have you offer him your experience. Should he be having difficulty with the two stallions won in the list, 'twould be a boon if you were at his side to assist him. Surely I can expect this small boon from my oldest friend."

Coy rolled his eyes. "By Saint Cuthbert, I can see there will be no peace for any of us on this journey. I shall be glad to speak with Gwillem, for I trow his converse is sweeter than yours. I grow weary of your self-pity." Coy neatly wheeled his mount and dropped back to speak with Desmond's new squire. The boy was an eager lad and had both horses well in hand, riding one and leading the other. He was dwarfed by the size of the destriers, but the determined line of his mouth revealed Gwillem was going to give a good account of himself or die in the trying.

"Morn, Gwillem."

"Good morn, Sir Coy." Gwillem kept his eyes on the road ahead as he spoke.

"How fare you, lad?"

"I am well. Is aught amiss? Sir Desmond looks greener than a seven-day-old fish; have I done aught to vex him?"

Coy smiled at the youth's eagerness to please Desmond. It was obvious he thought the man hung the moon. "Nay, lad, you are not the reason for his ill humors. He is not pleased to take a wife by the king's command."

"I cannot fault him, Sir Coy. There was much talk in the stables of the woman the king has chosen. The Poison Flower, they called her. Four men have been ordered by the king to wed her."

Poison. The word rattled in Coy's head like stones in an empty bucket. Perchance Desmond was despondent over the upcoming deed for more reason than simply the bride's advanced age and her widowhood. Was he keeping the truth from Coy to shield him?

"Tell me what you have heard, lad." Coy's suspicion was roused. He glanced at Desmond, marking the defeated posture, the long face. Moments ago, his friend's misery was amusing, but now with Gwillem's words, Coy was no longer laughing.

"I have heard the lady kills any who wed her," Gwillem said simply.

"Why poison a husband when the king will only find her another?" Coy mused aloud. "Not even a highborn woman could expect mercy from Henry. And yet poison is a woman's weapon."

"Aye, my lord, I have heard the same. A man will use a knife and a dagger, but a woman will use a brew," Gwillem said with a wisdom beyond his years.

"Gwillem, do you love your lord Desmond well?" Coy asked, a plan forming in his mind.

The boy's head snapped around. His eyes were wide. "Aye, Sir Coy. He didn't care that I am slighter than most lads, he allowed me to become his squire." Hero worship rang in Gwillem's voice. "He is the finest knight in all of England. Besides you, my lord."

Coy grinned at the lad's attempt to be politic. "Then you would do a service for your lord? A service that may well put you at risk?"

The lad straightened his back and drew himself up to his full height. He was still woefully small on the back of the well-muscled war-horse. "I stand ready, Sir Coy."

"Good lad. Now take heed. Trust no man, woman, or child with what I am about to say. When we arrive at Sevenoaks Castle, you and I must keep a sharp eye on Baron Desmond. It will be necessary that one of us be with our lord at any hour before he eats or drinks."

"Before he eats or drinks? Do you fear the Poison Flower will try and kill Baron Desmond?" Gwillem's young face pinched in alarm.

Coy leaned near and lowered his voice. "Men have died at Sevenoaks Keep. If the rumors be true and the lady the source, it will be up to you and me, if you have the steel, to foil the intrigue. We will taste all that is given to Desmond and if there be intent to harm him, our own deaths will peal out the deed and warn him of it."

"I will be proud to serve Baron Desmond," Gwillem said boldly, but all the color drained from his young cheeks. His freckles were dark against the chalky whiteness of his flesh.

"I only pray if his new bride is the one behind it that I have the opportunity to slit the wench's throat with my own dagger," Coy said coldly.

* * *

"I will not do it, Giles. No inducement will force me to the altar again." Aislinn choked on her unshed tears. Pointisbright was curled on the bed, licking his paws, oblivious to the pain in her heart.

"It will not be an inducement but punishment the king will wield. He is not in a mood to have you gainsay him," Giles, the abbot of Tunbridge Wells, warned ominously.

"I will not."

"To refuse the king means the ax."

"I care not, Giles. I will go to my own grave gladly before I bury another husband. If another man dies, I will surely be openly accused of practicing black arts and set to burn. Death for me either way."

"Dear Aislinn, I will not let that happen; you have my oath upon it. I will not let you be persecuted. Would that I had the power to free you from Henry's grasp, but the king has spoken. After the carnage at Combwell Priory, you would do well to obey."

"Giles, I cannot allow the king's blindness to send another man to his death. I have to halt this curse," she cried.

"There is no curse, Aislinn." Giles's tone was impatient. "There are only the vicious rumors."

"How can you say that when four men lie dead? The people of Sevenoaks say I am cursed; you have told me of the horrible stories they tell about me. After the death of four men, I needs must believe them."

"Ah, Aislinn, do not allow the superstitious peasants of Sevenoaks to worry you." He crossed the solar and gently laid a reassuring hand upon her arm. "The men you wedded died of reasons having nothing to do with any curse. You must not allow yourself to think you were the cause. I have told you time and again, they were old and battle-scarred."

"Yes, but Giles, you have heard the talk. You have told me the folk of Sevenoaks say I have cursed red hair." She stared into Giles's kind face. "I would gladly be bald as a hen's egg if I could live as other women live."

"Aislinn. Poor innocent Aislinn. You have suffered much." He folded her in his comforting arms. She did not realize she was crying until he captured a tear on the end of his finger and gifted her with a sympathetic smile.

"Come. Weep no more. Let us have a cup of ale and some bread. You look as if you haven't eaten in days."

"If I sup in the great hall the bread sours in my belly. I cannot ignore the stares and fear in the people's eyes. I have ordered my maids away, and now my meals are brought to my chamber."

"And do you eat alone in your chamber?" Giles asked.

"Nay, I cannot." She shook her head. "I cannot eat, Giles. I am in too much turmoil over the king's decision."

"This nooning I will be at your side. We will break bread and laugh and decide what must be done to prepare you, for there is no way you can disobey the king and live, Aislinn. I love you too well to see you toss your life away. You will obey the king and marry once again. We will pray it is for the last time."

Three

Desmond looked up at the thick mural towers and rounded crenellated barbican of Sevenoaks Keep with a mingling of dread and admiration. He was here to claim a bride that he neither knew nor wanted. He was about to sacrifice his freedom on the altar of wedded servitude to a woman far too old to become the submissive, pliant wife he had always planned on taking.

It was not a pleasant thought.

And yet the keep was a plum. It was constructed of honey colored limestone, well designed and finely fitted. Men walked the battlements and scanned the visitors with hard, shrewd eyes.

Sevenoaks was a mighty fortress, a keep any knight would be proud to call his own.

While Desmond sat astride Brume and waited for the wall guard to raise the portcullis, a thick cloud passed over the afternoon sun. The small hairs along his neck stood on end.

Were the deep shadows an omen?

He grimaced at the thought. His intended bride was probably old, wizened, wrinkled, and as hard as granite. She undoubtedly would not fawn over him as his lady mother had done with Basil. It would be foolish to think she would bathe him, coddle him with his favorite foods, rub his back, and see to his comforts. If she had ever been so inclined, it was inevitable that she had ceased to do so with each successive husband.

"And as the fifth husband, I will be lucky to get a tepid ewer of water for washing on my wedding night," Desmond grumbled to himself. Of course, he could take a mistress. He could find one sweet and simple, but that would not solve his problem, for she could not see to his comforts in his own chamber. And his father had always warned that two women were twice as demanding as one. All knights learned early that women required more up-keep than a well-trained destrier and yet gave only half the satisfaction.

"Baron Desmond, we have been awaiting your arrival," a burly man-at-arms shouted as Desmond scowled at the keep.

"Did the king send word of my coming?" Desmond called back.

"Nay, the abbot of Tunbridge Wells arrived this morn. He bid us be alert and welcome Baron Desmond Vaudry du Luc."

Desmond's party trotted over the cobbled entrance and under the thick, powerfully built gatehouse. A glance overhead revealed a murder hole and hidden arrow ports. Sevenoaks might be a jewel to behold, but it had been built with defense in mind. These stout walls could keep foes out.

"And the unwilling within," Desmond muttered. "Many a fortress serves as a man's own prison." He felt as if his hide were shrinking upon his bones as the port-cullis was lowered behind him.

Within minutes a strong contingent of men surrounded the new arrivals. Pages and servants directed Desmond's entourage to the mews, and the stables.

"We have been told you are to wed Aislinn, widow of our good master Theron, may God protect his bones," the man-at-arms said with genuine enthusiasm. "We have welcomed three good and true knights here to wed her since Lord Theron's passing. The abbot has prayed them into the ground the morn after the solemnizing ceremony. I pray to the saints you will fare better than those men before you."

Desmond digested the man's words while a chill marched up his spine. With every eye upon him, he had the uneasy sensation of being measured for his burial shroud.

"I will say a prayer for your health and long life, sir. You, there, take that cow to the outer byre," he shouted to a boy tugging a milk cow along.

"Where is the mistress of Sevenoaks? She should be the one to cry welcome to her betrothed." The man was still focused on the cow when the abbot of Tunbridge Wells swept across the bailey, waving a jewel-encrusted hand exuberantly as he trotted forward.

"Baron du Luc, you have come at last." Giles clasped Desmond's forearm. "I have alerted the kitchens, the castle cooks are preparing a feast in your honor. A new cask of wine has been brought up from the cellar. Or would a bath be more to your liking? Sevenoaks boasts many garderobes and a private lord's chamber unlike any in England. I have kept the solitary key to the door under my own protection until your arrival."

When he paused to inhale, Desmond interrupted. "Abbot, your mount must have been winged to have beaten us here."

The churchman blinked. "Nay, I rode but an ordinary beast. Perhaps your reticence about the coming wedding made you set a pace slower than usual?" Giles arched a brow in open speculation. "You seemed little pleased with the king's wishes when last I saw you."

Desmond's temper flared, but he managed to keep his expression bland. "The blood staining the green dimmed my pleasure, but make no mistake, Abbot, I am the king's man in all things. It is his will I shall marry Aislinn, and so I shall. Where is she? I would meet the chatelaine of Sevenoaks anon."

The abbot wrung his bejeweled hands and suddenly looked stricken. Desmond did not miss how quickly the man's moods could shift. "Alas, she is in her chamber."

"Does she sicken, or is she of a mind to defy the king?" Desmond had no liking for subtlety. He cast an uneasy eye about the keep. Though he could not prove it, he had the feeling a hundred pairs of eyes were drilling holes into his armor. Was it his own conflicting feelings about the upcoming wedding, or was there some ill humor that dwelled within the thick walls of Sevenoaks?

"I fear she is but sick of heart. Aislinn is still overwrought by the death of her fourth husband, Sir Bartholomew of Lewes. She begs your indulgence and prays you will allow her to remain within her chamber— for a time. She has every intention of doing the king's bidding, but begs for a short respite so she may mourn properly." The abbot looked beseechingly into Desmond's eyes.

Desmond was touched by the abbot's obvious affection for his aging kinswoman, and by her devotion to a man who had been her husband for only a matter of hours. Even if she was a crusty old crone too set in her ways, her request spoke well of her. And though Desmond was loath to admit it even to himself, a surge of relief spilled through his belly. The meeting with his betrothed was postponed for a short while. Henry had ordered them wed, and wed they would be. But even a Plantagenant in full-blown rage would surely not deprive a woman a bit of grieving time.

"I will give her time to mourn. She may also use the time to accustom herself to the notion of another wedding. Until then, she may keep herself as she pleases. Pray relay my message to her, Abbot."

"Gramercy, Baron. You are a kind and generous man. I will deliver the message to Aislinn myself. After I see her I will make certain the lord's solar is in readiness. We will raise a cup together at tonight's feast in your honor." The abbot turned and swept across the bailey toward the main tower of the keep, his dark robes fluttering behind him like the wings of a great bird.

And when he disappeared into the strong stone keep, Desmond realized he had not asked for the key the abbot had mentioned. He would have to see his chamber later, after the feast—after he had made a quick inspection of Sevenoaks.

Aislinn stood at her window and watched darkness creep over the curtain wall. When the shadows were long, she covered her head with a length of dark cloth and bound the hated red curls tightly at her nape.

The full, large cloak concealed her body, and the hood covered most of her face. She would never be recognized as the chatelaine of Sevenoaks even if any should blunder into her secret world.

Aislinn barred the door of her chamber with a thick oaken plank. She put another log across the firedogs beneath the conical chimney and stoked up the glowing coals. Orange flames licked at the seasoned wood. The chamber would remain warm for hours.

"Come Pointisbright. 'Tis time." The cat looked up at her with yellow, marquise-shaped eyes. She scooped him up in her arms, and his ginger body was soon invisible within the folds of her cloak. The rough roll of his satisfied purr vibrated her hands.

She moved to the large wooden cupboard that dominated one entire wall of her solar. The hidden iron ring was cold and solid in her hand. She turned it one full circle. With little more than a whisper, a carved panel slid open. She stepped up into the huge, empty recess of the cupboard. When she turned another ring inside, the door shut behind her.

"Come you lazy puss. Tonight you may walk." She set Pointisbright down; he meowed and fell into step beside her. The corridor of stone was dimly lit by candles stuck into iron holders ten feet apart. They illuminated a dusty passageway of hewn rock. It beckoned to her—that secret world where she found her only solace.

Desmond sat at the head table with Coy at his side. Rush lamps and tallow torches mounted on iron spikes stained the blush of limestone with gray plumes of smoke. It was a gracious room with many high-arched windows along the upper walls. Behind the dais and great table was a lush tapestry. The evocative hunting scene had drawn Desmond's eye and admiration when he entered. Sevenoaks was built to withstand siege, but it did not lack in comforts, riches, or the latest conveniences in castle construction.

" 'Tis a rich holding you have been given," Coy remarked. "I trow the minstrel strumming in yon corner is skilled as any in Henry's court."

"His pock-faced fellow trills well on that ivory flute as well."

"Aye. It has been years since Theron of Sevenoaks went to God, and yet this keep shows no ill effects. The seneschal must be a man with skill," Coy observed.

"Or the chatelaine." Desmond had an image of a stern faced virago who ran Sevenoaks with precision. She would not be the kind of woman to humble herself for her lord's pleasure.

"Mayhap. Look you, no hound treads through this hall. The bulrushes are no more than a sennight old."

Desmond found himself becoming more melancholy.

If Aislinn was responsible for the well-ordered dwelling, then she had done a fine job as each new lord came, died, and was buried beneath the chapel slabs. Definitely not a woman with a soft, pliant spirit.

Serving wenches and young boys brought trenchers of meat, distracting Desmond from his assessment of the hall. Ewers of wine were filled from a tapped oaken cask at the far end of the hall. The keg was presided over by a stern-faced tapman with sharp eyes. Every drop would be accounted for, Desmond had no doubt. For good or ill, this demesne was soon to be his. He found himself oddly proud of it and at the same time wished his bride-to-be were not so efficient. He would give much to gain a young, inexperienced maid that he could school in castle management and bed sport.

But it was not to be. He reached for his tankard, wishing to drown his disappointment with wine.

"I have a great thirst this eve," Coy said when Desmond's hand closed over nothing but air.

"So it would seem, my friend," Desmond said. "You have developed a strong liking for the grape."

"Sevenoaks boasts a fine cellar, if this is an example." Coy laughed, tipping Desmond's own cup to his lips and drinking.

"Are you so hungry that you must eat from my trencher and drink from my cup as well as your own?" Desmond asked.

Coy laughed and snagged a bit of meat from Desmond's hollowed-out bread bowl.

"I trow the journey has made me overhungry." He swallowed quickly, the brawn going down his gullet whole.

"So I see."

As soon as a serving wench topped off Desmond's cup, Coy snatched it up and drank from it again.

"Coy, that is my wine cup you quaff from—again," Desmond said with a frown.

"Oh, so it is, Desmond. My apologies. But I have taken only a small sip," Coy said and placed the cup back in its place. "There is no harm done. Drink."

Desmond shook his head. Coy was nobly born to the Brambourgs of Northumberland. He was not a mannerless lout. This behavior was no doubt due to fatigue and the day's journey.

"Since you are thirsting, you may have all in my cup. My appetite has fled. I have an aching head and want nothing more than to be done with this meal." Desmond had endured the castle folk's curious study of him all evening and now he was weary from it. They all smiled, but their eyes gave him so much silent pity, he was loath to look at one more face. It was as though they observed him on his funeral pyre. And yet not one among them seemed to think the empty chair on his other side—the chair where their mistress should be—was unusual in the least.

Did Aislinn often keep herself absent from the hall?

"Matters are not right in this keep," Coy grumbled, giving voice to Desmond's own troubled thoughts. "I see something akin to fear in the eyes of the castle folk, and I have heard stories."

"What do you hear?" Desmond wondered if it was his arrival that had unsettled them. Or was there more—something Henry did not mention? He had instructed Desmond to inspect the keep and put all to rights. Mayhap that was his royal way of hinting at some deeper problem.

"I have heard . . ." Coy continued as he took a bite of a small yellow apple set before Desmond. He put the rest of the apple back on the wooden platter. ". . . that the lady of the castle is feared as a practicer of lethal brews and potions. Some say she even has a shapeshifter that aids her with her sorcery."

"It is their own lady they fear, not me?" Desmond leaned his chin on his palm and listened.

"You are welcomed, but 'tis obvious they pity you. They believe you are not long for this world."

"What causes such feelings among these people?" Desmond mused aloud. "Has the death of four men so stricken them, or is there more we do not yet know?"

Coy shrugged. "The rumor heard at the Priory of Combwell was that Aislinn is wicked. Gwillem heard it mentioned she has hair the color of flame—devil's hair, they call it. The proof of their fear is the four strong men who now lie 'neath the chapel floor."

"Humph. Red hair wicked? I never heard as much. Many maids have red hair." Desmond snorted. "If the wench is as old as I suspect, then I trow she uses herbs and dyes to maintain the illusion of youth. Her peculiar red hair color is probably no more than the result of advanced age, vanity, and a poor decoction of dye which has turned her hair an unnatural shade of crimson. I fear the king has ordered me to bed a crone." Desmond sighed in abject misery.

"She is probably so ugly that mounting her caused the men to welcome an early death." The thought of a toothless, wrinkled wench who had a yen for active bed sport was so repulsive that Desmond shot up from his chair.

Coy could not help but laugh at Desmond's description. He sputtered, nearly choking on the hastily chewed bit of apple. Silence descended over the hall. Every eye was on Desmond. He stood stiff and uneasy behind the long table.

"Finish your sup. I am fatigued and wish to take air to clear my head. It was a fine meal—you all have done yourselves proud." Desmond's voice carried from the beams to the outer doors. A cheer went up among the castle folk before they went back to their meals.

"I will go with you." Coy made to rise and accompany him.

Desmond laid a hand on Coy's shoulder to halt him.

"Nay, good friend, sit and eat. Quench your thirst and slake your hunger. You may have what you have not already eaten of my trencher."

"But my lord, I would watch your back," Coy said earnestly.

"There is no need. This keep has many wonders, including a lord's chamber with a stout door and stouter lock. The abbot gave me the key as I came into the great hall. No page, squire, or serf is allowed to sleep within the chamber. Most odd, but I have it from the abbot that the room is quite desirable. He assures me he has inspected it himself. I must confess, Coy, the promise of privacy is a welcome boon. I welcome a night without your constant snoring and talking in sleep," Desmond quipped with a taunting smile.

"I do not talk in my sleep or snore." Coy bristled defensively. "Why do you keep saying I do?"

"Ah, yes, you only take in air so loudly it sounds like snoring." Desmond laughed and clapped Coy on the back. "Be at ease, good friend, I am jesting with you."

"Then I may share the lord's chamber?"

"Nay, you may not."

Coy frowned darkly. "Do lock and bar the door, Desmond. I will sleep on a pallet in the hall outside your chamber."

Desmond chuckled at Coy's sudden concern. "I will be safe enough. You need not worry for my health until I wed Aislinn and take her to the marriage bed. And then, if my theory is correct, I may indeed die of disgust, fright, and revulsion, but such is the lot of a loyal knight."

"Do not jest about so serious a matter." Coy's face was grim.

"Stop fussing as if I were a stripling youth and you my wet nurse. I am a grown man, well seasoned by life. I am most capable of seeing myself safely through a single night alone."

Coy flushed at Desmond's sharp words. "As you wish." He clamped his lips together. Desmond turned away.

"But I like it not," Coy grumbled.

"Ah, I knew you would get in the last word," Desmond said over his shoulder while he made his way from the crowded hall. He felt the sting of eyes upon his back, but that was nothing compared to the disappointment that twisted and turned in his heart. He had finally admitted to himself that he longed to find a romantic love like Rowanne had with her rogue husband, Brandt. He had fully expected to find a comely maid in the first bloom of her womanhood who would cherish and worship him. But he had sorely misjudged his fate.

He was a knight of the realm, a baron, and as a nobleman he needed the king's approval to marry. With his adopted parents' death came the du Luc fortune and the fat barony of Mereworth, ancestral home of the du Lucs since the Conqueror had come from Normandy. The holding paid a hefty tax to the crown, and from what he had seen so far, so did Sevenoaks. Desmond would have been nine kinds of a fool to think Henry would let him continue to run randy and solitary for much longer. Barons, like maids, had a duty to breed sons and daughters for the good of England.

So Desmond would wed and bed the much widowed crone Aislinn because the king willed it. There was no question; there was no option. It would happen even if she was as wrinkled as a dried fig. This was a marriage of obligation, not affection.

"And since she is set in her ways, I may as well forget

any dreams of winning her regard, her heart, and her love. I will have no tender heart to dote upon me."

Desmond made his way outside, gulping in drafts of cool, fresh air in an attempt to stave off the bitter emptiness that gripped him. He walked briskly, beyond the main bailey, around the motte, past the mews, toward the comfort of full darkness. Without thought of where he was going he ambled on. Over the greensward, beyond the buttery, kitchens, and stables. But while he walked, his thoughts turned to Aislinn of Sevenoaks. 'Twas not her fault she was strong and hearty enough to outlive all her husbands. It was no more than odd coincidence they died after the wedding night.

Wasn't it?

Desmond was sure it was not her doing that brought them to this sorry end. She had no more choice in the matter than he. The king decreed. She, like Desmond, was bound to obey or suffer consequences. Giles, the abbot, said she was heartsick. And with just cause. Desmond had no doubt the poor, frail, aging soul had suffered much.

He made one full sweep of the castle grounds while his mind turned over the facts. He pictured a dried-up drab with frizzled hair, dyed a hideous shade of vermillion, clashing with her careworn features—a woman long disabused of the notion of love and happiness. She would be past the age of childbearing.

Every one of Desmond's desires had gone up like smoke. There would be no nubile young nymph to pamper and love him, and there would be no children to comfort him in his old age.

What a sad future he saw in his mind's eye.

"How she must hate Henry's plans," Desmond mused. "The woman has buried four husbands and yet the king

is not done with her." Through his own self-pity, a shaft
of sympathy for Aislinn pierced Desmond's heart. He was
ashamed for thinking only of himself.

"She is not even allowed to grieve properly, for here
I am, ready to drag her to the marriage bed before her
last husband is barely cold in his vault."

Drained of his burst of restless energy, Desmond
leaned against a low wall and silently cursed himself.
How could he be so craven? What if it was his own sister,
Rowanne, in such a broth? Had he not learned how tender
a woman's heart could be? It was not Aislinn's fault she
never conceived an heir after each ill-fated bedding.

Desmond glanced overhead. The moon was rising over
the thick outer curtain wall. Shafts of silvery light sidled
over the crenellations, gilding the interior of the castle
grounds. From the battlements above, Desmond heard a
stirring. The clank of metal and murmur of low voices
told him men vigilantly guarded the wall from the para-
pets above.

"At least all within is safe this night." He shoved himself up from the stones and ambled onward through the
courtyard of the castle. A cloud passed over the pale orb
in the sky. The night darkened. He found his way more
by the instincts of a warrior than by real sight. He was
aware of the close shelter of greenery near his face. The
air around him became more fragrant as he continued
using the night vision honed in battle. Suddenly, like a
great pearl floating to the surface of the sea, the moon
slid free from the clouds.

A sturdy wall of box hedge shielded his view left and
right. Desmond was in a maze of hedges. He walked
farther, intrigued by the whimsy of his surroundings. He
turned left, then right, walking through the maze. His
boot soles crunched over crushed stones. Here and there
a wild vine or flower sprouted out of the center of the
path, and he wondered how long it had been since anyone

trod this avenue. One more turn and he pierced the hidden heart of the maze.

Flowers, vines, stone benches, even the sparkling gush of water from a fountain drew his eye. A tall metal sundial sat on a raised dais in a sheltered cove beside a bench. Desmond had seen similar gardens while on Crusade, but never had he expected to find such within the thick walls of Sevenoaks. Where his shoulders brushed against petals or his heels bruised stems and leaves, a light fragrance wafted from the night-blooming flowers.

"Where are you?" a soft, girlish voice whispered, blending with the perfume of the garden. "Pray do not hide from me—not tonight of all nights."

Desmond stiffened at the fervent plea in her request. He stood within the hidden garden while his warrior's instincts prickled with wariness. His eyes searched the moon-limned darkness to find who else occupied this sanctuary.

The sound of stones rolled beneath a foot brought his hand to the hilt of his dagger. He stood waiting, listening.

A cat meowed. Desmond looked down to see a large, well-fed feline twining in and out of his booted feet.

"Pointisbright? Where are you?" The same light voice drifted from behind an arbor of flowering vines. It rubbed on Desmond's skin like a skein of silken thread. He scooped up the cat. On tiptoe he moved in the direction of the woman's enticing voice.

"Pointisbright, do not vex me. Come at once." Her request was compelling, her tone spiced with feminine impatience. Desmond enjoyed impetuous maids.

A shadowy form appeared beside the vines. Her back was to Desmond. She was swathed in a heavy, dark cloak, almost invisible in the night except for the scent of exotic oils and the natural musk of a woman. Sexual awareness sizzled through Desmond's veins.

"I believe this must be Pointisbright." Desmond

stepped from the shadows, holding the cat out before him as a shield—or an offering; he did not know.

He heard a rapidly indrawn breath as the woman spun around. A voluminous hood hid her features from head to toe.

"Pray, give me Pointisbright." She reached out.

He studied her hands. They were slim, well formed, with long fingers. Quick as a wink, she took the cat from Desmond.

"Who are you?" the soft, melodic voice demanded. "How did you get here? Who told you about the maze?" More than a little surprise and disbelief spiced her questions.

Desmond grinned inwardly. The maid obviously thought her garden safe from outsiders. And she had the arrogant assurance to believe she should know every man who dwelled within Sevenoaks Keep by name.

He liked her at once. She was feisty, petulant, and enchanting.

"Ah, what question shall I answer first?" Desmond was of a mind to tease and banter with this mysterious maiden. She was as fragrant as the flowers of the garden, and more interesting because her face was still unknown.

"Mayhap I should ask a question of you: Who are you and how did you come to the maze without me seeing you enter?"

"As I asked you first, you are obliged to tell me." She drew herself up and squared her shoulders within the cloak. Though he could not see her within the sheltering folds of the hood, he could imagine a look of petulance on a lovely, young face. It intrigued him all the more.

"How did you gain entry to this garden?" she demanded in a breathy whisper. "Who *are* you?"

Sexual desire pooled low in his belly. He had to know the face of the woman inside that hood and cloak.

Intending to sneak a peek from a different vantage

point, Desmond, ever the gallant, stuck out one leg and delivered an exaggerated bow, flourishing his hand and dipping low. The position allowed him to look up into the hood. The night and shadows defeated his purpose. He still could not see her face in the moonlit night.

"I am Desmond Vaudry du Luc, Baron of Mereworth, at your command, lady. I have been sent to take your mistress, Aislinn of Sevenoaks, to be my wife. And now, my mysterious maid of the garden, I demand to know, *who* are you?"

Four

Moonlight limned his thick, tousled, golden hair like a lover's caress.

Desmond Vaudry du Luc. The name hung like poison dragon's breath between them.

This was to be her fifth husband? This was the king's latest choice for her? Could it be true?

He was young: strong and handsome. He had nothing in common with the aging knights the king had sent before.

Jesu, this was a man who could breed sons and daughters, not an elderly warrior in need of a nurse and healing medicaments.

Desmond's shoulders were wide, his smile beguiling. The leg he had graced her with was thickly muscled, supple as any worthy knight could wish for. She had no doubt he was able to ride well, wield a sword with honor, and bed a woman with lusty skill.

She wanted to turn and run from him—flee from the vision of manliness. A sharp pain twisted inside her chest to look upon him and think of the four men before him. She wanted to flee, but her feet would not move. Her heart thumped against the inside of her chest so hard she thought she might faint. The king had chosen someone near her age, a man in his prime, a man of wit and charm.

The man she had longed for—but it was too late.

She would have to take his life, and that she could not do. Aislinn could not carry the burden of another's death.

Her opportunity for happiness had been squandered by her fickle king and her cursed red hair. Hope was long since cold and dead. She would not risk this man's—or any other man's—life in an effort to find contentment. No matter what punishment King Henry might decree for her disobedience she would not marry again. Not even this man, this golden knight who tempted her with his blue eyes and finely wrought body.

She would put her head on the block first.

Being so near to Desmond made her heart ache. To look upon him opened a raw wound that had not healed but festered in her soul. His twinkling gaze brought back the foolish dreams of the past. She tried to harden her heart against the memories of her youthful expectations. It was painful to see him and consider what *might* have been—what happiness she *might* have known. With a strangled sob, she turned to escape from the pain she felt. A strong, warm hand on her shoulder restrained her.

"Wait—don't go. I will not press you for a name if it distresses you so, but pray stay with me a while. I did not wish to drive you from this beautiful garden."

She swallowed hard, trying to deny the heat and comfort that radiated from that manly touch. Oh, what a strong, wide hand he possessed.

"As you wish," she heard herself say when every fiber of her being warred with itself. Her head cried out to save him. Her heart bade her stay and savor each blissful moment in his company. Each time he glanced at her, part of her heart warmed and opened like a night bloom seeking the moonlight. She was a withered blossom until now, until Desmond Vaudry du Luc found her secret world—her maze, her refuge—and smiled upon her.

"I know not what troubles you so, lady, but since you are reluctant to tell me your name and I must call you something, allow me to give you a title befitting this moment, this night, this mystical march of time." Desmond inhaled the sweet fragrance of the garden and allowed his eyes to drift beyond the sundial and upward over the ragged edge of the hedge wall. Stars twinkled brightly overhead, occasionally disappearing behind a veil of clouds only to reappear again as if conjured by a wizard's hand.

"I shall call you my maiden of the stars." He reached up and extended his hand as if he might capture a handful of those twinkling lights.

"You should have a necklace of stars, my maid. You should wear a fat pearl that glows like the moon." He stared at her a moment and then he laughed.

Aislinn could not breathe. She believed he could pull down the stars. He was bigger than life. Desmond was the image of what every young maiden dreamed of wedding—when trusting maidens foolishly believed that happiness could be attained with wedding.

But Aislinn knew better. The deaths of four men proved to her that dreams of gallants and years of wedded bliss were only folderol. She could not stifle the whimper that left her lips.

The little gasp of pain took Desmond's breath. She carried a deep pain in her soul. He had the uncanny but certain knowledge she had known great loss and tragedy. He longed to be the man to make her smile and forget her anguish. He was driven to help her. And still he had not seen her face. How could he feel such a connection to a woman whose face was a mystery?

As if he had willed it, she tilted her head toward the sky. The moonlight seeped into the folds of the hood, and finally he saw her clearly.

Her eyes were pale. Green? Blue? He could not be sure. Perchance they were a shade of tarnished silver—exotic, unusual. In any case, they were pale and intriguing.

There was a deep, pervading sorrow in her expression. She was not old by any measure, but a single tear on her soft cheek made him think she no longer believed the poet's version of her life.

Did she follow the dictates of Courtly Love? Had her heart been given to a man who was not her husband? A dozen such questions hammered at Desmond's mind as he studied her pale face. And as he memorized her features, it hit him that *this* was the maiden of his dreams. She was young; she was beautiful. An innocent sorrow filled her face. Here was the kind of woman he had aspired to wed. Here was a virginal maiden he could teach the pleasures of bed sport while she came to love him. She would be devoted, submissive . . . she would be perfect.

"Are you wed?" Desmond heard himself ask with no finesse, no preamble, and no sense.

Her soft, thick brows beetled into a frown. Long, wispy lashes swept down over those fascinating pale eyes.

"I am not wed now and shall never be." Her soft voice rang with a finality that chilled him. How could one so young and frail be so resolute?

Jesu, with each passing moment he grew more curious, more sexually aware of her. A woman this lovely should be laughing and spurning the attentions of a dozen randy swains instead of just one randy baron. He longed to hold her hand, to whisper love words in her ear until she blushed and let him steal a kiss.

Why was she here? Alone? Sad? Who was this vision? He wanted to kiss her.

Her lips were firm, not overfull and pouty. Desmond had never favored women with too-full lips. This enchanting maiden had a surprisingly strong mouth with a square, fearless chin set in the pale oval of her face. Her hair was obscured from his view.

Was her hair golden?

Or perchance her tresses were the soft, tawny brown

of a dormouse's fur. Surely not black, not with lashes so subtle in color and velvety in texture.

Would she be shocked if he rubbed his lips over the soft flesh of her eyelids? Would she slap his face if he placed one kiss on the tender lobe of her ear?

Why was her forehead swathed in cloth? Had she been ill? Had her hair been fever-shorn?

He cared not if she were bald. It mattered little. This maid would still be uncommonly fair.

He wanted to kiss her.

"Do you come here often?" he asked, but what he really wanted to say was, *May I kiss you? Would you come into my arms? Could I tempt you to sin with me beneath the stars?*

"Aye, I come here at night—every night. When I wish to be alone." She looked him straight in the eye. There was a strange wariness about her, like a knight with armor at the ready.

He grinned at her subtle command for privacy. She was not a servant; that was obvious not only by the soft, pale hands that held Pointisbright, but by the way she spoke, the somewhat haughty way she chose her words.

Was she a highborn virgin who bided at Sevenoaks as companion to Aislinn? The daughter of some nearby baron? Was she fostering here with aging Aislinn to learn the skills of a chatelaine? Perchance some young relative of one of the dead husbands? His curiosity was hot and wild as he studied her face. And with each sweep of his eyes his desire grew.

She was comely and innocent. This girl was the flower of England—the kind of daughter many a man raised up and portioned off for a dowry so fat and plump it kept him well in his old age.

"Do you wish to be alone often?" Desmond took a bold, predatory step toward her. "Or do you say that because you think I will leave?" He inhaled deeply, imprinting her upon his memory.

Her own mystical scent blended with the herbs and flowers and the night. How good it would feel to touch her flesh and sculpt her beneath his palms.

"Because if that is the case, you have misjudged me." He leaned nearer and drew in her essence. "I am enchanted by you—you are a sorceress?"

She gasped and drew back. Her face blanched of all color. That virgin's response to his advance hitched his temperature higher. Though he was standing in the silvery moonlight, his skin was warm as if the sun of the Holy Land beat down upon him.

"I am accustomed to being by myself. I am more suited to being solitary." She neatly avoided his question about wishing him to leave. Though the maiden was skittish and modest, she had politely spared his feelings. It was a testament to her breeding and good manners, he thought. Or did she really want him to stay? Did she feel even a small part of the hot, dark passion charging the garden? Could she not feel the wild pull of desire?

"I am frequently alone." She lowered her head. The hood slipped over her face.

He wanted to see her again. *Had* to see her face—now. Desmond reached out and put his index finger beneath her chin. She was trembling.

"Let me look upon you, maid of the maze." He raised her head. "You are more pleasing than a young man's dreams. But why do you tremble so? I will not harm you."

"I am not afraid," she said softly.

"Then this will not shock you." He gave in to his impulse and quickly stole a kiss. The faint scent of mead was on her breath. How good it would be to hold her—to pull her against him and let the contours of their bodies fit like a puzzle.

The yowl of Pointisbright and the sting across the back of Desmond's hand brought him back to reality. He reeled back a respectful distance. His scratched hand stung. In the moonlight he could see the glisten of his own blood.

"Jesu, are you hurt?" she gasped. "Pointisbright has never done such as that before. Perchance your boldness frightened him."

"Only a bold man would dare to steal a kiss when you have a lion to protect you." He was excited, aroused, interested in this strange woman who claimed to come to this solitary garden each night. He could feel the heat and hard nudge of his own erection in his braies.

"Why did you even try?" she asked with such honesty that it speared his heart.

"A maiden as lovely as you should be kissed well and often."

She blushed. Even in the night he could see the color in her soft, downy cheeks. "Are you always so rash and foolhardy?" she countered.

"Perchance I possess more courage than brains, or so my friends tell me. But when I tell you that you are beauteous and desirable, you may believe me."

"You speak folderol," she said with shy conviction.

"Nay, I speak truly. Such a maiden as you should be the object of ballads and poetry; men should make fools of themselves in your name."

Desmond came near again. The tomcat hissed a warning. "Easy, fearful beast."

She smiled. It was a tentative thing, as if she smiled little, or had not done so for a long time. Desmond risked the wrath of Pointisbright once more. He reached out and gently rubbed the pad of his thumb over her bottom lip.

"I would tease more of those sweet smiles from your lips, fair maiden, for even as your lips lifted, your eyes remained bleak and mournful."

She opened her mouth to speak. Coy's voice rang out,

shattering the silence of the night. He called to Desmond from somewhere far beyond the hedge maze.

"My friend Coy beckons to me." He turned toward the sound.

"I beg thee, do not answer. This garden is secret." Desmond's back was to the lady as she spoke with a sort of breathy fear in her voice.

"No one knows of the existence of this maze," she continued. "You must not let it be found, my lord. Pray, do not reveal this secret. I beg you."

He was still standing with his back to her, listening to Coy's call. "Come, lady, I found the maze; it cannot be too much the secret. I want you to meet my boon companion—" A rustling of greenery caused him to turn.

The garden was empty. Only the smell of bruised leaves crushed underfoot and the exotic scent of a frightened virgin remained.

He might have imagined the entire incident except for the stinging scratch on his hand and the soft, sweet touch of her lips seared into his memory.

How had she disappeared so quickly? It was as if she had vanished like a puff of smoke. Where had his maid of the night gone? And how?

With Pointisbright in her arms, Aislinn ran through the passage, nearly guttering the candles as she went. She had never encountered anyone in the garden before—not ever. The hidden route from her chamber was known only to her. Theron swore none living knew of the maze. All these years no men had ever found the portal from the outside to the heart of the garden.

"But Desmond Vaudry du Luc did," she murmured. "He is an uncommon man. But will he keep the secret? Or is he now revealing all to his friend?" A nettle of fear

stung her. If the maze was found, then soon the secret
passages would be revealed.

"Thereon bade me keep them secret," she told Pointisbright. "I know not why, but Theron insisted, and I
gave him my solemn oath."

Her breath was coming fast when she turned the final
corner and began to climb the hidden steps back to the
lady's chamber. Soon she saw the rim of light showing
through the cracks around the panel that hid the passage.
She stepped inside and turned the heavy ring. The corridor behind her closed.

Her empty chamber was as she had left it; the fire was
low, most of the logs now burned to ash in the hearth.
The outer door was stoutly barred against any intruder.

She remembered Desmond's face, his voice. His touch
was still hot on her skin, his kiss still vivid on her lips.
Her hands were shaking as she shrugged off the heavy
cloak, letting it fall with a whisper to the stone floor.

She put Pointisbright on the floor and pulled the covering
from her hair. Great heavy locks tumbled over her shoulder,
catching the light, glimmering like fire as the curls
bounced free, reaching as far as her chatelaine's belt.

What would Desmond have done if he had seen her
hair? Would he have cringed in fear or sneered in distaste? Would he have offered up a prayer of protection
for his soul and life, as Giles said the castle folk did?
Pointisbright padded to the bed and leaped onto the furs.

*None could ever know I was outside my chamber. For
Desmond does not know me—I did not give my name.
He does not know I am Aislinn, the cursed, red-haired
woman he has been ordered to wed. The woman that will
surely cause his death.*

She could keep him safe if she never saw him again.
But her heart's desire was to see him. As soon as possible.

* * *

Several times Desmond found himself at a dead end, staring at a thick, thorny wall, forced to backtrack and try another direction. Time lost all meaning as he turned this way and that, trying to free himself from the tangle of greenery and the grip of the tall, solid hedge. He wondered if he was truly lost in the maze. He no longer heard Coy calling his name. He assumed his comrade-in-arms was seeking him elsewhere, perchance inside the castle.

There was no true danger to Desmond, of course. If the worst happened, he could simply hack his way free with his dagger, but that was not what he wanted to do. He wanted to solve the riddle and master the maze.

"I want to prove to myself I can navigate the labyrinth so I may return again," he mused aloud. "For I have a desire to walk in this garden and spend more time with the winsome virgin who blushes so pretty and yet spurns my company."

His thoughts drifted back to the maiden's exit. She had disappeared like mist over a mere. He walked and concentrated on the path, and when he failed, he tried again. Finally, with the moon in a much lower position, Desmond emerged from the tangle, little worse off for his efforts.

He glanced back at the hedge. The entrance to the maze was well disguised, barely visible even though he knew what he was looking for. Unless one was purposely searching, he would never see the opening. The thick, flowering vines and hedge appeared to sit before a solid wall of stone. The construction was admirable and masterfully executed. He could well believe that none knew of the secret garden, as the shy girl claimed. But how did she know about it? And why did she beg to keep it secret? More about her was intriguing besides her winsome form and beseeching eyes.

"I have to see her again." He glanced up at the stars overhead. "And I will keep her secret. It shall remain our own confidence. When the night comes again, I will be waiting for her in the heart of the garden under the magic stars."

The abbot of Tunbridge Wells had not exaggerated the richness of the lord's chamber. The privacy and design was beyond unique. Never, even at Mereworth, had Desmond enjoyed the luxury of such a well fitted-out garderobe. A smooth stone slab with a hole cut into it was hidden behind an ell of stone and plaster. Though a bit cold on his bare arse in the morning, because of the slits in the stone walls for ventilation, the garderobe was much preferable to a pot or a pit.

Theron, it seemed, had been a lord of rare taste and a man of unusual abilities. The large posted bed sported thick, heavy curtains. Small coffers lined the walls. A finely chased silver ewer and matching bowl for washing sat on a wooden commode. On one wall a massive, intricately carved closet spanned the entire width of the chamber.

There was something to be said for Sevenoaks's peculiar custom of keeping the lord's chamber private. Desmond had not listened to snoring, farting, or mumbling throughout the night. Outside the bed hangings, the room had been as peaceful as within. There had been no pallets on the floor, no unwanted companions, no servants overanxious to do his bidding. Desmond had puzzled over the rows of carvings on the cabinet—like dancing men beneath a crescent moon—before he drifted off to sleep. Alone, without servants or companions. Alone with his thoughts of the maiden in the maze.

He had simply been alone. It was not a common occurrence in these times, when many dozens of people shared the baron's keep and did his labor in exchange for food, clothing, and protection.

Desmond had woken feeling rested and refreshed in a way that was exhilarating. When he stepped out of his solar into the stone corridor, he found it empty as well. The stones were cool and silent.

He was beginning to like the strange keep of Sevenoaks. It had much to offer, from beautiful mysterious virgins to privacy.

Desmond turned the heavy key in the escutcheon of his chamber door, hearing the heavy mechanism of the lock fall securely into place. Then he hung the key from a thong on his dagger belt. His gaze slid to the other door on this level of the keep—the entrance to the lady's chamber. It was closed, as it had been when he climbed the stairs last night.

"It would appear the elderly Aislinn is still abed," he remarked to himself. "Our meeting will be postponed yet again." A wicked thrill of relief sizzled through him. He had not been anxious to meet his aging bride, but he was even less so since the comely young lass had captured his interest in the moonlight. Desmond was more than willing to put off the meeting for as long as he might. Perhaps he could avoid the deed for months. While he pondered that possibility, a meow drew his attention. Pointisbright ambled over and began to twine and weave in and out between Desmond's ankles.

"Ah, my feisty friend." Desmond picked up the cat and stroked him until he purred. The scratches on his hand were red and puckered this morning. "So you are a mere kitten when I am not stealing kisses, heh? Where is your beauteous mistress? Is she below stairs breaking her fast? Will you climb into her lap and reveal her to me?"

The cat purred louder as if in answer. Desmond chuckled. He was suddenly eager to move among the folk of Sevenoaks. With any luck at all, he might discover the mysterious maid of the maze. Would she be as enchanting in the light of day, or had it been a trick of the night? The strange surroundings and circumstance of their meeting had been a delicious temptation, but would that remain?

He bent and set the cat on the stone floor. "Go, find your mistress. Lead me to the lady of the night." The cat gave him a dour look and dashed back the way they had just come—not down the stairs to the feasting hall. A wave of disappointment crashed over Desmond. The cat scampered into an alcove notched into the corridor. He lay down to catnap. There would be no revelation this morn.

Feeling much less ebullient, Desmond trudged off to the hall to break his own fast.

The great hall was a hive of activity as knights, servants, men-at-arms, and his own personal entourage of loyal Mereworth men broke their fast with bread and ale. Many women sat together at various tables. He studied each face, but none were familiar. None was the lovely virgin of last night.

Coy sat at the raised dais at the far end of the hall. Desmond's gaze slid to the largest carved and draped chair—the lord of the manor's chair. The abbot of Tunbridge Wells was seated in the chair where the lord of Sevenoaks should reside. A cold feeling of unease gripped Desmond.

The abbot was evidently playing the part of the lord of the manor while Aislinn kept herself locked away. Desmond had no reason to be vexed by that, and yet he was. A strange, hot flash of territoriality surged through him. He was not yet the true lord of Sevenoaks, and would not be until he wedded old Aislinn, yet seeing the abbot in the lord's chair set his back teeth on edge.

He was stunned by the revelation: he wanted Sevenoaks. It hit him in a cold moment of clarity. He coveted Sevenoaks and all it entailed. It was more than just Henry's desires; Desmond wanted the demesne with its secret gardens and private chambers.

But to have the holding, he must wed the aging chatelaine, Aislinn.

A question seared through Desmond's mind. What would he do about the maid of the maze when he took Aislinn to wife?

Five

Desmond was still trying to reconcile the strange conflict of emotions when the abbot spoke.

"My lord baron, I trust you slept well?" Giles's ruddy face was wreathed in a sunny smile. He did not rise from the chair he had usurped. "Did you find the peculiarity of the chamber too lonely for your tastes?"

"The solitude was most refreshing." With a lift of his brow, Desmond pulled out the chair meant for the chatelaine of the keep and sat down on Giles's left. "I see *this* chair is empty," he said pointedly.

If the abbot of Tunbridge Wells understood Desmond's vexation, he was a master at hiding his thoughts. He smiled blandly and ate a fig.

"I pray you will allow my dear cousin a few more days of rest while you settle in here at Sevenoaks." Giles tore off a hunk of fine, white manchet and dipped it into his wine. "She is a tender soul and is still grieving."

"I have no wish to cause the widow more distress by rushing her mourning period." Desmond nodded when the servant offered to pour him a goblet of wine. He turned and focused hard on Giles. "But make no mistake, Abbot. Henry has ordered me to take her to wife and to the possession of this keep. I am his man and will do as I am bidden on all accounts."

Giles blinked. "Of course, Baron, I beg pardon if I gave offense. I would never oppose the king's will—"

Desmond waved his hand in the air in a gesture of impatience, suddenly disliking the churchman for reasons he could not name or explain. The stories of the abbot's ambition came unbidden to his mind. It was said his greed knew no limits.

"I am not so quick to take offense, Abbot. I am a man who speaks plain; I expect those around me to do the same. If you have anything to say on the subject of my wedding your cousin, then I give you leave to say it now."

"You are most generous," Giles said, sipping from his goblet. "My only concern, of course, is for the peace and happiness of my cousin Aislinn. She has suffered much."

"Then you may rest easy, Abbot, for I wish only to do my king's will. It is not my intent to cause Aislinn unease. Once the wedding and bedding are done she may continue her life as before."

"Are you saying you will not hold her to the vow?" Giles asked with a strange, quizzical frown.

"I am saying I do not intend to dominate her life. So long as we both do as Henry wishes, we should rub along well enough. Aislinn will find me an agreeable mate. In fact, with Mereworth so near I will probably spend a great deal of my time there and monitor Sevenoaks as is needed. It is evident that whoever has been overseeing Sevenoaks is more than capable."

"Ah, I had not expected this from you, Baron," the abbot mused softly.

"That is a strange thing to say, Abbot. What expectations could you possibly have of me at all?" Desmond reached for his wine, but his fingers grasped naught but air. Coy was holding his goblet.

"God's bones, Coy! I am beginning to think you have forgotten all the manners you ever knew," Desmond sputtered in amazement. "Give me the accursed cup."

Coy looked guilty, then alarmed. Pale liquid splashed on the fine linen table covering as the cup fell from Coy's fingers. It hit the bulrush-covered floor. Desmond leaped up, wiping at the wine soaking into his tunic and hose. Beside him the abbot did likewise, holding his heavy gold cross away from harm. Desmond was sure it could not be so, but for a moment it appeared that Coy had purposely released the cup of wine.

"Coy, meet me in the yard anon. I fear you need to hone your reflexes with a little sword practice, for you have become as clumsy as a newborn calf—unless there is some other cause?"

"Nay, my lord. 'Tis as you say. I have too long been without a sword in my hand," Coy said quickly—too quickly, by Desmond's reckoning.

"Aislinn, open the door; we needs must talk."

She lifted the heavy bar from the door and let her cousin come inside.

"Morn, Giles. How fare you?" she asked, noting the stain on his fine robes. Giles was usually loath to be seen in anything less than pristine garb. Something awful must have happened to bring him to her thus.

"You needs must put aside these foolish notions, Aislinn. You must marry Baron Vaudry du Luc immediately."

Her heart fell. She remembered the golden man from the maze. How could she marry him and see his life forfeit?

"Nay, Giles. I will not wed him."

"But Aislinn, I have spoken with him this morn. He assures me once the wedding and bedding is done he will return to Mereworth." Giles smiled happily as if that should somehow please her.

"What are you saying? Does he wed me only because the king decrees it?"

" 'Twould seem so. He has little interest in Sevenoaks; 'struth, he seems to have little interest in a wife." Giles clapped his hands together. "Think of it, Aislinn, you may wed him and he will leave. You will be free to do as you wish and finally free from the king's demands. Does this not please you?"

"Nay, Giles, it does not. For you seem to forget. None of my husbands ever lived to see the light of day after the wedding. Why would you believe Desmond Vaudry du Luc will be any different?"

Aislinn made her way through the secret passage that connected her chamber to the lord's solar—Desmond's chamber. Just the thought of it made her insides quiver with a strange anticipation. After Giles left she had been buffeted by painful emotions. She wanted to see Desmond again, but she did not want to jeopardize his safety. The next best thing was to go to the chamber where he slept.

When she reached the barrier, she ran her fingers along the wall until she found the iron ring. She turned it and heard the heavy bolt slide free. The panel carved with marching knights slid back into the carved pocket recess in the stone wall. Pointisbright padded at her heels as she emerged from the tall, rough-hewn cabinet.

She had not been here for years. There was no reason to come—until she met Desmond in the garden and he captured her thoughts.

She glanced around. The solar that Theron had built was the same and yet it was different. It was now occupied by Desmond Vaudry du Luc. A few personal items were strewn carelessly about the chamber. A suit of armor had been propped carelessly against a low, wide commode. Though shiny and clean, it bore dents and scars of hard battle. There was a small hole in the lower breastplate. She shuddered when she thought of how it must have come to be.

Feeling like a naughty child, she continued to look and touch. Each article made her feel as if Desmond was with her. It was mystical, almost spiritual, but she felt it all the same.

A small carved ivory casket sat on a low chest at the foot of the curtained bed. She lifted the lid of the coffer. Inside lay a few loose jewels and a closed bag of soft leather. Her eye was drawn to one stone in particular. It was rough and unpolished, but when she picked it up the sunlight from the window fractured into a thousand points of colored light.

"Lovely as a rainbow," she told the cat, who jumped on the bed to get a better view. Pointisbright pawed at her hand. "Nay, puss, you may not have it."

The sudden sound of swords clashing caused Aislinn to jump. She dropped the crystal back into the chest and moved to the open leaded windows that matched those of her own solar. Below in the greensward, a group of men and youthful boys crossed swords. Some were crudely carved wood, others were metal but rough-wrought, the tips dull, meant for practice only. The sound and sight had not been heard since Theron died. Aislinn was enthralled. She had always been exhilarated by the sight of men's bodies as they flexed muscle and won at contests of strength.

To the left of the practice green a quintain made of straw and sacking had been set up. Nimble riders were taking turns jabbing at the device and trying to escape before being clouted in the back of the head by a weighted bag as it swung around after the blow.

She smiled when one lad managed, somewhat comically and awkwardly, to land two blows to the quintain before the bag swept around, smacked him full force, and unhorsed him. He lay there, sprawled out like a felled roebuck. A small trickle of blood came from his nose.

"Do not look so glum, lad. E'en the best of horsemen has tasted dirt," a laughing man advised him.

Desmond Vaudry du Luc—the man she was ordered to wed.

Her heart lurched inside her chest. Desmond's laugh was a deep, mellow sound full of camaraderie and affection. He was even more glorious by noonday sun than he had been by moonlight.

"Your blow was well placed, Gwillem." He stabbed his sword into the dirt. Then he offered his hand to the fallen lad. "Come, gain your feet and let me see if you are injured."

Without conscious thought, Aislinn found herself leaning out the narrow portal of flared stone to get a better look. The fresh, warm air caressed her face and brought Desmond's deep, throaty laugh and gentle words to her ears. The wind caught strands of her hair. She impatiently swept them away from her eyes lest they obstruct her view.

"Gwillem, you did well against the quintain for a first attempt. I trow tomorrow you will do even better."

"But I was unhorsed, my lord. The bag of stones felled me." The boy rubbed the back of his head.

"Next time you will know what peril to avoid." Desmond grasped the boy's chin and turned his face this way and that. "Knowledge is sometimes a painful thing."

"Aye, my lord, most painful," Gwillem agreed. Desmond clapped him on the shoulder and laughed again. The boy swiped impatiently at the slow trickle of blood on his upper lip.

Aislinn's heartbeat grew heavy and rapid in her breast while she watched. What strength, what tenderness! He was an uncommon man. She could not take her eyes from him.

"Your blow was well timed, if perchance a bit too ambitious. Land one solid blow. That will be enough to make your opponent totter in his saddle and give you time to duck his thrust." He reached out and tousled the boy's hair with his fingers.

Aislinn's knees went weak as water. The memory of his touch was as fresh on her skin as it had been last night in the hidden garden. Her heart had leaped—skipped a beat—when he lifted her chin. How intimate it had been when he rubbed her lips with his thumb. That touch had made her deepest woman's parts heat and weep with need.

"And when he kissed me, by the saints, I thought I would surely die from pleasure. And fear—for him."

Desmond laughed again far below. It drifted upward on the soft breeze, bringing waves of longing to Aislinn. Her stomach tightened into a hard ball. She feared for his safety, though to see him now was to deny he was only a mortal man. As in some great legend of old, the sun glinted on his fair, thick hair, turning him to a golden vision of manly splendor.

He was nigh onto being a god in her eyes. He seemed invulnerable. But once she had thought Theron was also invincible.

Like a pagan deity, Desmond retrieved his sword from where it was stuck into the earth. He wove it to and fro, rending the air with a high-pitched whistle. His thick wrists showed strength and supple power with each quick slice.

What dark, sinful pleasures did those hands possess? What satisfaction would his touch bring?

Another man, leaner and darker, suddenly appeared at the edge of the practice field. He, too, carried a sword.

"Ah, you have come for your trouncing at last, Coy." Desmond wore a wide smile that pierced Aislinn's heart. How could he have so completely conquered her soul after only one meeting? What was it about him that made her blood sing with need and her battered mind yearn for what she could not have?

"Come, Coy, but have a care, for you are as clumsy today as ever you have been. I will have your liver on the point of my blade in a nonce."

Coy. So this was the friend who called to him last eve. Had he revealed the maze? Something twisted inside her at the thought.

"It is time to give an accounting of yourself, knave. Not since you were a green youth have you been as thoughtless of your lord's care as you have been since we arrived here. Unless there is more to the story?"

"Lo, I am ready to meet you blade to blade," Coy said, giving a stiff salute with his sword.

Though his words were stern, Aislinn could see that both Coy and Desmond smiled broadly. She didn't understand the way men found sport in banging at each other with sword, mace, and pike, but the two men were playful as puppies as they squared off in the middle of the practice green. Soon all the young squires and castlemen were lined around them, watching, yipping encouragement to one or both.

"He finds such joy in being alive," she acknowledged aloud. "He laughs more, smiles more, takes more happiness from a summer's morn than any man I have ever beheld. Or is his delight in life because he is yet young and has his life before him? Does he feel as immortal as he appears?"

And then he stripped off his tunic. Sunlight skimmed his taut, muscled chest and flat, rippling belly. Parts of her body she had thought numb suddenly thrilled with excitement. Her breasts felt weighted and heavy; her lower belly clenched.

Jesu, he was beautiful. She wanted him.

If he weds you he will die, the dark voice inside her reminded.

A strange, hot yearning flowed through her veins when she looked upon Desmond Vaudry du Luc. He was the husband she had always yearned for. The thought of being bedded and claimed by him made her tremble with anticipation. His body pleased her, his face, manner, and actions pleased her. He aroused her, made her want him with carnal lust the likes of which she could not confess to Giles.

"But if he weds me then his life will come to an end. If I do what Henry commands, then that beautiful man will be snuffed out like a candle in a strong wind."

Coy and Desmond rushed each other with a whoop of manly bravado. Their blades sang a discordant song as they thrust and blocked. The metal rang harshly with each blow. Aislinn gripped the sloping stone of the window portal, enthralled, mesmerized, and a little afraid that Desmond would not be fast enough—that the edge of Coy's blade would find his flesh, that his arm and strength would fail him.

"Desmond is reckless. Just look, Pointisbright, look how he ventures himself. He was nearly skewered on the point of Coy's sword on that last thrust."

Desmond swept low and jabbed. Coy leaped back but twirled and thrust again. His blade could not help but find Desmond's heart.

"Desmond, have a care!" Aislinn screamed.

A quick flick of Desmond's wrist sent Coy's weapon flying. It struck the verge point first. It swayed harmlessly back and forth like a bulrush gently stirred by the breeze. A masculine roar of appreciation filled the training yard, but Desmond was looking upward, scanning the tower with sharp eyes. His eyes searched the curve of the tower wall.

Aislinn felt the heat of his focused gaze upon her. She

jumped back away from the window. It was too late; he had seen her.

She ran into the cabinet. Her hand was shaking as she used the ring to seal the wall. Her heart was in her throat while she raced back to the safety of her own chamber.

He had seen her; she was sure of it.

"Are you staring at the window in the lord's own chamber?" Coy squinted up at the empty portal.

"Aye."

"And do you have a purpose?"

"Aye." Desmond tossed down his sword and ran toward the keep.

"What did you see in that window?"

"A face." A woman's face. And a flash of flame red hair.

"Indeed? Someone you know?" Coy looked doubtful. "In your own solar?"

"Aye."

"But is the lord's chamber not locked?"

"And with a single key to open the door, or so some would have me believe. But I will learn what is amiss and how any face could come to be in that particular window," Desmond told his friend as he hurried through the keep, ignoring the inquiring looks of the castle folk. He stepped over startled drabs gathering old rushes; he sidestepped young boys carrying baskets of wood for the hearths.

"Baron? Is aught amiss?" the abbot of Tunbridge Wells asked when they swept by him like a whirlwind.

Desmond offered no explanation to the inquisitive churchman as he and Coy took the stone stairs to the upper floor two at a time. He could hear the patter of the cleric's feet behind him. Now all three charged toward the lord's chamber.

"Sevenoaks is a keep filled with too many mysterious wenches. And one of them is in my chamber," Desmond

grumbled. But he found the outer door locked solid. The
key to the lord's chamber was on his belt. He slipped the
thong and placed the key into the lock plate of the solid,
studded oaken door. The inner workings clanked loudly
as they slid free.

Desmond flung wide the door of his chamber, ready
to confront Aislinn, to demand her explanation—to learn
why all at Sevenoaks lied about the single key and why
she invaded the solar but would not receive him.

He stalked into his solar. He spun around, checking
every corner, even going into the ell that concealed the
garderobe.

The chamber was empty—except for the ginger tabby,
Pointisbright, curled into a ball in the center of Desmond's bed, grooming himself.

"By the Rood!" Desmond exclaimed.

"There is no woman here, Baron." The abbot looked
at Desmond with smug satisfaction. "As I have told you,
there is only one key to this door."

Pointisbright peered at him. He yawned and tucked his
head in preparation for a nap. Desmond glanced at his
belongings. The jewel casket lid was open. He had not
left the chest open. And Pointisbright had been outside
the door *after* Desmond locked his solar door. It was no
mistake, nor his imagination.

He had seen a woman's face in his window. Since there
had been a flash of red hair at the window, the face could
only have been Aislinn's.

"There is only one key, Baron du Luc, and you hold
it in your hand. The story is well known. Theron had the
lock and the key fashioned while on crusade by a Turkish
craftsman. He had a foreign builder come back to England with him. The builder fit the lock to door, which
you can see is as thick as the breadth of a man's hand.
There is no other like it, or any locksmith that knows the
mechanism's workings. in all of England. If the key is

lost, the only way into the room is to hack through this sturdy English oak."

Desmond narrowed his eyes at the churchman. Was he not spending an inordinate amount of time explaining a simple door and lock? Did he lie? But to what purpose? Desmond had it in mind simply to ask the abbot, but for some reason he held his tongue. His gaze lingered on Pointisbright, protective lion of the mysterious maiden.

"Mayhap it was no more than a trick of the light. My eyes deceived me." Desmond's thoughts had turned to the maze. He did not want to arouse the curiosity of the castle. He did not want anyone to discover the maze and the maid until he learned more himself.

"And the cat?" Coy asked. "Did you bring the cat in to share your private chamber?" His dark eyes gleamed with suspicion.

"It is obvious he came into the chamber before Baron Desmond locked the door," the abbot provided helpfully. "There can be no other explanation for it."

"Aye, it must be as you say, Abbot—if there is but one key," Desmond said softly. He knew very well where Pointisbright had been when the door was locked. But until he solved this riddle he would keep his own counsel.

There was only one explanation; someone else held a key. The chatelaine of Sevenoaks, which was proper. But why go to such lengths to make is seem as if Aislinn did not have access to the lord's solar? There was some intrigue afoot regarding the lie; that was plain.

Desmond picked up Pointisbright. Aislinn herself had found access to this chamber, and that was when Pointisbright slipped inside. No woman could pass through walls of solid stone, and Desmond did not believe in magic. If there was mischief at work within Sevenoaks, it had nothing to do with sorcery.

Six

The long, sunny day crawled by. Aislinn nibbled of the bread and cheese and drank a little of the ale left outside her door, but she did not leave her chamber. And when Giles came at nooning and rapped lightly on her chamber door, she pretended not to hear him.

"Aislinn, we must speak." His knock and his voice grew more insistent, but she remained silent, hoping he would think she was sleeping. Finally she heard him move away, his heels thudding dully on the stones in the corridor between the lord's and lady's chambers.

It was the first time in her memory she had not obeyed Giles's summons, the first time she had kept her door barred against him. And yet she *had* been disobedient to her cousin, in her own way. She kept secrets from him, protecting all the information Theron told her before he died.

"Theron was my lord husband; I was bound by the laws of God and man to do as he bade me," she justified her actions. "But Desmond Vaudry du Luc is not my lord and master, yet I feel such a loyalty to him. How can that be?"

She marveled and argued with herself over the strange puzzle of her emotions. Though she could hardly believe it, Desmond Vaudry du Luc had taken her heart from her with his first spoken word.

"It was like a troubadour's lay."

The image of his body glistening in the bright sunlight while he fought his friend, Coy, made her throat dry and tight. Aislinn had never known such a feeling. It was frightening and reckless. And though she was timid because of its dark force, she yearned to know more of it.

"I want him as a woman wants a man. After all these years and all these weddings I finally lust for a man."

Aislinn had once been content to do her king's bidding: to marry for political advantage and reasons of state. She had no illusions about *desiring* her husbands. Of course she wanted to be bedded so she might bear children, but when she looked at Desmond she wanted to be bedded for reasons having nothing to do with procreation.

She longed to feel the strength of his body. Her hands itched to know the texture of his skin, the quality and thickness of his hair. It was like a sickness, a need.

But she could never have him. She could not risk him by wedding him, and Aislinn would never sin against God by swiving without marriage.

So she held the hot, lustful yearnings in her heart. They grew until she was nearly ablaze with longing. It would be another secret she would carry to the grave: this wild, heedless hunger for Desmond, and Theron's confidential information about the walls of Sevenoaks.

"Come, Coy, let us ride out and see the lay of the land." Desmond strode through the great hall, pulling on his leather gauntlets as he went. He was fitful, itchy, and restless to his very soul. The only way to dissuade such a mood was to mount Brume and ride hard across the greening fields. He had been idle too long—surely that was the reason his skin prickled and burned.

"As you wish." Coy leapt to his feet, ever ready for any adventure.

Gwillem quickly readied their mounts, and side by side they thundered across the drawbridge. Sunshine was burning off thick, vapory mist in the dales and valleys below the keep. It shifted and swirled, skimming along the earth like dragon's breath. It was a beautiful and mysterious sight; ribbons of fog rising over the meadows. And then as the haze lifted, there appeared a thatched roof.

"Look, a simple crofter's cottage." Coy lifted his hand and pointed.

"Let us take our ease there. Brume will likely want a drink of fresh water. And 'twill give me an opportunity to meet the crofter. I want the folk around Sevenoaks to know I am in residence, should they have need of me." Desmond reined Brume toward the cottage.

"Lo, inside. The new lord of Sevenoaks is here," Coy boomed out.

It was quiet. No cry of welcome sounded from inside. No sheep or goat stood in the small enclosure attached to the house. No ribbon of smoke rose from the hole in the reed-thatched roof.

" 'Tis quiet. And yet the dwelling does not look neglected or deserted."

"Aye, I wonder if something is amiss." Desmond swung from his saddle, tossing his reins to Coy. Instinctively he flung his cloak over his right shoulder so his sword arm would be free. "Lo, inside the cottage. Is all well?"

At length Desmond pulled the latch string and shoved open the door.

The cottage was dimly lit by the watery shaft of light coming through the smoke hole in the center of the roof. A low table and a single bench sat along one wall. The rough plank rafters were hung with drying herbs, blooms, stalks, and stems of every variety. A rude cot sat against the back wall with one thin blanket.

" 'Tis empty and yet has been occupied recently," Coy said when he had dismounted and peered over Desmond's shoulder. "There are no spiders spinning in the corners. Nor dust coating every surface."

"Aye, and neither is there a single flagon, bowl, or pot. Yet the scent of the herbs is fresh." Desmond turned and shut the door securely at his back, replacing the latch string as he found it. "Mayhap the occupant has gone on a journey. They might have taken their household goods."

"Aye, we will come again another time."

With one last look at the small empty croft, Desmond mounted Brume. With Coy at his side, he continued his journey to survey the countryside around Sevenoaks.

Aislinn paced the stone floor of her chamber. Each step counted down the slow drift of sand through the hourglass on the low oak chest. When the sun slid below the crenellations of the battlements on the curtain wall, she quickly wrapped and hid her hair, then pulled on her cloak. Night had not fully engulfed Sevenoaks, but she could not wait any longer. Her stomach was knotted with impatience as she hurried down the steps and through the cool stone corridor to the garden below.

Though it was foolish and reckless and potentially lethal, she prayed Desmond would find his way to the heart of the maze again—the heart of her soul.

"Silly goose, what a dreamer you have become. He came once by accident. Since it was built, no other man has ever found the heart of the maze."

"By the saints, I am ready to take my battle-ax and hack my way through this wall of brambles," Desmond cursed aloud when he found himself in a dead end of greenery for the sixth time since he entered the mouth

of the maze. It had been gloaming when he began; now
the night was fully dark, the cooling mists of evening
hanging near the top of the hedges.

He dragged his hand through his hair in frustration.
Then he turned to backtrack and start again to solve the
riddle of the labyrinth. He stared up at the sky overhead.
The stars were twinkling like polished jewels.

"I found it without knowing what lay at the end last
time; surely the way is not lost to me now that I am aware
of the treasure in the heart of the garden."

Disappointment and a measure of desperation pricked
at him. He took a deep breath.

"I must find it. I must see her again."

The rustle of leaves drew his eye to the darkened path-
way behind him. A pair of green-gold eyes winked at
Desmond from the roots of the privet hedge.

"Pointisbright, lion of the garden." Desmond squatted
and ran his hands over the cat's body, watching tiny
sparks fly from his fur as it crackled beneath Desmond's
palm. "If you will play the part of tracker and guide, I
vow to see you richly rewarded with thick, fresh cream
each night."

The cat looked up at him and blinked twice. Desmond
could almost swear the canny creature was considering
the offer. Then, with a flick of his raised tail, he turned
his haughty backside and padded down the green-
shrouded corridor of the hedges.

"Lead on Sir Mouser of the hedge." Desmond broke
into a trot to keep pace with Pointisbright through shadowy twists and turns. He knew it was foolish and the
chances slim that a fickle feline would truly guide him,
but in moments Desmond emerged in the center of the
maze.

Sitting on a stone slab beside the sundial, so still that
she might have been hewn from rock herself, was the
object of his interest.

Pointisbright jumped up into her lap and meowed. Desmond's boot crunched a twig underfoot. She looked up. Shadows made her eyes mysterious and unreadable within the folds of the heavy hood that covered her head.

"You came," she said. "I dared not hope you would. One part of me prayed you would not. 'Tis not safe for you to be here."

"I am soon to be lord of Sevenoaks, and if I am not secure within my own demesne, then where shall I be?" Desmond strode to the bench and took her face between his hands. He bent and captured her lips. He kissed her with all the lustful abandon of a man who has spent all day thinking of a woman who fascinates and tempts him. The frustration of the maze and his eagerness to find her had made his blood hot, his expectations high, his loins heavy with desire.

He wanted her utterly.

Her surprise at his brazen action was evident. She was stiff and unsure. It made him more determined to win her, woo her, warm her cool facade. He deepened the kiss, tasting her gently, sampling her. With a soft sigh she melted into his embrace. Her mouth held the subtle flavor of spiced fruits and honey. Like a ravening wolf that has tasted its first blood, Desmond thrust his tongue between her barely parted lips, probing, seeking.

He lifted one knee and placed it on the stone slab beside her. Her body nested near the juncture of his thigh. Her mouth was on a level with his tarse and stones. He throbbed with need. It was so tempting to lay her back—to claim her body on the cool, smooth stone, to ram his tarse deep into her sheath, to slake his lust. . . .

"Jesu." She wrenched herself free. The urgency of her voice brought him back into his right mind. Her eyes were wide, uncertain. His heart was pounding, unrelenting. He fought to master his instincts when all he wanted was to behave like a rutting stag.

"You are a man who moves swift and sure. I am not accustomed to dealing with one such as you. I have no experience in this kind of . . . love sport."

"Sport?" Desmond's heart was pounding like a hammer on a stone.

"Aye, this lovers' play. It is new to me; I have no experience in these matters. I fear you go too fast."

"Do you fear me?" He fought to cool the lusty heat coursing through his veins like molten metal. He had intended to question her about his chamber, to find if she knew of an extra key held by Aislinn, but now he didn't really care. Aislinn could have a dozen keys and he would not care.

"Fear? Aye, I have a great fear when I am near you, but not the way you imagine," she admitted in a husky whisper. A flicker of some unknown emotion appeared in her eyes.

"Green," he pronounced in wonder.

"Green?" She repeated it in a way that made him think he had wounded her. Did she believe he mocked her and called her *green* because she was a pure and chaste virgin.

"Your eyes are green," Desmond explained quickly. "I did not know, could not tell. I knew they were a pale color, but I did not know the hue. I wager your hair will be the color of warm honey."

She stiffened and jerked free of his embrace, scooting by him, rising from the bench, leaving him there with one leg propped on the cold, hard stone slab. She pulled the sheltering hood more firmly about her head. Her arms wrapped about her middle. Desmond did not know what had shattered the ensorcellment of the moment, but it was surely gone. He swiveled and lowered his rump to the slab. Now he sat sideways with one knee up to his chin, studying the maiden. He plucked a night-blooming flower from the climbing vine nearby and attempted to act as if her leaving had not wounded his soul. He glanced around the garden. Moonlight shimmered along the metal face of the sundial as he feigned interest in the device.

"Unusual face on yon dial," he commented casually.

"Aye." Her one-word answer was stiff, her posture even stiffer.

"Have you been long here at Sevenoaks?" He made no move to touch her. But even though he remained motionless, she stood stiff and unyielding by the bench.

"Aye, a long while."

"Indeed. Did you know the original lord—Theron, I believe he was called?"

"Aye, I knew him. He was a kind man." She was observing him from beneath the long fringe of her lashes.

It was not much, but each answer contained a few more words than the last. He was a patient man; battle had taught him to be able to invest hours of his time in order to achieve his objective. If it took all night and tomorrow to have her speaking freely, then he would spend it willingly.

"Tell me something of him. I see unique details of architecture and styles here at Sevenoaks I have not seen since I returned from Crusade." Desmond did not care what she said, only that she spoke. To watch her filled him with a strange, hot appetite. It was enchanting to watch her, to inhale the subtle delicacy of her essence in the quiet, star-filled night.

"My lord Theron had been twice to the Holy Land," she finally offered.

She was a woman who thought much and said little, as if each word needed to be chosen carefully, tried and savored before she spit it out.

"Ah, a fellow Crusader? That would explain the rare contrivance of the sundial and the rich appointments in the lord's solar."

"Aye, he was a warrior but he had a scholar's heart and soul." She suddenly relaxed. Like a nymph floating on water, she closed the gap between her and the device. Her fingers trailed over the exotic face of the sundial.

"When he returned to England he was ill for many long months. His wounds were nearly mortal. He spent an entire winter at Battle Abbey, where the holy men nursed him back to health. He came nigh to death that cold winter. When he recovered he came finally to Sevenoaks, where his Moorish craftsman had been working and awaiting his arrival. Theron brought the best of what he had seen outside England's borders to his own keep."

"Yet the keep does not lack defenses." Desmond was babbling, content to watch her face while she spoke. A little line between her brows indicated when she was being thoughtful. She pursed her lips ever so slightly just before she answered. It was immensely satisfying to learn these secrets about her.

"Theron said he had much to protect within the walls, some treasures seen and more unseen," she said softly as if repeating the old lord's words exactly. Desmond found himself wondering, with a sense of dread and jealousy, how well she had known Theron. Was she his leman?

"He was proud of the design and the comforts he had duplicated. The Moorish builder made sure the midden pits and garderobes were properly designed. He was a master craftsman, and he missed his homeland so much that he tried to recapture a bit of it with this garden for his own sake." She glanced around.

"He built the maze, not Theron?"

" 'Tis said they spoke of it together, but the plants and the fountain were the Moor's selection. It is special—unique. It was meant only for the lord and lady of the keep. A false wall was built to hide the greenery until it grew to sufficient height to confound the curious."

That explained how the maze had remained a secret. "And none of the castle folk were curious?"

"At the time Sevenoaks came to Theron it was little more than a ruin. The laborers were brought from Peavensey. When the maze and the castle were complete, the Moorish builder returned to his home. The other men returned to the coast or went on to other places to earn a crust. I know only one man to have worked the puzzle of the maze. You."

"Only you and I hold the secret of the garden?" Desmond said. "I like it much. I am pleased you and I share a secret."

Her heart tumbled within her chest at his words. She would share so many more secrets if she dared. She longed to share the secret of her virginity with this man who was forbidden to her.

"You are a mystery yourself, my maid of the maze. I know nothing of you, not even your name. There are too many secrets in Sevenoaks."

"What do you mean?" Aislinn asked.

"This very day I beheld a fleeting image of a red-haired woman in my own locked solar. I have heard it said the chatelaine of this keep has striking red hair."

Aislinn swallowed hard. Did he know? Was he playing puss and rat with her?

"A red-haired woman, you say?"

"Aye, I caught only a fleeting glance, but I know the tresses were red. I have seen no woman with hair that shade, so I must assume it was Aislinn, but if so, how did she find entry into my chambers?" He said it more to himself than to her.

"Do you think she used some evil power to gain entry?"

He could not help but laugh at her stricken expression. "Nay, I think she possesses a key." He chuckled and watched her expression change.

"A key?" That adorable line appeared between her brows.

"Aye, a key. Why must there always be a broth of intrigue

and superstition? The explanation is usually a simple one. Think you Theron died without giving a copy of the key to his wife? What lord would withhold the key to his chamber from his lady wife?" Desmond chuckled again.

"It sounds so reasonable," Aislinn agreed.

"Aye. Aislinn has a key. She went inside and Pointisbright, the opportunistic feline, followed her and remained when she left."

"How did you arrive at that conclusion? How can you discount the stories of her sorcery, her wickedness, and her unnatural hair?" Aislinn asked, her heart still in her throat. Desmond's cool logic did make her fears seem small, foolish, and ignorant.

Desmond shrugged. " 'Tis what I would do—will do. When I am wed I will be honor-bound to share secrets with my lady wife."

Aislinn's heart kicked again. She felt a yearning so deep and raw, it brought tears to the backs of her eyes.

"And will you share secrets with the woman the king has ordered you to marry? Will you share your deepest and most sheltered secrets with Aislinn?"

Desmond rose from the slab. He looked down on the woman encased in the folds of the sheltering cloak. "I have only one secret I will keep from my wife, maid of the night, and that sweet, dark secret is you." He pulled her into his arms and she came willingly. Desmond kissed her hard.

It was quite late or very early, depending on one's point of view. Desmond had not slept more than a few minutes through the night. Upon rising, he accidently woke Coy when he stumbled over his sleeping friend, who still slept outside his door like a faithful hound. Now the two men were alone in the great hall. The minstrels, strummers, and performers were absent, still sleeping in the dark hours before dawn. Soon the castle would rise and the hall would be full, but for now it was quiet—eerily silent.

Desmond reached for a heel of yesterday's bread to break his fast, only to find Coy's greedy hand already upon it. "By the Rood, Coy, I have had enough of this! You will tell me what is behind this spate of ill manners and gluttony, or by my beard, I will banish you from my sight and my holdings." Desmond clamped his jaw and waited.

It was no idle threat he made. He could no longer ignore these daily offenses in the name of friendship. Coy must learn who the master of Sevenoaks was.

Coy frowned. He swallowed. He frowned some more, then he heaved a great burst of air from his lungs and said, "I beg your pardon, Desmond—"

"Nay, Coy, you will not offer me flummery nor humbly beg my pardon. I will have the truth of your actions, or I vow on both my family names, you will be gone from Sevenoaks by nooning."

"God's bones, you make it hard to be a right friend to you."

"The reason, Coy—now."

"I fear you are to be poisoned," Coy growled. "There, now you have it—the truth you wanted. What shall you do with it?"

"Poisoned?" Desmond blinked and sat back in his chair. "Me? Poisoned? You taste all my food and drink because you fear a plot to do me to death?" He struggled to keep from laughing. He had imagined any number of foolish reasons, but none so nodcocked as this.

"Why do you fear I will be poisoned?"

"Think. The four men who wedded Aislinn before you have all died on their wedding night. They could have been given lethal herbs. I fear you will be next, and so to thwart the plot I have been making haste to sample all your food and drink before you put it to your lips."

Desmond could not quite digest this joint. He stroked his jaw and studied his friend. It was plain Coy was telling the truth—as he believed it. "Ah, but if you are correct then I am safe until the night I wed."

"I was not of a mind to take that risk with your life," Coy snarled. "Though to see how you thank me, I wonder that I bothered."

"You were ready to lay down your life for me?"

"I love you like the brother I never had," Coy said with a crooked grin and a flush of color to his craggy cheeks.

"Though it warms my heart to know you hold me in such high regard, you may be at peace, Coy. There is aught to worry about. The four men died because they were to a man battle-scarred and world weary. Their time was come. They had lived long and adventurous lives. They did not meet their Maker any sooner than most men. I would wager they cheated death longer than most. All of them were well above forty years."

Coy shook his head, his dark, shaggy hair whispering along the padded and rolled collar of his brigandine vest. "I wish I could take comfort from your words, but I do not believe it, Desmond. I have a feeling of doom. Now that you know, you must let me continue to taste your food and drink."

"Nay, Coy. There is no plot, no intrigue. I am not going to be poisoned, and you are to cease this foolishness. I will tolerate no more of this *coddling*. I demand you stop worrying like an overloving nursemaid. There is no danger to my life, no matter what gossip you have heard to the contrary. There is no plot, no intrigue, and no danger to me. This is nothing more than a busy keep with the usual problems of day-to-day life. There are no hidden passages, vast and wondrous treasure, or sinister plots to kill the lord of the manor."

Seven

"As lord of Sevenoaks he must die," Aislinn said miserably. "His time grows shorter with each passing day. You have told me of these rumors with each of my dead husbands. It cannot be different now."

"You are talking foolishness. You cannot spend the rest of your life locked in this chamber in order to avoid Desmond Vaudry du Luc." Giles cast around a gimlet gaze. He was irritable and jittery, his mood making Aislinn wish she could ask him to leave so she might go to the peace of the garden.

"If I wed him he will die!" Aislinn shouted. "I will not do it."

"The king has ordered it. You are in his hand. You must wed and be bedded anon." Once again he studied the room, running his finger over the stones by the hearth. "And he vows that once he is wed he will go to Mereworth Keep. He will leave us—you—in peace, Aislinn."

"You mentioned that before." Why did Desmond's vow to leave her make a pain twist in her heart?

"There is no reason for you to avoid taking the vows," Giles said cheerfully. He ran his gloved hand over the incised stones on the hearth. "He will leave anon."

"I refused to wed him to save his life."

"What? Aislinn, this is foolishness. You cannot defy the king."

"I could offer to give up all I own to enter a convent. Henry would allow that, I believe, if I gave over all my coin and Sevenoaks. I would rather lock myself away as a nun before I see Desmond die."

"Nay, you cannot." Giles whirled to face her. "You must not forfeit Sevenoaks."

"Giles, think. If I enter a convent, then no other man will die. Desmond Vaudry du Luc will be given another woman, and Sevenoaks will be in Henry's control. Did you present this to him as I asked you to when you were at court?" Aislinn studied Giles's face. For a moment she thought she saw a flicker of something—*guilt?* But then it was gone.

"Dearest Aislinn, Henry has a score of keeps. He does not want Sevenoaks; he wants you to wed Desmond Vaudry du Luc. You have no choice; you must wed again." Giles's eyes were wide and Aislinn was stunned to see how much he feared for her.

"Then I am prepared to remain locked in this chamber until the king pulls Sevenoaks down around me, if it means sparing his life."

Giles looked hard upon her. "You do not speak like a woman who has little knowledge of a man. You sound and act as if you know him well and have formed an attachment. Have you met Desmond Vaudry du Luc?"

Aislinn swallowed hard. She could not let Giles know of the passage and the garden. She had kept her sacred vow to Theron all these years and would do so until . . .

"Giles, I know you have me watched. And I love you for caring so much for me and worrying so that you take no chance with my safety, but you know this outer door has not been opened for me to receive Desmond Vaudry du Luc. Or are you now ready to believe the wagging tongues that say I can turn myself into a rook and fly?"

"Do not be foolish, Aislinn. I do not believe in such ignorant gabble."

"Then the eyes you employ within my keep have told you that I have not come below stairs or supped in the great hall since his arrival. And you know this outer door has remained locked." Aislinn salved her conscience by skirting the truth with her lies. She didn't want to admit it, but she was bothered by Giles's attitude about giving the crown Sevenoaks.

Giles rubbed the smooth pate of his tonsure in a gesture of impotent frustration. He stepped nearer to Aislinn. He tilted his head and studied her face while he fingered the heavy gold cross at his neck.

"Of course, you are right. You would truly have to be the witch people accuse you of being to escape this chamber."

His words brought a chill of dread up Aislinn's spine. She unconsciously touched the covering on her hair.

"Pray do not say such things, Giles, even in jest. I may be accursed, but it is through no fault of my own. I cannot help the color and hue of my hair. You know I am no believer in potions and spells."

"I well know it, but locking yourself away in this chamber does not help to quell the wagging tongues of Theron's old householders. The less they see of you, the greater their fear of you grows. They spin stories that make you seem the veriest harpy. Come, sup above the salt this eve and silence them all before Desmond's ear has been bent with tales of your wickedness. Once you meet him and sample his charms, perchance you will be more willing to say your vows and let him get back to Mereworth."

"Has Desmond heard the vile lies?" Aislinn asked as a corner of her heart tore in agony. The one man whose regard she craved was the one man whom she could not openly meet.

"I know not; I only know that the longer you delay

the first meeting, the more likely he will be to believe all that is said about your wickedness when he does hear."

Desmond walked through the bread kitchen and beyond to the building where the meat was roasted. As he passed drabs and workers he heard the murmur of whispered comments. He was an object of curiosity, but he had been made to feel welcome. By bits and bobs they had come to accept him, even though he had not yet wed Aislinn. The odd thing, and something he could not explain, was that none who called Sevenoaks home had ever said one unkind word about Aislinn. He heard no rumors, or talk. And yet Coy said that Gwillem had heard much about her, and the virgin in the garden spoke of rumors and tattle.

He found himself pitying Aislinn more and more, but he could not deny that he was grateful she had sequestered herself in her chamber. For her absence allowed him to enjoy his maid of the maze without guilt . . . almost.

It was a hot-and-cold current that ran in his heart. The chivalrous knight in him knew he must protect the honor of his betrothed, but the swain who had become enchanted with the maid of the maze was more than a little cheered by the respite Aislinn's continuing grief had allowed him.

He would eventually have to wed Aislinn, but for now he cherished the nameless vixen in the garden and lusted for her. Mayhap he should simply bed the wench. Once he had her, it was likely he could break her hold on him. Desmond was not proud of his fickle nature, but that was the way of his heart. When a woman took hold of his ardor and interest, the only way he could be free of her was to rut her often and well until his yearning and desire for her waned. It was naught to be proud of, but Desmond was not one to deny the truth about himself, good or ill.

"Lord Desmond, have ye come to sample a bit o' my

cookery?" A toothy crone with bright red cheeks managed a clumsy bow of respect.

"Something does smell passably tempting." Desmond peered in the large door of the roasting room.

"Ah, that would be me own crusty meat pie fresh from the fire. Would ye like a taste?" She held a golden-brown pasty in her hand.

The aroma was too much for Desmond to resist, or was it that he had just become a weakling—first for a nameless maid and now for food?

" 'Tis the best in the shire." She puffed out her already ample bosom.

"A bold claim. You offer me no choice. Now I must taste it and judge if you be boastful."

"Truthful I be, me lord. See for yerself."

Desmond took the morsel and bit into it. Spices and hot juice flowed over his tongue.

"A bit of beer to wash it down? We keep no ale in the meat house, but a hearty beer brew rests in that vat by yon door."

Desmond grinned. "Beer would be welcome on this warm day."

The cook nodded to a young lad who was badly crippled. He managed to swing his body between two padded crutches made of rough-planed timbers. One horribly deformed leg never touched the stones but stayed hitched across the other knee. The lad quickly ladled up a frothy jackmug and handed it to his lord with a sketchy bow and an eager grin.

"And who are you, my fine lad?" Desmond asked when he took the mug.

"I am Tom, my lord." The boy bowed his head.

Desmond drank the yeasty brew and licked his lips. The remainder of the pasty pie was gone in three big bites.

"How judge ye?" the cook asked.

" 'Tis no boast. 'Tis the best pasty in the shire. Tasty as you claimed," Desmond said, licking juice from his fingers.

"Since 'tis to your liking, you may come here at this time each day and one of me pasties will be waiting for ye." She tapped her finger at the side of her nose and winked. "But tell no other or the wrath of the entire castle will come down upon me head. Me meat pies are a treat that many covet and few receive." The cook straightened her shoulders, her ample bosom straining the stained cloth of her work gown.

Desmond laughed. "I will keep it our secret only, Mistress Cook. And now, where will I find the milkmaids at this hour?"

She squinted one eye and grimaced at him. "Ye don't look like a man who sops his bread in milk. I would think ye to be a lusty gut."

Desmond grinned at her brazen assessment of him as her eyes sketched over his form, lingering for a moment on his codlings. "I have a debt to pay and it can only be paid in fresh, sweet cream," he said with a chuckle.

"Then young Tom here can show ye the way to the milkmaids. And remember, let no one know of the bargain struck this day."

Tom swung himself out of the kitchen and awaited Desmond on the pebbly path beyond the cooking-house door.

"Tell me, Cook, how did the boy come to be so twisted?" Desmond asked in a discreet whisper to spare the lad embarrassment.

"A heavy cart rolled over his knees. He was like to die but was saved by one of the healing monks at Battle Abbey, though on days when his broken knees ooze and drain I wonder that they did him any favor. Poor Tom." She shook her head, dabbed at her wet eyes, and went back to basting a haunch of brawn.

Desmond left the kitchen, walking slowly so Tom would not be obliged to hurry in his strange manner of going. Whoever had saved his life must be a master healer indeed.

Aislinn worked her stitchery, combed her hair, nibbled at the food left at her door, but her heart beat within her breast only for the time when the moon would rise.

"I am a fool. Why do I torture myself by thinking of a man I cannot have?"

Pointisbright yawned and continued to groom his ginger fur, evidently not impressed by human affairs of the heart or by his lovesick mistress.

"I should defy Giles and leave Sevenoaks. If I went to a nunnery and pled for entrance, surely Henry would allow it."

Aislinn rose and walked to the windows of her solar. Even these no longer gave her the pleasure they once did. Now she had to approach them cautiously since Desmond had glimpsed her in the window. She took care to creep up only from an angle and to stay well back so there would be no chance of his recognizing her. It was only by God's grace he had not seen her features clearly enough to know she was the girl from the maze.

The sun was no longer visible over the battlements. Praise be to the saints, it was time. Giles would be at his evening prayers, and the castle folk busy preparing for the meal that marked the end of the day. None would come to pound upon her door, to demand a word or plead with her to present herself to Desmond.

With trembling fingers she braided her hair and covered it with a cloth, binding it well at the temples and nape so no hair would escape. Then she slipped into her heavy dark-gray cloak. When she was about to enter the cupboard, a sharp knock on her outer chamber door halted her. She froze with her hand on the iron ring.

"Aislinn, it is Giles. I must speak with you."

She bit her bottom lip. If she let him in, he would wonder why she was garbed to go out. But if she did not respond, he would wrangle with her on the morrow.

"I am preparing for bed, Giles. I am fatigued."

"It is yet early; you must speak with me, Aislinn. What has come over you? Open the door."

She worried her bottom lip. Giles sounded angry. "If what you must say cannot wait until the morrow, then speak now."

"Must we converse through this closed door, Aislinn? Surely you may let me, your own cousin and confessor, into your private chamber."

"Giles, I am dressed only in my shift. 'Tis unseemly for a churchman to look upon me thus," she lied. "We can talk on the morn."

"Nay, Aislinn, we cannot. I have been summoned to Tunbridge Wells. I must leave anon."

"Is there trouble at the abbey?" She stepped nearer the door, laying her palm flat on the smooth wood.

"Trouble? Nay. Simon the younger and Eleanor are at Tunbridge. The lady bids me come and attend her. It seems she has developed some weakness of the stomach."

"And what King Henry's spoiled sister wants, no man can deny?" Aislinn said softly.

"As you say, I am in no position to deny her request. Though her husband is no favorite of the king, Henry does well love his sister and would not welcome my refusal if she is truly ailing."

"Simon de Montfort is no favorite of mine, either. Like his father, I think he is too much the warlord," Aislinn said without thinking first. Theron had once warned her that de Montfort's blood was warlike and dangerous; he had counseled her to stay clear of all bearing the name.

"As a man of the Church, I cannot indulge in such pronouncements of judgment as you may enjoy, Aislinn. I must ride all night to answer the summons. I am a man of God. I am bound to comfort and heal. Still, I am concerned for you. I want you to make me a vow ere I go."

"And what would you have me vow, good cousin?"

"I want your vow that you will not meet Desmond until I return."

"Only this morn you were urging me to come out of my chamber and meet him in the great hall, to share his trencher and his wine. You were most anxious for me to meet him." Aislinn wanted to continue meeting Desmond in the garden in secret, but she had no eagerness to reveal herself openly as the cursed red-haired wench Aislinn and see his attitude toward her alter.

"I have changed my mind on the matter. You cannot defy the king, but I do not want you to meet Desmond until I am by your side. Swear to me, Aislinn. Give me your solemn vow you will remain safe behind this door."

"Giles, you should not worry about me so."

"Aislinn, give me your solemn promise. I cannot leave Sevenoaks without it."

"As you wish, I give you my vow. Lady Aislinn of Sevenoaks will not meet her betrothed, Desmond Vaudry du Luc, before you return from Battle Abbey."

Desmond stepped back into the shadows of the corridor and pulled the tapestry over the alcove. He had been about to go to his solar when he heard the abbot speaking. The churchman's insistence that Aislinn open the door had intrigued him. By luck he had found a hidden cove from which to listen to the entire exchange—something that was not Desmond's custom. The thick door had distorted Aislinn's voice, but Desmond had heard her words. Now he stood behind the fabric and pondered Giles.

"I begin to think the abbot is much too interested in the welfare of his aging cousin," Desmond said. He would speak with Coy tomorrow about the abbot, but tonight the lure of the maze would not be ignored any longer.

Desmond stood just within the hedgestile that marked the beginning of the maze, completely hidden from view without and within. It was a marvel of engineering: in plain sight, and yet it fooled the eye so completely that none had even been compelled to investigate. In his hand Desmond carried a wooden bowl of fresh, thick cream sweetened with a fraction of a dram of fine port.

"I trow the milkmaid deems me daft or else into my dotage." He chuckled aloud, but it was worth her pity—or scorn—if his plan worked. He leaned over and placed the bowl on the loamy earth. He reasoned that Pointisbright was probably out hunting in the moonlight.

"That canny puss ever seems to be available when I need him, I pray 'tis so this eve."

Desmond stared up at the summer sky. It was a right English summer, the kind that poets sang of but Englishmen rarely experienced. The scent of blossoms from the apple and pear groves in the common was thick and fragrant in the night air.

It was a night for lovers. A night made for seducing virgins.

Desmond marked a few constellations, though he had been a poor scholar and could remember only a handful. It occurred to him that he should have remembered more, staring as he did so often at the heavens, but he had spent his youth training as a knight, not a mariner, and so with the folly of arrogance he gave little dedication to the study of the heavens.

A rustle of leaves drew his attention from the sky. The

path was dark and not easily seen. Desmond squinted, trying to make his night vision more acute. He dared not bring a light lest he give away the delicious secret of the maze to any who might see him and be curious about his purpose.

A pair of feline eyes winked from the stygian darkness. A throaty meow broke the silence.

"Ah, Pointisbright, faithful fellow. Come, look how I repay my debt to you for service rendered to your lord." A spark of hope mingled with anticipation. If the cat proved reliable, then Desmond might swive his virgin before the sun rose over the battlements.

The cat ambled over and delicately poked his nose into the cream. He withdrew and licked his whiskers.

"Come now, fine fellow. Do not play the fickle puss. Have your cream and then be my guide."

Pointisbright hesitated as if deciding whether the offering was suitable. He blinked at Desmond once and then began to lap up the thick liquid.

Desmond stood with his arms crossed, watching the cat devour the dish of cream. Would the cat walk into the heart of the maze or simply go in search of a fat mouse to top off his sup? If the cat failed him could Desmond find his own way? He thought that by now he might be able to remember the route, and would try it alone if the tom proved unreliable, but 'twould be much quicker if the puss cooperated.

Pointisbright finished the cream and looked up. He meowed once, as if aware of his human companion's desires, and turned toward the path. Quick as a hunter on the scent of prey, he ran down the crushed stone.

Desmond trotted behind the cat, feeling both a little foolish and giddy as a green, stripling youth at his first assignation. His heart was beating hard with anticipation when he emerged.

She was standing in a shaft of blue-tinged moonlight.

The huge cloak concealed her form, but from some strange inner source Desmond knew her form, the delicate curves, the nubile shape. He did not even try to hide his excitement.

"I have come to you again." Desmond was hot, itchy, and very aware of her. He dropped to one knee before her. "I fear I have lost my senses over you. I am like a man possessed; I have no will, no wish to be anywhere but here with you in this secret garden."

Aislinn's heart contracted the moment Desmond prostrated himself before her. Then he spoke and she died a little inside. Those were the words every maid longed to hear, but now she knew only sorrow. Her soul was filled with a deep, abiding pain. She could never marry this man who spoke love-words and kissed her senseless. She could not, come damnation or the axman.

"To love me is to taste death." Tears choked her. She could not tell him. She must leave him before she lost her strength and succumbed to his charms. "I am as lethal as poison to you."

She darted away from him before he could gain his feet. Quick as a blinking eye, she vanished behind a vine-covered trellis. Desmond was after her in a nonce. He heard her small feet pounding on the leaves and gravel of the path and then . . . nothing.

He stopped and listened. No sound. No rustle of leaves. No scent of her remained. He turned and looked at every empty corner of the maze. She had vanished.

Desmond was buffeted by his lust and his frustration. No woman could walk through brambles or stone.

"I believe this maze is touched by magic—or at least my virgin is. But I will find her identity and where she goes if I have to pull down the very stones of Sevenoaks to do it."

Eight

Desmond was in a fine, high temper. He had spent the past couple of days training his men, and Sevenoaks's own guard, until sweat poured down their faces in rivulets. His sword arm was burning from the effort of wielding a blade as he met worthy challengers. And still his blood was hot and high.

"Desmond, we have been at our weapons without rest for nearly four hours," Coy said, his breath coming in harsh rasps. "Are we expecting to be overrun by pagans?"

"I am not yet ready to cease," Desmond growled and swung his blade at a shield target, slicing the wood cleanly in half. He knew he was in a loutish temper because of his lust, but that did not make him any less furious. The nut of his puzzle was simple enough to see, but not so simply solved. He was commanded to wed one woman, and though his action surely branded him a coxcomb, he was enthralled by another. His dreams of a young, dutiful wife could be answered by the virgin in the garden, but his fate lay with the aging Aislinn.

He was silly to be in agony. A man should simply accept his lot in life and be done with it. Desmond was mentally berating himself when a party of men rode into the bailey. The abbot of Tunbridge Wells led a small entourage including Hadwaine, the Sheriff of Kent, who carried the royal warrant on his livery. Mereworth was in his jurisdiction, so Desmond had met him when his parents had died. Behind him rode a noble couple. Fine silks and jewels glistened on their clothes. The lady's face was familiar; she bore the same striking features as all Plantagenets.

Desmond took a step toward the gate to give welcome to Henry's sister when a great crash brought him spinning around. One of the younger knights lay in a heap on the ground, his arms and legs tangled with that of his destrier.

"He is skewered!" Coy shouted in alarm.

Desmond ran to the injured lad as fast as his legs would carry him, guilt for his selfish, mean-spirited attitude spurring him on. If he had not been in a high dudgeon of anger this would never have happened.

"By the Rood, is he slain?"

"If he is the fault is mine. Had I not been stewing in my juices, I would've heeded your warning. The horses are tired, the men exhausted. If that good knight dies and that fine mount is crippled, the shame lies upon my head."

The knight writhed and moaned in pain. A broken lance protruded from his shoulder, having pierced his body just below his collarbone. The horse was up and seemed to be sound of limb.

"We need healing herbs," Desmond said as he fell to his knees beside the knight.

"There is the croft that lies in the dale below Sevenoaks. Mayhap whoever lives there has returned. But even with healing herbs, who has the skill to use them?" Coy asked.

"I do," the abbot of Tunbridge Wells proclaimed. He and his party had gathered around the wounded man.

"You are trained in the healing arts?" Desmond asked.

"I am well versed in all manner of injury. I spent many years at Battle Abbey tending the wounded that returned from Crusade. The sin of pride is mine, for I can say I lost few men."

"We found a croft with many physics nearby. I can go and bring what you order," Coy said.

"There is no need. All that is required grows within the walls of Sevenoaks," Giles said.

"Do what you can, good Abbot. If you save this man's life you will have my gratitude," Desmond promised. "Ask of me what you will and it will be granted."

"How can I refuse such an offer?" the abbot said as he retrieved a bag from the pommel of his saddle. He began to issue orders with all the command of a general in battle.

A litter was brought. Under the abbot's instruction, the young knight was carried into the keep.

"I hope the churchman is as good as his boasts." Coy's dark face was wreathed in speculation.

"As do I. If the lad dies it is all because of my lust for a woman I cannot have."

"What woman?" Coy's brows rose.

"A woman of mysterious ways who does not exist in the light of day," Desmond said, stung by his own self-ishness and guilt.

The fallen knight was laid out on one of the huge tables in the great hall while the abbot stripped off his cloak and his fine gloves. Desmond was somewhat surprised to see the cleric wore a simple tunic and hose, covered with a light shirt of mail beneath his holy garb. Without his robes he looked more the simple warrior than a gentle man of God. It was only sensible, he supposed, to wear some protection, but then again, did Giles not believe that God was his shield?

"Tell the cook to bring as much boiling water as may be had, and lengths of clean linen," Giles ordered over his shoulder. "And send someone to the physic garden by the chapel. I want fresh yarrow, fever-wort, and spider-webs."

Coy leaned near to Desmond. "He seems to know the difference between a dirty cloth and a proper bandage. Not since the Crusades have I seen so much attention to cleanliness."

"Aye, he works much in the same manner as the healers at Acre," Desmond agreed. "And he seems to know exactly where to find the proper medicaments inside the keep."

With steady hands Giles took hold of the splintered shaft protruding from the knight's shoulder.

"Cut away his gambeson," Giles said in a clear, authoritative voice. "And do not be meek about it. I needs must stanch the blood flow lest he die."

Several brawny men-at-arms applied knife blade and muscle to the padded and reinforced garment. Soon the lad was stripped to his braies. Crimson stained his pale body and dripped onto the rushes beneath the long plank table.

"Where is that boiling water?" Giles roared.

As if conjured from the harsh and commanding power of the abbot's voice, ewers of steaming water appeared.

"Now where are the herbs? And a pestle and mortar? Make haste. Make haste. Don't be timid."

The wounded knight's moans echoed to the rafters when the shaft was ripped free of his flesh. Giles seemed oblivious to his torment. He focused his attention on the bloody rent. Taking no heed of the man's thrashing, he bathed the gaping hole; then with quick movements, he worked herbs and spiderwebs into a thick paste and forced them into the hole.

Mercifully, when Giles's fingers probed the wound, the knight slipped into insensibility. With blood dripping from his hands, Giles shouted new orders. He worked surely, and in due time the lad was swathed in clean linen bandages. His lips were pried open. A good, strong mead, fortified with more mysterious herbs and laced with thick cream, was slowly poured down his throat.

He was pale, but his chest rose and fell in a steady rhythm of breathing.

"The color of his gums attests to the fact the bleeding has not been mortal," Giles informed all who would listen. "He will live; I have saved him." Giles wiped his gory hands on a strip of huck toweling, smiling in satisfaction. "He needs must be put somewhere he may be watched. There must be no draft, but the air must be fresh, not stagnant."

"There is a small chamber off the kitchens that might serve," Tom offered, swinging to the front of the crowd on his crutches.

Giles looked at the boy and frowned darkly. At the moment when Desmond was going to offer his own chamber, the abbot nodded at Tom.

"Just so. The ovens nearby will keep him well warmed, and with door and windows kept open he should be well enough. See he is settled. Not too jostled—easy; lift him easy. I will bring a potion to aid his sleeping at nightfall." Giles smiled at Desmond. "I have not worked thus for years. 'Tis good to know my knowledge yet serves me."

"You trained while on Crusade?" Desmond asked.

"Nay, I was in service at Battle Abbey. Many returning knights and local folk needed my skills."

"Ah, then you must know crippled Tom, the lad there." Desmond indicated Tom, who swung between his crutches and led the way for the men bearing the wounded knight.

"Nay, I do not know him," Giles said quickly. He did not look in the boy's direction.

Desmond wondered how the abbot could be so sure he did not know Tom—or mayhap he did. But why would he lie?

"I am grateful you were here, Abbot. 'Twas a fortunate

happening that your business at Tunbridge Wells did not keep you overlong."

"Ah, the reason I returned so quickly slipped my mind in the heat of healing. Simon de Montfort bade me bring him so that he might meet the new lord of Sevenoaks."

"The earl of Leicester? Married to the king's sister?" Desmond asked, knowing the answer before Giles spoke.

"Aye, the same. He is of a mind to sup with you and enjoy your hospitality for a time. He will soon be journeying to Oxford to attend parliament."

Desmond clenched his hands into fists. The last thing he wanted was the schemer de Montfort here. There were whispers on the wind of a counsel of powerful barons wishing to adopt provisions of limitation on the king. 'Twas said in darkened corridors they intended to tempt the king with a fat war chest for the younger prince's bid to seize the Sicilian crown. The coin would be the incentive to force Henry to sign the document. Desmond had no desire to be caught in that broil. For even if Henry did give in, it was only a matter of time before Prince Edward took the throne, and Desmond was certain that he had a long memory.

"You forget, Giles, I am not yet lord of Sevenoaks. I have not wed the lady Aislinn."

"Then mayhap 'tis time the wedding was done. And who better to witness the ceremony than the sheriff of Kent and the king's own sister and her husband?"

Desmond was being pulled in many directions. He wanted the power that wedding Aislinn would bring him, but he wanted the freedom to pursue his mystery virgin. He ran his finger around the collar of his tunic. It felt much smaller and tighter than it had a moment ago.

Aislinn swallowed hard and leaned against the stone wall for support. It had been a horrible thing to watch as the knight and horse went down. His screams of agony were worse. Yet Aislinn had been unable to pull herself away from the window portal. Giles, wonderful Giles, with his faith and his skill at healing, had been there. Pride engulfed her when he took control and saved the knight's life.

"How many times did Theron tell me he owed his very life to the skill of the monks at Battle Abbey? I think it must have been Giles himself who saved him."

Her pride in his success was tinged with bitter envy. Aislinn would give much—all she possessed—to have the skill and ability to save a man, one man in particular. She would give her very soul if she could both have and save Desmond Vaudry du Luc.

She pulled herself away from the window when the knight was carried away. Within moments she could hear the buzz of activity outside her door. As the castle folk came and went, Aislinn heard snatches of conversation. All among them were in awe of Giles's skill and Desmond's kindness. Desmond had sent riders to the knight's family to bring them the news. And a noble and his wife were now enjoying the hospitality of Sevenoaks.

She leaned her forehead against the sturdy oak door and closed her eyes. It would do no good to hope or pray that she might somehow join the life outside her chamber. Fate had given her cursed red hair and she was doomed to be alone.

Or Desmond is doomed to die. There is no other course.

The night's supper was a great din of noise and merriment. Not only were the noble de Montfort and his wife honored guests, it seemed the entire keep celebrated being alive after death had come so close to one who dwelled inside Sevenoaks. And yet the gilt chair beside

Desmond remained empty. He found himself oddly melancholy because of it. This was Aislinn's keep, her folk. He had assumed the mantle and role of lord, yet he was a lord without his lady and only a figurehead until the wedding.

It rubbed him the wrong way that Aislinn never partook in the joy of her own demesne. She should be here to laugh and flirt and garner praise for the skill of her cousin. All in attendance should flatter her for the tasty dishes and the fine wine being served. The king's sister should ask about her health, her desires, and the upcoming wedding.

Why did she not take her place at the high table? Surely her mourning period was nearing its end by now. Or was there some other reason Desmond had not yet figured out? It was a riddle. Gwillem and Coy swore she was a plague upon the keep, and yet not a single word had been imparted to Desmond of cruelty administered by Aislinn's hand or word. It was almost as if the story was smoke and fable. But if it was no more than rumor, then who among the castle folk hated Aislinn enough to destroy her reputation by starting them at all?

"I hear you have no liking for the king's choice of wife for you." Simon de Montfort leaned around his lady wife and speared Desmond with a look.

"I have yet to meet the lady and therefore cannot say if she pleases me or no," Desmond said bluntly.

Simon and the abbot exchanged a glance. The look upon their faces made the hair on the back of Desmond's neck prickle. It was foolish, he knew, but he suddenly had the same gut-clenching sensations he experienced before going into battle.

"You have not yet laid eyes upon the wench?" de Montfort said in disbelief. "Does she hide from you?"

"My cousin has been mourning the death of her last husband," Giles interrupted.

"But you would obey my brother, the king?" Lady Eleanor asked. "This delay in meeting is not some plot betwixt you and Aislinn to thwart him, is it?"

"In all things, my lady, I am loyal to the crown. I can assure you that I have had no converse with the lady Aislinn." Desmond toyed with his goblet.

Lady Eleanor gave her husband a satisfied look; then she speared a bit of meat from her thick bread trencher.

"You have barely touched your food, Baron du Luc. And with so many savory dishes gracing the linen, I am surprised," Lady Eleanor observed, and he realized he was being watched—closely.

"When one as beauteous as yourself is nigh, all other hungers flee in shame." Desmond used the courtly manners taught to him by his adopted lady mother, Alys du Luc. In truth, Cook had provided him with two thick meat pasties after he had gone to check on the wounded knight. He and Tom shared a story or two while they devoured the pies and two cups of yeasty beer. Now Desmond had no appetite, but having given the cook his word, he would keep their tasty secret.

"You must eat, Baron, lest you sicken," the abbot advised. "I would not see another of Aislinn's husbands fall ill."

Hadwaine, the sheriff, coughed behind his hand. "If another of Aislinn's husbands falls ill, the king has ordered me to hold a thorough inquiry."

Giles's eyes narrowed. "Indeed, this is news. And what kind of inquiry?"

Hadwaine's tone was dire. "I am to subject both the keep and all within to . . . questioning."

The word lingered like a taint in the air. Many in the room knew that some methods of extracting the truth bordered upon torture.

"Ah, but Baron du Luc looks hale and hearty. I do not think he is in danger of dying," Simon de Montfort said.

"But neither is he wed to the lady yet," Eleanor quipped. "And history shows us all the men in her life stay healthy until they take her to wife."

"I doubt one has to do with the other," Desmond snapped.

"Indeed?" de Montfort asked, his brows lifted in unabashed astonishment. "Then you do not believe the rumors Giles tells us?"

Desmond thought Giles paled a bit, but the cleric remained silent.

"Aislinn has been wedded to aging knights, all carrying the scars and wounds of past battles. I think it is little more than happenstance that they died on their wedding night," Desmond defended his betrothed.

"Then you do not believe Aislinn has earned the name of Poison Flower?" Lady Eleanor asked.

"Nay, I think she is the victim in a sad travesty of fate. And if it please you, lady, I would prefer that you did not refer to my betrothed thus." Desmond was willing to risk the wrath of the king himself. He was not going to hear Aislinn spoken of badly when she was not even present to defend herself.

"As you wish. It is good to see the lady has a champion." Eleanor dipped her head and gave her husband a look full of secret meaning.

Desmond was growing tired of the banter. He was anxious to leave, casting about for any excuse, when he spotted Coy.

"My man returns. If you will pardon me, I have business to attend."

Before anyone above the salt could object, he was up and striding toward Coy, thankful for any diversion to free him from a table of royal vipers. But when he neared Coy, he saw a look of worry in his friend's eyes.

"We must talk, Desmond."

"Tell me."

"There is a plot afoot to align the barons once again. Rumor has it that Sevenoaks Keep will be the meeting place where they will draw up the document to present at parliament and to the king—and that young Simon is the leader."

Nine

"I will not have it." Desmond slapped his fist into the open palm of his other hand. "I will not have Sevenoaks and Mereworth drawn into endless political intrigue and tedious plots to emasculate the king and diminish his power."

"And yet you can do little to halt it. You have no real power until you wed. Perchance you should leave here, Desmond, return to court, and beg the king's ear." Coy's brow was furrowed.

"And tell him what? That his brother-in-law is a snake? That there are barons who want more and more?" Desmond shook his head. "This he knows well. William Briware advised the Lionheart, King John, and then Henry. He placed an ear in every corner of every baron's hall. There is no doubt Henry knows all. Nay, I needs must stay and protect Sevenoaks."

"And Aislinn?" Coy asked softly.

"And Aislinn," Desmond agreed, though the image of pale-green eyes and dewy skin flashed in his mind. He had no ill feeling toward old Aislinn, but his heart and mind had become engaged with the mysteries of Sevenoaks—and the beautiful young woman who was nearer to his ideal of a wife.

A slight movement caught Desmond's eye. "Abbot, you need not hide in the shadows. Pray, join us."

The abbot of Tunbridge Wells separated himself from the long cleft of wall near the castle well. Desmond was sure the churchman had been listening to Desmond's thoughts on de Montfort's activities.

"My lord, I was seeking a private place so I might pray and contemplate," the abbot explained smoothly.

"And did you find such solace?" Desmond looked into the abbot's eyes and saw deceit shining there.

"I, like most men, struggle with my conscience. Do you, Baron? Do you find yourself torn over what is right and what is *expected* of you as a knight of England?"

"I am pleased to give Henry my forty days of service each year."

"Ah, and about other things—about his demand you wed?"

"I am anxious to do my king's bidding as well as to establish myself as lord of Sevenoaks. There is no struggle within me."

"And about Simon . . ."

Desmond had no patience with Giles's mincing around the subject of the earl and his intrigue. "Even though I am not yet lord, I hope all who dwell inside the walls of Sevenoaks are loyal to the crown."

"When you are officially the new lord, will there be more changes?" Giles asked. "You spoke once of going to Mereworth."

"I do intend to spend much of my time at Mereworth, but I will tolerate no subversion or intrigue—from anyone, no matter how high or lowborn, at Sevenoaks. If I must lower the portcullis and remove all visitors, I will. If I deem Lady Aislinn would be more secure at Mereworth, then I will see her installed there in comfort."

" 'Tis easy to see your hackles are raised over Simon's presence."

"Nay, I offer bed and bread to all who travel, even scheming earls. My hospitality does not extend to meet-

ings and gatherings that will pull in the unwary, the innocent, and the defenseless. Such affairs put all here at
risk, especially Aislinn. I will tolerate no traitors, whether
they wear church cloth or no," Desmond said bluntly,
leaving no question that he knew of the rumors regarding
the documents for parliament and that he questioned
Giles's part in it.

Giles stiffened. He understood Desmond's meaning. If
need be, the abbot would be put to the road as quickly
as any tinker or drover. Desmond saw a hot flash of anger
in the abbot's eyes.

"I will leave you now, Baron. I will speak with my
cousin Aislinn and tell her to ready herself for the wedding anon."

"Aye, do that, Abbot, for I think her mourning time is
soon to be at an end."

Desmond stopped to check the health of the wounded
knight. As he expected, Tom was by the fallen warrior's
bedside.

"He is healing, I trow," Tom whispered when Desmond
lifted the corner of the bandage and looked at the wound.
There was no red, puckered flesh around the jagged hole,
and no flush of fever stained the lad's cheeks. There was
no doubt that Giles's boast was indeed truth: he knew
much of herbs and healing.

"Does he sleep so soundly all the time?" Desmond
asked Tom when the sound of their voices and Desmond's
touch caused not so much as a stirring.

"Nay, sometimes he is troubled. The abbot gave him
a draft of herbs but a bit ago. First the knight babbled
and thrashed about. He spoke of his youth; then he settled
into a deep slumber."

"Indeed, it seems he sleeps peacefully as a babe. None
would know his wound was nearly mortal—it does not

cause him much pain now." Desmond watched the even rise and fall of the lad's chest. There was some dark notion niggling at the back of his mind, but he could not readily grasp the thought.

"Are you off to the dairymaids, my lord? I can fetch your cream if you like." Eager as a young pup, Tom swung up on his crutches. He was amazingly fast for one so grievously crippled.

"You know about my cream?" Desmond asked.

"Oh, aye, my lord. I saw you fetching it afore sundown. I will tell no one that you have a fondness for it; if any should ask I will say you drink only ale—strong ale."

Desmond could only smile at the lad. Tom expected Desmond to be secretive about the cream because it was not a manly drink. If only the lad knew it was bribery for a feisty cat.

"I trust you to keep my secret, good Tom." Desmond patted the boy's strong shoulder affectionately. Tom's ground-down front teeth attested to the level of pain he endured each day, and yet he never complained, never shirked a duty. Cook had told Desmond that below the most shattered part of the crooked knee the wound had never healed properly and frequently wept pus and vile corruption. Yet the boy was ever cheerful and willing to work.

"I know how to keep a secret, my lord; I have many secrets in my head. I have been learning them and keeping them since before I had these." Tom jiggled his crutches.

"Then I know I am in good hands." Sevenoaks was riddled with secrets both great and small. What was one more silly secret about a tankard of cream for a helpful puss?

* * *

"I expect you to be wed by month's end, Aislinn." Giles sat on a Roman-style chair and studied her over his goblet of wine. He had brought her supper but Aislinn had been able to swallow little with Giles badgering her about the wedding.

"I have said I will not marry him, Giles. Nothing has changed. I will not wed Desmond."

"I have been patient, Aislinn, but you must cease this stubborn refusal. Simon de Montfort, Earl of Leicester, and his lady wife will be in attendance for this wedding, as well as the sheriff of Kent."

"You make it sound as if highborn witnesses will somehow change the outcome."

"Desmond Vaudry du Luc will be fine."

"Aye, he will. Desmond will not fall victim to this curse because I will not wed him. You cannot force me, Giles." She set her wine cup down and began to pace. The flames of the fire were too high, making her chamber too hot and close, but before Giles had come she had been preparing her chamber to leave and go to the maze. Now the moonlight glowed silver through her glass windows and she longed to be away from here—away from her cousin.

"Jesu! I grow weary of you, Aislinn. I know what is best in this matter. Do you no longer trust me?" Giles stood. His body was rigid with anger, but to his credit he only narrowed his eyes at Aislinn.

"I—I trust you," she said with a reluctance that surprised her.

His gaze narrowed even more, as if bringing something about her into sharp focus. "Really? It has been weeks since you confessed. Would you like to do so now? Would you like to make confession to me?"

"Nay. I would like only to go to sleep, Giles, my head is aching."

"You are too headstrong, cousin. I cannot force you to

wed, as you say, but mark me. The king is not some mewling pup to be ignored. He carries the hot temper of his grandmother, Eleanor of Aquitaine, in his blood. Do not vex him, Aislinn, lest we all taste his wrath."

"Are you certain I cannot forfeit Sevenoaks to him? I would gladly give it up and join an order—"

Giles reached out and gripped her wrist. His fingers were strong and bit into her flesh. "Do not try it, Aislinn. I warn you." He turned and left her before she could react to his strange behavior. Giles was not himself, and she could not imagine why he was so short, and so cruel.

Could he be involved with Simon and his scheme? Aislinn had heard talk about Giles's power, but she had never seen him as a politician. But tonight . . .

Oh, but what did she care? Her world had narrowed to the space of a garden. She counted three beats of her heart before she rushed to the door and threw the bolt. There had been a moment when she'd sensed violence in Giles, but surely she was mistaken. When their parents died in the same sinking ship, he had cared for her. He had ever been kind. It was Giles who arranged her wedding to Theron.

No, surely she was mistaken. Giles was her rock in a world full of stinging tongues and schemers.

An owl called, pulling her attention to the windows. Night was full upon her. She bound her hair, grabbed her cloak, and made for the maze with Pointisbright on her heels, praying she was not too late—praying Desmond would be there, and all the while hoping for his sake that he would not be.

Aislinn's breath hung in the back of her throat as she watched Desmond. Unobserved, he rubbed his fingers over the sundial. His tawny brows were furrowed, the craggy lines of his jaws taut. He was enchanting—heady as strong mead, more addictive than sin.

Desmond could not see her from her vantage point within the passage. She held her breath and slipped silently from the stones. When she turned the hidden iron ring, they began to shut with a little whisper of limestone.

Pointisbright dashed by her and ran toward Desmond. She froze. If he turned now he would catch her—would learn of the secret passage. Almost at the moment the stones found their mates and disappeared, Desmond turned and saw her.

"Do you appear by magic?" he asked softly, their eyes locking. Even in the thin light, she could feel the power of his gaze upon her.

"I have been here watching the path. I know not what means you take to reach this maze, but I know it is not the same path I take." He reached out and extended his fingers, stopping just short of touching her.

"Are you spirit? Or mayhap a nymph that lives only here among the flowers?"

"I am flesh and blood." A little voice in her head bid her tell him all, but she could not. She had given her solemn vow to Theron and would not break it. "Do you think I walk through stone?"

He finally touched her face. He rubbed the back of his knuckles down her cheek, to the curve of her jaw.

She shuddered beneath his touch.

"It matters not how you came, only that you did. Come, let me enjoy the pleasure of your company, sweet maid of the maze, for I must soon wed and will no longer find succor with you."

He took her in his arms and kissed her passionately. And all the while he was initiating her in the ways of love, she knew in her heart their time had surely run out.

Desmond wanted this woman. It mattered not that he

did not know her name, or that she grew more mysterious each night. He wanted her.

His body tightened and heated. He kissed her deeply, dipping his tongue into her mouth, running it along the edge of her teeth. She gave a little sigh of submission and he knew he could have her—he could take her. He could swive her until sunrise.

But his honor would not let him.

He lifted his head and stared at her. Had there ever been a maid with more kissable lips? Or one more elusive and mysterious?

"Nay," he said as he lightly touched the bottom of her mouth with his thumb. "I cannot dally with you and marry another. Forgive me."

He turned and left the maze as fast as his feet would carry him, with the maiden softly calling his name.

Desmond walked through the tall arched doors into the keep. From his vantage point he could see into the great hall. The earl of Leicester, Durham, Seddenham, and Falsey were all breaking bread and hatching plots at one end of the great table. They gave him a cursory glance and went back to their conversation as if his presence was of no consequence to their plans. Their behavior would have been intolerable even if he had not been itching from lust and guilt and sexual frustration.

"They take advantage since Sevenoaks has no true lord." Coy slipped from a corner and stood beside Desmond. "There is much speculation and worry among the castle folk."

"What hear you, Coy?" Desmond fought to ignore the heat in his braies, the fury in his heart.

" 'Tis said fifteen barons will come here to meet and draft their document before they journey to parliament at

Oxford. The king will be little pleased with any involved in their folly."

"You, my friend, have become a master of understating the obvious," Desmond said darkly. "If Henry would kill for the loss of a cook, what will he do about treason among the nobles of England?"

" 'Tis said they have purposely chosen Sevenoaks because the keep is without a true lord and Aislinn has no husband to guide or protect her," Coy said, giving life to Desmond's own thoughts.

" 'Struth, I can no longer think of myself alone. The time for being selfish is at an end." Desmond turned and headed toward the upper chambers. He was no love-struck swain, ruled by his tarse. He was a man with responsibilities. Sevenoaks folk needed a strong hand to lead them lest they fall into a pit of vipers and incur Henry's wrath. Aislinn did not deserve to be dragged to the axman because she was not young and virginal.

"It is time to do my king's bidding. 'Tis time I took the lady to wife."

"Lady Aislinn, I would have a word with you—now." Desmond knocked on the door of Aislinn's chamber. "Lady, you needs must obey me. 'Tis time we met."

Nothing but silence from within.

"May I be of assistance?" Giles hurried toward Desmond, his eyes wide, his robes flowing behind him.

Desmond turned back to the door and knocked again, ignoring the cleric. Was Aislinn so elderly that she could not hear the summons? Could it be that her hearing had been lost along with her youth?

"Aislinn, open the door and admit your betrothed."

"Come back on the morrow—" Giles began.

"Nay, I shall meet my betrothed anon. I do not need

your assistance, Abbot; go find a soul to comfort—or a plot to hatch."

Giles's mouth tightened into a grim line, but he did not rise to Desmond's bait. "Perchance Aislinn is early to bed," Giles provided smoothly, though there was a glimmer of unease in his eyes—or was it simply anger at Desmond's dismissal.

"Mayhap that is the case, but the time has come, Abbot. If you have ways of communicating with your cousin that I am not privy to, then tell her our wedding will take place."

"When?"

"By eve on the morrow. And then as soon as I may, I will take her to Mereworth. There is too much intrigue within this keep to suit me. I will not have the lady in danger." Desmond waited to hear the churchman's objections. Instead, the smile that blossomed across Giles's face stunned Desmond.

"As you say, my lord. I will rouse her somehow and make haste to see she is prepared both to wed and to travel."

Desmond nodded stiffly and turned away. He had expected the abbot to object. He suspected the churchman had aligned himself with de Montfort and preferred Sevenoaks without a lord. That the abbot was eager for the wedding, and eager to have Aislinn far away at Mereworth, made his stomach clench. Perchance he had misjudged the man. For it seemed he was most anxious to see Aislinn and Desmond wedded and gone.

The sun rose and Sevenoaks ignited with activity. All within had a duty to perform to see their lady wed by evening. Even Desmond and his men spent their time making sure their tunics were brushed and their mounts readied so the wedding party might leave immediately.

And now that Desmond was no longer counting the hours before he could meet his mystery woman in the maze, they seemed to move in the same fashion and pace as before. His infatuation was foolish when he really thought about it. He had seen her less than a half-dozen times; he had never learned her name or anything important about her. She was little more than a phantom of the night—a vision conjured by his longing for a young and dutiful wife.

"Why then does my heart grieve at the prospect of binding myself to Aislinn and never seeing the virgin again?" he asked himself as he scraped a sharp blade across his beard. Why did he see flashes of the maiden's sad eyes each time he closed his own?

" 'Twas no more than lust and a foolish fancy. 'Tis time to surrender. I will not have a young wife, nor children to dandle on my knee in my old age. I must do my duty to Henry and to Aislinn."

Desmond washed and dressed his hair, selected a proper jewel as a token for Aislinn, and quit his chamber without the giddy anticipation of most men about to be wed. Though he took little joy in the task, he went early into the hall below to toast with the noble guests and await his bride.

After a respectable amount of mead had been consumed, the assembled earls, ladies, and highest castle folk gathered on the steps of the Sevenoaks chapel. The brew had brought about the bluff glow of good cheer. All those gathered in the bailey were laughing and joking as they awaited the arrival of the lady Aislinn. In the fullness of time the cheery banter lessened. Jests and laughter became sporadic. Soon there were whispered rumblings of concern.

"This bodes ill. If my lady bride is so vain that she is late for her own wedding, I trow I will be a man much abused," Desmond said lightly. A round of hearty laughter eased the tension.

Desmond supposed the elderly Aislinn was doing her best to tame the hideous red hair. A chilling vision of frizzy, artificially hued locks coiling like snakes around her wrinkled face momentarily gripped him.

"She will be here anon," the abbot of Tunbridge Wells said with confidence. "I informed her myself of the time of the wedding."

"She must come," Lady Eleanor said. "To do less than offer complete obedience to my brother is suicide."

A few in the crowd of barons and earls showed their bravado by laughing at the macabre remark. But Desmond marked a few pale faces.

"A woman who has buried four husbands surely has a strong instinct for survival," Simon de Montfort said. "I cannot believe she would disobey and invite Henry's wrath."

"I will go and bring her anon." The abbot left in a flurry, his flowing robes billowing on either side of his legs as he took the stairs at a gallop.

He was gone only moments. His cheeks were stained red. His eyes narrowed. "My lord Desmond . . . I can't—that is, I know not how to say—"

"The lady Aislinn will not have me?" Desmond provided helpfully.

A hush fell over the nobles. Wide-eyed ladies blinked in disbelief.

"That cannot be . . ." Lady Eleanor began.

"But 'tis true," the abbot said. "Aislinn refuses to wed. She says under pain of death she will not have the baron Desmond Vaudry du Luc."

A stunned silence descended. No man, woman, or child spoke, or even stirred. And then he could stand it no longer. Desmond threw back his head and laughed heartily at the absurdity of it all. He had finally decided to wed the aging crone with hideously dyed red hair, and she threw his magnanimous gesture in his face.

"She will not have me. 'Tis a rich farce. Rich and deadly indeed. But I admire the lady—she has a spine of steel and a valorous heart."

Ten

"Do you realize what you have done?" Giles roared. "I cannot be responsible for the consequences of this madness!"

"You are not responsible, Giles. I am." Aislinn could hear her cousin pacing outside her locked and barred door. The fury in his voice both stunned and frightened her, but she would not be bullied or forced to change her mind.

"You know not what you say. God's bones! The king will have your head and the head of any who share your blood."

"Ah, so it is your own neck you worry for and not mine? Be at ease, Giles; I hardly think the king will notice if one much-widowed woman does not wed again. He will be busy with his cathedrals or his son's wars, and if he does take notice I will be sure to advise him you tried your best to sway me. Now leave me in peace."

"I demand you open this door and present yourself below stairs for the blessing and wedding. You *must* wed and bed Desmond Vaudry du Luc, and it must be done today. He wishes to travel before dark."

Aislinn stepped back from her side of the door. The emotion in Giles's voice was not feigned. She had never seen him in such a fine temper. Surely he did not believe the king's wrath would extend to a powerful churchman.

'Struth, the king well favored Giles. Nay, he was in no true danger, she was sure. But if that was true, why was he in a roaring rage?

"Aislinn, you will wed Desmond Vaudry du Luc and you must do it anon."

Aislinn's taut nerves snapped. "I will not have him, Giles. Do you hear? I will not wed Desmond Vaudry du Luc. Not this day, not any other day. Now cease bullying me!"

"If you do not open this door, by the saints I swear with my own hands I will hack it to pieces and drag you to the steps of the chapel by your hair."

"Over my cold, dead body," Desmond said. He leaned against the hard stone wall.

Giles, the abbot of Tunbridge Wells, spun around, his face turning green as a toad's spleen when he saw Desmond lounging no more than an arm's length away. "My lord Baron, I did not hear you approach."

"Obviously, Abbot." Desmond had been listening to this argument for long minutes, completely unnoticed by Giles. He folded his arms across his chest to keep from throttling the abbot.

"Now that you are facing me, let there be no mistake of words between us. I may not be lord of Sevenoaks by virtue of wedding the lady Aislinn, but I am a knight of the realm. No man, even a man of the cloth, will force a woman to wed against her will."

"But the king—"

The clatter of boots on the steps announced the arrival of Hadwaine, the sheriff of Kent, and Simon de Montfort with his lady wife, Eleanor. They were round-eyed and eager to hear more drama.

"She will not have me. It is that simple. Whether Henry will pull down the very heavens because of it, the lady will not have me. She does not think I will suit. And while there is breath in my body, no man will force a woman to the altar against her will. Not even you, her cousin."

"You know not what you say—"

Desmond pushed himself away from the stones and stalked toward Giles. He grasped the abbot's tunic front and pulled him near. "Aye, I know what I say. I will kill you if you bring one more moment of grief to the lady's door." Desmond released his grip and turned away in disgust. He pushed himself through the gaping group of barons and strode down the steps.

Aislinn stood with her ear to the door of her chamber. Never in her life had anyone defended her like Desmond had. And he had done it for her.

Not for his virgin of the maze, but for me, for Aislinn. She slid down the door into a heap on the hard stone floor. She pulled her knees to her chest and allowed the tears to come.

"I love him more each day—a man I can never have."

The tension within the walls of Sevenoaks was thicker than the cream Desmond placed before Pointisbright that night. He stood just within the hidden entrance of the maze, fighting a war with himself. He wanted to see his mysterious maiden, but a new conflict flourished within him.

Today his betrothed had laid claim to a chunk of his heart.

With her courage and her determination, Aislinn, the aging bride he did not want or need, had won his admiration, respect, and loyalty. It was not often that Desmond found a woman who could inspire such unabashed awe. Aislinn, regardless of her age or looks, was *sans pareil.*

Without equal, he mused.

He had not felt such a rush of reverence since he'd heard the story of his brave, doomed mother and how she had tried to save her three children from slaughter at the hands of de Lucy's assassins. Aislinn, it would seem, was cut from the same ell of cloth: a woman of virtue, of principle—a woman who would face death rather than give up her convictions. His heart swelled with pride for the woman who refused him.

"I am sorry she will not have me," he told Pointis-bright. "A man would be fortunate to have such a female as his helpmate and his lady. With such a woman at his side, any man would feel like a king. Such a woman would breed sons and daughters to comfort a man in his dotage."

But Aislinn was old. There would be no children . . . and still his feelings toward his unwanted bride had changed, melding into both pride and disappointment. He would have her—willingly, gladly—because she had a valiant heart and spirit. But she would not take him.

And because of that, Desmond could not enter the garden. Even when Pointisbright finished the cream and ambled down the leaf-strewn path, Desmond could not follow—not now, maybe not ever again.

If he did, he would feel disloyal to Aislinn, a woman who was too honorable to be wronged by a man who was smitten by lust for another woman.

That, he could not and would not do.

Aislinn stared at the sundial in silence. The half-moon was high and Desmond had not come.

"But why?" she said to Pointisbright, who shared the cold stone seat with her. "Now that Aislinn has refused to have him, why will he not come to me?"

The confusion in her mind was like sharp daggers, cutting away at her confidence, tearing rents in her heart. One part of her was ecstatic that Desmond had risen in defense of Aislinn, while another part of her wanted him to come to the maze in search of her, the nameless maid.

She was both women and she was neither. It was a terrible, sharp twist in her soul. If he but knew she was the same woman . . . "But he cannot know," she announced sadly. "I love him as the maiden and as Aislinn, but he does not care a groat for either."

Desmond was pacing the floor of his private chamber in the dark when the rider came. He saw the torches flicker and sway like liquid gold against the stygian fabric of night as the guard yelled the alarm. A few moments went by and then the creak and grind accompanied the lowering of the drawbridge.

He raced down the stairs to see who would be given admittance at this late hour, knowing it could not be good tidings. There was a murmur of voices, the creak and clang of the mechanism lifting the portcullis followed by the sound of rapid footsteps over paving stones. Just as Desmond reached the outer doors of the keep, a man rushed forward and went down on one knee.

"Baron Desmond Vaudry du Luc?" A black-armored knight clapped his fist to his heart.

"Aye."

"I bring greetings from King Henry. He and his entourage arrive on the morrow." The black knight pulled a vellum scroll from beneath his dark cloak. He put it into Desmond's hand.

"From the king. For your eyes only, Baron."

"Gramercy. Please, take food and drink and ease yourself for the night; you have the hospitality of Sevenoaks." Desmond's grip tightened on the scroll. He marked the curious and uneasy gazes of Hadwaine, Giles, and most of de Montfort's barons as the knight found his way to the kitchens for refreshment.

"If there are any among you who suddenly have cause to leave before sunrise, pray do not feel any need to make your apologies," Desmond said with a lift of his brow.

One stricken look of panic was exchanged, and a goodly portion of the barons quit the hall in a buzz of whispers.

"No matter what punishment Henry metes out, it will be worth the pain to have that nest of vipers gone from this keep," Desmond muttered as he climbed the stairs to his empty chamber.

The scroll was a royal proclamation bearing the heavy wax seal of Henry himself. Desmond broke the seal and unrolled the skin, his heart thumping loudly in his chest. He scanned the writing and heaved a great sigh.

"So, it has come to this," he murmured to himself. "Ah, but what did I expect?" The ancient ogham stones and the prophecy of the Vaudrys flashed in his mind. "Mayhap the old legend is true. Perchance I may rise from the dead." He chuckled darkly.

Suddenly his chamber was too tight, too confining. He strode to the door and flung it open. Out in the hall he could hear the sounds of the barons making preparations to flee before the king arrived.

"Like rats on a sinking barge." He locked his private chamber door, wanting nothing more than to ride Brume. "One last time."

Aislinn turned the ring that opened the panel in the lord's chamber. She crept inside. Desmond's presence washed over her, filling her with desire. She missed him—missed his voice, his laugh, the way he made her pulse beat a little faster.

A vellum scroll was lying on the chest at the foot of his bed. She saw the royal seal.

"It would be wrong to read it," she told herself even

as she reached out and picked it up. Her eyes scanned
the rich lettering. With a softly spoken oath, she dropped
the parchment and ran back to the corridor. "I never expected Henry to go this far."

Sunrise splayed golden rays over the upper edge of
Sevenoaks's crenellations and found the folk within hard
at their labors. The chambers vacated by the fleeing barons had been aired, linen freshened, and new rushes
spread upon the floors. Pigs and lambs had been slaugh-
tered. The fires in the meat-cooking house were blazing
like Satan's own.

"Lord Desmond, I have your pasties ready for ye."

Desmond walked to the long, scarred table and
plopped down on a battered stool.

" 'Tis proud we are to be entertaining the king, and
make no mistake, the food Sevenoaks will serve shall be
of the best quality. I have been up since before prayers
basting the stag and rubbing lamb with rosemary and bay.
The meat will be tender and tasty. Ye'll not be shamed
by the Sevenoaks larder."

Desmond smiled, but he could not work up much enthusiasm. "I am quite sure the king will find nothing
amiss with your cooking."

"Pray, my lord, are you ailing?" Cook asked. "You
have not touched yer pie."

"Lord Desmond, are you in need of physicking?" Crippled Tom swayed near, putting his weight on the crude
crutches. Desmond felt a surge of pity for the pain he
must endure each day.

"Nay, Tom, I am not sickening. Pray, do not let my
mood spoil your good humor. Be of good cheer. Before
the king's arrival I want you to have a fine new tunic."

"Oh, my lord, I could not—"

Desmond waved his hand to silence the boy's protests.

"Nay, do not gainsay me. Go to the stable and find my squire. Tell Gwillem to find tunics for you both, if not in my chests, then Coy will have extras. A baron must have his best men properly liveried."

Tom's face flushed. Then, in a rare moment, the tension and pain seemed to ease from his young face. In that tiny march of time Desmond saw what the lad might have looked like if a wagon wheel had not crippled him and left him grinding his teeth in torment. He was a strapping boy with a plain, honest face full of loyalty and bluff kindness.

"I vow I shall repay you," Tom said shyly. "Though I may be a cripple I am stout of heart, my lord."

"I have no doubt of it. Now be off with you. Bathe your body and don your new clothing; the king will be here anon." Tom swung away quickly, obeying Desmond's command.

"Ye be a good man, Baron. Not many's ever showed the boy a kind word afore ye." Cook patted at her eyes with a corner of her head covering. "Now you follow your own words, if I may make so bold. Go, bathe your face and don proper garb for the king's arrival."

"As you say, Cook. A man must do his king's bidding or be ready to suffer the consequences," Desmond said with a dry laugh. He wondered whether his bravado and humor would be with him when the king and his favorite axmen rode beneath the portcullis of Sevenoaks.

Heralds and outriders announced the king long before the dust from his entourage's tail climbed over the horizon. Every living soul within Sevenoaks, save the castle's own chatelaine, stood within the bailey awaiting the monarch. The inner courtyard was a mass of humanity.

"Cor, what a crush!" Coy and Desmond stood cheek

by jowl with the schemer de Montfort and his lady wife, Eleanor.

"The folk of Sevenoaks will be retelling the events of this day to their grandchildren," Desmond said.

"Aye, seeing the king is a rare experience. It is a matter of pride to open the castle gates to the monarch of the land."

"Almost as spectacular as a beheading. I have heard he travels with nigh onto a hundred. Feeding them will likely strip the larder," Desmond growled. It was a fact that many a baron was brought to the verge of beggary by lavish entertainments for the crown as the king and his attendants rode about the land traveling to and from his favorite holdings.

Tom and Gwillem appeared among the crowd. Gwillem elbowed a path and Tom swung into the gap. They worked well together. Desmond noted they were clean, their wet hair plastered and slicked against their skulls. An unlikely pair: the small, straight boy and the tall, crippled lad. They slowly worked their way nearer to Coy and Desmond.

"Ah, my best men here to attend me," Desmond said loudly. All eyes turned. The other folk moved aside and a wide corridor opened before the boys. The blushing duo obeyed their lord's command.

"My lord, we should not rise above ourselves," Gwillem said sagely.

"Nonsense. I want my three best men at my side on this day of all days. A man should have his most trusted men at his back on the day of his wedding—and the hour of his death." Desmond was determined to put on a good face, though he was less than jolly.

Coy cast an uneasy glance at Desmond, but before he could say anything the king's heralds cleared the gates. The horns blew and three knights entered. Then, as cleanly as Moses parting the waters, the mob created a corridor. The king, in full royal plumage, appeared riding a fine prancing chestnut stallion. At his flank, tall, regal with a hint of cruel dignity in his pale eyes, rode Prince Edward, the "Longshanks." At his tail, knights in flashing armor, litters carrying noblewomen, and carts full of personal items poured through the gates of Sevenoaks. Though the bailey was large and expansive, big enough to let the castle animals graze and fatten without inconveniencing the household, that green suddenly seemed small. The throng swelled to the very curtain walls. Pennants, banners, and heralds blowing horns filled the lower bailey.

"Lord preserve us," Lady Eleanor whispered. "My warrior nephew accompanies his father. There will be blood spilled within the walls of Sevenoaks Keep if I know that one's habits."

"Desmond Vaudry du Luc," the king's herald bellowed. "Step forward and receive your royal gift from Henry, King of England."

Desmond stepped forward, heartened that Coy, Gwillem, and even Tom swinging on his crutches were behind him.

"Sire." Desmond bent his leg, bowed his head, and submitted to his king.

"Enough, enough, gain your feet, my good fellow. See what we have brought you." The king clapped, and a covered litter borne by sweating squires was brought forth. "These are from my private flock at Winchester."

The cover was yanked away to reveal a pair of peafowl. The iridescent blue-green of the cock's neck feathers caught the light and turned the fine feathers to jeweled hues. Royal peacocks were a coveted item, a symbol of favor.

"You are too kind, sire," Desmond said.

"I have heard that you are not yet shackled to the lady of the keep. It is true?" The question came from the prince as he speared Desmond with his bird-of-prey eyes. He did not blink, he did not smile. His was a face of stone as he waited for Desmond's answer.

" 'Tis true," Desmond said in a clear, strong voice, never looking away from that hard gaze.

"She will not have me." Desmond's lips hitched up, and he could not suppress his grimace. It was the tenderest irony that a woman he had not wished to wed had refused to wed him.

The king frowned darkly at Desmond's words. "You received my royal proclamation telling you of our arrival?"

"Aye, sire."

"I expected better from you, Vaudry du Luc."

" 'Twould seem your will means little to this Poison Flower of Sevenoaks," Prince Edward taunted. "She flaunts your will in your face."

Henry's expression darkened. "There will be a wedding or their will be a chop. Let all hear what I proclaim. If at sundown Lady Aislinn does not present herself at the steps of Sevenoaks chapel to willingly wed Desmond Vaudry du Luc, his head will roll." Henry swiveled in his saddle. "Now, sister of mine, attend me and tell me what mischief your husband is been at. William Briwere's spies tell me the tentacles of your husband's intrigue reach all the way to court. 'Tis said Simon opposes my new fair to be held at Westminster. Is this so?"

"Nay, brother, he does not oppose, only fears that a fair scheduled to last a fortnight will cause the loss of income from the usual fair at Ely. He worries for you, brother, for that will cause a loss of revenue to the crown. The bishop of Ely is likewise minded."

"Ah, and because a bishop gives sanction you think I shall be swayed? Your lord husband is more a merchant than even I thought, Eleanor. Did your bishop tell you the fair I propose is to honor St. Edward? The people

love him and our good bishop of Ely should do the same,"
Henry snapped.

Eleanor dipped her head and smiled slyly at her
brother, the king. "I fear you will beggar us all in order
to rebuild old tombs at the minster and honor the saint.
Some say the dead in London have finer quarters than
the living."

The king's face was a study in anger and disbelief. But
he schooled his features and smiled coldly.

"Westminster will be rebuilt; the fortnight fair will be
held. And I doubt your claims of beggary, sister, for your
cloth is fine and your jewels plentiful. Now, do not try
and turn my mind from the original question. I will meet
with you anon, and I expect a full accounting of that
rascal earl you are wedded to."

She swept into an elegant bow, her face like stone.
Then she stood and lightly placed her hand on her
brother's forearm. The king and his sister walked side by
side up the steps and into the great hall. Desmond
watched the flood of advisors, lords, and ladies following
at a respectful pace. And behind them all came Simon,
the much discussed but unacknowledged earl.

"He does not look happy," Coy said near Desmond's
ear.

"Happiness is a fleeting thing," Desmond commented.
He felt a surge of pity for Simon, until he remembered
his own fate.

"Come, I will walk with you," Coy offered.

"To where?" Desmond asked with a lift of his brow.
He could finally breathe again now that most of the king's
entourage had disappeared into the keep and the crush
of bodies had lessened.

"To Lady Aislinn's chamber. She must be made
ready—by force if necessary."

"Nay, Coy." Desmond frowned at his friend, somewhat
surprised that his boon companion could even consider

what he suggested. "Did you not hear what I told her cousin Giles? I will not be party to forcing any woman to wed."

"Aye, but that was before. The king will take your head if she does not wed you."

"I will force no woman. Whether it means my life or not, I will take no woman to wife who does not present herself willingly."

"By the Rood!" Coy exclaimed. "Are you so tired of life?"

"Nay, I am not. 'Struth, I have much to live for, but I will not live at the expense of seeing my convictions murdered."

"You are a fool, Desmond, or do you believe that prophecy carved into the stones near your ancestral home? Do you think you truly can rise from the dead a second time?—for if you do you are surely wrong." Coy stalked off, mumbling curses about cruel princes and fickle women as he went.

"Lady, you need not speak, just listen to what I say." Desmond spoke through the lady's chamber door. "The king has arrived, but I want you to know that I meant what I said. You will not be forced to wed."

Desmond leaned his head against the rough, studded planks. "I have made arrangements for your safe travel to my home at Mereworth after the king is gone—he plans on taking Sevenoaks for the crown. Do not fear. You will not be placed into a nunnery; I have seen to that." He did not say the words *after my head is gone from my body,* but they were in his mind. "You and any of your household who wish shall be cared for and protected at Mereworth."

Aislinn leaned her head against the door. She choked on the hot, dry lump in her throat. Jesu, why did Des-

mond have to be so honorable? She had read the proclamation; she knew that Henry was threatening to pull
down Sevenoaks stone by stone. And little did she care
about that, but to hear Desmond tell her of arrangements
for her care and safety as if . . . as if he would not be
alive . . .

"Be at ease, lady, and know that whatever happens, I
have admired your courage and determination. God be
with you, Aislinn."

She heard the soft thud of Desmond's boots as he
moved from the door. She stood there with her palm
pressed against the rough wood and tried to ignore the
pain twisting in her heart. If only, *if only* she were not
cursed.

"Lady?" A new voice called softly, followed by a
knock. "Lady Aislinn, do you hear me?"

"Who are you?" Aislinn asked.

"I am Coy of Brambourg, friend of Desmond du Luc.
Lady, I must tell you what has come amiss."

"I know of the king's proclamation," she said.

Coy clenched his hand into a fist. He would like to
hammer down the door and drag the wench out by her
hair. It was not fair that Desmond should suffer because
she was a fickle harpy.

"Then you are aware the king will see his will done
in this matter or Desmond will die?"

"What? What say you? I know only that Henry threat-
ens to confiscate Sevenoaks. If this is true, why did your
lord not come to plead with me himself? Why did he
send you?"

"He did not send me, lady; I am here of my own account. I love him as a brother and think he is wrong in
this matter."

"How so?"

"He vows he will take no wife by force. He would

rather die than sully his honor by seeing a woman forced to wed him. He is prepared to meet the axman this day."

"Your lord sounds very noble."

"Aye, he is, lady, noble and strong. Will you come? Will you save the life of my lord Desmond?"

"Have you not heard the rumors about me?"

Coy shuffled his feet. He had not expected such directness from a woman—from *this woman*.

"So you have heard the talk that I am wicked and evil. You know they call me the Poison Flower?"

"Aye."

"Then isn't your lord Desmond in mortal peril if he weds me?"

Coy swallowed hard and digested her words. "It may be as you say, lady, but know this. Desmond will surely die by the ax this eve if you do *not* wed him. I know not if you are a practicer of poison or if four of your husbands were simply old and frail, as Desmond bids me believe. But I do know the king will not change his mind."

A short silence was Coy's answer. Then he heard the soft voice say, "I will think on what you have said."

Eleven

A full-grown ox was spitted. A dog in harness turned the mechanism to evenly roast the beast as he chased after a joint just out of his reach. The bullock crackled and sizzled, browning over the flames. At the end of the hound's labors he would be rewarded with a chunk of meat and a big joint still holding the marrow.

The entire meat kitchen was in use as eels were poached in honey wine, plucked geese were being stuffed, and a score of blackbirds were being spiced for the king's favorite dish.

Desmond barely found an empty space to perch upon. Tom leaned on his crutch and watched in silence while Desmond ate his daily meat pasty.

"My lord, yer look like a man going to his doom, but have heart, do not despair," Cook said. "The lady will show herself. She is not unkind. She will not let you lose your head."

Desmond's head came up. "You know her?"

The cook crushed chestnuts with a pestle, making a fine flour to roll venison strips in. "Oh, aye, when first she came to Sevenoaks to marry our dear lord Theron she was a bright little sprite. A quick smile and a kind word were ever to be had from our lady Aislinn. She oft visited the kitchen to ask about me health."

"What happened to change that?" Desmond asked, wondering why Aislinn had chosen to lock herself away.

"After our lord Theron's death, she began to change a little. I never knew where the stories started, but one day, as if shot from a bolt of lightning, rumors were whispered about the lady."

"No doubt some of the castle folk."

"Oh, nay, my lord. All of Sevenoaks loved her and pitied her. Nay, the stories were odd. The rumors just were."

"What sort of rumors?"

"Odd-like, it was. 'Twas said that any maiden with hair the color of flame was wicked and should be shunned. I never heard such afore. None of Sevenoaks had ever believed the likes of that. The abbot offered up special prayers and such like to combat the evil. Soon the lady stopped coming to the kitchens. After the next two husbands died, she stopped coming below stairs at all except to eat in the hall. Then, after the last death, she shut herself away in her chamber. I see food is taken up each morn and nooning so she will not suffer. The poor little mite."

Desmond had wondered who made the arrangements for Aislinn's comfort and meals. He thought it might be Giles who made sure she did not hunger. Strange that the very people who were supposedly terrified of Aislinn had cared enough to see to her daily needs. It was more of the deepening mystery, but soon Desmond would be free from earthly cares and woes. Henry would take Sevenoaks, and it would be his privilege or curse to solve the riddle or see the keep in ruins.

"I will have another pasty, Cook," he said when the last crumb was licked from his fingers.

"Your appetite is good today, my lord. That is a good sign."

"Should this be my last meal on earth, then I wish it to be your pasty pies."

"Never say so, my lord—"

"Nay, we will speak of it no more, Cook. For now I am content. I have good food, good company. Tom, will you join me in a last tankard of beer?"

With a smile of pride and affection, Tom made as if to rise.

"Nay, keep your seat. I will pour and see if I am half so good as you." Desmond did manage to pour out two mazers of beer without spilling a drop on the stone floor.

"To my best boon companions. May you live long and well." Desmond tipped up the mug and drained it. Then he had another. Perhaps the brew would dull the ax's edge.

Desmond looked right and left to make sure he was not seen. With so many new people in the keep and most of them busy with the king's arrival, it was unlikely he would be noticed. That justification and several tankards of ale had made him risk one last visit to the maze. He hoped to find his virgin so he could tell her himself that she would be welcomed at Mereworth.

He darted behind the concealing greenery and walked briskly down the path. He reached the heart of the maze, but it was empty. The gurgle of the small fountain and the chirp of birds plucking nesting material from the vines were his only companions.

A feeling of melancholy dark and thick as a cloak forced him down to the slab of stone near the sundial. Desmond's eyes wandered over the time keeping device. It was oddly constructed, different in some subtle way his mind could not bend itself around. Idly he ran his fingers over the surface, wondering why he should care about something so mundane as a sundial when he was to die.

Mayhap it is because my own time is drawing to a close that I choose to think of counting hours.

Desmond prayed that he would not shame himself. He prayed for strength and courage when it came time to place his neck upon the block for the king's justice.

"You look finer than most of the men in the royal entourage," Coy of Brambourg said as he entered Desmond's chamber.

"Aye, 'tis true, my lord Desmond," Gwillem agreed. He began to straighten the chamber, making neat his lord's belongings.

Desmond had bathed in the huge tub lined and padded with linen around the top edge. Using a rough brush, Gwillem had tidied his best tunic, embroidered with the badges of both Vaudry and du Luc.

"A man should meet his Maker looking his best."

"We are here to attend our friend before his wedding," Coy said with a determined frown. "I cannot believe the lady will let you perish."

"Ah, but the lady does not know of the king's intent. She is never below stairs and does not know of Henry's promise," Desmond countered as he straightened his girdle and wrapped the long end of leather around. Gwillem used the brush to smooth the tunic over Desmond's shoulders.

"Gwillem, do not fuss. You both should go and entertain yourselves," Desmond urged.

"Nay, we will stay and walk down with you," Coy said, plopping down on the big bed. He bounced a bit. " 'Tis soft and large enough for good bed sport."

Desmond turned and frowned at his friend. He was acting as if Desmond's wedding was a fait accompli.

"Your mood has lightened. Have you been much at the wine?"

"Nay, I have a feeling the lady will not fail you," Coy said.

Desmond scowled at Coy. "What deviltry have you been at, Coy? You remember what I said? No woman will be forced."

He smiled evasively. "Aye, I remember. No lady will be dragged to the chapel steps, not even to save your neck."

"Coy, you give me pause. Was it not you and Gwillem who were wolfing my food and wine recently, sure that I was to be poisoned?"

Coy colored hotly and sat up stiffly on the bed. His swarthy face was somber. "Scoff if you must, but I still think someone in this castle may be using herbs and potions to do the lords to death."

"To what end?" Desmond asked sharply. "Name me one person who has benefited overmuch. The Church, the crown, and the lady Aislinn all have received a bit, but by no means enough to commit murder four times over."

"We may not yet know the reason, but I still believe the threat exists. It would please me if you did not drink before I taste your brew tonight."

Desmond smiled and clapped a hand to his friend's shoulder. "After my head leaves my neck, you will worry no more about what passes my lips."

A handful of sly-eyed barons had remained with Simon de Montfort, and they, along with the king's traveling retinue, filled the upper bailey and crowded toward the steps of the holy place. The greensward leading to the chapel of Sevenoaks was resplendent in color from their cloaks, tunics, and jewels. Tonight they would be entertained, either by a royally commanded wedding or by a beheading. Each was greeted with equal enthusiasm by Henry's court.

Men, women, and even children had gathered, the spectacle of blood and seeing the king and prince too great a lure to ignore.

Henry III's court was a broth of intrigue. His son, Prince Edward, was every inch the warrior. All could see the tall, well-muscled prince chafing for the day when he would deal with the fractious barons, earls, and scheming clergy. Into the midst of this intrigue, Desmond presented himself with as much dignity and aplomb as he could muster. The din of voices, laughter, and conversation was loud as Coy walked beside Desmond to the spot where the king sat waiting.

Suddenly, Coy's former confidence was gone. He was pale, his lips beaded with a line of sweat.

"Chin up, Coy. I am determined to meet my death with courage."

"But not like this, Desmond. To die in battle is one thing, but to lose one's head because the king is in a bluster is another," Coy growled into Desmond's ear. "Say the word and we will make a fight of it—back to back we can take down a dozen at least. You may die, but at least you will do it with a sword in your hand."

"Nay, Coy, lift not a finger on my behalf. After all, a man eventually dies; at least I will provide a little spectacle for this coldhearted mob."

"Would that I had your salty humor." Coy looked around at each face as if committing them to memory. "I had hoped—I was sure the lady—"

"Leave it, Coy. The lady will not have me." Desmond took the first step. By the time his foot touched the second riser of worn limestone, an eerie, strained silence had fallen over the crowd of onlookers.

"Ah, Vaudry du Luc, I see you are well ready. I am

pleased. Now, if the lady will show herself, we can have the abbot of Tunbridge Wells say a prayer for your health and get to the business of the feast. My stomach growls." The king was in fine spirits, it would seem.

"Sire, about Sevenoaks. I would be honored to purchase the keep—" the abbot began, waving his brightly gloved hands in the air. He wore a pair of gauntlets fashioned from fine kid, dyed bright saffron yellow. In the wash of sunset they were garish and ugly.

"Abbot, be silent. Do not be impatient to see du Luc into his tomb." The king raised a hand and gestured to the west. "The sun is not yet beyond the horizon. We will wait—a bit."

"Aye, Father, there is no rush," Prince Edward said with a lift of one brow. "The axman can work as well by torchlight as by gloaming."

Desmond heard Coy swallow hard beside him. He turned to watch the golden-red orb slip behind the cover of the crenellated castle battlements. It was a beautiful sunset, the kind every man should see his last day on earth.

Twelve

A strange, hushed murmur began in the crowd. It grew, rose, and fell like ocean waves crashing upon a rocky shore. Desmond heard his own name whispered by many lips.

He turned to see why.

There, swathed from head to foot in a pale ivory veil of intricate lace, opaque yet not quite see-through, walked a small woman. The veil appeared to be many layers of cloth, folded and arranged to conceal, held in place by a gold circlet at brow level.

Desmond could see no sign of the woman's features, but within the folds of gauzy fabric he spied the muted tones of long, red hair.

"Aislinn?"

"Lady Aislinn." The king raised his bejeweled hand in welcome. "You were nearly too late, but well enough in time to save Desmond's neck. Come, let us get on with it; the celebration feast is waiting."

Without a word, the small, concealed figure climbed the two steps and stood beside Desmond. She appeared to be something not of this world. He found himself recalling the rumors of her sorcery. At the same time, his heart swelled again in pride.

This was a woman who had strength and courage and *compassion*. She was willing to take a man she did not want to save him from the block. She was willing to sacrifice herself on the altar of marriage in exchange for his life. He did not feel worthy of such a noble lady.

"Abbot, hasten the prayer," Henry snapped. "My supper awaits."

Giles began to pray. His voice rose and fell as he intoned heaven and all the angels to deliver happiness to the couple. The prayers went on for long moments, and then it was simply over.

Desmond was wedded to Aislinn of Sevenoaks.

"Done. And about time," Henry said.

" 'Tis a pity, the axman is new and needs practice. He might have done the deed in less than five chops, like his last attempt." The tall, regal prince's face was broken by a wide smile. He offered Desmond a wink and continued.

"I know not whether to offer you my pity or my wishes of happiness, du Luc. Some say marriage is far worse than a speedy death."

"I will soon find out," Desmond replied. He was filled with a strange burst of affection and gratitude for this woman, his wife. Aislinn was no longer young; judging from the form inside the thick covering of lacy cloth, she was quite small and frail. His aging wife would need care and understanding. There would be no laughter or bed sport or making of babies to carry on Desmond's line. He could not have any of that, but to repay her for this day's work she would have his concern, respect, and fidelity.

He silently swore an oath on his family honor to see it done.

Giles, the abbot of Tunbridge Wells, extended a hand as if to handclasp with Desmond, but the king suddenly stood and put himself between Giles and the couple.

"I am anxious to sample the fare of Sevenoaks Keep. Let us get to our tables." The king's voice was loud and

was a subtle command that most obeyed, obediently
trooping toward the great hall. "Go you now, Baron, take
your bride to the upper chambers and consummate this
union. It is my royal command."

"But sire, the feasting—the mead—we have not drunk
their health—" Giles lurched forward, grabbing at and
missing Desmond's shoulder. "And Desmond planned to
take Aislinn to Mereworth."

"Abbot, do you gainsay me?" Henry asked in a decep-
tively light tone.

Giles's eyes were wide, his hand shaking. He acted
like a man much beset by worry, but Desmond could not
imagine why. "Nay, sire, but if they desire to journey to
Mereworth this eve—"

"Nonsense. There will be no travel this eve. I wish to
see this wedding sealed, sanctified, and consummated before the morrow, when I leave for Eltham Palace. I command the couple will take themselves to the lady's
chamber now and get the bedding done. Prince Edward
and I will slumber in the lord's chamber this eve. Do you
have the key, Desmond?"

Desmond nodded and removed the key from its thong.

"Fanciful bit of iron." The king turned the metal creation, designed with many loops and holes, in his hand,
studying it. At length he placed it in Prince Edward's
hand.

King Henry raised his hand. Two of his royal guards,
bristling with weapons under the royal livery, stepped forward.

"I will brook no more arguments, delays, or deaths at
Sevenoaks. If my fine Desmond is not hale and hearty
on the morrow, more heads than one will roll, beginning
with the lady and all of her bloodline; on that you have
my promise."

"Ah, then perchance there is hope the axman may yet
get his badly needed practice. If our lord Desmond does

not survive the night, the block will be much used on the morrow," Prince Edward said with cheerful anticipation.

Desmond turned to his bride and took up her hand. It was cold and stiff. Under armed guard they made their way through the thinning crowd and up the stairs. Desmond's own hand was none too steady as he grasped the round iron ring and opened the thick oaken door. With a whisper of sound, the lady Aislinn silently entered her own chamber. Desmond barred the door with a thick cross beam. He turned and looked about.

No fire burned in the hearth. Her chamber, though smaller, was much like his own, done on a more feminine scale but with the same heavy carved cabinetry on one wall and the same fine leaded windows.

Desmond was stung by his neglect. He should have ordered a fire laid, fresh linen covered with flower petals, her favorite foods provided—but then, he had not expected to need food or fire or even breath after sundown.

"You have saved me," he said simply. "Lady Aislinn, I know not what to say. I would have had it otherwise. I would have spared you this . . . chore of wedding me." Desmond nearly choked on the words. How noble she was! How could he ever hope to repay her? "Gramercy is too small a word."

She had not moved since he barred the door. She stood there, small, regal, and silent. It unmanned him.

"My throat is parched. Would you take wine with me?" He spotted a slender ewer and two goblets on a low chest.

The lady hidden beneath the gauzy material nodded with a whisper of delicate pale lace.

"Remove your veils while I pour us wine. Be it ill or well, we are now husband and wife. I would be gladdened to look upon your face, lady, and look into your eyes while I once again give you my thanks."

Aislinn's heart was beating so hard, she feared it might come through her chest. Disbelief still gripped her soul.

She had done the unthinkable. She had married Desmond to save him from the king's axman. And by wedding him she had doomed him to die like the other four men who had married her. Now they stood in her solar and she was trapped.

"Come, remove your veil, lady wife."

Wife. The word was a sweet torment to her ears. She wanted to be Desmond's wife in every way. She wanted him to mount her, to claim her, to join their flesh and their souls.

When he learned who she was and what fate awaited him, he would hate her.

"Lady Aislinn?" Desmond's voice was both curious and demanding. She loved the sound of it. Here in her private chamber it was even more compelling, more forceful, more commanding than in the secret garden.

"Come, do not be shy."

She turned away from him. There was no place to run, not even if she used the secret passage. He would find her.

Her fingers were trembling when she removed the heavy gold circlet from her head. She could feel his eyes upon her. Jesu, she was frozen with fear and longing. Her hands were cold and clumsy. The seconds passed, each one marked by a painful thud of her heart. The material drifted like gossamer clouds until at last it was gone. He was right behind her. She could feel the heat from his body.

Desmond stared at Aislinn's back. She was compact, trim. Perchance a woman could keep those narrow hips and tight, rounded flanks when she had not borne children, but the hair . . . the comely hair was a rippling river of shining flame-colored curls. Could an aging crone keep tresses like that?

He put his hands on her shoulder and slowly turned

her, though some part of his mind knew what he would see.

The green eyes were wide, the strong, kissable lips slightly open. She was looking straight into his eyes.

"By the Holy Rood, it is you!" His eyes flicked over her face, her bosom, down to her tiny feet and back again.

Quick as lightning flashes then dies, so did every emotion from joy to fury sizzle through his soul.

" 'Tis you," he repeated numbly.

"Aye." She twisted the lace veil in her fingers, determined not to quell when his gaze turned cold. Then his lips flattened into a hard line of anger and she died a little.

"What manner of jest have you played upon me, lady?"

"I played no jest."

"Meeting me night after night, never divulging your true identity . . . you played me false."

"Nay."

"Why did you keep your name from me? Why did you have to be forced to wed me when you found my lips and hands pleasant enough in the maze. If I was good enough to toy with in secret, was I not good enough to wed?"

Aislinn swallowed hard. "You cheapen our time in the maze with your words, but I understand it is because you are angry."

"Aye, I am angry. Why, Aislinn? Why did you not tell me who you were the first night?" Desmond's heart squeezed so tight in his chest, he thought it might cease to beat. Here was his mysterious maid of the maze and the lady Aislinn, whom he admired. Or was she the Poison Flower, who had buried four husbands, in the same satiny flesh?

Betrayal clawed at his pride. He loved her. Nay, he hated her.

She was his vision, his dream. Nay, she was his nightmare.

With the lovely young Aislinn he could have sons, daughters, and a biddable young wife who would learn to love him to the exclusion of everything else in her life.

If he could but forgive her.

"Did you laugh behind my back whilst you played your charade?"

"Nay, never—"

"You would not have me, you said. You would not have me when I waited at the steps of the chapel in front of Mereworth and Sevenoaks folk alike. I played the fool."

"Nay, I could—"

"Not until Henry vowed to take my head and your precious demesne down stone by stone. Is that why you wed me? To save Sevenoaks?"

"Nay, 'twas—"

"Save your lies, Poison Flower. Save all your denials, for now we are wedded. You will have me now, by God's teeth."

Desmond took her into his arms. He put one hand on the slender nape of her neck and forced her to accept his kiss. He was angry; he was hurt; he wanted her with his very soul.

He had dreamed of this moment. His body had conjured a thousand dark and sinful dreams each night about his maiden of the maze and the moment he would bed her. Well, now she was his by the law of man and God. He could do as he wished with her. He had the right to take her body.

He forced her lips open. They parted, whether willingly or no, he did not know or care. He thrust his tongue inside her mouth. It was lightly honey-spiced from mead.

"So you drank a brew to fortify your courage before you came to the steps of the chapel. Do you need more now, little vixen? Will a tankard of mead make the bedding easier to endure?" He gazed into her face. It was the same and yet somehow different. The halo of hair made her different in some way he could not explain. In the back of his mind he thought of Aislinn, the woman who had courage and faith and determination.

He searched her face, trying to reconcile the rush of his own hot blood and the cold sting of her betrayal. "Why didn't you tell me?"

She did not answer. Her eyes were wide; her breath came in quick, shallow gasps.

"You want me. By God's holy blood, you want me as much as I want you." He sounded more surprised than he wished to. Did he covet her or did he hate her?

Perchance a bit of both at this moment, when his blood pumped hot and thick through his sack, and his tarse was so hard it was painful to endure.

"Say you want me, Aislinn, maid of the night, Poison Flower. Whoever you are this moment, say the words. I would have you beg me to be inside you."

He would show her that he was no man to trifle with. He would show her the wages of such folly. He would make her beg for release. He would . . . he would give her pleasure. He would worship her body with his own. He would show her that she pleased him in spite of all that had happened. She was still the same brave and valiant Aislinn who had wedded him to save his neck—and she was the enchanting maid who had looked so sad beneath the stars.

"Say the words."

She remained silent, her eyes skimming over his face. She was stock-still, staring at him with wide, round eyes.

"You will be my lady wife in all ways, Aislinn." His voice was rough from the heat of his own desire. With a low growl, Desmond picked her up. He strode to the bed and positioned her in the center of it.

"Disrobe for me, Aislinn," he commanded. To keep

himself from reaching out to assist her, he crossed his
arms at his chest and took a stance. He would wait; he
would give her a chance to come to him willingly. She
wanted him; she would come to him; she would beg him.

Aislinn swallowed hard. This was what she wanted.
She had yearned for the bliss of marriage. For years she
had prayed for a husband to take his rights upon her body,
to fill her with his seed, to give her children and purpose
to her days.

But was Desmond doing so because he wished to share
her flesh or because he was under order of the king? Or
was this a man's fashion of revenge upon her because
she had shamed him? The cruel questions played in her
mind over and over like an endless chant.

Would he be dead by morn?

"Aislinn?" His harsh voice made her start. "Obey me."

"Aye, my lord husband." She began to tug at the laces
at the side of her bliaut. Her fingers were clumsy and
slow. Her heart beat hard and fast within her breast. One
tie would not give. She pulled at it in frustration.

Would he be dead by morn?

Did she dare take her pleasure and hope for a child?

Would he be dead by morn?

What kind of soulless wanton had she become to think
of a morrow or babes without Desmond? A hot tear
plunked onto her hand.

"Tears?" His voice was flat, without emotion. "From
the stalwart Aislinn? Woman's tears from the lady who
sacrificed herself to save my head?"

"My lord—"

"How I yearned to hold you, to have you beneath me.
But you were not the innocent, virginal maid I thought,
were you? You are a widow—much widowed. The marriage bed is no stranger to you, is it, brave Aislinn?"

Her breath caught in the back of her throat. She looked
into his face. This was a side of Desmond she had not

seen. He was seething with fury. His eyes were a study in cold fire. There was also pain and want and a raw emotion she had never seen on the face of a man. He felt betrayed. She wished she could erase that expression, but she could not bear to tell him.

"I am cursed. It is my red hair." The words were out before she realized what she was saying. She could not call them back. "I am cursed, and like the other men who wedded me, you are doomed to die on the morn."

He stared at her for one full heartbeat. Then he began to laugh. His hearty baritone startled her. It echoed off the stones. "Cursed? Red hair is now a curse? What folderol is this, Aislinn?"

" 'Tis true. You will die before morn."

His lips twisted into a grimace. "Should I take your words as a threat or warning?"

She wept harder. It was bad enough that she had confessed the truth, but to have him laugh at her as though it were some dark jest was more than she could bear.

Desmond hated women's tears. They unmanned him, made him helpless. He would rather face an army of Saracens on the hot desert sand than hear a woman weep. In battle he knew what to do; he would fight; he would do the things a knight had been trained to do. But when women shed tears of sorrow . . . he had no training, no skill. He was impotent, no better than a eunuch in a harem in the face of such sorrow.

He was momentarily distracted by a light, quick knock on the outer door of the chamber. Desmond was grateful for whoever interrupted, though he could not imagine who would disturb the lord on his wedding night.

He lifted the bar and opened the door. There was no one in the corridor. A wooden tray of food sat by the door. He brought it inside and placed it on a low commode near a large carved cabinet nearly as big as the one in his own chamber. When he turned, he found Aislinn staring at him with red-rimmed eyes.

"I never meant to put you in danger," she said softly. She took up a great tress of red hair. The thick strand curled around her fist as if it were a thing alive. "This is my curse."

Desmond had never seen anything more enchanting. She was pink-nosed, red-eyed, her gown was only half laced. Thick tangles of blazing curls twined around her slender neck and shoulders. She looked like a maid who had been tumbled in a byre—or who should be swived in her own bed by her husband.

His tarse and stones reacted like any man's would at the sight of her, but he resisted—barely.

"Where have you heard such nonsense?"

"People say—"

"Who has said?"

"Giles tells me of the rumors." She sniffed in a most unladylike fashion and his heart tumbled inside his chest.

"Aislinn, you have tried me sorely. You have played me like a foolish swain."

"I never meant—"

"Are you a sorceress?"

She stared at him gape-jawed. "Nay."

"Yet four men died—you say because of your red hair. I believe it not. If you thought to dissuade me from bedding you with that ripe tale, then you are much mistaken."

" 'Tis no tale, but truth. I am cursed."

"Never!

"I am! All who have married me have died before we even shared the marriage bed." Her green eyes rounded.

"What say you?" His question was little more than a whisper.

She clamped her beautiful lips into a hard, straight line.

He could tell she was no longer in a mood to talk. Or perchance she had talked too much.

"Is it true? Are you yet a virgin?"

She averted her eyes and blushed a fine rosy hue, and he had his answer, much to his astonished delight.

"Jesu." This news made his sack even heavier with lust. He had thought the king was wedding him to an old crone who had long-since given herself to a string of husbands. He had almost given up his dream of a young, fertile wife who would dote on him. But now, with her hastily blurted words, he realized he had been given a blushing beauty with her maidenhead intact.

Jesu! His dream of wedded bliss was within his grasp. He could have her maidenhead; he could fill her with his seed; and while she bore him sons and daughters, he would teach her to adore him.

His heart swelled. His blood heated. He had been given a prize beyond reckoning. Henry surely believed as Desmond had—that Aislinn had been bedded by one or all of her four dead husbands.

His head was spinning. But then he realized, it was most odd that she had not been bedded before they died. The king's bawdy joke about her killing them with her insatiable sexual appetite was far from the mark.

"Aislinn, does anyone know you are yet a virgin?"

Her cheeks blazed a deeper vermilion. She shook her head, the thick mane of hair whispering along her shoulders. "I was too shamed to tell anyone. Even Giles, my confessor and dearest cousin, does not know how unnatural a female I am. 'Tis a part of my curse. I am untouched—unloved."

Desmond reached out and tipped up her chin. "You are not unnatural. Aislinn, though I am much vexed by you, you may trust me in this. Red hair is not cursed, and the silly gossip you have heard is foolish tittle, no doubt meant as a cruel jest."

"How can you say that when four men have died?"
She shivered.

"There must be another cause that has nothing to do
with the hue of your hair." He wanted her with an intensity that shook the foundations of his manhood. But how
could he take her when there was such fear and sorrow
in the depths of her eyes? He could not take advantage
of her. He steeled himself against his lust.

"Aislinn. Maid of the garden. Two women in one body.
Tell me why you believe such nonsense abut your hair."

"After Theron died, the gossip and the whispers
started." She gestured in a manner that made her appear
frail and helpless. Desmond longed to take up his sword
and hack through the people who had hurt her. And yet
he remembered Cook's words. When Aislinn first came
to Sevenoaks she had been happy, accepted. Her hair had
been just as red then as it was now.

"One of our greatest queens had red hair. Remember
Boudicca?"

She looked at him with a sharp, raw pain in her pale-
green eyes. "Desmond, would that I could believe, but
four men lie beneath the chapel stones. They all wedded
me and died."

Desmond frowned and thought about all the accounts
he had heard. Each of her husbands had perished in a
seemingly different way, on their wedding night. That was
the only common thread—the wedding of Aislinn.

He glanced at the tray. There was a ewer of dark wine,
sugared fruits, and rich, dark bread. Coy's vigilance and
his tasting of food and wine suddenly flashed in Desmond's memory. He had made light of his friend's cau-
tion, but perchance Coy had been right on the mark.

"We shall not eat or drink this night," he said as he
moved away from Aislinn and lifted the bar from the
door.

"That will be no hardship. All on the tray is not to my

162   *Linda Lea Castle*

liking. I prefer light wine and manchet, and I detest sugared fruit. Cook must be in her cups to have forgotten."

Desmond wondered about that as he picked up the tray and put it outside in the corridor. Then he made the door fast again. Or perchance Cook had not made the food.

"Now we are safe, here in your chamber. There is only one way in and one way out. No menace can gain entry."

Aislinn's eyes slid to the carved cabinet. The truth about the passages between her chamber, the lord's solar, and the maze crowded the back of her throat. Desmond believed there was only one door. But she knew otherwise. She had to make him realize that his life was in danger. If he did not heed, he would be dead before the sun rose.

Thirteen

The knock on the door brought Aislinn bolt upright in the bed. She blinked as if unsure where she was. A little gasp of surprise—or was it terror—left her lips when her eyes skimmed over Desmond.

"You . . . you live," she whispered.

"Aye, if you could call this aching state I am in as living." He had spent the night pondering the situation within Sevenoaks Keep while sitting in a chair of Roman design. Now his shoulders and neck were stiff. He rotated his head and heard the crack of bones. He stood and put his hands over his head, stretching his cramped muscles.

"My lord Desmond?" An unknown voice called from outside in the corridor. "Are you well, my lord?"

"Aye."

Desmond could practically hear the gasp of shock on the other side of the thick oaken door. It would seem that Aislinn was not the only one expecting to find a corpse.

"Aye, my lord. I was told if you lived—that is, the king would see you below stairs anon."

"Prithee, tell him I, and my lady wife, will attend him within the hour."

"As you say, my lord."

Aislinn had not moved. She was staring at Desmond with round, shock-filled eyes. Her thick curls were a blazing halo around her pale face as she clutched the bed coverings in white-knuckled hands.

"Your face tells me you expected to find me dead by morn." He lifted one brow.

She swallowed and blinked as if his voice had woken her from a strange waking dream. "Aye. Nay. I know not whether to believe you are real or whether I only imagined you."

"I am flesh and blood."

"Would I could believe it." She ran her fingers through her tousled hair. Desmond's breath caught in the back of his throat. Her nipples showed clearly through the fabric of her half-laced tunic. She was kissable, and all together too swivable.

He found himself moving to the side of the bed like a man in a dream.

He pulled her to him. She was pliant, still drowsy and sleep-drugged. His hands found her plump, firm breasts; he held them almost reverently. It was God's blessing that his wife was young, supple, and virginal.

"You may believe, Aislinn. I am no figment of your dreaming mind."

He kissed her hard, driving his tongue deep into her mouth. His body warmed and hardened with the sheer pleasure of holding her.

His wife. His lady. His curse?

She moaned softly. Her body became liquid in his arms. Aislinn might be untouched and virginal, but a river of passion flowed beneath her pale, translucent skin. He wanted to churn the waters until they overflowed in a mighty, torrential flood.

He wanted this maiden as he had never craved another. His pride was still stung by her deception. Oh, he believed her story of fearing for his life, but being a man— and he was, after all, only a man—he could not

completely ignore the nettles that pricked him and called
him a fool for being led down the path of deceit.

He broke the kiss. Aislinn wore the drowsy flush of a
woman in full passion. He could flip her on her back and
tumble her in a nonce.

But he would not. Not yet.

He steeled himself against the pounding of his own
heart. His ears were full of the roar of hot blood and lust
when he stood away from the bed.

"Desmond?"

"Ready yourself, wife. We go to meet the king." He
turned away and strode to the window. When he heard
Aislinn's heavy sigh and the rustle of cloth, he nearly
shamed himself right there. His tarse pulsed with need,
but his man's heart denied the plea. He released the iron
latch and opened the portal. The cooling gust of fresh air
cleared his head—a little.

Within one turn of the hourglass, Desmond emerged
from the lady's solar with his bride on his arm. He did
not know how she managed without a maid, but she had
donned a bliaut of the finest venetian velvet, the hue of
a rusty sunset. At the neck there was fine scroll stitching
of black silk. Her hair was a healthy, glowing tangle of
curls that fell down her back and bounced near her buttocks. At her brow was a circlet of tiny pearls.

She was pale, tense as a bowstring, and beautiful as
the first sunrise. Desmond had never felt so proud and
full of confusion as he did when, side by side, they descended the three flights of curving stone stairs and
stepped into Henry's royal presence.

To watch the faces of those gathered around the great
hall was enlightening. Coy's face was a study in sheer
relief. Prince Edward wore the mien of slightly annoyed
disappointment. Henry was smugly satisfied; his will was

stronger than death. De Montfort and his lady Eleanor seemed genuinely surprised and pleased. Giles—ah, now Giles—was the most revealing. His expression was a mixture of humor and impatience. He did not seem in the least surprised to see Desmond breathing.

"Ah, Desmond and Lady Aislinn. Come, come. Sit at my right. We will share a loaf and a tankard." Henry smiled broadly.

The couple obeyed the monarch's summons. Aislinn's hand was shaking inside Desmond's. To her credit, her back was straight, her chin up as she climbed the dais to take her seat.

She was courageous as Boudicca. A woman that minstrels should sing about. Poets should write odes to her and that mass of curls that shone like a fiery beacon.

"Lady Aislinn, the reports of your haggard appearance and wasting due to grief have been much exaggerated." The king looked pointedly at Giles. " 'Struth, Aislinn, you are more lovely than last I saw you," Henry flattered the blushing lady at Desmond's side.

"By the Rood, I trow a woman who is able to blush after wedding five husbands is a rare joint to nibble," Prince Edward said with an upward lift of his lips. "I begin to see you received a better bargain than first I thought, du Luc."

Desmond nodded. "My wife is an endless source of joy and amazement to me."

Aislinn cast him a glance from under the soft brown fringe of her eyelashes. Desmond found Coy watching them.

A hot loaf of white manchet was put before the king. The smell wafted in the air. Aislinn's stomach growled. At that moment, Desmond realized he believed Coy's notion of poison four times done.

Yet not even a hardened murderer would risk poisoning the king with his entourage and the prince in residence.

Edward, it was said, agreed with Simon's father when he had said, "kill them all and let God sort them out." Desmond hesitated until he saw the king tear off a bit and pop it into his mouth. Then he broke the loaf in half for himself and Aislinn.

The king's tankard was filled from the same ewer that held Desmond's and Aislinn's wine. He watched each sip, each swallow, and only when every morsel had been tasted by someone else did Desmond allow Aislinn to eat.

He leaned near her ear. "We break our fast as man and wife for the first time, but I promise you, it will not be the last."

She looked at him, her lips quivering slightly, and he knew she had no faith in his pledge. Why did he have to want her with such white-hot intensity? Why did he have to admire the way she sat unflinching beneath the scrutiny of the entire hall, all the while expecting to be a widow with his next breath?

"I confess it, Father, I am much disappointed," Prince Edward said with a sigh that was pure royal ennui. "I have heard tales guaranteed to chill the blood in a man's body. Rumors of wickedness and evil have abounded the last five years."

"What say you? Speak plain." King Henry focused his full attention on his son and heir.

"Desmond Vaudry du Luc is hale and hearty. Or if he be spirit, then he has a better appetite than most ghosts that walk."

Titters of laughter rippled through the hall at the prince's jest.

"It would seem all the apprehension regarding Aislinn's wedding to du Luc was simply the foolish chatter of bored drabs—or jealous folk," Prince Edward said in a loud, commanding voice.

All eyes riveted on Aislinn and Desmond. She stiffened beside him, but she did not look away or quake under the scrutiny of the prince. She had the heart of a warrior, and she was winning Desmond's regard with every breath.

"Tell us, lady. Does Desmond live and breathe because he is young and does not suffer from festering wounds?"

"I saw no such malady on his body," Aislinn replied boldly. "He is sound of limb and strong of heart."

The prince chuckled. "Spoken like a woman who has tasted bliss in the marriage bed, I trow. Evidently the task of bedding you was not enough to cause his heart to cease beating like it did the other four." He turned to his father, the king. "As I said, if you sent her a man that was young enough to survive the bedding then all would be well. Too young a mare and too old the stallions—that has been the problem."

Hot blood rushed to Aislinn's face. She ducked her head, unable to meet the prince's lewd, bold gaze lest he realize she had not been bedded.

"You have made the lady, blush, my son," King Henry said with a throaty chuckle. "But you have made a point. For five years I have heard the stories of mysterious death within Sevenoaks. Now I will hear no more. Lady Aislinn is settled, wedded, bedded, and her husband looks able to continue the tasks. Desmond Vaudry du Luc is now lord of Sevenoaks and all within. Give them both your fealty and respect."

His words had the finality of a bell pealing over all those within hearing. Not a person breathed, moved, or even blinked for a tiny march of time.

"And now," continued the king, "I can devote my attention to fickle sisters and their rebellious husbands." Henry glared at Simon and Eleanor. " 'Tis time to get my household and kingdom in order, and I needs must start close at hand."

The weight of five years of torment rose up from Aislinn's shoulders. Desmond had managed to survive their wedding night. And in the harsh light of day, with Henry's and Edward's words, she began to think it had all been a bad dream. None at table seemed to think her hair was cursed or that she was evil. In fact, she saw shy smiles from the folk—even the serving women she had recently banished from her solar.

King Henry clapped his hands. Flutes, harps, and strummed instruments filled the hall with sweet sounds. Laughter and gentle conversation began here and there at tables below the salt. But Aislinn could not allow herself to hope—to look at Desmond and think they might have tomorrow and tomorrow after that.

"Come, show me all the wonders of my new keep, lady wife." Desmond stood and offered his hand to Aislinn. She looked at it as if it were a foreign thing, or perchance the offer of walking about in the day was strange to her.

"Go, go," Henry ordered. " 'Tis a wife's duty to obey her husband's every wish."

She obediently put her fingers into his palm. They were small and cold. She was pale, her skin like the softest of flower petals against the stark russet of her velvet gown.

"As you say, my lord."

They left the hall hand in hand, with the sound of music at their backs. At the moment sunshine touched her face, Aislinn pulled up short. She had not been out in the day for longer than she could remember.

Her world had shrunk with the death of each husband until at last she had her chamber, the secret passages, the view from her window, and the maze at night. Now Desmond, by his will or a whim of fate, had changed all that—at least temporarily. Life beckoned to her now, tempted her. But did she know how to reach it?

Was there a way to grab happiness, or was she still shackled by her secrets? Desmond seemed to think that surviving one night proved he was safe, but she was not so sure. She could not simply let go of all she had believed in the blink of an eye.

She was not ready for that—not yet. She needed more time with this man, more time to learn his ways, to see if her heart, so long denied hope, could trust in him—trust in the promise of a future.

"My lord, I would go where you take me this day. Show me the bits and pieces of the life you brought to Sevenoaks."

He studied her face a long while. Then he nodded stiffly. "As you wish, my lady. You will meet my trusted men and my horse, for next to a wife they are the most important things a knight may possess."

"Possess?" Aislinn repeated.

"Aye, you are mine now. I will protect and provide for you as I do my men and Brume."

"And what am I to do, my lord, while I am being protected, provided for and *possessed?*" Aislinn was not sure she wanted to hear Desmond's answer since he had measured her up and fitted her worth somewhere near his stallion.

His expression was complete astonishment. "Why, you must love me, of course. That is what a wife is to do—love and cherish her lord husband."

Later in the stable, he patted his dapple-gray horse affectionately. "He is stout of heart and limb. He can gallop in the lists all day and be ready for the same on the morrow. Brume is battle-trained and not bothered by the scent of blood," Desmond boasted.

"Just like you to laud the virtues of your horse when a beautiful woman stands at your side." A tall man with dark hair and slightly almond-shaped eyes appeared. His body was lean and well muscled. It took Aislinn a moment to recognize Coy.

"Coy, come meet my lady bride." Desmond gave Brume one last, affectionate pat. " 'Tis fitting she meets you first, since you are my oldest friend."

"Brandt would be grievously wounded to hear you name me best and oldest friend."

"Ah, Brandt is indeed my friend, but he is also my brother-in-law. Besides, he is far away on the northern border of England; you are here, so I will call you best." Desmond chuckled.

"I pledge myself to your safety, Lady Aislinn. As Desmond's wife you have my fealty. I would lay down my life for you." Coy executed a bow.

"Sevenoaks has seen too much death and mourning." Aislinn shivered at the reminder. And once again she wondered how Desmond could so easily discount years of evidence about her curse. Was he right or was he rash?

"Come, Aislinn." Desmond beckoned. Her heart leaped at the sound of his voice. "I have several more men I would have you meet this morn."

She went obediently, but her mind was torn. Aislinn was not as able as Desmond simply to shrug off the feeling of doom.

The men she met were no more than lads. Aislinn thought they should still be sharing their hearth with their mothers, but she held her tongue as the smallest, Gwillem, gave her an elegant bow. The other lad, Tom, was unable to move so nimbly because of the crutches. She remembered seeing him when Theron first brought her here.

"I am not so nimble as Gwillem here, but my heart is

strong and I am keen of wit and sharp of eye. I am your man unto death."

"Valuable traits, I am sure, but please let us have less talk of death on the morn after my wedding." Desmond frowned, and Aislinn caught him giving Coy a meaningful glance. Was he not as secure as he would like her to believe? Or was there some secret she was not a part of?

That niggling thought took root in her mind and grew. Now when Desmond and Coy spoke to each other, Aislinn was sure she heard some hidden meaning. It made her wary, and with that wariness she recalled her vow to Theron. He had bidden her keep Sevenoaks's secrets— and keep them she would.

At nooning the prince sought out Desmond. He wore the same sharp expression he had at breakfast. It was a trait all his line carried: the ability to be looking through a man instead of at him.

"Baron, the king and I take our leave this day. We have much enjoyed the hospitality and entertainment of Sevenoaks."

"I am pleased, my lord," Desmond said, feeling a little disgruntled that the drama of his life was entertaining.

"The lord's solar is a most unusual chamber. Even in Aquitaine and Anjou there are none quite like it. Though I endeavored to solve the riddle whilst I was in it, I confess I failed at finding the source of the dancing lights."

"Dancing light?" Desmond repeated, feeling like the village idiot.

The prince smiled smugly, obviously pleased to know more secrets than Desmond. "Ah, I wondered if you knew of the story. I am gratified to know my ears do hear all. The castle folk of Sevenoaks tell that on the darkest of nights, long before the dawn, a ghostly light is seen dancing in the window of the lord's chamber."

"More foolish stories, I am certain." Desmond was tired of gossip.

"Perchance it is only a story told by bored drabs and old men," Edward agreed. "But consider, it is the only story not involving the lady Aislinn or her dead husbands. I find that singular detail most interesting. Would that I had more time to pursue the riddle, for I am ever intrigued by a mystery."

The prince's words had merit. It was especially odd that of all the dire stories, this particular tale had never been repeated to Desmond. Did Aislinn know of it? Had her helpful cousin Giles told her this legend, or did he keep this tender morsel from her and only relay the stories that wounded and hurt her? It had not escaped Desmond's notice that Giles had a habit of telling her outlandish tales about her "curse."

"You may rest easy, my prince. I vow to solve the riddle in your stead."

"Just what I hoped to hear, Baron. Keep ever vigilant, and be assured my father is not unaware of your efforts on his behalf regarding the pack of ambitious barons and their plans for parliament." Prince Edward gave Desmond a haughty, cold smile. He strode off, his long legs eating up the ground at an amazing pace. His words hammered at Desmond's mind.

"Another damned mystery within the walls of Sevenoaks."

"My lord, will you retire to the lady's chamber this eve or to the lord's solar? If it be the lord's solar, I needs must have the key to lay a fire for you." Gwillem stood at Desmond's elbow. All dining at the high table turned and looked at Desmond. He could practically feel the heat of embarrassment radiating from Aislinn beside him.

"I will be in my lady wife's chamber. I found my stay most pleasant and would wish to repeat it—many times."

A knowing murmur swept through the hall. From the lowest serf to the highest ranking knight in Desmond's service, he saw a smile of understanding and . . . *approval?* If any among them feared her or her hair, it did not show in their actions.

"My lord, is this more of being *protected* or *possessed?*" Aislinn whispered near Desmond's ear. Her warm breath smelled of the wine they had shared. Her presence was pleasing, and he drank it in, imprinting her on his soul.

To the casual observer it would appear they had their heads together making love-talk. And thanks to Coy's surreptitious sampling of everything put before the couple to share, none would even see they had not eaten or sipped anything that was not first tasted.

Desmond felt a bit foolish to be so vigilant, but he was willing to risk his dignity, and Aislinn's pointed observations, if he could solve the riddles of the keep.

All afternoon as he and Aislinn walked the bailey and enjoyed the sunshine, he kept hearing the prince's words. Could the ghostly light in the lord's solar be connected with four untimely deaths?

"My lord?" Aislinn was looking expectantly at Desmond.

"Aye?" He could drown in the cool green of her eyes. She blinked and his breath hitched in his chest.

"I beg permission to withdraw to my chamber." Her eyes flitted over the hall. She was uncomfortable here, and yet she held her head high and met every eye with valor. A surge of pride for Aislinn swept through him. She had not put herself on display before these people in a long while. She only did so now because he had wedded her and it was expected. What courage she possessed.

What sons she could breed.

Desmond rose and pulled her up beside him. "My lady and I will retire to our chamber. The seneschal shall tap another barrel of wine. Enjoy yourselves."

A loud cheer went up through the hall. Tankards were thumped on the table, creating a booming refrain. He looped his arm around her slender waist and kept her near him as they climbed the three flights to her chamber door. She did not object to his bold attention, but neither did she relax against him. The moment they were inside, Desmond put the bar on the door. Aislinn exhaled a breath of sheer relief.

"Was the meal so poor?" he asked, his eyes skimming over her form, lingering on her breasts, her tiny waist, the chatelaine's keys that hung at the apex of her thighs.

"I had forgotten how it was at high table: the noise, the gossip, the intrigue. I find it *exhausting*." She sat down heavily upon the side of her bed, nearly invisible within the heavy hangings at each tall post. All that Desmond could see was the curve of her knee and one pale ankle peeking from beneath her bliaut. It set his blood ablaze. He walked to the edge of the bed and gazed down at her. Aislinn was surely the greatest mystery of all the mysteries of Sevenoaks.

"Aislinn?"

"Aye, my lord." She tilted her face and met his gaze. Her bottom lip trembled.

"What do you wish from life?" He flexed his fingers, trying to resist the urge and impulse to rub the pad of his thumb over that lush bottom lip.

Wish from life. Desmond's words were so foreign to Aislinn that for a moment she had no comprehension of what he had said. His body was hard and tempting. His face was pleasing and manly. She had not thought of a future for so long, her mind could not readily understand the concept.

"Aislinn, what do you dream of? What joys do you hope to find in life?"

A hot sting of tears behind her eyes came unbidden and unwanted. She blinked rapidly, but they would not be stanched. His question had the effect of rubbing salt in an open wound.

"I do not hope or dream, my lord. Not after burying four husbands. Joy is not meant for me."

"But once, surely . . . when you were a young maid. What did you dream of when you were a girl?"

Was she ever a girl? It didn't seem so. It seemed as if she had gone from being a babe to being the widow of Sevenoaks. There had been few hopes or dreams since that time. And yet, for a small march of time, mayhap a sennight or two, when Theron had been alive . . .

"Aislinn?" Desmond allowed himself to come a bit closer. His hand burned to touch her cheek, to cup her face and taste her sweet mouth.

"There was a time long ago I dreamed of being a wife and mother," she finally whispered.

His breath hung painfully in the back of his throat. Was that not the most simple and basic of all women's dreams? Was that not what he yearned to give her?

"Let me remove the shadows of pain from your eyes." He finally allowed himself one touch. He grazed her cheek with the backs of his knuckles, feeling her silken flesh against his rough, war-hardened hand. It had the effect of softening his heart. All his annoyance with her for deceiving him flitted away.

"Confide in me, wife."

Aislinn's heart ached. The urge to reveal all of Theron's secrets tugged at her. The desire to unburden herself and show him all the strange and peculiar wonders of Sevenoaks was a great temptation. When he touched her, it was as if she had not will or strength to resist him. This submission of her very soul was new and frightening. She had never felt like this before, and it terrified her. She was saved from the sweet pull of his powerful will by a short, soft knock on the outer door of her chamber.

Desmond frowned and called out, "Aye?"

No voice answered in return. He strode to the door and opened it. A wooden tray containing a mazer of wine and a tankard of fresh, thick cream sat on the stone floor. He smiled to himself. Crippled Tom had no doubt brought the tray, since only he knew of Desmond's trip to the milkmaid each day.

"Come, lady, have a cup of wine." Desmond picked up the goblet and offered it to her. A bit more wine might ease the tension in her face . . . or loosen her tongue and allow her to reveal what it was that made her look so sad.

"Do you suffer from complaints of the stomach, my lord?" She peered curiously at the thick cream.

"Nay. I repay a debt owed." Desmond poured out the thick cream in the bottom of the tray. "Come, Pointisbright, and receive your reward."

He looked up to find Aislinn watching him with a strange expression on her pale face. Mayhap he had found a way to begin to win her trust. She tipped up the goblet and drank deeply while Pointisbright lapped up the cream.

"Aislinn, come, ready yourself for bed."

She yawned. Desmond was stung by guilt. The maid was exhausted. He had expected too much of her when they inspected the keep. She was not accustomed to walking all day. He realized with a jolt how different they were: these soft, pliant women who looked to their lords for safekeeping.

"Come, sweeting, let me help you out of your gown. You seem too sleepy to manage alone." He scooped her up and carried her to the bed. Her head lolled against his collarbone in a gesture of complete submission. The wild tangle of her curls twined around his arm. She was soft and liquid in his arms—pure temptation. The scent of her hair, her skin, her very essence made him drunk with desire.

Jesu, how he wanted his lady wife. And how it pleased him that she was willing to bend to his will. She was nearly boneless in his arms. He laid her gently on the bed and slid her soft goatskin slippers from her feet, marveling at how small and well shaped her tiny toes were. He would kiss each knuckle and feather kisses up her instep. Would the pulse spot on her ankle be a location of erotic sensation for her? Desmond kissed her ankle and rubbed his fingers up her calf to the tender inside of her knee.

She moaned and murmured his name. Only then did he stop and look at her face. He frowned and moved nearer her head. She was sinking into slumber. Perchance it was the last tankard of wine after an exhausting day. Compassion and a frisson of annoyance engulfed him.

He wanted her, but not half-asleep. He did not wish to bed her when she was drowsy with wine and exhaustion. Desmond had never favored a compliant swiving.

"Desmond?" She sighed.

"Aye, I am here." He unlaced her outer bliaut. She moaned softly and snuggled her cheek against his shoulder.

The small action sent his temperature soaring on wings of hot lust. She was everything a man could want. Her body was smooth and firm, her limbs well formed, her skin creamy and pale as moonlight.

With his teeth grinding together like millstones, he managed to free her from her outer tunic and soft inner bliaut. She was clad only in a soft, sheer shift. With great effort he forced his hands to his sides. Her breasts pushed gently against the fabric with each breath. Her lips parted, looking dewy and soft as the petals of a flower.

He could take her. If he stayed another moment he *would* take her.

Like a man fleeing a burning room, Desmond strode to the door and lifted the bar. He turned back and gazed at her perfection one last time. Her hand was fisted near her cheek, Pointisbright was curled into the crook of her knees. Desmond was being slow roasted over the fires of hell and his lust. He had to get out now.

With only a sliver of moon, the night was dark. The hidden greenery that disguised the maze managed to thwart Desmond twice before he found the opening. He had no notion why he was going to the maze, since his lovely maiden was fast asleep in her bed.

Bed. The word made the blood throb in his sack. He wanted her, but some niggling voice in the back of his mind told him he could not be completely happy until the unsolved mystery of this place was revealed.

He could barely make out the shapes of hedge and stone slab. He reached out and placed his fingers on the rough, oddly designed face of the sundial.

Did the moor fashion it in the way of his homeland? Desmond still had a question about the device, but he could not quite formulate what it was that poked and nettled at the edge of his mind.

A night bird swooped by, followed by its mate. A cricket began its song and was soon answered. Frogs peeped in the low bog near the moat. Desmond was surrounded by the sounds of nature. His body thrummed in rhythm to the cadence old as time.

He thought of Aislinn in her chamber above. She was his wife. He could take his rights upon her body and end his torture.

I want her to trust me so she can learn to love me. I want her to ask me to take her maidenhead. More the fool, I want her to tell me what haunts her soul and causes the bleak pain in her eyes.

He tilted his head and counted the stars overhead. He saw a yellow flash from the corner of his eye. Desmond walked to the corner of the maze and looked up, peering into the night. A glow flared in a window.

"In the lord's solar window."

Desmond forgot about the stars and Aislinn as he hurried to the entrance of the maze and made his way back to the keep. He moved quickly and quietly up the three spans of stairs to the lord's private, *locked* chamber. He used his key and opened the door.

The room was dark and empty, but the scent of smoke still filled the air. He used flint to light a candle.

All his belongings were there. Nothing had been taken.

So the ghostly light is not that of a thief, but someone who seeks something within this chamber. But what and why?

Fourteen

"Desmond! Pointisbright is dead!" Aislinn's voice brought Desmond sitting bolt upright, his sword drawn by instinct. She stood before him holding the limp body of the tomcat. Her hair curled wildly; her eyes were filled with unshed tears. Her brows furrowed in sorrow, cut Desmond's soul like a sharp dagger.

"Dead? But how?" He sheathed his sword and took the cat from her trembling fingers. He laid the creature on a low commode and found Aislinn's polished mirror. He held it before the animal's nostrils and saw two tiny spots of fog appear.

"He is not dead but in a deep, deathlike sleep. See, there is a little breath."

She leaned close and peered at the mirror. "But why?"

"That, lady wife, is a question I cannot answer—yet."

The great hall was buzzing with activity when Aislinn and Desmond came below stairs. He had bidden her to tell no one about Pointisbright, telling her that the animal must have gotten into some noxious herb, but she knew it was a lie. The wine had been pale and to her liking and dosed with a sleeping potion, just as the laced cream Desmond had given to Pointisbright.

But why? Why? The question hammered at her heart. Surely her new husband had no motive for drugging her.

Who could have done such a thing? She did not want to let herself believe what her heart feared.

Desmond felt Aislinn tremble at his side. She was doing her best to hold back tears and to keep her chin high. He was prouder of her each day. Most women would have been consumed with questions and weeping about the pet, but not his brave Aislinn. And thank the saints, for how could he have told her the truth? How could he tell her that someone within Sevenoaks could so easily slip potions into the lord and lady's drink? He was angry. He did not relish this feeling of impotence, and he vowed to do something about it.

"I should ask Giles to see to Pointisbright," Aislinn whispered as they entered the hall. "Perhaps his healing would extend to an animal as well as to the injured."

The abbot was seated at the high table, no longer in the lord's seat but near enough. His eyes were narrowed as they slid over Desmond and Aislinn on his arm. There was menace in that sly gaze.

"Nay. I forbid it," Desmond said shortly. Aislinn's step faltered slightly.

"My lord?" She looked into his face in confusion.

"There is no need, Aislinn. Pointisbright is a strong cat, and the abbot has the wounded knight to tend." He could not tell her that his heart contracted painfully at the thought that she might be in danger—or that he was powerless to move until he had proof of misdeeds.

"As you say." She ducked her head, hoping that Desmond did not see how angry his words made her. She was not even bedded—valued somewhere in the region with his horse, and now he ordered her about like a castle drab. Aislinn's anger was simmering, and as it grew hotter, those hated suspicions took form.

"Tell me, Aislinn, where does Giles sleep?"

"Sleep, my lord?" Now was he determined to harass her kinsman? What scheming did her new husband plot?

"Aye, he spends much time here at Sevenoaks. Does he possess his own chamber?"

"Aye, my lord. It lies at the back of the chapel, so he may minister to those of the keep. I have oft told him he should find more suitable quarters above stairs, but he says he needs must be available at all hours."

"Hmmm," Desmond said without explanation. There was something about the gleam in his eye that made Aislinn uneasy. Since waking she had been fighting the suspicions that lurked at the edges of her mind, but now they would not be quelled.

She had been dosed with a sleeping draft. Who had the opportunity?

Desmond. The name was cold and solid as stone. Only her husband could have given her and Pointisbright the potion. But why? Why did he want her sleeping? Or did he want her dead?

She denounced that possibility. If he had wished her dead, there were a hundred ways and as many chances. Only yesterday he had snatched her back to safety when one of the stones on the upper battlements slipped beneath her feet.

Nay, she would not believe he wanted her dead. But mayhap he did wish her to be out of his way . . . for a time.

But why? And why the cat?

Was he aware of the passages within Sevenoaks's thick walls? Could he be playing puss and mouse with her? Did Desmond want her heavily dosed with a sleeping draft so he could examine her room and find the secret ways? Or was it something in the maze?

"My lord, I have no appetite. I would go and see to Pointisbright if you will allow it," she said abruptly, without having tasted wine or bread. She wanted to go to her chamber and ponder the reasons for Desmond's strange behavior.

"Aye, you should do so," Desmond said absently. "I will send Gwillem with bread, cheese, and fruit. You should remain in your chamber all of this day."

His brow was furrowed as he placed one quick, chaste kiss to her forehead and walked out of the great hall. She watched him go while her heart tore a little more deeply. First he barked orders; now he dismissed her as if her presence was an unwanted bother.

Desmond found Tom in the meat kitchen with Cook. "Morn, lad. You look fit this day."

"Aye, my lord. The abbot gave me a sleeping draft. I hardly felt my aching leg at all last eve."

"Lad, did you have the potion with you when you fetched my nightly drink?" Was it all an accident? Did Tom, swinging on his crutches, trying so hard to please, accidently spill his own potion into the wine and cream? Desmond chided himself for seeing villains and plots where none existed.

Tom's eyes flicked from Desmond to Cook and back again. The lad's face flushed. "Nay, my lord. I did not fetch it last eve. Forgive me. I took the draft and was asleep. I will not be so careless again, I promise."

"Nay, lad, do not fash yourself. It is of no consequence." So Tom did not bring the tray, and he had made no arrangement to have someone else do it in his stead. It was a relief to know Tom was innocent, but now a prickle of battle-awareness climbed Desmond's back.

Someone within the walls of Sevenoaks was playing a dangerous game. And he was fairly certain he knew who, but the question of *why* was no nearer to being answered.

Desmond, Coy, and Gwillem rode around the common

and to the fields of Sevenoaks. The rich, dark soil had been turned, and now fielders were sowing. Small boys ran behind, covering the seeds quickly lest the flocks of rooks, pigeons, and larks eat them all before the smallest lads, armed with stones, could pelt the winged thieves.

"For a man with a lovely wife, you seem much troubled." Coy's mount matched Brume's pace as they rode well away from the castle common.

"I am much troubled," Desmond said bleakly.

"Why so?"

"I must now admit it. You were on the mark when you suspected a poisoner, Coy."

Coy's face was a study in fury. "By the Rood, I will have the wench's head! Does she think to make herself a widow another time?"

"Coy, cool your blood and watch your tongue. 'Tis not my lady wife who brews potions and decoctions. In fact, she herself was given a sleeping brew last eve. That which was meant for me went to the cat."

Coy pulled up on the thick leather reins. His stallion resisted the harsh treatment, coming to his back legs with his iron-shod hooves flashing in the sun. "It could just as easily have been poison and not a sleeping draft."

"Aye, that fact chills me. Aislinn might be lying in the chapel now—and if not for the cat, with me beside her."

"Who do you suspect?"

"I fear 'tis the abbot of Tunbridge Wells. The nut and kernel of my problem is finding a cause."

"He is a powerful force. You must not move against him without irrefutable proof, lest Aislinn be widowed again when Henry takes your head."

"Pointisbright is stirring, Aislinn." After two days in a deathlike state, the cat was twitching his way back to consciousness.

"I feared he would never wake." Aislinn put her palms together and held her hands near her face. She looked so small and vulnerable. Desmond wanted to comfort her, but he held himself in check. He could not share his fears with her and put her in greater danger, and so he watched and waited.

"Come, sit by me while your lion wakes. I am of a mind to hear a story."

She blinked at him as if he had uttered insensible words. "A story, my lord?"

"Aye. Tell me something of Theron, your first husband. Tell me more about the building of Sevenoaks."

She hesitated. Was that a shadow of guilt that flitted across her eyes? Why did her every thought and gesture seem secretive and guilty? Or was it all in Desmond's own mind? Surely Aislinn would not have taken a sleeping potion willingly.

"Why do you have such curiosity about Theron?" Aislinn asked.

"He must have been a most unusual man. The more I see of Sevenoaks, the more I appreciate how unique the design. Was Theron a man of letters?"

"Nay. He was a warrior."

Desmond did not know what he was looking for, but it seemed as if the mystery started with Theron's death—and Aislinn's first wedding. What did Giles want?

"The Moor he had build Sevenoaks may have left some scrolls, but I never saw Theron reading them."

"Would they be the plans to Sevenoaks?"

The color blanched from her face. She hesitated for a moment—a very telling hesitation. "I—I know not. Giles keeps those items in the chamber he uses here within Sevenoaks. Why do you ask?"

"I have a desire to see the plans of the keep, if they exist. Why does Giles have them?"

Aislinn looked up at him, her eyes wide with fear. He

regretted the suspicion that coiled around his heart, but he felt it just the same.

"It was the chamber the Moor used, or so I am told. Giles simply did not clear it out when it took it."

"And why did Giles take that chamber?"

" 'Twas nearest to the chapel and so natural that Giles put it to use while he is in residence. I told you this before. Why do you ask me these questions, my lord?"

"I beg your pardon, lady. I did not realize I was doing so. Forgive me; I am no ogre." He reached out and touched her cheek. It was soft and smooth, cool as marble. "I wish you would not fear me."

She jerked back from his touch. "I—I do not fear you," she stammered.

"Then why do I see terror behind your gaze? And why do you tremble so when I am near?" Desmond trailed his fingers down the curve of her jaw, holding her lightly with his other hand. She pulled against his gentle restraint. "And why do you try to pull away from me when you never before did so in the garden maze?"

"I—it is just—I cannot say, my lord."

"Could it be because you are yet a virgin? Does the prospect of giving me your maidenhead frighten you?" His finger followed the column of her throat and skimmed along the top of her bliaut. Wool thread had been looped along the edge of the linen, and he toyed with it, dipping his fingertip deeper into her shift. "Or is there some other reason you quake with fright?"

"I am not frightened." She would not give voice to her true fears. She could not trust him, but she did desire him.

He tilted his head and regarded her. "Then if you are not frightened, perchance you are *eager* to learn the ways of bed sport."

Aislinn's cheeks turned crimson. He had been fighting

the urge to kiss her, and now with the flush of maidenly embarrassment, the battle was lost.

Her lips were warm and supple when he allowed himself that first delectable contact. It took only moments for his blood to ignite with the familiar conflagration of lust.

She is your wife. You are free to take your rights.

The wicked little voice in his head wasted no time giving him all the reasons why he should give in to his desire.

Aislinn gave a little moan, but whether of pleasure or fear he did not know—or care. His hands found her waist, then slid up to her breasts. He kneaded the soft mounds beneath her bliaut.

They fit well together, he thought in some dark recess of his intellect, for at this moment he was a beast of pure sensation. His heart beat heavy and quick inside his chest. His blood flowed swift and hot through his body, pooling in his tarse and stones.

He wanted her. He wanted to strip her bare and see all of her body. He did not wholly trust her, but then, when did a man need to trust his wife to swive her?

Without really formulating the notion, Desmond began to divest her of clothing. The bliaut went easily and was quickly followed by the undertunic. She whimpered slightly when he tugged at the shift, but he swallowed the sounds of her protest.

And then he broke the kiss and beheld her.

Jesu, the sight of her body so fresh, innocent, and available nearly unmanned him. Her skin was so pale it was nearly translucent. The thick mane of red hair curled around her lush breasts in a caress he envied. He could see a fine tracery of bluish veins in her paps. The nipples were a soft pink-russet color. The nipples were large—the better to suckle his babe after he planted his seed within her.

He wanted to do so now. He wanted to break her maidenhead and plow her deeply. His seed would grow and become his heir. And when she had his child at her breast she would love him. It was the inevitable way of marriage. He would protect her, give her children, and she would cherish and dote upon him.

He was eager for that.

His eyes flicked to that softly furred portal where her passion and virginity rested like a hidden treasure. Like the hair on her head, it was also concealed by fiery strands. They were a bit paler in hue, enchanting and unique. With one hand he put pressure on her thigh until she yielded and opened fully to him.

He beheld a delicate flowering of flesh. Moisture glistened on her skin. He put his fingers over her mons and felt the heat. She gasped in shock when he slipped one finger inside her. He brought it to his lips and tasted her juice. The musky attar of her perfume made him harden to the point of pain.

"Aislinn, lady wife, I want you."

She did not look away, but her pupils grew larger, her lips parted, and her breath caught.

He could take her with no resistance—he recognized the signs of acquiescence. She would welcome him. He would place his shaft at the opening of her quim and she would welcome him inside. They would be one flesh; they would be one soul.

He could take her now.

But he could not. Damn his honor and his suspicion; he could not do it.

Desmond stood away from his lady wife while every nerve ending and muscle in his man's body cried out to take her. He wanted her, but he dared not allow himself the sweet, drugging bane of lying with her. Not until he found out whether she knew of Giles's deadly skills, and whether she had assisted him in some way or only kept silent as he did his worst.

"Cover yourself, Aislinn," Desmond managed to croak out before he turned and fled her chamber in a haze of red lust.

When Desmond was gone, Aislinn breathed again. "He does not desire me," she whispered. "He must find me repulsive with my red hair and pale skin."

And yet the way he had touched her, *tasted* her. Jesu, she had no notion that men did such things. Could he do that if he did not find her appealing? Did men do such? She wondered what else was she ignorant of.

I thought I knew what to expect in the marriage bed. But the moment Desmond had undressed her and touched her, she realized how wrong she had been. She was as a newborn babe compared to the wondrous things he knew.

Each touch is more delicious than the last. He shocks me and yet he makes me yearn to be shocked yet again. But he does not want me. He drugs me and ignores me.

She pulled her shift over her head and sat staring at the carved wood that hid the passage from her room to the lord's solar.

Would I had the skill to make a lover's potion, for if my lord Desmond does not take me soon, I shall be the one to die from unanswered passion.

Coy and Desmond stood within a sheltering ell of stone and watched Gwillem. The lad had agreed to do his lord's bidding without question. He took a deep breath and rapped his knuckles against the rough wood door.

Giles, the abbot of Tunbridge Wells, answered immediately. His eyes were sharp as he looked down on the small lad.

"Aye?" The tone of his voice was far different than the usual sonorous whine he used during daily prayers. It did not hold holy benevolence or mercy, only impatience.

"I wish to confess my sins," Gwillem said loudly.

"Go away. Confess after prayer this eve. I will be in the chapel then."

"But I cannot live with my shame until then." Gwillem hung his head dramatically. Coy elbowed Desmond in the ribs and nodded at the lad's ability to act.

"What have you done that is so dire?" The abbot seemed a bit more interested.

"I have shamed myself. I have taken food from the larder of my lord."

"That is not much of a sin."

"I have done other things," Gwillem said quickly. "There is a pretty kitchen maid. I followed her and . . . and—"

"Yes, yes, go on."

"I cannot do it here. I must confess in the chapel. I need to be on consecrated earth to unburden my soul." Gwillem had desperation in his voice.

Giles frowned and glanced back into his chamber. Then he sighed. "Oh, very well. Run on ahead and I will meet you anon."

The door slammed in Gwillem's face. He was smiling as he scampered around the building toward the chapel. Within a moment Giles appeared. He turned and shut the door. And then, while Coy and Desmond watched in amazement, he flipped the great cross at his neck and inserted the long bar into the escutcheon plate. The sound of a lock mechanism falling into place was as loud as the crack of doom.

Desmond looked at the key hanging from his waist. And suddenly he knew there was more than one lock his own key would open.

As soon as Giles was gone, Desmond and Coy went to the door of Giles's lair. Desmond slid his own key into the lock and the door opened smoothly.

"Now we know how he could gain entry into the lord's

solar," Coy said with a lift of his brow. They slipped inside the chamber and shut the door. Stacks of parchments and shelves of books were everywhere. Though small, the chamber was hardly spartan in appearance. The bed was well padded and covered with sleeping furs. The floor was strewn with fresh-smelling herbs. A great branch of candles stood on a commode.

"But why? What is it about the lord's chamber that has moved our churchman to lie and slip sleeping drafts into Aislinn's wine and the cream thought to be for me? He may indeed be guilty, but why?"

"And why a sleeping draft instead of poison?" Coy observed dryly. Desmond continued scanning the open book on a low table. It was a beautiful illuminated manuscript. It detailed the great battles and deeds of a knight.

"Theron of Sevenoaks," Desmond said, running his finger along the lettering. "It is an account of Theron's time on Crusade."

"What about Theron's deeds has so captivated the abbot's notice?" Coy said with a frown.

Desmond leafed through the book, suddenly stilling as his eyes moved down the script.

"What, what have you found?" Coy asked. "Does it shed light on the lady's lies?"

"Nay, but I think I may have found the reason Giles searches the lord's chamber by night," Desmond said darkly. "It seems our lord Theron brought back a sultan's ransom in plundered treasure. And if this account is to be believed, it is enough gold and jewels to make any man a king in his own right."

Aislinn stood at her window and watched the door of Giles's chamber with her heart in her throat. She saw Giles leave; she had seen the way Coy and Desmond clung to the shadows like thieves not wishing to be seen. And she had seen them enter the chamber.

But Desmond is lord of the manor. He has no reason to skulk—unless he is up to some dark intrigue. Her thoughts returned to Pointisbright. She and Pointisbright had been given a potion to make them sleep.

My husband gave me a potion. But why? What is he about? Is my dear cousin Giles in danger from the man the king has wed me to?

Aislinn turned from the window and went to her wardrobe. She selected her finest gown of blue silk trimmed in squirrel fur. It had been too long since she had made herself visible within the walls of Sevenoaks, but she could hide no longer.

Desmond needs to know I am chatelaine of this keep, and that he cannot do harm to Giles or any of my people without dealing with me.

Fifteen

"Ah, his color is good. Though he still sleeps too long, I trow." Desmond leaned over the wounded knight, checking his wound while Tom looked on. "You have done a fine task of seeing to his wounds."

"I did little. Giles brings the potions and herbs, and all I need do is see they are given at the right time and amount," Tom said modestly. "He is a master healer; each year his skill grows."

"Have you known Giles long?" Desmond asked.

"Since the wagon broke my knees. I was taken to Battle Abbey. Most had little hope I would live, but Giles—he was not the abbot then—would not give up. I remained abed many long months."

"Indeed, I trow that was a hard task for a lad to endure pain and lay abed when you wished to be out in the air and sun."

"Nay, 'twas no burden, for the abbot gave me pain-killing herbs, and I shared my fate with many returning knights. The fog in my head kept me from aching, and I had the stories of their glory to entertain me. 'Twas where I met my lord Theron. When I was able to stand again, he bade me come to Sevenoaks to live."

Many thoughts were swirling through Desmond's head when he entered the great hall that evening. Giles was

surely behind the ghostly light the prince spoke of, but was
he responsible for the deaths of four good and true men?
It did not fit with his reputation as a skilled healer. For
such a man, the pressure to kill would have to come from
a powerful source. Could the quest for treasure be enough?

Aislinn trusted Giles without question; Desmond knew
that. What would happen if he did bring down the powerful cleric? Could she ever forgive him if that came to
pass?

His thoughts were dark and boded ill when he glanced
up and found his wife watching him. She sat at the high
table, her thick red hair curling about her shoulders like
a fine mantle. The shimmering blue of her gown made
her pale skin even more ethereal. 'Twas as if an angel
had deigned to sit at Desmond's side.

Except the expression in her eyes was anything but
angelic when their gaze met. Jesu, he felt a shock, as if
standing too close to a lightning-charred tree. His skin
heated; the hair along his forearms stood on end; his
heartbeat hastened.

She was furious, and her anger crackled around her,
giving her an aura of feminine power.

He wanted her; for good or ill he wanted her. But only
a fool would allow himself sweet pleasure when she
might be aware of Giles's actions.

His heart was thrumming like a siege engine. He swallowed his lust and put one foot in front of the other.

Aislinn's intention had been to present herself and be
visible, to make Desmond aware of her power and her
station while she watched and listened and learned what
mischief he was about. But now as he strode toward her,
his tunic fitting his wide shoulders like a second skin,
and his muscled legs tensing and flexing with each step,
she grudgingly admitted that her joy in seeing him was

real and physical and could not be denied. The pit of her stomach tightened into a hard ball, and the soft, secret places of her womanhood tingled.

She wanted him. She was a fool because she wanted a man who had drugged her and lied to her—a man who practiced stealth and deception.

"My lady, you look well this eve." Desmond took his place at her side, feeling the heady intoxication of her aura. She was even more beautiful with the flinty gleam in her eyes. Her face was serene, but Desmond felt the surge of fury beneath her cool facade.

It made her more magnificent—more enticing and more unattainable. His heart tumbled in his chest, and his tarse solidified into a shaft of hot steel. Jesu, 'twould be a long meal with his erection pulsing in his braies.

"And you, my lord, are you well this eve?" Aislinn tried to ignore the thrill she experienced when his hand lightly touched her arm. How easily he touched her, both flesh and soul, but she must not let down her guard. "You have been busy this day, my lord, going about Sevenoaks, opening doors and learning much."

Desmond looked at her sharply. His eyes flicked over her face as if he were searching for something. Then he smiled slyly. "There is much to learn about Sevenoaks, and many hidden things, as we both know."

"As you say, my lord." Aislinn felt a moment of unease. She put her hands before her on the table to steady them. Had his words been carefully chosen because he knew about the passageways, or did he know she had observed him violating Giles's chamber?

" 'Tis good we have reached an accord so early in our union. It makes our time together all the sweeter." He turned her hand and lightly touched her wrist, drawing sensuous circles on the tender flesh.

"And will you return to the lord's solar this eve, my lord? Or have you enjoyed enough of my company?"

His smile cooled a little. He placed a hand on her shoulder, liquid fire trailing down her throat, making her breasts heavy and taut with awareness. He was a man, with a man's touch and a man's power. She was hard put to ignore the effect he had upon her.

"Nay, wife, I will spend this night and many nights to come in your chamber."

"Ah, 'tis always a joy to hear that marital bliss and contentment have been found in the marriage bed," Giles said happily as he took his usual seat. His smile was genuine. "Let us toast your continued happiness with my lovely cousin, my lord."

He grasped a ewer and poured wine into the lord's and lady's cups. Desmond looked at the liquid. It could be laced with poison or a sleeping draught. He was considering what to do about the possibility when Coy suddenly stumbled and draped himself across the table, upsetting both cups, staining the pure white linen of the table covering a pale pink.

"Ah, Coy, clumsy as ever, I see," Desmond said with a small smile and wink of gratitude.

"Forgive me, my lord; I am such a bull, I beg your indulgence. Lady, forgive me; I am forever at your service. Allow me to bring a fresh ewer of wine and pour for you myself." Coy bowed low and backed away, with Giles glaring at him.

Aislinn delayed her departure from the great hall as long as she could. But when only Giles and her husband remained with her, she knew the hour was at hand.

She stood, but her legs were none too steady. The wine seemed more full-bodied than usual, it had gone straight to her head. Desmond reached out to steady her, but she instinctively avoided his touch.

"My lord, with your permission, I would retire." She

did not know whether she resented his concern or relished it. Either way, she did not wish him to touch her.

"As you wish. I will join you in your chamber anon." Desmond did not even look at her. She felt neglected and strangely bereft, even though she was sure she did not crave his attention. Suddenly, he grabbed her hand. He looked up at her, his gaze burning into hers with an intensity that made her tremble.

"Lady wife, take care not to bar your door, for I will join you in your chamber."

"As you say, my lord," Aislinn managed to answer without her voice quavering, but she was trembling inside. How he had looked at her! Jesu, there was heat and power in his eyes.

She turned and fled—too quickly to be ladylike, but she had to reach the sanctuary of her chamber and compose herself. But how could she steel herself against his potentency?

"He will wish to bed me this eve, and as his wife I must submit. But this is not how I would have it. Jesu, I am a fool, but I want his respect, trust and affection."

"Your lady wife had the appearance of a doe caught within a bowman's gaze when she ran from the great hall," Coy said with a half smile as he separated himself from the shadows and met Desmond by the curtain wall. "She behaves more like a quaking virgin than a jaded widow."

Desmond said nothing. His friend glanced at him with shrewd, knowing eyes.

"By the Rood!" Coy looked Desmond full in the face. "It cannot be, and yet I read your eyes clearly. You have not bedded the wench."

"No man has," Desmond said softly, toying with the

fine, sharp edge of his eating dagger. "She is a virgin bride."

"How can this be? Four husbands before you—how can this be?" Coy repeated to himself.

Desmond shrugged and attempted to school his features. If he was not careful, his boon companion would read the signs and know that Desmond was about to burst into flame from wanting his virginal wife. " 'Tis part of the mystery of this damned place. Each husband died before even mounting her."

Coy's brow furrowed. "If 'tis poison, then the dose must have been given long before the couple climbed the stairs. This is something to ponder, my friend."

"As you say, 'tis something to ponder. Cook might be able to remember the fare of each feast; the pantler might know the wine."

"I will begin inquiries on the morrow."

"Aye, but tonight position yourself near the chapel and remain there. After my wife is asleep, I will watch the lord's window and see if our friend searches again. We will share our information tomorrow."

"After she sleeps? You do not intend to bed her this night?" Coy asked with an arched brow.

"Your nose grows too long, my friend; take care it does not poke so far into my business that I must trim it for you." Desmond flicked his blade back into its sheath. He glanced up at the lady's chamber window. The glow of a candle flickered on the small glass panes. Heat poured through him like a fount.

Aislinn stood in her shift staring at the tray on the low table. It had been waiting outside her door when she arrived. A tankard of pale wine—her favorite—and a mazer of thick cream.

"So, he means to drug me again. Jesu, what kind of

a dastard is he?" She ran her finger around the rim of the mazer. The cream glowed pearly fresh. The light from the cresset lamp cast shadowy lights in the wine she was sure contained another brew.

I know not which I dread more, the prospect of being drugged or bedded. Aislinn wanted him; of that there was no doubt, but she realized that even after four husbands she put a high value on her virtue and her maidenhead. 'Twas not something she wished to have taken while she was insensible, and neither was it something she wanted to surrender to Desmond simply because he was her lord husband.

A stubborn kernel of defiance took root in her mind. She would not be drugged—she would not be bedded. Not this night, or any night until she was ready.

A sound made her turn. And there he was, her lord husband, looking too manly, too handsome, and too treacherous.

"Aislinn?" His voice was deep and pleasing, like the purr of Pointisbright. "Await me in the bed."

"Nay, my lord, I will not."

His eyes flicked over the tray and lingered on her hand on the mazer of cream. "As you wish, I am a patient man. Do we share a cup first?"

"If you desire, my lord." Her heart tore a little. Why did he play this charade? Did he want her or not? Did he want her drugged for some darker reason?

The expression in Aislinn's eyes was unreadable to Desmond. There was a sadness and vulnerability about her that called to his soul. And yet he glimpsed another side to her: a defiant, rebellious tilt to her small chin. She meant to defy him about something, he could sense it. Was it the bedding? Would she give him a potion to delay the bedding?

He did not want to think that way, but there was her hand on the cup of cream, her long delicate finger tracing round and round the rim. Had he entered as she dosed the cream? But he had told her it was for the cat. Did she think that he had only given it to Pointisbright on that one occasion?

She lifted the cup of cream and handed it to him. "Drink, my lord husband." So she did believe he drank the thick stuff.

He lifted the goblet of wine. "I will drink only if you will join me, wife."

They stood there, staring at each other in tortured silence. The air crackled with some unspoken promise. He saw her lips move in silent speech, and he willed her to say what was on her mind.

But she did not.

Aislinn felt the sexual tension coiling within Desmond's body as waves of his manly heat poured over her. The cup in her hand was hard and cool in comparison with the fire in his eyes. She could not think, could barely drag air into her lungs. If she sipped the wine, she would be helpless against him. If she sipped the wine, he would be in control.

"I must go to the garderobe." She ran behind the ell of stone and dashed the wine into the hole. Relief sluiced through her now that the tainted brew was gone. She leaned back against the cool, rough stones and swallowed her sorrow.

The moment Aislinn went to the garderobe, Desmond lifted the iron latch of the window. He poured the thick cream down the side of the stone wall, watching it ripple harmlessly over lichen and moss.

I will not be lulled by her beauty, and I will not sleep this eve. My lady wife cannot poison me if I do not drink the potions she gives me.

Sixteen

Aislinn returned from the garderobe. She tipped up the goblet as if draining it before she put it on a low chest. Desmond pulled his tunic off and tossed it over a stool. She had moved to the far corner of the room, clutching the bedpost, watching him with round eyes. Why did she treat him as if he might ravish her at any moment? Jesu, he had done nothing to inspire her nervous glances and frightened demeanor.

Desmond decided to ignore Aislinn and play the part of a man under the influence of a brew. He feigned a loud yawn. Then he flopped clumsily into the chair that had been his bed since the wedding. He raked his fingers through his hair and let his eyes drift shut. After a time he lifted one lid enough to see Aislinn. She was still watching him with a taut, contained intensity that made his blood burn. He faked a manly snore and pretended to succumb to the effects of the sleeping draft he had poured out the window. It was torture to make his own body appear loose and languid under the heat of her unwavering stare.

Aislinn watched Desmond's honey-colored lashes fan over his sharp cheekbones. She let out an unconscious sigh of relief and appreciation when he fell into a deep sleep. It was glorious to have the freedom to look at him. Her eyes roamed greedily over his taut, lean torso. There

was a scar, white and puckered, on his lower ribs. She
remembered the armor in his chamber. It had a hole in
that region.

Jesu! His face might be that of a golden angel, but she
should make no mistake; her lord husband was a warrior.
He was battle-scarred and combat smart.

But was he sleeping? Or was he pretending to sleep?
The rogue! If he gave her a sleeping draft, then he was
only feigning slumber, waiting for her to succumb to the
brew in the wine she had tossed out.

He stirred.

Aislinn quickly lay down on the bed. She did not
bother to take off her bliaut and slippers, hoping he would
think the tainted wine had overtaken her quickly. She shut
her eyes and forced herself to breathe slow and deep.

Desmond peeked at Aislinn through one barely
cracked eyelid. She had looked at him for a long time;
evidently her confidence was bolstered because she
thought he slept from the potion.

Or did she?

She would have no reason to take a sleeping draft herself, but by the way she had taken to her bed, it was
obvious she was very tired and slumber overtook her almost immediately. Her breasts rose and fell in a deep,
even cadence—the unmoving sleep brought on by a draft
of herbs. Her full bosom made the bliaut pull taut across
those soft, enticing globes. Oh, how he wanted to suckle
her nipples; he wanted to taste the honey between her
legs.

He squeezed his eyes tight and counted the thud of his
own heartbeat. When Aislinn did not move for long minutes, he opened his eyes and quietly rose. He yanked his
tunic over his head and went to the door. With one backward glance of regret, he slipped silently from the chamber and out into the empty corridor.

The moment Desmond was gone, Aislinn sat up in her

bed. The rogue—the cullion—the blackguard! A hot flash of indignant rage swept through her. How dare he give her potions and decoctions and pretend to sleep. How dare he try to render her senseless and then leave her alone.

She ran to the wardrobe and turned the iron ring. When the panel opened, she slipped inside the portal.

I will not be locked inside the walls of Sevenoaks while my lord husband has the freedom to walk in the night. He may have his foolish intrigue, and welcome to it. I will spend my time as I did before he came into my life.

Desmond was to meet with Coy later at the stable, but now he found his feet carrying him on a familiar journey. He had to think, he had to sort his thoughts and reach a conclusion about the tray of wine and the mazer of cream. The solitude of the maze beckoned to him. There he could have peace, and there he prayed he would find the solution to his confusion.

He entered the sheltered greenery and turned right, left, right, left, and left again. When he reached the heart of the labyrinth, he went straight to the sundial. The mysterious markings unlike any he had ever seen, belonged in this place of intrigue and suspicion.

But I cannot believe Aislinn was the one to slip me the sleeping draft this night. Else she would not have taken one herself. We were given the draft by another? He walked to the dark corner of the vine-covered wall and picked a night-blooming flower. Though he told himself it was a small thing to know his wife was guiltless, his heart sang with relief. It meant much to know she was innocent of wrongdoing. He was smiling as he thought of her body, so lush, so ripe. A grinding sound nearby made him flatten himself into the dark recesses of the foliage. His gaze went to the keep wall. It was solid, the stones well fitted and mortared . . . until a door appeared.

An uneven march of stones, large enough for a horse and rider to pass through slowly, separated itself from the wall and swung inward. From that dark aperture stepped the lovely Aislinn of Sevenoaks. She turned and touched something, and the door disappeared with a light grinding, as if she did have the gift of magic.

Desmond's confidence in her shattered like a poorly made glass. She was bright-eyed and fully awake—hardly the unwitting victim of a sleeping potion.

Disbelief warred with rage in his heart. His lovely wife had pretended. *Why?*

Aislinn strolled from blossom to blossom, inhaling the fragrance of the garden. Her face was serene, her bearing regal. She seemed completely unconcerned with the events of the evening. If she felt one twinge of conscience at having deceived him, she showed no sign of it.

She was so beautiful with the small sliver of moonlight limning her smooth jaw, the stars reflecting on her vibrant hair.

He was furious, but he still wanted to possess her. He wanted to drag her to the dark, loamy earth and make her squirm and plead for sexual release when he drove her to the point of madness. And then, when she was nearly liquid with desire, he would have the truth from her sweet, lying lips.

"I must have the truth before I bed her, but by my sword I will have that virgin's body," he whispered to himself while his blood did a slow, simmering burn. He was hot from anger and from animal lust as he watched her tend her flowers, check her vines. She hummed a soft tune as she did her night gardening. When she had made one full route around the maze, she went to the wall. When it opened, she stepped inside. He followed her and ran his hands over the closed stones. Beneath his palms he felt the incised carving of letters, partially covered by moss and lichen. He found four lines of deeply chiseled words, but it was far too dark to make them out. Beside them he found an iron ring.

"By the light of day I will return here, Poison Flower. I will strip the secrets from Sevenoaks until you are the only mystery that remains. I vow it on my honor as a knight."

Coy paced back and forth in front of the stables. The sound of boot heels on the paving stones near the stable sent him to the covering shadows. He drew his dagger and waited.

"Sheath your weapon, old friend." Desmond stepped into view and revealed himself. "What did you see?"

"The abbot came from his chamber with a scroll."

"And somehow he gained access to the lord's solar, for I saw the dancing light of a candle in the window."

"Would that we could see through stone and see what he does in that chamber, for I grow convinced four men have died because of it," Coy mused.

" 'Tis sad to think their lives were held so cheap," Desmond said with a violent oath.

"More troubles you than just the crafty churchman, methinks."

"You know me too well." Desmond grimaced. "I fear my lady wife is in this broil up to her lovely eyes." Desmond was the only man to marry Aislinn who had not died, but why? "What was different about my wedding?"

"The king, prince, and royal axman attended yours," Coy said with a dark chuckle.

"Aye, the king attended and ordered me to take my lady wife directly to the bride's chamber. We shared no feast and no toasting. I was ordered to the lady's bed-chamber and thereby left the lord's solar empty."

"Ah, I see the direction of your mind. On the morrow I will speak with Cook and find out if the others feasted, and who was in attendance for the toasting."

"I would wager much that the abbot made the last toast to all those good and true men."

"But is that enough to take to the king?"

"Nay, we will need much, much more to challenge the abbot of Tunbridge Wells before Henry's court and advisers. And I would know why it is my wife could drink from the same cup and not die."

When Desmond returned to the chamber, Aislinn was abed. The candle had burned low, almost to the point of guttering. It cast long, sensuous shadows on her face. Her fist was curled beside her cheek, her lips slightly parted. She was either a master at pretending or she was really sleeping now. Pointisbright was still weak from his ordeal, but he lay beside her and let out a little growl of warning when Desmond reached out to grasp one thick red tress between his thumb and forefinger.

"Are you angel or minion of the devil?" Desmond whispered. He rubbed the silky strand between his thumb and finger, releasing the fragrance of flowers into the air.

He wanted a woman who did not trust him and whom he did not trust in return.

When morn came, Desmond rose and went directly to the maze. He found the wall and the chiseled stones where the secret door had appeared. With his dagger he cleaned away years of moss and lichen. It took some time, but finally the words were revealed.

The time is marked when the moon is ripe
Surrender the Stars and carry a light
The lord and lady share a floor
Riches untold behind the door

Desmond read it over more than once. It was an intriguing lay. Was the reference to riches the reason four men had died?

"Is this the reason Aislinn has kept the secret passage hidden from me?" he wondered aloud. " 'Tis time to force her hand and find if her heart is cold and hard as these stones."

Desmond went to the great hall and found the castle folk breaking their fast. The abbot was there, but he was dressed as if to travel. He wore a fine cloak of deepest purple over his holy robes. A pair of bright saffron gauntlets completed his attire.

"Ah, Baron, I am glad to have a word with you. I am leaving this day."

"Leaving?" Desmond doubted the cleric's words. "Where are you bound?"

"The wounded knight desires to return to his home so his family may care for him."

"Is he well enough to travel?" Desmond was responsible for those in his care.

"If we go by cart and journey at a slow pace. He grieves for a glimpse of his home. It is my duty to see his soul healed as well as his body." The abbot dropped his eyes and tented his gloved fingers.

"I am more concerned for his flesh than his soul. Can he endure the pain?" Desmond could well imagine the horrors of bouncing in a poorly sprung cart over rutted roads.

"I will give him a potion that will bring on a deep

sleep. 'Tis not far to Rye. By the time the brew wears off, he will be among his kin."

"You are able to judge the time and affect of your herbs?"

The abbot began to walk. "Aye. Come with me, and I will show you."

They walked through the great hall; Coy frowned darkly as they passed. He did not follow closely, but Desmond was sure he was there in the shadows. The morn was bright when they stepped outside to walk the short distance to where the knight rested near the meat kitchen.

"Morn my lord, Abbot Giles. I have been keeping him well covered as you instructed." Young Tom stood his vigil beside the knight's bed.

"You have done well, Tom," Desmond said. Giles did not even respond, and it seemed odd to Desmond, for Tom had known him since childhood.

"I am most pleased with the method I have found for relieving pain," the abbot said, tugging off his gloves. He carefully folded them in half and hung them from his girdle beneath the vibrant purple cloak. "I brew down the herbs into a paste and then apply it near the wound."

The knight was awake but appeared to be in no distress.

"See, he is awake and yet not awake." Giles lifted the sheeting and Desmond saw the glob of herbs on the lad's chest. "The herb juices slowly soak into his skin and keep the pain away for many hours. Soon he will lapse into a deep sleep that will almost appear as death."

"You are truly skilled." Desmond thought of Pointisbright. His sleep was so sound that it mimicked death.

"I will fetch men and we will see the knight loaded into the wagon. Tom, bring Coy and Gwillem to assist us."

Tom nodded and swung off on his crutches. He never complained and was always quick to do Desmond's bidding. He was well liked by all, and everyone took time to give the lad an encouraging word. Except for the holy man. Giles had never said more than two words to Tom as far as Desmond knew. It niggled at the back of his mind, but he could not grasp the reason why.

In a short while, the wounded knight was placed on a thick pallet of straw covered with soft furs. He never moaned or reacted, only stared into space. And then, just as Giles had predicted, he closed his eyes and appeared to be asleep. When all was completed, the abbot climbed into the cart and took up the reins. He looked up at Aislinn's windows and waved with his bright saffron gauntlets.

"I shall be gone at least a sennight, mayhap more," he said in parting.

Desmond watched the cart roll under the portcullis and out onto the verge.

"Strange that your lady wife did not come to see him depart," Coy said. "Ah, and I spoke with Cook and others. Giles was never at the final toasting."

Desmond looked up at Aislinn's window. She returned his gaze, her hair blowing like living flame in the morning breeze that whipped around the towers of the keep.

" 'Tis time I had a word with my lady wife," Desmond said as he strode off. He was tired of secrets between them. Instead of waiting and wondering, he was going to do what he should have done from the start. "I am going to demand the truth from her, and one way or the other, I shall have it."

Desmond tried Aislinn's door and was surprised when it did not open. He tried again. It was not just old wood swelling; clearly the door had been barred from the inside.

"Aislinn, open the door," Desmond said, tapping on it.

"Nay, my lord." Her voice was sweet and dulcet.

"What?" He did not believe he had heard her right. "Aislinn, open the door. 'Tis time we made things betwixt us clear."

"Nay, my lord. My door will remain barred, but you are correct, there are matters that must be sorted."

"Aye, now open the door, Aislinn." His patience was wearing thin.

"Nay, my lord," she said sweetly. "I would know why you felt the need to give a sleeping potion to me and poor Pointisbright. And until I know what plot you hatch, my door remains closed."

Desmond was taken aback by her words. It was a natural assumption, but to hear her accuse him of giving her a sleeping draft was unsettling. He wanted to look into her eyes, to have her see the truth of his words when he denied it.

"So you do not deny it? That is something at least," she said.

"Aislinn, there is much we need to talk about. Open the door." Desmond's voice had risen in anger and frustration.

"Nay, my lord husband. I shall remain within, and my door shall remain locked to you until you give me satisfaction and confess your reasons."

Desmond's blood heated with rage. His first instinct was to bring a battle-ax and hack down the door, then to ravish his disobedient little wife. But that was the way of a cullion and a man without honor. He must be more clever.

His lips broke into a smile when he thought about the maze. Aislinn could not resist the lure of the garden. He could be patient.

"And I will be waiting for you, sweeting. I will be waiting," he murmured to himself as he turned away from the locked chamber door.

"Whatever lures our cleric here, it is truly well hidden," Coy said as he crawled over the floor of the lord's chamber. "I can find no loose floor stones, and the hearthstones are solid."

"Aye, 'tis a puzzle." Desmond thought of the strange words carved into the wall of the keep—just one more conundrum to add to the secret maze, a secret passage, and a wife who barred her door.

"Well, my friend, I would go have a tankard of ale and some bread before 'tis all eaten." Coy gained his feet and dusted the knees of his hose.

"Aye, go. I will see you on the morn. I have little appetite and wish to walk a while and ponder what we have learned."

Aislinn was feeling the heady intoxication of power as she leaned out her window to watch the stars twinkle in the sky. She had done it; she had taken her fate into her own hands. She had not needed Giles's help or her lord husband's permission. And though her bold move to bar Desmond from her room had seemed strange and reckless, she was glad she had done it.

"I am mistress and chatelaine of Sevenoaks, and I will not allow any man to rule me, give me potions, or command me against my will," she said aloud.

Pointisbright meowed his agreement and rubbed against her leg. She had been giving him choice bits of eel and fish that Tom had procured from the kitchens. Now Pointisbright's strength had returned. Yesterday Aislinn had gone into the orchard and picked fruit, some of it still green, so it could ripen in her chamber while Desmond was busy in his solar. She had taken steps to have untainted food. She would have no need to eat or drink anything he left for her.

"I will not be given anything against my will again. And my lord husband will learn to respect me. I shall not be ordered or taken or ignored. He will be at supper in the great hall now, Pointisbright. We can go into the garden and enjoy the night away from all danger and prying eyes."

As she walked down the rocky corridor, her goatskin slippers whispered on the dusty stones. Over the past sennight, Aislinn had done a lot of thinking. And she had finally realized that what Giles said was true. There was no curse upon her hair. Desmond had proved that by staying alive on the wedding night and beyond. It had been no more than foolish, ignorant babbling of crones and drabs.

"But I have let it poison my life and destroy my confidence. No more."

She was young, alive, and mistress of a mighty keep. The king and prince had smiled upon her, and their approval had erased any stain upon her reputation caused by the death of her four husbands.

"I am the mistress of my own fate and circumstance. I am married to a man who is sly as a fox and slippery as an eel, but I shall thwart him in whatever dark scheme he has plotted. All I must do is think with my head and not my heart. I shall keep myself away from the power of his lips and his hands and his body until I have divined what he is about."

Pointisbright purred within her arms as she reached the final door and opened it into the garden. She took a step, inhaling the enchanting perfume of the night. Then she felt the ironlike grip upon her arm.

"Ah, lady, I have been waiting for you."

She looked up into the face of her husband, Desmond Vaudry du Luc. And then he bent his head and swallowed her shriek of fright and frustration as he claimed her lips.

She struggled against him—against herself. His mouth was hot, demanding. She let Pointisbright slip from her arms.

There was little gentleness in Desmond's touch as he pulled her tight to his body. He pushed her hips against his pelvis, the hard ridge of his staff undeniable within his hose.

Aislinn felt her own body begin to respond. She knew if she allowed him to touch her, to fondle her breasts, to caress her, that the war would be lost. Desmond was potent, irresistible. He was like sweet poison that she had no power to resist.

"Nay, I shall not—" She pulled away from his kiss. But there was his mouth again, taking her protests, sapping her strength, her will. With each beat of her heart, she cared a little less about Desmond's duplicity and a little more about the exquisite pleasure that flowed through her body.

His hands were magic; there was no other explanation. The lips he used to draw her soul forth were firm, warm, and insistent. The fingers that found secret places and hidden sensations were gentle and strong.

"Aislinn, my stubborn, secretive wife. I will have you tonight. I cannot deny myself any longer." His breath was warm as he sipped kisses along her chin, her throat, and her bare breasts.

Jesu, when had she lost her clothing?

It mattered not as he drew her down to the stone bench, now covered with her cloak and her bliaut. It mattered not one bit that he suckled her with insistence and longing until a deep chasm of want and need pooled low in her own belly.

"Aislinn, beauty, you are mine by right and law." His

voice was rough and husky as he laved his tongue over her nipples, now swollen and sensitive with desire.

"Open for me, sweet. Open for me so I may taste your sweet honey."

Aislinn's mind did not comprehend, but her body did. Without thinking, she spread her thighs. He was there above her, a creature of silvery light and dark shadow. She felt more than saw him. His gaze burned a trail over her belly and down lower, lower until suddenly he kissed her—there.

Such heat! Never had Aislinn known the fever of eroticism; now she burned with it as Desmond's wicked tongue schooled her in desire, longing, need—*pleasure*.

Wave after wave of delicious, hot satisfaction rolled over her, bending her body, molding her to him. Her hips arched; she had no thought of it. Her core pulled at him; she had no control to stop it. He led the way and her body followed.

"Aislinn, Aislinn," he moaned. She whimpered with need when he left her.

Hot, hard, and swift, something impaled her. She tightened and tried to scramble away, but he was there, holding her, soothing her, coaxing her to trust him.

The feelings were sharp, new, raw, but suddenly Aislinn's body was no longer her own. It shattered into a fragmented vessel of intensity, so brilliant and so primal she could only scream.

But Desmond found her mouth and swallowed the sound. There were only the night animals and the soft swoosh of a bird in the garden as Aislinn gave up her maidenhead and her resistance to her husband.

Long minutes later, Aislinn stirred beneath Desmond, and he began to harden again. He had taken her with such urgency there on the stone slab beneath the stars, but now as his head cleared, he regretted it. She should have had a bed, sweet fragrant beeswax candles, a soothing bath, and mulled wine.

"Did I hurt you?" He moved, taking his weight upon his forearms and lifting himself off her body slightly. She was so small, so delicate. He had taken her with all the lust of a rutting boar; now his conscience stung because he had been so ungallant.

"Nay," she said in a breathy voice that was foreign-sounding to her ears. In the soft, pale light of the moon, their gazes locked. Something hot, primal, and possessive passed between them.

"I do not regret taking your maidenhead, Aislinn, but I regret that it was not done with soft furs, love-words, and the glow of candles," he said earnestly.

His words made her want to weep, so she changed the subject. "How did you know about the passage?"

"I once saw you emerge like a fairy creature. You flitted from bloom to bud like a woodland sprite. It was enchanting."

"How long have you known?"

"Since the night you pretended to be drugged and came straightaway to the maze."

"You tried to give me a sleeping potion," she accused, her body stiffening beneath him. She did not make any attempt to be rid of him or to remove his body from inside hers, but her eyes blazed with anger, and the hands that gripped his shoulder tightened.

"Nay, sweeting. I did not. For a time I thought perchance you tried to dose me, but I realize that was not the case."

Her eyes flitted over his features, questioning, judging, weighing his words. "But if you did not and I did not . . . then who?"

"Wife, I find my head is too full of you to think and talk of intrigues and potions. Let me love you again in a proper fashion and allow me to lie with you in the lady's chamber."

"You ask my leave?"

"I beg it."

He kissed her mouth before she could reply. Gently he began to move inside her . . . in . . . out. Gloriously she responded. Her hips met his in a slow dance of exquisite pleasure.

"Aye," she whispered in his ear.

Whether it was her assent to let him stay with her, or her plea that he continue moving inside her, he was not sure. They fit together as if crafted from the same hunk of flesh. He felt powerful, protective, manly. She made little mewling sounds as he satisfied her yet again.

Slowly they separated, becoming two souls again instead of one. He stood and righted his hose. Aislinn stood and untangled her clothes from the bench. It was an enchanting moment: the moon above, the sounds of the night insects and birds.

And then she turned to him, and he nearly died from the sight of her.

A pale shaft of moonlight limned her breasts, the slight swell of her belly, and her long, sleek legs. Part of her face was in shadow, but he could see her eyes.

Desmond was stunned.

For in those beautiful pale-green eyes he saw the truth; he had brought her sexual release and satisfaction—and no more. Her innermost woman's soul was untouched, unmoved. She pulled on her bliaut and stood, leaving the laces trailing at the sides.

"Aislinn?" He was shaken, unsure of himself. How could a woman experience such shattering pleasure and keep her heart apart?

Her smile was cool, self-possessed, and confident. He realized she knew exactly what she was doing.

"My lord?" Her brows arched gently. They might have

just been sharing a warm fire in a room full of castle folk for all the intimacy he saw in her face and eyes.

The vixen might have been a virgin, but she had the power and instincts handed down from Eve. "Aislinn, what we just shared—"

"Aye, my lord, 'twas wondrous. The king was correct. You are a stallion among men. We must do it again some time soon."

She pulled on her tunic. Then she turned and, with her head held high, walked back to the stone wall. She disappeared inside and the stones swung shut, leaving Desmond alone in the maze, feeling as if he had been hit with a battle mace.

Seventeen

Aislinn stripped off her clothes and washed in scented water from the ewer. Her hand was shaking and so were her legs.

Desmond did things, knew things about her body that she had no inkling about. He was a wonderful lover; the sensations he awoke in her were thrilling.

"And I could clout the blackguard in the head for having such knowledge about me," she grumbled aloud.

"He values me not at all. He does not trust me. He thinks more of his stallion than he does having me as his wife." She washed until her skin was pink and stinging, but she could not erase the memory of his magical hands upon her skin.

"My lord husband is a rogue. He thought I tried to give him a sleeping potion, or so he says. How can I believe him? How can I trust him?"

Her thoughts swept back in time to Theron. Good, solid, trustworthy Theron. He had warned her about trusting men. And now she realized that because of the great difference in their ages, he had known this day would surely come.

"Theron had known I would be at the mercy of a skilled lover who was unscrupulous. But I do remember your counsel, Theron. I do remember. I will not share

Sevenoaks's secrets with a man I do not trust and who does not have trust in me."

Desmond stood in the garden feeling like a spurned lover. He had never felt such heat and passion during the act of love.

Or such utter contempt from any woman when we parted. It was not in his experience. Women, especially women who had been satisfied, were pliant and soft. They wanted to cuddle and be stroked like a tabby.

"Not Aislinn."

He sat down on the slab of stone, still warm from her body, and ran his hand over the surface. A shiver of shared sensation ran through him. "She took her pleasure and left me like a used trencher."

Desmond's pride was battered. Bruises to his confidence, the likes of which he had never known before, stung him. He had been used like a stallion to service a mare in season. It was a painful thing. A small voice in the back of his mind suggested he had done the same to maidens more than once, but he refused to examine that possibility.

Desmond rose from the bench and began to pace. He wanted his wife with the same fervor as before, but like a child who has touched fire, now he would be more wary. And while he was nursing his wounded pride, he glanced up. A ghostly light danced from within the lord's chamber window.

"And our good Giles is gone to Rye, so it cannot be him that searches. I have been a fool on two counts: first by thinking I knew where the danger lay; and second by thinking my lady wife would give her heart to me just because I swived her."

* * *

Dawn found Desmond still sitting in the garden maze. He had spent the night thinking and had come to realize he was a fool. Only a doddering swine would have expected a woman like Aislinn to suddenly give herself, heart, mind, and soul, after a good swiving.

"Stallion, indeed." He repeated her words, spoken with such cool disdain. His pride withered, but in spite of it all, he admired Aislinn. She was like Boudicca in more ways than just her flame-colored hair. She had a warrior-woman's heart. Aislinn was the kind of majestic wife any man would be proud to have on his arm.

"If only she felt the same about her lord husband," Desmond said glumly. And then, like the shaft of bright light reflecting off the sundial, he knew what he must do. He must win the lady's regard and respect.

And show her that I trust her. Surely then she will learn to adore me—to love me.

Later in the morning Desmond saw Coy approaching. "By the Rood, I have never seen a longer face. What vexes you, Desmond?" Coy sauntered to the low stone wall, where Desmond sat beneath an apple tree. "You should be happy. The abbot is not within Sevenoaks, and in his absence there is a good chance we will solve this riddle."

"I doubt that, for we have been sniffing in the wrong direction."

"How so?"

"I saw light in the lord's solar last eve. If Giles was on the road to Rye with the knight, then he cannot have been above stairs. Mayhap this place is haunted."

"I do not believe in ghosts." Coy frowned. "Perchance the abbot was not on his way to Rye."

Desmond glanced up. "'Twould mean he would have to leave the knight alone on the road."

"Aye, but if the sleeping draft had been given, then even the knight would not know of it."

"True." Desmond nodded.

"But 'tis not the riddle of Giles that vexes you, is it?" Coy flopped down on the turf and began to cut an apple with his dagger.

"My lady wife does not love me," Desmond said, expecting to hear words of pity from his friend. Instead he was given a harsh cackle. Coy's face was contorted in amusement.

"She is your wife, not your mistress; of course she does not love you. Sometimes I think you took one too many hits in tourney and your brains have been scrambled." Coy tapped his temple.

"Rowanne loves Brandt." Desmond felt the sullen jealousy of a stripling youth when he thought of Brandt and how Rowanne doted upon him. What was happening to him?

"Ah, but that is a most singular situation. Few men even receive a passing affection from their wives. Get a mistress if you want love-words and fawning looks. Wives are for land, political strength, and well-bred sons."

"I don't want a mistress to love me. I want Aislinn."

Coy shook his dark head in annoyance. "For pity's sake, bed the wench and get this fever from your blood."

"I have bedded her." Desmond concentrated on the apple core he held, as if it could answer all his questions.

"And?"

"And she said we should do it again sometime soon."

Coy doubled over in gales of laughter. He squirmed on the turf. He kicked his legs.

"Coy, you test me sorely." Desmond did not see the humor of his situation.

"It has finally happened, though I expected to have a long, white beard before I saw it."

"Saw what? And get up; you are causing the castle folk to gawk at your foolishness."

"The great lover and dashing swain, the 'stallion of England,' as Henry named you, has met his match in one tiny red-haired wench. You have lost your heart."

Desmond tossed the core as far as he could. "Do not be daft. Of course I have not lost my heart. That is what I have been saying. It is the duty of a wife to love her husband, not the other way round. My wife does not love me."

He refused to believe what Coy was saying. He did not love Aislinn; it was simply that he wanted her to love him. He wanted fawning looks and obedience and smiles of shy, erotic memory. "And if it kills me, by the Rood, I am going to have her love."

Aislinn watched Desmond in the orchard below, and her heart kicked.

Arrogant cullion. Does he now relay all to his friend? That would be the way of the lowborn knave. She turned away from the window and closed her eyes. Instantly she saw in her mind's eye the sliver of moon and the fiery intensity in her lover-husband's eyes.

It was wondrous. And I would know those feelings again—often. I would have my lord husband bed me nightly, and I would bear his children, but I will never, ever give up my heart to him. For Theron was right: to give my heart means the loss of my soul.

Desmond had spent hours mulling over his problems and had finally come to the conclusion there was no easy path for him to his wife's heart. Aislinn was not like any other woman he had ever known. She was courageous and honorable.

"And more stubborn than Brume when he does not want new shoes on his feet," he grumbled, and idly nibbled his pasty.

"Did you say summat, my lord?" Cook asked.

"Nay."

He remembered Aislinn's face when he had brought her to see his warhorse. There had been a moment when she had looked almost disappointed. But what could he have said or done to wound her?

Tom was perched on his high stool, assisting Cook in any fashion as he might, occasionally casting a look in Desmond's direction. He scooted off his stool and swung on his crutches. He poured out a mazer of beer and handed it to Desmond.

"You have not eaten much of the pasty, my lord."

"I have little thirst or appetite."

"Do you sicken, my lord?" Cook asked, wiping her hands on her full linen skirts.

"Nay, 'tis not an ailment of the body," Desmond admitted.

Tom and the cook exchanged glances. "Ah, so that is the way of things," Cook chuckled and ground herbs in a stone bowl.

"What way of things?" Desmond frowned at the smiles on their faces. What could they know that he did not?

"An affair of the heart, my lord?" Cook slapped a haunch of lamb onto the table and rubbed rosemary and thyme into the pink flesh.

"Are you conversant in affairs of the heart, Cook?" Desmond's question was sharper than he meant it to be.

She wrinkled her nose and placed her hands on her hips. "I know what all women know, my lord." She squinted her eye at him.

"Which is a sight more than many lordlings know, if I may be so bold as to say so."

Desmond grinned at her effrontery. She was a brazen

crone, and perhaps wise. "Tell me, then, good Cook. How does a man win the heart of a woman who likes him little and needs him not at all?"

"Sit down, my lord, and I will give you the recipe for winning a lady's heart."

Desmond was whistling a tune as he took the stairs two at a time. He went to Aislinn's door and rapped smartly.

"Wife, ready yourself. We ride." He turned and took two steps before the door swung open.

Aislinn's face was a study in confusion. Her hair tumbled about her shoulders in big, loose curls. "What do you mean, my lord? I have made no such appointment."

"Ah, but you are my lady wife. And as such, you owe me your loyalty and obedience—at least in the small things of life," Desmond added with a wink. "Now ready yourself, for the horses are waiting in the bailey."

Aislinn opened her mouth to protest, but Desmond swiftly disappeared from sight. This was just the sort of command a cullion such as her lord husband would issue. She should shut her door and put the bar on it . . . and yet the day was fair and she had not ridden in a long while. It was foolish for her to hide behind her door and miss out on the beauty of the day.

"As you wish, my lord. I will take my pleasure in the day and allow you to think you are the piper who plays the tune." She braided her hair and caught it up in a golden ring. "But you will soon learn I will dance the steps only if I wish."

Desmond was waiting on the steps when she emerged from the keep. Aislinn's hair was caught in a thick braid that bounced down her back as she lightly took the steps. She was wearing a modest gray bliaut and a simple cloak of brown wool. If it had been her goal to look plain as a wren, she failed, for the pale translucency of her skin, and her vibrant hair, were more lovely than jewels and silk. It was difficult to keep from reaching out and pulling her to him, but Desmond remembered Cook's advice.

"I am told this palfrey is settled and surefooted." Desmond lifted Aislinn up onto the mare's back. He took the opportunity to trail his fingers down the inside of her thigh. Her expression did not change, but she shivered. He took a small measure of satisfaction from that telling sign.

"Brume is much in need of exercise," he said as he climbed into the saddle. He was still using his bulky jousting saddle and armor, since he had yet to return to Mereworth. But today he would remedy that.

"Where shall we ride?" he asked sweetly.

She turned to him, the picture of serenity, her green eyes steady on his face. " 'Tis up to you, my lord."

"I was hoping you would say that. Let us begin and I will reveal our destination later."

Her eyes rounded, but he gave her no chance to gainsay him. He kicked Brume, and the palfrey matched her pace to the stallion that led her. They loped across the drawbridge and down the verge.

The land was green with life. Tender sprouts of rye, wheat, and barley lay in the dark, loamy furrows. Young boys with slings and rocks kept the birds away, making a game of their chore.

"The harvest will be good this year," Desmond commented as Aislinn's eyes skimmed over the fielders. "Sevenoaks will not know hunger this winter."

Brume leaped a small runnel of water. Aislinn's mare did the same. Aislinn was not prepared, however, and slipped sideways, losing her seat and hanging on with round, wide eyes until Desmond snatched her into his arms.

"My lord!" she said indignantly while she tried to shove her bliaut down from where it bunched at her thighs.

"Lady wife, I cannot let you fall into the mud. The pigs have been herded into the forest to forage for acorns; I would not have you eaten."

Aislinn's head spun around. Swineherds were controlling the pigs with long staffs and dogs.

"My horse—"

"Will follow Brume. She is nearly in season. Do you not feel his interest in her?" Her braid was coming loose as they rode. Strands of her hair flew like a fiery pennant. The scent of exotic oils and her own musk wafted to his nose. He warred with himself as his arm tightened around her lush body.

Aislinn glanced at Brume's head. She made a small O of surprise when she realized that the stallion was making whiffling noises at the palfrey, who scampered obediently, keeping pace with the mighty destrier.

" 'Tis nature, sweeting. He is hard and ready for her— as I am for you. Have you heard of the *liaison de chevalier?*"

"Nay."

"Let me show you." He let Brume have his head, knowing the stallion would pick his way home to Mereworth. Desmond's fingers found Aislinn's moist cleft.

Her head lolled back onto his shoulder. She moaned. He could feel the heat growing at the juncture of her thighs. It was delicious having her in front of him while the rocking motion of Brume's great strides rhythmically put his sex against her soft, rounded arse.

"Aye, show me, my lord husband. Teach me," she said in a breathy voice.

"We needs must move you around." She weighed little,

and so 'twas easy for him to lift and turn her toward him.
He slid her bliaut and tunics up to her waist, baring her
sweet, soft quim to his view. Her head was bent, and she,
too, was looking at herself as he unlaced his hose and
freed himself from his braies. He was hard as a spear.

"Do you trust me, Aislinn?" he asked.

She lifted her chin and looked him straight in the eye.
"Nay, my lord, I trust you not, but I am willing to let you
teach me the ways of love. I can share great pleasure with
you, but I will not give you my heart."

So, the little vixen was willing to throw down the
gauntlet, to make it plain how matters lay between them.

"Very well, lady wife, then let me give you what I
may." And on Brume's next step, Desmond gently lifted
her and impaled her on his stiff member. She gasped and
clung to his shoulders. He kicked the stallion, increasing
the pace, the motion, the pleasure.

"But by the time I have schooled you in all the ways
of love, my beauty, I will have your heart. I vow it."

She gasped and dug her small gloved hands into his
shoulders, looking back behind him as they rode over the
uneven dales with Brume leaping the runnels. Each time
the horse landed, Aislinn gave a little cry of pleasure as
her body was settled more fully on Desmond's lance. He
was settled deeply into her.

"My—my lord," she gasped.

"Aye, 'tis good," he growled.

"Aye, but my lord, there are riders behind us."

He shoved himself into her, taking deep satisfaction at
her indrawn breath. "They are but our escort to the borders of Mereworth, lady. Fear not, they have been told to
stay well back except in case of danger. They cannot see
what we do."

"Mere—Mereworth?" Her speech was thick and
slurred with her building passion. The high jousting can-

tle of the saddle at her back kept her tight against Desmond's groin.

"Aye, lady wife. We are bound for my ancestral home. With all the intrigue and plots at Sevenoaks, I will not risk your safety another day."

Desmond put his hands on Aislinn's waist and lifted her higher. He released his grip. The motion of the stallion and her weight settled her hard against him. She moaned. They reached the pinnacle of the pleasure in unison, shouting each other's name as the towers of Mereworth came into view.

Aislinn was still shuddering but she managed to clear her head and take stock of her surroundings.

"My lord, pray turn me round, else your folk will wonder."

"As you wish." He lifted her and turned her. She began to right her skirts as he pulled the laces taut on his codlings. A smile curved Desmond's lips. He had taken his bride twice now, and they had yet to know the comforts of a bed.

"Why did you not consult me about this journey, my lord?" Aislinn asked with a flinty edge to her voice. The soft purr of desire was gone now, and he saw her scan the scarred and solid facade of Mereworth with anger in her green eyes.

"I wanted none but Coy and my trusted guard to know our destination."

"But I have no gowns—"

"All you need will be found within Mereworth. My lady mother was a female with a taste for clothes. Her gowns, though a bit out of fashion, will serve you well."

"I would return to Sevenoaks anon."

"Aislinn, I did not give you a sleeping potion. I did not give Pointisbright a sleeping potion. Think you I will continue to see you at risk when someone within the walls of Sevenoaks is using herbs to kill?"

"Kill? What do you mean? Pointisbright has recovered, and I, though I am angry—"

"You could have been given enough of the sleeping brew to bring death." Desmond pulled Brume to a stop outside the wide, deep moat. He nodded to the man on the gatehouse wall, who recognized him instantly.

"Aislinn, 'tis time you and I had an understanding of events. I will see you settled and then we will talk."

Aislinn glanced up at the castle while the drawbridge was lowered across the green water of the moat. Mereworth was squat, gray, and solid. Vines climbed up the southern wall, thick and glossy as the scales on a dragon's back. It was not a pretty castle, but it did give the appearance of strength and protection.

She turned her head sharply and looked at Desmond. His mouth was set in a hard, determined line. His hair was still as golden, his face as fair, as when first she saw him, but he was different. No longer was he the smiling rogue, but beneath the facade she saw the hard core of the warrior and protector.

When she turned and faced the gate, it was with a sense of well-being. She did not trust this husband of hers—not completely, not if she had her wits—and yet she knew that within his arms and within these walls she would be safe.

"My lord Desmond, 'tis happy we are you have come home." A grizzled man with sharp eyes and jaggedly cut hair approached. About his waist was a great ring of keys.

"Galen, my seneschal. This is my lady wife, Aislinn of Sevenoaks."

"Milady." Galen executed a deep bow. "I shall make preparations for a feast and ready the lord's chamber."

"Ready the lady's chamber as well," Aislinn said, leveling a look upon Desmond.

Desmond inclined his head. "As my lady says, Galen, and have a bath brought to her chamber. The trunks containing my mother's belongings are to be opened and the gowns freshened."

"As you wish." Galen turned and bellowed orders in rapid succession. Soon the bailey was a hive of activity, but each person who came or went looked up at Desmond and smiled warmly.

"You are well loved, I see."

"Mayhap after a time within Mereworth you will come to feel the same for me, lady. Dare I hope it?"

" 'Tis always good to have hope." Aislinn refused to make promises to this rogue. "I am waiting for us to have converse, as you said. There is much to settle between us."

"And we will do it anon . . . after you bathe me as is the custom among ladies of the keep." Desmond's smile was lecherous as he dismounted and pulled Aislinn down from Brume. The little mare had obediently kept pace with the stallion, and now that he was free of his human burdens, the horse turned his attention to her. He whiffled, snorted, and nipped at her.

"Come, lady, let us leave Brume to mount his mare."

Aislinn looked into Desmond's eyes and felt the sexual magnetism of him sluice over her. His words brought back images and sensations that made her middle flutter.

"Put Brume and the mare into the lower common, where they may dally as they wish."

"Aye, my lord." Galen stripped off the saddle while another lad did the same for the mare. And then, before the horses had been moved to the grassy common, the stallion moved to the mare and mounted her. Aislinn could not help but remember the sight of Desmond's arousal—so primal, so like that stallion. She shivered as her body responded to the thought.

"Come, lady, our bath awaits." Desmond nipped the soft skin of her earlobe. "And I would teach you more in the ways of love before our feast."

She could not find the strength or the will to protest, for she wanted him inside her again.

The lady's chamber was comfortable, but it had no glass windows—only arrow ports. There was no garderobe discreetly hidden behind an ell of stone, but a pot tucked under the bed. There were, however, heavy, richly colored tapestries on the walls, and thick furs strewn across the floor and the bed. The tub that had been carried up and filled was a huge oaken vessel with a padded linen rim large enough to sit at least four knights. Steam rose and winnowed through the arrow ports on the outer wall.

Aislinn felt as if she were under siege. Desmond looked at her in a way that was different: enticing and possessive. Even when she did not mean to do so, her body answered his silent call. His eyes moved over her form greedily as the maids and serving lads poured sweet oils in the water.

"You may leave," Desmond said in the general direction of the servants. They silently retreated from the chamber.

"Now, lady wife, come, do your duty. Remove my clothes and bathe me," Desmond commanded in a soft, winning tone.

Aislinn swallowed. She knew it was her duty, but this was a service she had never performed. Still, how difficult could it be? She started at his padded gambeson, unbuckling the taches and freeing the side so he could assist her in slipping it over his head.

"Sit, my lord, and I shall remove your boots."

He did as she commanded, never once taking his eyes from her face as she knelt before him. The air grew hot and close in the room, no doubt because of the steaming tub in the middle of the floor and the tiny arrow ports for ventilation.

"Aislinn, you are flushed," he said matter-of-factly.

" 'Tis warm, my lord." She grasped his boot heel and pulled. The boot slid free. He wiggled his toes, which drew her eyes up his ankle to his calf and beyond. There was a discernable bulge in his hose.

"Are you warm, Aislinn? Does your body burn?"

She glanced away from that enticing set of codlings and quickly grasped the other boot.

"Does your sweet quim ache for me? When Brume mounted the mare, did you remember what it felt like to have me inside you?" His voice was smoother than spiced white wine.

"Aye, my lord," she admitted honestly, shutting her eyes and savoring the thrill that started low in her body.

"Come to me. Let me show you more of the ways of love, my beauteous Aislinn."

She stood on shaky legs. He stripped off his hose and braies. Then he removed the long tunic that had modestly covered him. He jutted proud and hot from a tangle of golden-brown curls.

"You are well endowed and manly, my lord husband." There was no shame in her words, only appreciation and gladness that he was able to do to her the things he did. She might not trust him—was afraid to love him—but she was willing to be pleasured by him.

"Come, let me play the lady's maid for you." He unlaced her bliaut and pulled it over her head. Then her undertunic and shift followed. She was bare except for her feet.

"I have been wanting to feather kisses up those dainty ankles for a time now." He lifted her foot, letting his eyes skim over the nether regions of her now exposed body. He removed the slippers. Then he lifted her and deposited her into the tub.

"But my lord, I—"

"Shall do your duty and more, my lady wife. Have no fear of that."

He climbed into the tub with her. Then he pulled her to him. She felt the silken slide of his tarse against her buttocks as he settled her back to his chest and into his lap. With one hand he fondled her breasts, causing little sparks of sensation to travel from her nipples to her belly. The other hand had found the front of her cleft and was gently parting her tender flesh. She gasped and arched when a finger slipped inside her.

"Ah, you are tender yet from your ride," he purred in her ear, nipping the skin on her nape, sipping kisses down her neck beneath her hair. "Ride my hand, dearest Aislinn. I am willingly your stallion."

His words and his touch ignited something wild and wanton inside her. She was shocked but not shocked. She was afraid but not afraid. Within Desmond's encircling arms she felt alive, powerful, and anxious to do what he bade.

"Let me see if I may . . . ah, yes, one more finger will fit, but tightly. I feel the bud of your desire, Aislinn. Do you feel this?"

He touched a part of her that made her gasp. She could not breathe, could not think. There was nothing in the world but Desmond and that core of need and want that he flicked, teased, and caressed so expertly.

She pushed harder into his hand.

"Ah, yes, sweeting. Show me the best way to please you. I shall endeavor to please you in all things, Aislinn."

Madness was overtaking her now. She writhed, unmindful of the splashing water that lapped over the edge. She pushed harder and began to move in a sensuous motion that increased her pleasure.

When she felt the hot tide of release upon her, Desmond lifted her body and impaled her from behind.

Somehow they were spooned together. She thought of the stallion and the mare, and her body grew more excited because of it. He was deep within her, at the very core of her being.

"Now, Aislinn, I will show you another level of passion." And as his hand fondled her bud of desire, he drove deep into her. "I will plow you deep and often and plant my seed in you, lady wife."

She could no longer hear or comprehend his words. She called out his name in ecstasy, and though she did not wish it, her secret heart heard his words and embraced them. For that had long been her heart's desire: to have a child conceived in love.

Desmond gently washed her body, cleansing her of his juices while she lazed, boneless and satisfied in the hot water. It had cooled to a pleasant heat, and neither, it seemed, was anxious to leave the tub.

Her eyes drifted over him and she felt . . . she was not sure what she felt. She did not love him. She would not let herself love him or trust him. To do so would be the apex of foolishness, and Aislinn was not a foolish maid. But she had reveled in the power of his body and his skill as a lover, and would do so again.

"I never knew that bed sport would be so . . . so interesting," she said with a sigh.

"Interesting? Hmm, I shall take that as a compliment." He chuckled and looked at her with a strange glint in his blue eyes. "There is much you still do not know, Aislinn, but I will show you and teach you. I want to teach you."

She sat up and looked at him, assessing him critically. He was handsome, but certainly there were men fairer of face and form. What was it about him that wrung such feelings—such raw lust and consuming hunger—from her?

"Aislinn, we must talk now. There are things that must be said." He scooted to the opposite side of the oak tub and swiped his hand down his face, sluicing water from his jaws. His hair was wet, the tips dark brown and dripping. He needed to scrape the rough beard from his cheeks and chin. He looked a little dangerous and very, very desirable.

"There is a killer at Sevenoaks," he said without preamble.

"And who has died?" Suspicion twined in her head like the wisps of steam from the water.

"Four men." Desmond looked at her sharply. "The four men who wedded you before me."

She sucked in a breath. Since the king had left, she had not thought about the deaths of her husbands in quite the same way. She did not realize until this moment that she had let go of the torment, no longer carried the horrible weight of guilt.

"How cruel of you to mention them. I will not allow you to say I am cursed."

"There is no curse, Aislinn, not on you or Sevenoaks or any of your husbands. Their deaths had naught to do with you."

"Then speak plainly, husband. Your words are like riddles to me."

"Riddles indeed. And I think a riddle is at the center of this tangle. Do these words mean anything to you?

"The time is marked when the moon is ripe;

Surrender the stars and carry a light.

The lord and the lady share a floor;

Riches untold behind the door.

"Have you ever heard that spoken, or read it anywhere at Sevenoaks?"

She paused and averted her eyes. It was nothing more than the briefest intake of breath, but Desmond saw it.

"Nay. Is it a riddle of your making? And what has that to do with murder?"

"It is carved upon the stone door you use to enter the maze. Covered by moss and lichen, it must have been cut into the stone at the building of Sevenoaks."

Aislinn shrugged, but she no longer met Desmond's gaze. "What has that to do with murder? I still do not understand."

"I did not give you a sleeping draft. I believe you did not attempt to give any potions to me. If that is true, then someone wanted us both sleeping."

"How foolish. Who would wish such a thing?" She toyed with little shimmering pools of exotic oils floating on the surface of the water, avoiding his gaze altogether now. But was it because she knew more than she was saying or because he brought up painful reminders of the past?

"It is my belief someone wanted us both insensible so they could have leave to inspect the lord's chamber without fear of being caught. I believe that is the reason all the men died. They were going to take you to the lord's chamber to bed you; is this true?"

Her brow furrowed. He could see her reaching back in time to each wedding, scouring her memories. "Aye. Preparations had been made for the bedding to take place in the lord's chamber."

"And each time you were widowed you closed yourself up in your own solar to grieve, leaving the lord's chamber unattended."

"This is flummery. There is only one key; there has ever been only one key."

"So you say, and yet each night lights are seen in the lord's chamber. Some of the folk think it is a spirit, but I believe it is someone searching—searching for the riches behind the door that are mentioned in the lay carved into the stones."

She finally looked up and met his gaze. "Is that what you wish, my lord husband? Are you after riches? Is that the reason you risked death to wed me?"

He studied her face but did not answer. Her words hit harder than a fist. She really did not trust him—'struth, she had little regard for him at all except as a lover. It was a bitter draft. Or did she dance around the truth because she knew all about the chamber, the lay, and the riches? Once again a small seed of distrust was planted in his mind.

Eighteen

"My lord, 'tis good to see a wife finally at your side." A plump matron with several chins bowed before the great table. "I had begun to think I suckled a eunuch."

"Aislinn, this is, Meg, my old nurse." Desmond stood and leaned far across the table. He deposited a kiss to her forehead just below her head-covering of starchy linen. Her face softened and her eyes filled with watery tears.

"He was a trial to me sometimes, lady, I can tell you that; but now in my old age he is a blessing. I only wish his mother and father had lived to see this day." Genuine tears welled in the woman's eyes. She scuttled away, dabbing at her cheeks.

"What happened to your parents?" Aislinn heard herself ask. She did not want to know, did not want to ferret out details about his life—it would only make him seem more flesh and blood, and the Lord knew she did not need that.

"On a holy pilgrimage they contracted a killing fever. They were buried together in France." Desmond's words were tight and he discreetly swiped at the corner of his eye. "But the du Lucs were my adopted parents. My real mother died when I was very young. My sire a few years ago, before I learned of my lineage."

"May I know the story?" Why did she ask? Why did

she care what caused his face to pale and his eyes to fill with pain?

"I was a babe still suckling when our castle, Irthing, was breached by an enemy. My mother was ravished and died trying to protect me, my sister, Rowanne, and my brother Lochlyn. We were taken away. The tale is tangled and cruel. Suffice to say, all thought the children dead but my father. The threat was made that if he made any attempt to free one, the others would be killed. Ancient ogham stones near Irthing promise the Vaudry children will rise from the dead and are destined to love only once."

He stared into the wine in his goblet as if looking back into the past and reading those stones.

"And have you, my lord?" Aislinn asked.

He glanced up. "Have I risen from the dead?"

"Nay. Have you loved yet?"

"Not yet, my lady. Not yet."

Aislinn's heart skipped a beat. Then suddenly, a stronger beat filled the air. Lutes, harps, and small, deep drums were being played. The low tables were cleared and shoved back against the wall. Fresh-faced maids and handsome young swains clapped their hands and took opposite sides of the room.

"Come, lady, stand away from the table, lest you be swept against the stones." Desmond chuckled and lightly looped his arm around her waist.

"My lord, lead us in the dance," a young serving maid pleaded. Her request was joined by other voices, some sweet, some coarse with the first flush of manhood.

"How can we refuse, wife?" Desmond grinned at Aislinn. He grasped her hand.

"My lord, I have not danced in years—"

"Then 'tis past time. Come, lady wife, take a turn with me and let the folk of Mereworth learn to love you for your grace and beauty." His words were so sweet, his manner so winning, she could not refuse.

Aislinn felt clumsy as a green girl of twelve when Desmond bowed to her with a flourish and offered a leg. She tried not to respond to the flexing of his thigh muscles, or the lusty twinkling in his eye, but her body ignored her mind. She knew what manly flesh was hidden beneath the edge of his tunic.

His hand was firm and strong as he led her. She began to do the almost forgotten steps. Every face in the hall was joyous as she and Desmond lightly skipped past them and twirled to the end of the line.

She stood with the girls and clapped as another couple followed the same route, skipping and twirling to the finish. Desmond's eyes were upon her. He grinned and clapped while his gaze stripped her bare.

Jesu! He was a courtier when he wished to be. And he was the lord of a castle that knew joy and merry-making. Aislinn tried to remember a time in her life when she had danced and giggled. After her parents drowned, she had been raised by a nurse, with Giles overseeing her day-to-day activities.

There had never been this kind of jubilation. And she realized with a painful wrench of her heart, she had missed much in growing up as she had.

"Come, lady, now you must dance with each of the knights of Mereworth." Desmond spun her out to the center of the floor. A line of grinning warriors stood patiently waiting. They were young and old, tall and stocky, and each one looked at her as if she were a tempting sweetmeat.

"But my lord—"

" 'Tis the custom, lady. And what better way to meet the men who are sworn to protect and uphold you?" Desmond nodded and the seneschal Galen took her into a turn around the floor. Laughter, clapping, and stamping of feet accompanied her journey.

"My lady," Galen said with a bob of his brows, "we hope you find Mereworth to your liking."

"I—'tis a most merry keep," she finally said.

"Aye, merry and happy we are that our lord has taken such a comely wife."

And with that welcome, Aislinn found herself introduced to the folk of Mereworth. She was complimented, flattered, and twirled until her head was spinning. Each knight, retainer, and high-ranking servant introduced himself and then galloped her around the great hall with a vigor that took her breath away. Her hair was heavy and damp on her nape, her feet tender and sore, by the time the great, fat tallow candles sputtered and went out. And yet the hall remained bright. She glanced at the arrow ports on the top level of the hall and saw the pinking rays of dawn.

She had danced all night.

"Gramercy," Desmond roared. "You have my thanks for giving my lady wife a warm welcome." He looped his arm around her as the last knight twirled her toward her husband. "Now we must see she takes her rest. After the cows are milked and the animals tended, you all may have a day of leisure."

A loud roar echoed through the hall. Empty tankards were banged on the wooden tables against the wall.

"Desmond, I am asleep on my feet," she said with a happy sigh.

He smiled down at her. " 'Tis the first time you have called me Desmond except in the frenzy of passion."

"I beg pardon . . ."

"Do not be foolish, Aislinn. I like the sound of my name on your lips when you are being lusty, and now as well. Come, let me aid you, wife. I am here for you in all things." He scooped her up in his arms to the hoots and cheers of his men. With a throaty laugh, he climbed the stairs to the upper chambers.

Aislinn curled into his shoulder and yawned; she was asleep before he reached their solar. Her sweet mouth curled in a small smile of happiness.

Aislinn heard the clatter of dishes. She opened one eye. A young girl with butter-colored braids was moving about the chamber. She glanced up and froze when she met Aislinn's gaze.

"Oh, lady, did I wake thee?" she said in a soft, girlish voice. "Pray forgive me—"

"Is it morning?" Aislinn swiped her hair from her face and sat up. She did not remember coming to bed.

" 'Tis long past nooning, my lady. Lord Desmond ordered a bath for you upon your waking. 'Twill be here anon."

The mention of a bath brought a warm flush of remembered passion to Aislinn's body and mind.

"He also ordered fresh ale and warm bread. I have it here, lady. May I brush your hair?"

"Brush my hair?" The words chilled Aislinn.

"Aye, lady, I have never seen such glorious hair. All the maids in Mereworth are talking about your hair. We all wish we had been born with tresses that look like flame. Hilde asked her mother if there might be herbs she could rinse her pale hair in that might change it to a like hue." The girl smiled guilelessly as she chattered.

Aislinn's eyes burned from unwanted tears. Never in her life had she received such a sweet, heartfelt compliment.

"I promise not to pull if ye would let me dress it for ye."

"What are you called?" Aislinn asked softly.

"I am Megret. Lord Desmond says if I please ye I might have the privilege of becoming your maid."

"Megret, you please me much. And aye, you may brush my hair, though I warn you it is a tangle and oft has a mind of its own."

The girl giggled and found an ivory comb on a small commode. Aislinn assumed it was more of Lady Alys's finery. She rose naked from the bed, feeling a little shy, but Megret simply held a thick velvet-and-fur robe for her to slip into. She moved to a low padded bench by the slender arrow ports. 'Twas surprising how gay and cheerful the solar seemed in spite of the lack of sun. Candles burned in iron holders, and cresset lamps hung from a great circle of iron in the arched and domed ceiling.

Megret began to untangle Aislinn's hair, taking care not to tug or pull. It was wonderful to have someone minister to her, but what was more astounding was the feeling of acceptance and belonging.

She sucked in a startled breath.

"Oh, lady, did I hurt you?" Megret asked.

"Nay, Megret, 'tis nothing wrong, a foolish thought caught me unaware." She could not allow herself to be seduced by this place and the lord who called it home.

Within the hour, Aislinn was bathed and her hair dressed in an elaborate coif of braids and curls that dangled over one shoulder. Megret beamed with pride as she finished the back laces of the pale dove gray gown that had been pulled from a chest full of gowns. Flower petals had been layered among the clothes and the scent lingered.

"Oh, lady, ye are a wondrous beauty." Megret clapped her palms together.

"I agree." Desmond lounged in the doorway, his eyes sliding over Aislinn from head to bare toe. Her entire body tingled each time Desmond looked at her. There was no way she could deny his appeal or his manly prowess. And yet she must withhold her heart and keep her secrets.

"But we needs must do something about your unshod condition, lady."

Aislinn bent over and looked at her naked toes. "Come here," said Desmond, beckoning her to a small coffin. He lifted the lid and moved aside a layer of fragrant herbs and flower petals. "I think these might fit."

Several pairs of soft kid slippers lay in the chest. He drew out a dark-gray pair, closed the chest, and patted the top.

"Sit, lady." She sat.

Desmond lifted her foot, taking the opportunity to skim his fingers over her ankle and down the arch. Her breath dragged into her lungs. Megret colored hotly and fled the chamber with a nervous, girlish giggle.

"My lord, you have shocked my maid," Aislinn said with a lift of her brow.

"Then 'tis well she left, for I may do more than simply touch you, and that would scandalize her utterly." He shoved up the soft fabric until it bunched at Aislinn's thighs. He touched her cleft.

"Ah, already wet for me," he said as he rubbed his fingers over her secret parts. "I would have a taste now." He went to his knees before her.

Aislinn opened her mouth to protest, but the words would not come when Desmond kissed her. Her breath hung at the back of her throat; she could not move, could not protest as his tongue delved deep and he tasted her. Her body was suspended in space and time while he flicked his tongue, hot, warm, and strong, over the bud of her femininity again and again. It seemed that if she moved she might shatter, or this gossamer web of sensation would surely vanish.

She could not risk either.

Desmond knew where to touch her, where to kiss, tease, and lick her to make her liquid in his grasp. Her thighs trembled, her insides shuddered. She was enfolded within the warm cocoon of awakening desire.

A little voice inside her head called him wicked to do such things, but a louder voice named him wondrous, skilled, and generous.

Aislinn no longer cared whether what Desmond did to her should be considered shameful, for she was not ashamed. She was reverent and joyous that he should be able to bring such sweet, drugging pleasure to her body with the merest touch.

Her body tightened. Her blood thickened. Her heartbeat slowed and strengthened.

Then, like a shower of stars in the sky, her ecstasy burst within her. She grabbed at his shoulders, clung to him so she would not drift off in the flurry of brilliance as her body became first taut with flame and then boneless with satisfaction.

She moaned his name. He gently pulled her from her perch on the low chest. The tangle of thick, soft furs cushioned her back as he laid her on the floor and spread her legs. With swift, urgent movements he freed himself.

He was pulsing, the head of his erection flush with the proof of his need. He bent over her and took her in one rapid, strong thrust.

"As if God created you for me. Tight—so tight and hot."

The lingering shudders of her climax met the ardent rhythm of his coupling. He rammed hard once, twice, three times while the tight coil of desire wound inside her.

"Aislinn!" he roared her name. Waves of bliss rolled over her. They rocked together in a frenzied mating, each intent on wringing the last bit of passion from the other.

"Ah, lady wife. Three times now I have taken you, and we have yet to find a bed for our coupling." Desmond rested his forehead against her own.

She could not help but smile.

The afternoon was spent in lazy companionship. Desmond showed Aislinn much of Mereworth, walking at her side with his arm looped around her waist. They ended up back in the lady's chamber, where they talked of foolish things. Arguing over which made the best pet: a hedgehog or a dormouse—and whether babes should be suckled by only their mothers or whether they should have a nurse.

"I want my babe to feed here, often and well." Desmond traced a lazy ring around her nipple. Through the thin fabric it was evident that it puckered in response.

"See, your body knows even now that my heir will suckle this sweet bud. Mayhap the seed has been planted and grows already." He bent his head and licked a trail where his finger had been, the cloth dampening and dragging against his tongue.

Her head lolled to his shoulder and she clung to him. She could not suppress the little moan of pleasure.

"My lord, the things you do—"

"Are meant to show you how matters can be between a lord and lady. When you have learned that I am capable of giving you all you need, then you will love me," he declared boldly.

Aislinn lifted her head. "And do you propose to love me in return?"

He smiled at her as if she were simpleminded. "Aislinn, 'tis a wife's duty to love her lord husband."

"And what is your duty to me?"

"To protect you from harm, to see to your comfort, to

give you pleasure in the marriage bed, and give you strong sons and daughters."

She frowned at his words, strangely saddened to hear him say such. "And in all that living and breeding, there is to be no love from you to me?"

"Aislinn, it is the way of things; surely you know that. Henry bade us wed, and we are wedded. I would lay down my life for you. I vow to protect and honor you."

"But you will not love me." She untangled herself from his arms and yanked her bliaut up over her bare breasts. "I am suddenly taken with an aching head, my lord. 'Tis time for you to leave."

Desmond looked confused and a little angry, but he gained his feet and walked to the door. "Rest. I will see you below stairs for supper. That is not a request, Aislinn, but my will."

He closed the door behind him with a loud thud. She threw one of her kidskin slippers at the door. "I hate you!"

Desmond shook his head at his wife's foolishness. She had much to learn about being wedded.

"Perhaps you do now, but you will grow to love me. It is your duty," he answered from the other side of the door. When he turned, Galen was approaching. If he had heard Aislinn's words, he gave no sign of it by his expression.

"The women are here, my lord."

"Ah, and do they look as if they will do?"

Galen's brow furrowed. "I am no expert in the ways of women, but if their appearance is any indication, I would say they are skilled beyond imagining."

"Good, good. I will interview all three together. The sooner I find what I need, the quicker I can settle all affairs regarding Aislinn and Sevenoaks."

Aislinn flattened herself against the door in misery.

Desmond's words washed over her. Anger and betrayal chilled her soul.

The scoundrel is going to find a mistress! She squeezed her eyes against the thought, but the pain remained. The only part of her marriage that was a boon was the wonderful time they spent coupled in passion. *And now he means to keep that from me and take a mistress?*

She opened her eyes and sucked in three deep breaths of air. When her head no longer twirled like a distaff, she pushed herself away from the wall. She retrieved her slipper and put it on her foot.

"Indeed, you may find another woman to share your bed, my lord husband, but you will not do it in secret," she said softly. Then she squared her shoulders and flung open the door. She marched down the hall toward the sound of voices. "I will be present when you 'interview' the trulls."

Aislinn stood out of sight where she could see Desmond's expression. He looked hungry, eager. It was like a lancet through her heart. Then, as if he felt her eyes upon him, he turned.

"Aislinn?"

She stepped into the doorway. "My lord husband, I have come to aid you in your selection of a mistress. If I am going to be sharing you, then I believe I should have a say in who I share you with." Aislinn planted her feet, ready to disobey him if he ordered her away.

One of Desmond's brows arched in an expression of mild surprise. "Aislinn, by all means come in and join our guests."

He swept his hand toward the women, and she finally took a good, long look at them.

Three crones sat side by side. They were gray, grizzled, and grinning with blackened stumps of teeth. Their eyes were sharp as a falcon's. One raised a gnarled finger and cackled.

"I trow I could teach the young cockerel a thing or two. If I had but known that was what the young lordling wanted, I would've worn my best gown."

"Aye, and combed yer hair," another drab cackled in mirth.

The heat of humiliation climbed into Aislinn's cheeks. She started to back from the room, but Desmond's fingers locked on to her wrist. He tugged her fully into the chamber. In a nonce, she was seated at her husband's feet on a plump bolster. No doubt, he thought the submissive position was fitting punishment for her brazen outburst.

"Come, lady, you wished to be a part of the discussion, so join us. Do not turn shy and maidenly *now*."

It took some long minutes for the women to cease sharing ribald, bawdy jests. Aislinn was miserable. How had she so confused and confounded his words?

"Ladies, please forgive my wife. We are newly wed, and she is yet jealous."

"I am not jealous," Aislinn snapped. She was not— could not be jealous of this vainglorious fool who said it was her duty to love him.

Desmond shrugged and gave a look to the three crones as if to say, "See how it is?" The old women nodded and murmured in agreement.

Aislinn decided she would be best served by simply being quiet. She clamped her lips tight and folded her arms beneath her breasts.

"I asked my seneschal to find the wisest wise women in my demesne. He said you three are the most learned, the most skilled and respected."

"Aye, aye," they agreed in unison.

Aislinn's mind was whirring. Wise women, healers, *witches*. She drew in a shaky breath. What could this all mean?

"If it would please you, I would enlist your aid in solving a mystery."

"What sort of mystery, my lord?" one of the crones asked, her seamed face all interest.

"A mystery of death and poison. I would learn what kind of poison can be given in secret that will kill each victim in a different way and at different times."

"Do ye ask for fast-acting potions?" another asked, as if the question was as common as removing warts.

"Nay, I believe 'tis a poison that works so slowly the one who administers it is never nearby when death comes."

"Ah," the three crones said in unison. They put their tangled gray heads together and murmured. When they separated, one said, "We will assist you, my lord. For a price."

"Name your price."

"Ah, that we cannot do. It is our way to aid you first and then, at some time when we are in need, we will ask for payment."

Desmond hesitated for only a moment. "Done. I agree to your terms. Ask of me what and when you will, and if 'tis in my power, you will have it. Now, tell me what you may about the poison I speak of."

Aislinn sat mute while the wise women listed herbs, flowers, roots, and barks that could kill. The manner of death they listed ranged from the gentle and painless sleep after sipping tea to sennights of watery bowels and bleeding gums brought on by a single prick of a poisoned thorn.

Her stomach roiled and churned. It was all she could do to remain in the room and listen to such brutal converse. She did not trust her husband, but Jesu, she never thought him capable . . .

"Aislinn, your knuckles are bloodless," Desmond remarked blandly, nodding toward her hands.

She glanced down and found she had gripped a bit of her bliaut in her fists. The death grip she had on the cloth was turning her knuckles white. With an effort, she released the gown and smoothed out the peak of wrinkles.

"Pray, continue, ladies," Desmond said after he had given Aislinn a moment of study.

Why was he learning all he could about poisons? Who was his intended victim?

She had opened her mouth to ask when the sound of a herald's horn rent the air. All heads turned toward the corridor leading to the great hall. Galen appeared, his face split by a smile.

"My lord, Lady Margaret has come."

Desmond leaped from the stool as if it were on fire. "Ready her rooms, Galen; make preparations for a feast. Have a bath sent to her with a selection of fragrant oils and unguents." He turned and speared Aislinn with a gaze.

"Come, 'tis time you met Lady Margaret."

Aislinn rose on shaking legs. So, now he had brought his mistress to Mereworth. She had been foolish to think it was the wise women, but now there could be no mistake. Not the way his face lit with a loving light. As the green bile of jealousy began to rise in Aislinn's throat, she had to admit she was near tears at the thought of sharing him with another woman.

You fool, you cannot be jealous of him!

How cruel the traditions and practices of men. Desmond expected to have her body and her love. He, on the other hand, was free to give his affection and his seed to a woman who had no duty to him at all. Aislinn was expected to make him a home, bear his children, and suffer his faithless conduct.

It was unfair and too common. Most noblemen kept mistresses, sometimes more than one. And usually they dallied with kitchen wenches and milkmaids on their estates. While their wives did all they could to make their homes comfortable and efficient, bore their children, and tended their wounds, the better part of them—*the whole of their hearts*—was given to another woman.

"I will not live thus," Aislinn muttered.

"What say you?" Desmond asked as he pulled her along. "I did not hear you clearly."

"I said I would like to have had warning of visitors so I might have donned a fresh gown and groomed my hair. I will not appear to be a drab, a lazy crone."

Desmond turned to her, his brow furrowed in a puzzled frown. "Aislinn, your hair has never been more beautiful. All you need do is let the sun shine upon it and all around you are held in thrall. Do not fash yourself. You are the most beauteous of visions."

How could he compliment her at a time like this? How could her heart swell with gratitude at his sincerity when he was dragging her along to meet his leman?

It was amazing—and a bit sobering. How could he have such an effect upon her when at this moment she didn't even like him very much?

The question went unanswered in her mind as he released her hand to embrace a woman. Aislinn was stunned to see that the woman was not young and nubile. She was still lovely, but time had marched a path across her face. Her waist was thick and her neck lined.

"Ah, Desmond, my love," she purred.

Did her husband's taste run to matrons? Surely not, for he was a lusty gut when it came to bed sport. She could not see him suppressing his ardor to accommodate an aging woman who could not match him stroke for stroke, fire for passion.

"And is this your wife?" The matron broke Desmond's embrace and grasped Aislinn's shoulders. "You are everything I imagined and more. I left Irthing as soon as we received word from court that Desmond was to marry." She bussed Aislinn's cheeks.

"We?"

Lady Margaret frowned and glanced at Desmond. "Have you not told her of your family?"

"I spared her some of the more melodramatic parts," Desmond said, and to Aislinn's surprise a flush climbed his neck.

"Then I must remedy this lack. But before I do, I am to inform you, Desmond, that your sister is breeding again."

Desmond grinned widely. "And how fares my nephew?"

"Gervais is a robust boy. I trow, if it were not for Gruffudd and his pack of fawning hounds, the child would run his parents a merry chase. But those alaunts love him well and follow him like his shadow. Brandt is hoping for a girl."

"Ha! That one will spawn hot-blooded sons."

"Oh, I do hope you are wrong, for he vows to keep Rowanne breeding until she brings forth a sweet-natured daughter for him to dandle on his knee."

"An excuse on Brandt's part, if I know my friend and brother-in-law. He only wants a justification for so much bed sport."

"Well, that may be true, but I would never say so." Lady Margaret grasped Aislinn's hand like a mother would a child's.

"Come, take me to your solar. We will drink Desmond's best wine and I will tell you all I know about this gallant rogue."

Aislinn saw Desmond's gulp of mild distress. For a moment he looked so human: so flawed—so handsome. She smiled at Lady Margaret.

"I would like that, lady. I would like that very much."

They entered the chamber, and Lady Margaret turned

to Aislinn. "What, my dear, do you want from your wedding that you are not getting?"

"I—but I have not said—"

Lady Margaret sat down on a bolster-covered bench and smiled. "You need not speak the words when the truth of your want is written all over your face. Now, sit and tell me. What has that scoundrel Desmond done to make the shadow of sadness linger behind your lovely green eyes?"

Aislinn blinked furiously in an effort to hold back her tears. They burned hot and salty, but she managed to swallow the hard lump and speak.

"I want him to love me."

"And he does not?"

"He says 'tis the duty of a wife to love her husband. But he has no liking to do the same."

"Young fool. Many a knight is raised to think the same foolish nonsense." Lady Margaret clucked sympathetically and took Aislinn's hands. "Shall I help you?"

" 'Tis not possible to make him love me," Aislinn said miserably. "I do not believe in love potions, and so I must endure what I must endure."

"Nonsense. Do not be foolish as he is. And don't be fooled." Lady Margaret smiled. "He is well on his way to worshipping you. All that is required is for you to assist him on his journey."

"Worshiping me?" Aislinn repeated in doubt.

"A blind man could see it, but let us move along. Have you always loved him?"

"I have not said so. I would be a nodcocked ninny to love him."

Lady Margaret smiled again. "As you wish, Aislinn. You do not love your lord husband. If 'tis what you choose to think, then I will not gainsay you." Margaret tapped her finger on her chin and frowned. "Desmond values courage, honor, and trust in his men. I cannot but think 'twould be the same qualities he would appreciate in a wife."

"Or a horse." Aislinn sniffed.

"Do not tell me that young cockerel compared you to his horse? Jesu, 'tis well I have come. We shall save him from his own foolishness. Aislinn? Have you given him your trust?"

Trust. The word hit like cold, icy wind. Nay, she had not given him her trust, and could not until . . .

"Ah, I begin to see the rub. You cannot fully trust Desmond, and you are afraid to openly love him. But mark me, lady, you cannot win his love unless you can give him your trust."

Nineteen

Galen bowed discreetly and whispered into Desmond's ear, "My lord, there are visitors at the gate."

"Visitors from where?"

"From Sevenoaks, my lord."

Aislinn's head came up. Lady Margaret was watching Desmond with open curiosity. It was no more than a quick nod in their direction, but all the knights seated at the side table rose and left the hall in force.

"You know my orders on this matter, Galen," Desmond said softly, picking up his goblet and sipping.

"Aye, my lord." He left without another word.

Aislinn stared at Desmond. "What does this mean?" she asked.

He lifted both brows, but his expression was far from innocent. "What, lady? I know not what you speak of."

"My lord, you were told there are visitors from Sevenoaks."

"Aye, 'twas the nut and kernel of Galen's words."

"So, will the gate be opened and the visitors brought to sup with us?"

Desmond took a sip of wine and looked Aislinn full in the face. "Nay."

She blinked and glanced at Lady Margaret. "I surely have misheard you, my lord, for I thought you said nay."

"Aye, I did say nay."

Margaret's head swung to and fro like the clapper of a great bell as she watched Desmond and Aislinn.

"Bu—but why?"

Desmond's gaze turned hard and shuttered. "Until I determine what kind of mischief is afoot and who is behind the treachery at Sevenoaks, none from that keep will be admitted to Mereworth."

"But—"

"Nay, lady, but me no buts. You are safe here in Mereworth. There is no danger of potions and poisons. And until I am ready to solve the riddle and bring the blackguard before King Henry, you will remain here, where you are safe."

"So, I am a prisoner." Aislinn slumped back in her chair. The truth of Desmond's words washed over her. She was safe—safe within a gilded cage. "I am to have no say in the matter?"

"None."

Aislinn gave Lady Margaret one desperate look; then she bolted from the great hall. Her slippers slapped along stone corridors as she climbed the curving stairs to the top of Mereworth. She threw open the heavy oaken door, ignored the startled looks of the castle guard, and ran to the edge of the battlements. The wind whipped her red hair from the thick braid, stinging her face, blinding her. She looked down at the brown ribbon of road beyond the drawbridge.

There was Giles and his personal guard from Tunbridge Wells. His face was a study in grim fury.

"Giles! Giles!" she shouted, but her hail was lost on the wind. Her cousin raised his fist and mouthed something. She did not have to hear to know he had just cursed Desmond Vaudry du Luc to perdition.

* * *

Day after day Desmond consulted with the wise women. They had taken a chamber for the brewing of foul-smelling decoctions and hellish-looking gruels. They used lanolin, extracted from wool, to make creams and pastes.

Aislinn stood in the corridor, peering in at the three crones, who babbled and mumbled words only they understood. Lady Margaret came down the hall. She discreetly positioned herself behind Aislinn so she could see into the room.

"My lord husband has gone mad," Aislinn whispered over her shoulder.

"Nay. He seeks only to protect you."

Aislinn turned and looked at Margaret. Her expression was sincere, and that confused Aislinn.

" 'Tis the way of men when they cannot find the words to tell a woman how they feel about her. To a man—especially a knight—keeping his lady safe is the ultimate illustration of great regard."

"Ha, my lord husband has shown me how he feels. He has locked me inside this keep; he no longer visits my chamber. His actions have been eloquent on the matter of his regard for me. He has undertaken this foolish quest because he thinks someone wishes him harm."

"Judge him not, Aislinn." Margaret tucked a wayward strand of hair behind her ear. "Give him time to solve this problem. He fears not for himself but for you."

"For me?" Aislinn repeated.

"Aye. Henry has let it be known: if one more man who weds you goes early to his grave, then you will lose your head. Desmond seeks only to protect you and solve the puzzle of Sevenoaks Keep."

Desmond stared up at the sky as the first twinkling star appeared. He burned for Aislinn by day, but at night, when the whisper of wind and fragrance of night-blooming flowers touched him, the thought of the maze and his maiden came to him unbidden with such force that he ached to hold her. How could one woman have so many facets?

He was walking the battlements, trying to tamp down his lust and sort his feelings, when he saw a flash of something pale at the sally port. He squinted into the night as a blur of pale color left the deepest shadow of the curtain wall.

"By the blood of the saints." He ran along the battlements, ignoring the inquiries of his men as he leaped from one level to another and sprinted to the stables. Brume snorted his displeasure at Desmond's speed when the bit was put into his mouth. Without saddle or blanket, Desmond climbed onto the destrier and shouted for the gate to be opened.

"I shall return anon with my lady wife. See that the sally port is barred and guarded from now on."

Brume's great stride ate the ground beneath him. Desmond could see the flash of movement in the moonlight. As he drew nearer, he could see the mare's tail blowing in the wind, and the tangled flames of Aislinn's magnificent hair.

"Aislinn, halt afore you are hurt."

"Nay, I will not be kept a prisoner," she yelled over her shoulder.

Desmond shook his head in amused frustration. He pulled up slightly on Brume's reins. He would let the mare run herself out. Mayhap by then his wife's temper would have cooled in the night air.

He let Brume set a pace that was comfortable. Desmond smiled at his wife's ability to ride. She was a wonder with her stiff-backed indignity and courage. She jumped a small runnel and kept her seat well. Then a young stag burst from a chestnut thicket. The mare shied and leaped to one side. Aislinn lost her balance and fell with a thud.

Desmond flew from Brume's back, cradling his wife's head in his lap. "Aislinn. Aislinn. Tell me you are not injured."

"I hope you are happy," she chided. "This would never have happened if you had not given chase."

He grinned down at her. The light from the half-moon poured over her face in a caress he wanted to duplicate.

"Ah, Aislinn. You are beautiful by day, but at night you are magnificent."

"Ha, you expect me to believe such flummery when you have not touched me in days? I wonder that you have not worn your gauntlets this night so you might be spared the feel of my flesh against your open palm."

"Little fool, I will show you how much I have craved to touch you."

Desmond plundered her mouth. She grabbed his hair on each side and kissed him back savagely. She met him with a hungry intensity that made his heart tumble within his chest. He and his wife might disagree on most things, but they shared a passion of the flesh that was precious and rare.

Her hands ran under his jerkin, kneading his chest, digging her nails into his muscles in a fashion that was a sweet, drugging pain.

"Let me disrobe for you and you may get a bigger handful, my lady." He yanked his padded jerkin off, then his boots and hose. She did the same with clumsy speed. They were hungry for each other.

"You have missed me," he quipped with satisfaction.

"I have missed your body. I will not say I have missed other parts of you." Then she pushed him roughly back onto the turf. It was damp with dew. She straddled him, taking the lead, kissing him hard first, then playfully. She nipped his lower lip and tugged lightly on it.

He tried to raise his head and deepen the kiss, but she stayed just out of his reach. He strained halfheartedly against her hands placed on each shoulder.

"Give me your lips," he growled.

"I will give you nothing, lord husband. You must earn it all: my body, my respect—"

"Your love?"

"Aye, if that be your aim, you must find the key to my heart. But do not expect me to solve the riddle for you."

"I found the key to the maze; I trow I shall find the key to your heart as well." With a grunt he flipped her over on her back, switching their positions. "Now, I will have that kiss, lady wife."

"As you wish, my lord." She let him take her mouth. And while he was occupied, she slid her hand down his flat, hard belly and grasped the manly part of him.

His head jerked back in surprise. His eyes were wide. He wore an expression that was a mingling of satisfaction and astonishment.

"You may take me, lord husband. You may pleasure me with this lance of yours, but remember: my heart is yet my own." She guided him to her softest parts. His gaze turned smoky with passion as he plunged inside her.

"Aye, lord husband, aye. Do it well." Her body clenched and pulled at him. She matched his pace, returned his thrusts. They rose higher and higher on a cloud of sensation until they reached the stars. With voices in unison, they cried out each other's names.

When it was over, they lay tangled in each other's arms. Desmond trailed a finger over Aislinn's nose, down her chin, and over one nipple. It tightened in response. Her skin was damp with the night mist.

"Are you now ready to say you love me?" he asked.

"Nay, I will not say it, for it is not true. I love our passion, but I will not be so foolish as to love you."

"Foolish wife, it is the way of things. A wife must love her husband."

"You say so now, but will it be days again before you come to me? And will you be wearing gauntlets?" she taunted.

He sat up so quickly, he nearly collided with her head. His eyes were bright, his face an expression of understanding.

"By the Rood, that is it!" He planted a kiss on her nose, her chin, the taut nipple. "A wife that is lovely and wise. You have done it, my love. You have given me the missing piece to the puzzle." He jumped to his feet and pulled her up after him.

"Come, find your clothes. We need hurry."

"Desmond, 'tis the middle of the night. What is our need for haste?"

"Aye, 'tis night. You needs must wake your maid, wake the whole of Mereworth. We must be on the road by sunup."

"Where are we going?" She found her tunic and pulled it on.

"To Sevenoaks. I know the how. And with luck and my wise women's training, I will soon know the who and the why."

He caught up her mare and lifted her onto the saddle. Then, with a whoop of joy, he flung himself up on Brume's wide back.

"Come, lady wife, let us not waste a moment."

And they were off, galloping side by side back toward the castle she had fled as though it were a prison.

Within one turn of the hourglass, the castle was a din of activity. Desmond insisted she bring all the gowns she liked, and such plate and finery as she might covet from Mereworth's vast wealth. Aislinn felt as if she were standing in the center of a whirlwind when Lady Margaret appeared, softly rumpled, rubbing sleep from her eyes.

"What, pray tell, is your lord husband about? The noise has brought me from my bed."

"We make haste to leave for Sevenoaks Keep anon." Aislinn quickly sidestepped a heavy chest being taken to a cart below. "He says he knows the answer."

Lady Margaret's attention sharpened. She was at once fully awake. "Here, you men. Come to my chamber. My chests are still packed and ready to be loaded."

"You—you are coming as well?"

Lady Margaret grinned, her face seaming prettily at the corners of her mouth and eyes. "I smell an adventure. I will not be left behind. For too many years I was kept apart from life—nay, I shall not miss this intrigue, be it good or ill."

And so in the fullness of time, they were loaded and departing the stout, reliable keep of Mereworth. Aislinn and Lady Margaret rode in a well-built, nicely padded cart that had belonged to Desmond's mother, Lady Alys. Leathern covers were brightly painted both inside and out, and a small oil lamp swayed to and fro, providing light as they traveled.

"What do you suppose has ignited this fire beneath Desmond's backside?" Lady Margaret mused aloud. She tapped her finger on her chin and stared unseeing at the lush bolsters around her.

"I know not. We were—" The memory of their lovemaking in the field brought heat rising to Aislinn's cheeks. "We were talking, and suddenly he gained his feet and bid me hasten."

"What were you speaking about? Do you remember?"

"N-nay." Aislinn could not tell Lady Margaret of the

converse. It had been about pleasures of the flesh and
how she would never love him.

"A pity." Margaret studied her with a sidelong look of
speculation. "Perchance I could have divined what made
him so anxious. But 'tis no matter. The sun will find us
at Sevenoaks's gates, and if I know Desmond Vaudry du
Luc, we are in for a lusty bit of excitement."

Excitement was not the word Aislinn would have chosen to describe her homecoming. It was more like organ-
ized madness as the caravan of carts and men-at-arms
from Mereworth poured over the drawbridge and into
Sevenoaks. The bailey swelled with men, goods, and animals. She was gratified to see her castle folk do all they
could to aid the unloading while the dray animals were
tended and food prepared for the travelers.

Coy and Gwillem were at Desmond's side in a nonce.
They had their heads together, speaking in low tones like
conspirators, when Giles appeared. He rushed toward
Aislinn.

"Thank the saints you are well." He swept her from
the cart. "I attempted to bring you home but was not
allowed inside the walls of Mereworth. Are you hurt?
What manner of chicanery is Desmond about, to lock
you up within his ugly keep?"

" 'Tis more accurate to say he locked you out, from
the accounts I heard." Lady Margaret stepped lightly,
without assistance, to the ground. She positioned herself
between Aislinn and Giles and stared up into his face
with narrowed eyes.

"And who, madam, are you?"

Lady Margaret's eyes hardened in a way that gave Aislinn pause. The lady's smile was still in place, but it was
brittle. "I am Margaret, widow of Thomas de Lucy, mis-

tress of Sherborne and Letchworth. And who, churchman, are you?"

Giles puffed up like a threatened toad. It was not to his credit that Aislinn saw barely suppressed fury in her cousin's face. She was reminded of the way he looked outside Mereworth's gates. There were sides to him she had never seen before.

"I am the abbot of Tunbridge Wells." He squared his shoulders.

"Ah, I will seek you out when 'tis time for my confession." Lady Margaret turned her back on him, dismissing him in a manner that left no doubt as to how unimpressed she was by his position. "Now, Aislinn, show me to your chamber, where we might refresh ourselves."

Aislinn was too stunned to do more than obey her request. But as she left, she caught a glimmer of malice in her cousin's eyes. For the first time in her life, she felt a frisson of dread regarding Giles. Something in that cold stare made her fearful for Lady Margaret's safety.

"What is the plan, my lord?" Coy leaned against the stones of the outer bailey, cleaning his nails with the tip of his dagger.

"Aye, my lord, we are ready to do your bidding," Gwillem chirped.

"And me as well, my lord." Tom swung around the corner on his crutches. His face was drawn and pinched with pain.

"I see I needs must school my emotions better. If you three know I am about to execute a plan to catch a fox, then so must everyone within the keep." Desmond frowned at Coy. "How have matters been since I left?"

He shrugged. "Each night a light shines in the window of the lord's chamber."

"Ah. So my absence was welcomed by at least one here."

"I have followed the abbot to the lord's chamber each night. Yet he was not within the walls of Sevenoaks, having taken the knight to his home when we saw the light on another occasion."

"Aye. 'Twould seem to be the logical explanation." Desmond turned the matter over in his mind. "But I wonder if you are not correct, and our abbot had a place where he could leave the knight and return to Sevenoaks unseen?

"We needs must be vigilant. Take care, all of you. No foodstuff or wine or ale shall be given to my lady wife that you have not personally supervised."

"And how about you, my friend? How shall we keep you from being poisoned?"

"I will only eat pasty pies and drink beer with good Tom and Cook. Though I am confident food will not be the manner or method of my poisoning."

"You speak as if you will be poisoned," Coy said.

"I am counting upon it."

A great feast was held in the great hall of Sevenoaks. The rushes had been replaced with fresh green stalks; new tallow candles sat in the holders. Lutes were strummed, jesters entertained, and the wine flowed freely from two freshly tapped casks. Aislinn sat at her husband's side and watched while he did not touch a drop of the grape or nibble so much as a crust.

"Are you ailing?" she asked.

"Nay, I have no thirst or appetite."

She stared at the goblet of wine and the trencher of savory spiced meat before her husband. The memory of being drugged played through her mind.

"Lady, would you share my cup?" Giles asked at her

elbow. But when Aislinn looked up she realized he was not speaking to her, but rather to Lady Margaret, who sat on his other side.

"Nay, red wine is not to my liking." Waves of tension flowed between the lady and Aislinn's cousin.

"If all our guests ate and drank as little as you, then the larders would ever be full," Giles snapped.

"*Our* guests? Pray, have I been misinformed? I thought Sevenoaks was the keep of Desmond and Aislinn." Lady Margaret smiled coldly. "Or do you have a prior claim I do not know about?"

Giles's face flamed. He stood up abruptly, his chair scraping on the stones beneath the rushes. "I must be about my prayers." He stalked off without a word to Aislinn or Desmond.

"My lord, if you would allow, I am feeling tired. I would retire," Aislinn said to Desmond. She could not shake the nagging portent of doom.

"Aye, take yourself to your chamber. Lady Margaret will be sharing it with you this night."

Aislinn looked from Desmond to Margaret and back again. She had not been told of this before. There were other chambers, many most comfortable and suitable for a lady of Margaret's position.

"That is wonderful news. I hate to be without company in a strange keep," Margaret said with a wide smile. She rose and stepped away from the table. "Come, Aislinn, let us go and sip wine and gossip in front of your hearth." Her words were so charming and heartfelt that Aislinn could not be annoyed, but she did feel the loss of her husband's company. For she still vowed to take her physical pleasure with him whenever possible. She told herself that was the only reason she felt bereft and lonely knowing he would not come to her tonight. She told herself that was the reason she choked back tears as she and Lady Margaret entered her solar.

* * *

Desmond's knees were sore and aching. "I cannot find a joint or a crack that would bring up the floor."

Coy and Gwillem, on opposite walls, rubbed their fingertips along the mortar. "It does seem as if the lord's chamber is tight as a well-swelled cask."

"And yet the poem . . . 'The time is marked when the moon is ripe. Surrender the stars and bring a light. The lord and the lady share a door. Riches untold beneath the floor.' "

"Sounds almost as if the beginning is outside in the moonlight. I trow I am puzzled." Coy scratched his head and yawned.

Outside in the moonlight. The words hit Desmond like a fist. *I have been a blind fool.*

"Coy, you and Gwillem take yourselves off to bed. We have searched enough this eve. Tomorrow we will begin again."

" 'Tis sense you speak. Sleep with your door barred in case someone decides to put a knife in your heart," Coy advised.

"Aye, I will sleep with one eye open," Desmond said, but his thoughts were upon the maze and how quickly he could evade his friends and find his way to the center of the garden.

For that is where the puzzle begins. He was sure of it. And he was also sure his wife knew more than she had ever said.

Aislinn waited until she was sure Lady Margaret was asleep before she rose and donned her cloak. She had not seen Pointisbright since her return and wondered if he might be in the maze. On tiptoes she crept to the cabinet and turned the iron ring. Then she slipped inside and closed it behind her. The candles had not been replaced, and the corridor was dark. She would need to get fresh tapers and replenish them on the morrow, but now she navigated by memory. Her fingers slid along the rough stone until she found the ring and opened the door. Desmond stood in the opening.

"Lady wife, I have been waiting for you." Desmond held Pointisbright in his hands. "We have both been waiting. Come, sit with me by the sundial and tell me the truth. Tell me all about the mystery of Sevenoaks Keep."

Twenty

She gasped, stepping onto the gravel path. "I know not what you mean."

"Nay, Aislinn, tell me no more lies." Desmond put the cat on the earth beside his boots. His fingers were like iron as they bit into Aislinn's shoulders. "The riddle of the lord's chamber is a riddle that begins here in the maze. Now tell me."

Aislinn looked into his face. Her heart warred with her mind. She could still hear Theron's ghostly warning: *Do not give up the secrets to anyone you cannot trust.*

"I know nothing of what you speak," she said stubbornly.

"Fine, then sit you down and I will tell you what I know."

"I have no liking to hear this. I came only to see if Pointisbright was here and safe. Pray, allow me to return to my chamber." She turned away, but Desmond grabbed her wrist and spun her back to face him. His face was hard. She had never seen him like this.

"Nay, wife. You will not leave." He glared at her. His eyes flicked hotly from her eyes to her lips, where they lingered. "Damn me, I cannot resist you, Aislinn."

He crushed her in a hard embrace. His lips found hers, the kiss hard, just short of punishing. His hands roamed over her body. In her mind she uttered her own oath.

Damn you, Desmond, for I cannot resist you either.

He pulled her from the path to the sheltering vines. Together they slid to their knees, the soft bed of leaves from the vines making a thin cushion. Of one mind, they stripped away cloaks, girdles, and hose until they lay naked in each other's arms. He kissed her throat, her breasts, her belly. Then he moved lower.

"Aislinn, this night we will settle matters between us. I am your lord husband and you will love me."

"Nay."

"You will not gainsay me by the time I am through." He picked up her hips and tilted her quim to his view. Then, like a man denied too long, he went down upon her, hungrily. She moaned as he kissed her deeply, laving his tongue over her bud and inside.

"Nay, Desmond, nay, I cannot take such pleasure. . . ."

"You have told me that is all you allow yourself. Then you shall have this and more. And by the time the sun rises, you will say you love me."

The fire in Desmond's soul was part frustration and part need. He was hungry for Aislinn—not just for her lush body, but for the words she would not say.

She must love him. He wanted her to love him. He needed her to love him.

Why it had become so important, he could not say, but it was vitally important that she love him. He did not want the affection and concern of a leman; he wanted love from his wife. It was as simple and complicated as that. Yet the stubborn little vixen was determined to withhold it.

As if Desmond could somehow turn her mind with his skill as a lover, he touched every inch of her body, tenderly, reverently wringing passion from her until it flowed like a rain-swollen beck.

He was rewarded by mews of passion. Her body arched

and bucked and met his dutiful mouth. Her juices flowed and her skin heated.

He could make her writhe with need and purr with satisfaction. So why couldn't he make her love him?

The question burned in his mind as he used his tongue and his fingers to bring her to completion. She was sated, boneless, sweetly mussed when she looked at him.

"Do you love me yet?" His tone was hopefully arrogant.

"I will admit you are a lover of great skill, but nay, my lord husband, I will not let myself love you."

He took it as a challenge. He slid his fingers inside her hot, smooth sheath, gratified when she moaned and moved a little toward him.

"You will, Aislinn; by all that is holy, you will."

He touched that hot, throbbing part of her. She stiffened. He teased her until she was moaning and thrashing her head back and forth. He poised himself above her and entered her.

He went deep—mayhap deeper than ever before. It was like seeking the unattainable as he thrust himself inside her. The more she held herself from him, the more determined he was to hold her close. It was an unsolvable puzzle, this strange conflict he had with his wife. Suddenly the blood coursing through his veins roared in his ears. He could hold back no longer.

"Come with me, sweet Aislinn," he roared into the night as she stiffened and rammed herself against him. It was the most bittersweet coupling he had ever experienced.

Some time later he looked into her eyes and said, "Now, do you love me?"

She looked at him a long time. Then she moved a

strand of sweat-dampened hair from his brow. "Ah, lord husband. I do not love you, but I will trust you."

He tried not to feel the sweet bite of her words. It was truly a gift with a sting in the tail. She trusted him, but she did not love him. Perchance he should settle for that alone; mayhap he was a fool to yearn for her affection.

"Do not look so wounded. I trust you, Desmond, and to prove it I will share with you one of Sevenoaks's secrets."

Aislinn rose and gathered her scattered garments. Desmond sat down and began to pull on his hose.

"There is no need for that, my lord husband. Remain as God made you; none will see." She went to the wall and opened the portal. " 'Tis dark, so take my hand."

Desmond scrambled to his feet, snatching up jerkin, boots, and braies. Then he grasped Aislinn's hands, feeling a thrill of excitement to be naked with his wife, being led like a blind child down a chilly corridor of stone. At length they reached stairs and climbed. A rasp of stone and it opened. They were standing in the lord's solar.

"Now I will show you more." Aislinn pulled him back into the corridor, and within several long paces he saw the glow of light around a doorway.

"Take care to make no sound, my lord," she whispered. The panel opened into her chamber. A fire glowed warm and cheery. Lady Margaret was breathing softly within the thick bed hangings. Silently Aislinn closed the opening. They stood alone, together in the stone corridor.

"So this is the secret," Desmond whispered.

"Aye, 'tis one of Sevenoaks's secrets. None but my lord Theron, the Moor, and I knew of it. Now you know."

"Come, let us return to my chamber; I grow weary of the dark," he said.

"As you wish, my lord." Aislinn took his hand and led him once again to his own chamber. When they emerged, he was full of questions. He was also hurt and angry that she had kept this from him. She said this was one of Sevenoaks's secrets. How many more secrets did the wench still hide?

Aislinn stood naked before him, as if she were as innocent as a lamb. She smiled, that knowing kind of smile that women often have and that men are loath to see.

It aroused him.

She moved to the bed and toyed with the hangings at one of the four posts. The picture was too much by half; the winsome, nubile woman with nothing but her wild, red curls to hide her lush body.

Desmond's tarse sprang to life. And since he was as God had made him, there was no hiding the effect she had upon him. Her eyes slid over his body, and that knowing smile grew more knowing.

"Cease, wife," he growled.

She tilted her head and studied him intently. "Do you want me again, lord husband?" she asked coyly.

"The proof of my desire is stiff before you," he said with a lift of one brow. How saucy the wench had become—how comfortable with her power over his flesh.

He glanced back at the portal they had come through. There was no joint, no seam, no mark to give away the location from the outside.

"Giles could have searched until Judgment Day and never found the portal," Desmond said aloud.

"What say you? You think Giles knows of this corridor? That cannot be. Only Theron and I knew—and now you because I trust you with this knowledge. You have kept the secret of the maze, and now you may add this one to it."

"I will keep the secret, sweet wife, but I tell you Giles has been seen searching this chamber by night."

She frowned at him, obviously thinking he lied. Desmond had no desire to fight with her, not when she was so near he could smell their shared musk and feel the heat of her body.

"How does it close?" he asked lightly, hoping to wipe that look of distrust and suspicion from her eyes.

Aislinn's breasts jiggled pertly as she worked the mechanism. The panel closed with a soft bump. They were alone in the lord's solar.

"This is how I knew what Henry commanded," she admitted boldly.

"And you were the one who came and locked Pointis-bright in."

"Aye, my lord." She nodded, and the tangle of fire-bright hair swung around her breasts, cupping them. Desmond could stand it no longer.

He stuck the taper into a stone dish, barred the door, and turned to his wife. "The time has come, Aislinn of Sevenoaks."

"The time?"

"Aye, 'tis time you were truly *bedded*." He strode to her and lifted her over his shoulder, kneading that fine, well-shaped bottom as he took her to the bed and dumped her in it.

"Tonight you find out what a bed is truly for."

She smiled that woman's smile again and lay back, opening herself to him. "Come, my lord husband, do your worst."

"Nay, you will have the best and more."

Desmond kissed the inside of her ankles, tickling a particularly sensitive spot with his tongue when she giggled. He sipped kisses over her calves to the soft, tender inside of her knees.

"Had I known you would reward me thus, I might have shown you the secret passages sooner," Aislinn said with a sigh.

"Vixen, you have kept secrets from me, but you will have no secrets of the flesh." Desmond lightly nipped the inside of her thigh. She moaned and her hips lifted toward him.

He used his fingers and teased her until the heat and moisture of her desire flowed over his hand. Then he poised himself above her and entered her—slowly—going deep and settling himself there with a satisfied grunt.

She sighed and looked up at him. Jesu, she was lovely, with her alabaster skin framed by the riotous red curls. The wild strands splayed out over his bolster and spilled down the side of the bed.

She was an enchantress. She was a witch. There was no denying that she had ensorcelled him from the first moment he saw her in the maze.

"Desmond, you are truly a master at bed sport," Aislinn complimented. She nudged against him, and his body answered in kind. They set a slow, sensuous pace. There was no hurry; there was no movement without the measured, deliberate design of what effect it would have. If he lifted himself away, she arched and met him, but all was done in a long, protracted manner that extended pleasure until it was molten-hot in their veins.

When he felt her body shudder and buck, his did the same. She tightened around him, milking him, drawing him deep inside her.

It was exquisite.

And when it was over, they lay in a tangle together. Her head was upon his chest, her long hair spilling across his belly and sex. Desmond kneaded the erotic flesh of her arse as they drifted off to sleep. And the last question in his mind was, *Does she love me yet?*

Morning found Aislinn wound in Desmond's arms and her own hair. She opened her eyes to find him watching her. The expression on his face was beyond curiosity. There was an intensity of wonder that lanced through her soul. She could not breathe, could not look away. All she could do was stare into his eyes. She felt his heart beating beneath her cheek. The rhythm was slow and steady. The deep boom spoke to something inside her. They remained as they were for prolonged moments. And then he gave her a half smile.

"Come, wife, let us break our fast. I am hungry after last night's activities." He gently untangled himself and stood. His body was hard, erect, and strong. For a moment she felt a strange, melancholy hunger. She wanted something just out of her reach of understanding. . . . She wanted . . . *to love him?*

Nay. It could not be. He was a wonderful lover, a wit and a gallant. She enjoyed his bed sport, but she would not—could not—give her heart to a man who would not love her in return.

Aislinn shook the thought from her head and rose. She busied herself gathering her clothing while Desmond went to the garderobe. When he returned, she did the same. They dressed in silence. When they were ready, he unbarred the door, and together they quit the lord's chamber. And ran straight into Giles.

"My lord, my lady." His eyes skimmed over them both in a manner that made Aislinn's blood chill. Why was he outside the lord's chamber? And why did he look at them as a hungry wolf looks at a newborn lamb?

"My lord Desmond, I did not realize you and the lady retired to your chamber last eve." Giles's eyes were narrowed in open speculation.

"Indeed, Abbot, I did not realize we needs must make you aware of where the lord and lady of Sevenoaks choose to take their ease."

Aislinn looked from one to the other. Desmond's expression was wary and cold; Giles was openly hostile.

"And you, cousin." Giles suddenly focused on her. "I was sure you went directly to your chamber and did not emerge from that door yon." He glanced toward Aislinn's chamber door. "How is that possible?"

"Abbot, you ask far too many questions. My lady wife does not answer to you," Desmond said abruptly. He placed himself between Aislinn and Giles, his tall, wide body preventing her from seeing Giles's face. "Do not think your common blood allows you to interrogate her."

His voice was hard, his manner . . . *protective*.

A strange thrill of happiness flowed through her. Desmond was intent on protecting her; the thought suddenly formed in her mind. And as she stood there, a little voice in her head asked if Giles could somehow be a threat. She was ready to ask as much—to step from behind Desmond's back and demand to know what Giles was all about, when the door to her chamber opened. Lady Margaret appeared. She looked at the trio with shrewd eyes.

"Good morn." She moved between Giles and Desmond, subtly insinuating herself between them. "How nice to have such a worthy escort. Mmmm, I smell fresh bread below."

She slipped her arm into the crook of Desmond's arm. He shot her a warning glance, which she ignored. Then she reached out and grasped Aislinn's hand with her free one.

"Come, children, take an old woman down to break her fast." And in a manner that was so neatly done that Aislinn was in awe, Lady Margaret swept them away and left Giles standing, angry and alone, in the corridor.

Twenty-One

The great hall was full, teeming with life and activity as it was each morning, but today it seemed different. Aislinn sat at the chair beside Desmond while invisible ribbons of connection bound them together. When he inhaled, she felt it. When he frowned, she knew it.

What could the reason be for suddenly being so aware of her husband? She had shared the pleasures of coupling before and never felt thus the morning after.

'Tis because you now trust him. 'Tis because you have shared a secret, a little voice inside her head provided.

"I would speak with you this morn, Aislinn," Giles said as soon as he appeared from above stairs. He cast one withering glance toward Desmond. "Alone."

Desmond's brow arched and he stiffened. Aislinn felt the restrained power in him. A surge of pride for her lord husband—her protector—sizzled through her.

"Nay, Giles, that will not be possible. I have promised to spend my day in the company of my lord, Desmond, but if you would like to speak with us both—"

"Aislinn." Giles uttered only that one word, but in it was a warning she could not ignore.

Perchance Desmond is right. Mayhap there is a side to Giles I have never seen.

Her cousin gave her one last quelling stare. "I find I have little appetite this morn. I will make ready to return to Tunbridge Wells. I think I am needed there more than here." He turned and left in a flurry of indignation.

"Methinks you have made an enemy, Desmond. Have a care and watch your back around that one," Lady Margaret warned.

Aislinn kept her word and spent her morning with Desmond. They went to the stable and Desmond sought out his squire.

"Gwillem, ready Brume and another horse for my lady. And bring a hawk."

The boy grinned as he did his master's bidding. In a nonce, Aislinn was mounted and riding beside her lord husband. He was a skilled falconer, she learned with pride. Soon they had a string of plump fowl hanging from the pommels.

"I trow Cook will do much with these," he said with a chuckle.

Aislinn reveled in his company, and when they were alone, she felt nothing but calm security; but she could not forget the scene at high table. Finally, her mouth opened and the words simply tumbled out.

"My lord, I begin to believe what you say—insomuch as something is not right here at Sevenoaks. I cannot believe my cousin Giles is involved in murder, but clearly there is a mystery. If it would please you, I would like to help solve the riddle of Sevenoaks. Command me, Desmond; tell me what I may do."

He leaned far out in his saddle and settled a lusty kiss upon her lips. "You could love me."

"Nay, my lord. I will love you not, but I will aid you in whatever way I can."

"Stubborn wench," he said roughly, but his face was split in a smile that softened his words. "Come, let us return to the castle and begin our search together."

They wheeled their mounts and rode wildly back to the keep. The ring of eight hooves thundered over the drawbridge, drawing the attention of all within the gate tower. Aislinn saw the happy, peaceful faces of her castle folk and felt a glow of pride. She and Desmond rubbed along well together, and the sorrow of her former husbands' deaths had been wiped away. And yet . . . there was the nagging suspicion that Desmond was right about a murderer walking the halls of Sevenoaks.

"Come, wife, let us go to the kitchens and find a morsel of food." Desmond laughed and lifted her from the lady's saddle. It had been years since Aislinn had come to the kitchen to walk among her people and sample bits of the cookery.

"But my gown is soiled, and my hair—"

"Is a wild tangle of flame—the way I like it." He looped an arm around her waist and pulled her near. The heat and comfort of being beside him made her knees liquid. Desmond was a rogue, and he demanded too much. Every thought, every action was about him: his comfort, his fulfillment. And yet . . . she found herself being engulfed in his charm and his self-centered affection.

He was a man like no other in her experience. And though she fought with all her soul to resist him, each day a little more of her resolve crumbled.

"Ah, Cook, do you have a pasty for me and my lady?" Desmond said when they entered the kitchen. The heat from the oven took Aislinn's breath. A hearty woman smiled broadly and served up two steaming pies on a wooden plate as if she had expected their arrival.

"I just happen to have an extra, my lord." She winked and Aislinn wondered if there had been a prior plan to bring her.

"My lady." The cook bowed low. "It has been too long since you came to see us."

"I . . ." Aislinn vaguely remembered her.

Desmond squeezed her hand and nodded his encouragement.

"Aye, it has been too long, Cook, but I intend to remedy my neglect and visit you often," Aislinn said.

"My lord, would you have a tankard of beer?" Tom swung into view. He nodded his head at Aislinn.

"Aye, two tankards, my good fellow."

"But Desmond, I have no liking for beer, only pale wine," Aislinn said softly, not wishing to hurt the crippled lad's feelings.

"Try it; you may find it appeals," Desmond urged with his most winning smile.

"As you wish, my lord." She suddenly wanted to please him, not because it was her duty but because it meant something to see his smile of happiness and approval.

Was this how it started? she wondered. Did loving begin with the smallest bit of affection and respect? Did it turn into a need to please? Would it end with her being enslaved by love to a man who swore he would never love her in return?

"Try this, sweeting," Desmond cooed as he held the pasty before her lips. She bit into it. Savory juices ran over her lips. It was delicious and made all the more tasty because Desmond held it. He chuckled deep in his throat and used the pad of his thumb to clean her lower lip. A thrill of hot excitement rippled through her core.

"Have some more. Cook makes the best pasty in the land; I have decreed it," Desmond said boldly, feeding Aislinn with all the sensuous care of a devoted lover.

This is what she wanted. She wanted a man who cared for her feelings and comfort. Loving would not be so bad if it was returned in kind. Could Desmond not see that?

They ate the rest of their food in silence. Aislinn sipped the beer and, as Desmond had predicted, it was yeasty and cool. He finished his food and licked each finger. Watching him suckle those digits made Aislinn aware of her body in a new and shocking fashion.

She wanted him to touch her thus. She wanted him to taste her and suckle her and bring her to pleasure as he had before.

Dare she ask for such a boon?

"Come, wife. Let us freshen ourselves." Desmond stood up and pulled Aislinn from her stool. She brushed against him and felt the hot ridge of his desire.

Mayhap she need not ask for the boon.

"Come, love, let us find a place to be private together," he whispered in her ear as they left the smiling cook and blushing Tom.

They started across the way and found Giles in the inner bailey, his horse loaded and ready for travel.

"I am taking my leave," he said shortly. "I will be better used at Tunbridge Wells. Keep you well, cousin." He mounted and wheeled his horse without saying a word to Desmond.

"And I will sleep better knowing you are gone," Desmond grumbled beneath his breath. "Come, lady, let us not allow your cousin's leave-taking to dampen our spirits or interfere with our newfound alliance."

When they stepped into the keep, the great hall was full of folk spreading rushes, drinking ale, discussing castle affairs.

"We could go again to the lord's chamber," he suggested.

"I have a better idea." She felt suddenly lighthearted. She refused to admit that Giles's leaving had lifted a burden from her mind. "You go to your chamber; I will go to mine. But we will meet in the maze."

"Ah, you are a saucy vixen. Make haste, wench, for I need you now." He kissed her hard, swirling his tongue into her mouth, hinting at the pleasures to come. Aislinn's body molded against him, pliant and willing. He swatted her bottom as he gently pushed her on her way.

Jesu, she would not love him.

"You, there." Desmond hailed a young girl carrying a ewer. "Bring hot water to the lord's chamber and my lady Aislinn's solar." Then Desmond turned and laughed as he took the stairs two at a time.

Aislinn emerged from the passageway before Desmond. She had rushed through her ablutions and donned a fresh gown. It was crafted from thin gossamer fabric. She had chosen not to wear a shift beneath, and the cloth abraded her nipples with each breath. She told herself it was only natural for a woman to revel in the pleasure her young, virile husband gave her.

While she waited, she walked to the sundial and looked at it. She rarely ever came to the maze in daylight. But now as she looked at the device, it did not seem to work properly. She glanced up. The sun was high overhead, but the shadow did not fall in the proper place on the exotically designed face.

"Most peculiar," she murmured, running her finger over the raised images crafted in the metal face.

"Aislinn." Desmond's voice brought her spinning around; all thought flew from her head. The sun gilded him, turning him into a magnificent golden god. His pale eyes seemed lit by inner fire; his manly face was ruggedly raw in the stark light of midday.

He strode to her and swept her into his arms. Their noses nearly touched as he gazed into her eyes.

"You are an enchantress." He tangled his hands in her hair, pulling and tugging her head into a more comfortable position for him to plunder her mouth. He kissed her—hard—branding her, taking possession.

"Have I told you how I love this wild mane of yours?"

he asked in a voice gone husky with passion. "Have I told you that I dream of being naked with naught but your hair to cover us?"

"Nay, my lord, you have not."

"I am saying so now, wife. Come, let us strip ourselves bare and lie in this garden of flowers with nothing but your tresses to cover us."

His eyes fastened on her breasts showing clearly through the thin material. He suckled one, wetting the cloth as he pulled her nipple into his mouth. When he released her, the nipple was hard, the cool, damp cloth clinging, causing her to shiver.

"I would have you bare, wife."

And with sure, deliberate movements, he unlaced her thin gown and pulled it over her head. Then he removed his own clothing and tugged her down to the leaf-strewn earth.

"Our bed, my lady." He pulled her atop him and took great handfuls of her hair and splayed it out to cover them. "And our canopy."

The feeling of the sun on her thighs and calves, the texture of Desmond's crisp hair beneath her, was a heady aphrodisiac. Aislinn moved her palms over her husband, emboldened by his words. She was powerful, a sexual creature who could take her pleasure as she wished.

"Use me, my lady," Desmond purred.

And she did. She grasped the hard, throbbing part of him and placed it inside her. Then she wriggled herself firmly down on him. His face was a study in pleasurable agony, but to his credit, he kept his eyes upon her and did not try to assist in her clumsy efforts.

"You shall surely kill me," he groaned when she finally settled herself deeply upon his staff. She could feel the prod of him deep within her. That alone was enough to send her passion soaring, but when he gently lifted her buttocks and then went deep with a sharp thrust, she nearly reached completion.

"Jesu, Desmond," she gasped.

His grin was an expression of pure, wicked pleasure. He was a satyr; he was a warlock. Surely there was hot, molten magic in his staff.

"Ride me, Aislinn; I will be your stallion."

"Nay, warrior you are, my lord, for I am surely impaled upon your lance," she replied. He had set a rocking pace for them. Each thrust of his hips drove him so deep, she wondered how long he had grown. But then all thought fled her mind as he bucked against her and stiffened. They clung together in the sunshine until the waves of satisfaction left them drowsy and sated.

Lady Margaret climbed the stairs to the solar she shared with Aislinn. It was nooning, but she had no desire for food, having eaten well when she broke her fast early in the day. When she reached the door, she discovered a small silver tray with a single goblet.

"Ah, pale wine, my favorite." She knelt and picked up the tray. "Desmond and Aislinn are most considerate of an aging matron's likes and dislikes. I must gift them with something truly magnificent before I return to Letchworth."

The wine was sweet and cool in her throat. In a nonce, the goblet was empty.

"Would that we might stay within this maze forever." Desmond toyed with the strands of hair covering his face. He held them up and looked at the blue sky between the fiery tresses.

"Desmond, do you really believe a murderer lives

within Sevenoaks?" Aislinn swirled her fingers in his chest hair, playing with the flat, hard nipple.

" 'Struth, with the sun overhead and you in my arms, I confess it does seem like a foolish thought."

"Perchance it was nothing more than cruel fate. Four men who wedded me died, but they were not young like you. Giles has skills in the art of healing, and he swore upon his faith that old wounds and age were the cause."

"Ah, Giles. But why does your cousin search the lord's solar by night?" Desmond nipped her earlobe and kneaded the flesh of one breast.

"Mayhap he does search, but does that mean there is also a murderer in the mix?"

Desmond levered himself up on one elbow. He looked into Aislinn's eyes. "I am unsure. Mayhap you are right. Come, let us return to our chamber and freshen ourselves for tonight's supper. You have used me so well I am hungered."

She giggled as he struggled to untangle himself from her hair. He rose up, tall, proud, and smiling.

"As you wish, my lord." She stood and pulled on her transparent gown, suddenly aware that she also could eat and drink. They walked hand in hand down the dimly lit corridor, kissing each other as they separated and each went to their own chamber.

Desmond turned to watch her disappear into the secret door, the light from her solar silhouetting every ample curve.

She was lovely.

She was screaming.

Her terrified voice brought him running to her side in a great leap. He was through the closet and into her chamber in a nonce. She stood with her knuckles shoved into her mouth. At her feet was Lady Margaret. Her lips were blue, her face white as newly fallen snow.

"Is she dead?" Aislinn whispered.

Desmond kneeled and put his fingers beneath Lady Margaret's nostrils. "She breathes, but barely." He scooped her up from the stone floor and placed her on Aislinn's bed.

"If we hoped to disbelieve a murderer walks these halls, then we can disabuse ourselves of that notion. Lady Margaret has been poisoned."

Twenty-Two

The trio of wise women were brought from Mereworth. They worked through the night and into the next day to keep Lady Margaret breathing. Brews, potions, and possetts were made, prayers were offered and vows of revenge uttered. And through it all Aislinn could no longer deny the obvious.

A murderer did walk the halls of Sevenoaks.

But who and why?

Surely no person of Sevenoaks wished harm to this sweet lady; of that Aislinn was certain. And Giles had made quite a show of leaving the keep before Lady Margaret was poisoned.

Lady Margaret was new to Sevenoaks. She was a guest, barely known. Slowly a thread of awareness wound its way through Aislinn's mind. No man or woman of Sevenoaks could possibly wish her harm, and if that was true, then there was only one other explanation. The wine had been meant for Aislinn and not Lady Margaret.

A cold chill of fear engulfed her. She shivered and looked at her husband.

He stood at the foot of the bed where the pale, barely breathing Lady Margaret lay. His hands were clenched into fists at his muscular thighs. The healers surrounding the woman laid poultices upon her neck and across her upper chest.

Desmond glanced up and met Aislinn's gaze. His eyes were stormy—full of tamped fury. She swallowed back her own tears of pain and confusion.

And then he opened his fists and raised his hands slightly. It was a small gesture, so subtle one might have missed it. He was offering her the comfort of his embrace.

Aislinn ran across the solar and into Desmond's strong, welcoming arms. They closed around her like a warm shield. No pain or harm could come to her as long as she was here.

"Shhh, do not weep. Lady Margaret is strong; she has endured more than this and weathered it all. She will live."

"Oh, Desmond, I do not weep for Lady Margaret. I weep because I am terrified."

He looked down upon her while using his finger to tip her chin up. "Why, lady?"

"Because I think the poisoned wine was for me."

His face hardened into stone. It was cold and terrible to behold the transformation. His eyes blazed with fury.

"By the Rood, if anyone dares harm you, they will be stretched, drawn, and quartered by my own hand."

She sucked in a strangled breath when she heard the heated passion in his voice.

Desmond kissed the top of her head. "You need not worry. I have pledged my arm, my body, and my life in your protection."

The most withered crone stepped away from the bed. Her face was grim.

"We have done all that may be done. If she lives through the night, she will live."

Aislinn heard a sound and realized only when Desmond's arms tightened around her that it was her own sob of pain and relief.

"Come, you need rest. I will take you to my chamber." Desmond gently led Aislinn from her own solar. She leaned on him, content to let him support and comfort her at this most terrible time. When they stepped inside, he pulled her into a kiss meant to reassure her. No more than a soft brush of his lips over her own.

"Aislinn, I am going to have food and drink brought from the kitchens that I am sure is safe. Then you must rest." Desmond left the room and she was alone with her thoughts—with her fears.

She remembered the chilling way Giles had looked at her. *But it cannot be Giles, since he left for Tunbridge Wells early in the day.*

Desmond opened the door with one hand, balancing a tray of fruit, cheese, bread, and pasties. Behind him was Tom, swinging on his crutches with a ewer in his hand.

"I have brought enough food to last for days, and fresh pale wine from a newly tapped cask. You will eat nothing but what Coy, Tom, or I bring you." His face was stern.

"So you believe the wine was meant for me and not Lady Margaret?"

Desmond did not answer; instead he put the tray on a low chest.

"Here, allow me to help you, Tom." He took the ewer.

"We will all do what needs to be done to keep you safe, lady," Tom said seriously.

The impact of his words made Aislinn's stomach contract. The memory of the sleeping potion being given to her returned unbidden. It was no accident—and it was not Desmond who did it. The time for denial was over. There was a murderer within the walls of Sevenoaks, and she was the next intended victim.

The next few days Aislinn barely slept. When the healers were below in the great hall taking their meals, she would use the secret passage to enter her own chamber and sit beside Lady Margaret. Her color was only slightly better. The wise women gave her liquid potions and kept drawing poultices on most of her body.

It was a sad time.

Desmond comforted Aislinn by night, both in the lord's chamber and in the maze, but by day it was Tom who told her stories and kept her from going mad with worry.

"Lady, would you care for another game of chess?" Tom asked, awkwardly maneuvering himself to a low stool. From the taut, controlled expression he wore, his broken knees were obviously hurting him.

"Nay, Tom. Today I would be entertained in another fashion."

"Anything you wish, lady." He grimaced and swung himself back up between his crutches.

"Come, take your ease upon the lord's bed."

Tom's eyes grew so round and large they appeared to pop from his skull. "I am not a knight, lady, but I also believe to take the lord's wife is a mortal sin. Ask anything of me, but that."

Aislinn smiled at Tom's honor and loyalty. "Be at ease, good Tom. I am not joining you on yon bed."

"Oh, my lady, pray forgive my impertinent tongue—"

"Hush, I would see you rest your leg, for I can see it pains you today. Worry not that you have offended me."

His face turned a deeper shade of crimson. "Lady—"

"Shh. Say no more. Take yourself there and find a position that gives you succor from your pain."

"But lord Desmond bade me entertain you."

"Fine, you may entertain me by telling me a story. Tell me something of your life before you came to Sevenoaks."

Tom's shattered body sank into the soft padding of the lord's bed. He laid his head upon a bolster and closed his eyes.

"I was eight when I fell beneath the wagon wheels. Before that time there was nothing of any import in my life. I rose; I ate; I helped in the fields. My life changed that day."

"Poor Tom, how you have suffered."

"Ah, but I also had the company of knights and warriors. No other boy could say that. I shared my days with Crusaders returning from the Holy Lands. What wondrous stories they could tell."

"Where was this, Tom?"

"At Battle Abbey."

Something niggled at the back of Aislinn's mind. "Tell me more."

"Friar Giles—he was not yet abbot—he gave me potions and let me lie on a palette between the beds of two great knights." Tom's voice had taken on a dreamy quality. His eyes were still closed. The tension in his face had eased, letting Aislinn see how young he truly was.

"The knights told many tales of their valor."

"It took your mind from your pain."

"Aye. At night was the worst. The potions to make us sleep did not work quickly enough, but they loosened the tongues of the warriors."

"Theron was wounded in the Crusades," Aislinn said absently.

"Aye, the sword cut across his chest oozed and pained him greatly. Few thought he would survive the wound-fever. Friar Giles used all his healing skills to save him. He spent many hours wiping his brow and listening to his babbling."

Aislinn sat up straighter on her stool. She had forgotten that Theron had spent a long time recovering at Battle Abbey.

"He talked about a great treasure he had found buried in a ruin in the desert. . . . He spoke of jewels . . ." Tom's voice drifted off and he succumbed to sleep.

Aislinn sat for a long time simply staring at his bent and broken body. Theron had been at Battle Abbey. Giles had been at Battle Abbey. She did not want to think of what those two things meant. And yet she could not ignore what suddenly seemed so obvious.

Giles had been at Battle Abbey. He had heard Theron speak of riches. Giles had been the churchman to officiate prayers at each of Aislinn's weddings. He had comforted her, told her of all the gossip and vicious rumors.

"Until I stayed within my chamber like a coward."

Just before Desmond took her to Mereworth, Giles had bidden her sign a paper deeding Sevenoaks and all within to the Church should anything happen to her and Desmond. She swallowed her pride, her pain, and her disgust and went to find Desmond. It was time they made a plan and executed it together, for now she knew why her wine had been poisoned.

"I will not let you put yourself in harm's way." Desmond slammed his fist upon the scarred oaken table. Coy raised a brow but kept his tongue.

"Desmond, it is the only way. We must invite Giles to return to Sevenoaks and we must do this. If we do not, we shall never have enough proof to take to the king," Aislinn said reasonably.

"If you are right, then he has tried to kill you—mayhap more than once." Desmond could barely suppress the fury he felt. "I will order the gates closed to him forever. He shall never have a chance to harm you again."

Aislinn felt a smile tickling the corners of her mouth. This was a serious business, and yet Desmond's rage and determination to keep her safe made her want to laugh and throw herself into his strong arms. Instead, she schooled her features and said, "My lord husband, we cannot do that. Forget that Giles is my kinsman; he is a powerful churchman. If we deny him entrance into

Sevenoaks, the deed will reach the king. Without proof, what shall we claim as our reason? Anything less than proving Giles's guilt or innocence would ruin us all. The gossipmongers will twist the tale until we are the ones brought before Henry."

Desmond's brows pinched into a frown. He was so stern and still, he appeared to be a statue carved of stone.

"You speak sensibly, lady," Coy said. "The abbot of Tunbridge Wells is rich and powerful."

"And if Aislinn's theory is correct, he wishes to be richer yet." Desmond uttered an oath. "How can a man as intelligent as Giles be chasing a mythical treasure? Surely he does not believe Theron managed to bring back a treasure in secret, and see that treasure hidden, again in secret. Such a bounty would have been found by now."

"Are you so sure 'tis not real?" Coy asked Desmond, his gaze sliding to Aislinn.

Desmond shook his head and chuckled. "Think, man, do not allow the glitter of mythical gold to blind you. If a treasure was here, wouldn't Theron have told Aislinn?"

"Mayhap." Coy's gaze lingered on her face, making her uncomfortable.

"And if there was a treasure to be had, wouldn't the lady have used it for herself?" Desmond demanded.

"Surely no woman could resist such temptation," Aislinn said softly.

"Exactly," Desmond said. "No, the treasure is no more than the fevered ramblings of an injured knight."

"We must invite Giles back." Aislinn reached out and lightly touched Desmond's sleeve. "We must bring him back and force him to move against—"

"I will not put you in harm's way."

"Nay, my lord, 'tis not I that will be his target. We needs must make it necessary for him to remove *you.*"

Desmond's jaw dropped. Aislinn's words hung like a veil of gloom.

"Me? Ah, I begin to see. In order to force Giles to move against me, he must first see me as an immediate threat."

"What was it about the other four men that made him do murder so quickly?" Coy raked his hand down his face.

"They took possession of the lord's chamber in a way I did not." Desmond's words were thoughtful. "I have spent my nights with my lady in her own private solar or at Mereworth. It has left the way open for him to search unimpeded."

"So now you must invite him back and make it known you intend to block him utterly. What can you do to put yourself squarely in Giles's path?"

Desmond smiled. It was cold, calculating, and made Aislinn's pulse quicken. "Send a rider to Tunbridge Wells. Invite my wife's cousin to attend me here at Sevenoaks."

"What reason shall the messenger give?"

"Tell him nothing. I am of a mind to see his reaction when he finds Aislinn alive and well. While he is absorbing that, we will tell the abbot that the lord's chamber is to be torn out and built larger in another part of the keep. If he truly believes a treasure is hidden there, that should make him desperate to see me dead and buried."

"I will go to the kitchens and speak with Cook. We must see that our larder is full of Giles's favorites." Aislinn smiled at Desmond. "And to make sure a supply of pale wine and savory meat pies will be made for us by her own hand before he arrives."

Desmond spent the rest of the day with the wise women at Lady Margaret's bedside. She was now awake for short periods, though she was not herself. She spoke of her youth and of her time locked within the walls of Sherborne Castle with Rowanne as prisoners. The reminder of how his sister had suffered only strengthened Desmond's resolve to keep Aislinn from harm.

He was gratified to know that she now believed him, and that they were working together to obtain proof to take to the king. He would need substantial evidence, for the king was not in a generous mood. His unruly barons had presented him an unpleasant surprise at parliament. Now Henry's power was even more limited. And it was rumored that Prince Edward was in a killing rage over the barons' treachery. Desmond did not want to find himself on the wrong side when that man came to power, for Desmond had no doubt Edward would see his own form of retribution exacted upon those who had wronged his father.

"We are ready, my lord."

The wise woman's voice drew Desmond's attention. "You have found an antidote?"

"Antidote? Nay, but mayhap a way to keep the poison from killing."

Desmond raised a brow. "From your lips to God's ears, for I have no desire to see my lady wife a widow."

"The abbot of Tunbridge Wells," the herald announced as Giles swept into the great hall. His expression was dour, his robes flowing as he swept a quick glance at the empty chair beside Desmond.

"My lord, I received your invitation. Has something happened to Aislinn?"

"I have not said so." Desmond let his gaze slide to the empty chair his lady usually occupied at his side.

Giles did not answer immediately. He was sly and cunning. It would take all of Desmond's planning and the wise women's skill to catch him.

"Why have you summoned me?" Giles asked.

Desmond drummed his fingers on the scrubbed wood

of the table. He had hoped—in vain, it would seem—that Giles would simply reveal himself. Now there was no choice but to play out the dangerous charade and hope he lived to see the end.

"I have great need of you and your skills, Giles—great need."

"Something dire has happened; I can see by your manner." Giles stepped forward, his expression altered. He became the benevolent churchman, willing to comfort. "You may depend upon me, Baron."

"Please sit." Desmond indicated the chair beside him. Giles hesitated a moment, his gaze sliding over the ornately carved wood. Did he think of Aislinn? Did he have one moment of regret that he had put poisoned wine in her chamber?

Desmond clamped his jaw shut. He wanted nothing more than to yank Giles from the chair and put a blade into his black heart. Instead, he poured out two goblets of rich, red wine.

"Drink, Giles." Desmond picked up his own cup and sipped.

Giles frowned. His impatience was showing. He picked up the goblet and took one drink. "Now tell me of your trouble, Baron."

"Oh, there is no trouble, Giles. We just wanted you here to bless the new lord's solar as it is being built. Tomorrow we begin pulling down the old one," Aislinn said brightly from behind Giles's chair. He started and jumped up, his eyes rounding like bowls. The goblet slipped from his fingers, the wine spilling, staining the scrubbed wood.

Twenty-three

"Aislinn—but you—"

"Aye, Giles?" she asked coyly, slipping to Desmond's side and leaning into his strength when her own flagged. If she had any doubts about Giles's actions, they were forever erased by the look in his eyes. He had expected to say prayers over her corpse. She had still held a glimmer of hope that they were all wrong—wrong when Tom said he saw Giles pouring a goblet of pale wine.

"You—you are looking well, cousin." He recovered with a cough.

"Aye, I am well. My lord husband takes my health and protection very seriously," she said softly. And she meant it. There was something warm, strong, and wonderful in knowing that Desmond would keep her from harm.

"We will have a feast tonight, and on the morrow we begin the work on the old lord's solar. I have brought extra craftsmen from Mereworth to take up the floor in the old chamber. We can mayhap reuse some of the stones." Desmond nodded to the new swell of men. The great hall was full, crowded from wall to wall with brawny knights and men-at-arms. They had been brought from Mereworth, but a large group had been summoned from Lady Margaret's keep, Letchworth. There was an impressive army at Desmond's beck and call.

"Aye, I will say prayers of benediction and protection

upon your venture. Now, if you will excuse me, I have something I must attend."

Giles swept from the room. Desmond nodded to Coy. Like a shadow slipping along a path, he faded from the crush of people and followed. Soon Desmond would know where Giles had gone and why.

"Now, my lady, we will spend every moment in the lord's solar, thereby preventing Giles from searching. If we are correct, he will have no choice but to kill me."

Desmond and Aislinn sat together on a low bench in the lord's solar. He had returned from seeing the wise women. His skin glowed and he smelled of wild honey.

"The wise women are brewing a new medicament for Lady Margaret."

Aislinn felt a stab of guilt. If she had been more vigilant—or suspicious . . . mayhap she could have prevented all this sorrow.

"Do not look so sad." Desmond made as if to tip up her chin with his knuckle, but at the last minute he closed his hand and did not touch her.

"Soon we will bring all to rights." She reached up and grabbed a handful of hair beside his ears. Then she pulled his face to hers. He kissed her, probing her mouth with his tongue. Aislinn was ashamed because even as she grieved for the four men who had wedded her, she could not deny the heat of desire that Desmond ignited.

Was she a wanton? How could she think of coupling when Lady Margaret lay ill and Desmond was prepared to sacrifice himself?

Later that night, Desmond opened the door to Coy's light, prearranged knock. He swept inside.

"He goes to the crofter's cottage on the edge of

Sevenoaks Hold." Coy stripped off his gauntlets and laid them on the chest. "Smoke was coming from the hole in the thatch when I left."

"Of course. The cottage was filled with herbs and roots," Desmond recalled with a frown. "I should've realized what we found in that place were the medicaments of a healer."

"Or a killer," Coy provided. "How is Lady Margaret?"

"She will live. She takes a bit of broth and ale, but her body trembles and is weak. 'Twill be some time before she is herself again."

"There is something else, my lord." Coy raked his hand down his face.

"Aye?"

"Tracks of where a wagon was kept beside the croft. They came straight as an arrow's flight from Sevenoaks."

"The wounded knight bound for Rye?"

"Aye. It looked as if the weight had set for some time. I believe he dosed the man and returned unseen to Sevenoaks to do what he wished while we thought the fox was elsewhere."

"Desmond, I am so afraid for you," Aislinn admitted, looking up into his strong face. The more she heard about her cousin, the less she realized she knew of him. "Is there no other way?"

"Nay, love. We needs must have proof."

"Have you so much faith in those three crones?" Coy asked, his dark brows knitted together.

"Aye, and in you and Aislinn. For it will be up to you to see I take no food or drink that is tainted. The rest will be up to my three witches and their magic armor." Desmond grinned grimly.

Aislinn dressed in the gown Desmond chose for her. It was sewn from a rare, deep black velvet, the full, draping cuffs trimmed in ermine and silver wire thread. At her throat was a silver mesh collar that went from collarbone to jawbone.

"Ah, wife, you are most beauteous," Desmond said. "Your hair is like a beacon."

"I must braid it now, if you will help me."

"Nay, leave it down. Let it flow down your back like a river of fire. This is how I like it best. Wear only a simple circlet at your brow." Desmond nipped at the lobe of her ear. "Now, I must dress for my feast." Desmond strode to a trunk and flipped open the lid. Then he pulled out a tunic of black velvet. The Vaudry coat of arms was worked in silver wire on the front. Down his left sleeve was the du Luc device.

"They could have been cut from the same bolt of cloth," Aislinn said in amazement.

"Aye, 'tis as if fate knew we would come to this night. Let us hope the rest of our destiny is written with a kindly hand."

The reminder of what was to happen chilled Aislinn and froze the small smile on her lips. Her stomach clenched painfully.

"Desmond?"

He pulled on his tunic and turned to her. Their eyes met in a sultry union. "Aislinn, if our plans should come to ruin—"

"Nay, do not say it."

"Listen to me. If I fail, then I want you to go with Lady Margaret to Letchworth. Galen and Coy will protect you. Leave this accursed pile of stones to Giles and never let him near you again."

"You will not fail. You cannot because—"

"Because you love me?" he asked.

"Nay, because I do not yet love you, you foolish peacock. If you will have it as you wish, and earn my love, then you needs must live—live for many, many long years."

He took her into his arms and crushed her into a hot, long kiss. Then he made tender, slow love to her.

As if it might be the last time.

The lute players sent strains of sweet melody wafting to the smoke-stained rafters of the great hall. Wine, sweetmeats, bread, cheese, fruit, puddings, and roasted meat of all kinds were in such abundance, the tables nearly groaned from the weight.

Aislinn ate nothing. She watched Desmond's cup and trencher—prepared especially by Cook under the scrutiny of young Tom—like a hawk. While Desmond had gone to his three wise women, they had made sure all was as it should be for the feast.

Giles sat at Desmond's side and smiled. He ate and drank nothing either, Aislinn noticed. Perchance he was afraid of spoiling his fine costume. He wore the opulent robes of his office, and bright saffron gloves completed his ensemble. Aislinn had seen the gauntlets before, but she could not place them.

"Smile, wife, this is a joyous occasion," Desmond urged.

"Indeed. Your lord husband is so prosperous that he is prepared to enlarge Sevenoaks," Giles agreed. "Why did you decide to begin with the lord's solar?" he asked blandly.

"The chamber is not to my liking. I would design a chamber large enough for my lady wife to share with me if she chooses. The chamber needs must accommodate two beds." Desmond settled a look upon Aislinn. She heated beneath his gaze.

Did he really wish to have her with him all night— every night? It was almost unheard of for a lord and lady to share one sleeping chamber. But then, it was almost unheard of for the lord and lady to have complete privacy when they slept, but that was the way of Sevenoaks. Mayhap another change would not be unwelcome.

"I would choose to be at your side, my lord husband," Aislinn said suddenly, surprising herself and Desmond. He smiled and winked. She knew he was silently asking her if she loved him yet. She shook her head nay, and he broke into gales of hearty, deep laughter.

"It would appear you share a private jest. Come, let us have another cup, and then I will perform the blessing upon you, Baron." Giles's voice was harsh.

"Aye." Desmond picked up his goblet. "I agree, Abbot, 'tis time."

Giles's voice droned on in a dry monotone as he evoked God's protection and blessing upon Desmond as lord of Sevenoaks. Aislinn silently prayed along with him.

Finally, the prayer was finished. Desmond smiled broadly as the castle folk cheered. Giles flicked a gaze at Aislinn, then he approached Desmond with his gauntlet covered hand extended.

In a flash of clarity, she realized where she had seen those saffron gloves. Giles wore them at all of her weddings. And then he shook hands with all her husbands—save one.

"Nay—" She took a step, intending to warn Desmond, but a strong hand stayed her. Coy was at her side, keeping her where she was.

"Nay, lady, you must not interrupt, nor make any move to warn him."

"I know how the poison has been given."

"What say you, lady?" Coy speared her with a dark look.

" 'Tis the gauntlet. Desmond must not touch the gauntlet."

She and Coy stared as Desmond grasped the saffron glove tightly. Giles smiled as he patted the back of Desmond's hand with one gloved hand and clasped him for long minutes with the other.

Aislinn's breath lodged in the back of her throat. Desmond was surely doomed.

Time had no meaning while Desmond stood holding Giles's hand. Aislinn pushed her way through the throng of castle folk, but when she finally reached her husband, Giles was moving away.

"I am fatigued. Pray forgive me if I take me leave now." Giles melted into the crowd of people.

"Oh, Desmond," Aislinn whispered in his ear. "You needs must hurry to the wise women."

"Nay, my lady, there is no time. For even as we speak I can feel the poison." He turned his hand over, staring at his palm. There was a stain. He looked at Aislinn and collapsed in a heap at her feet.

"Desmond!" She kneeled beside him. Coy was there in a nonce. He ran his hand over Desmond's face.

" 'Tis too late, my lady. My lord Desmond is dead."

Aislinn stared at the golden visage of her husband as the great hall began to tilt and shift. Then she remembered no more.

Twenty-four

Aislinn opened her eyes. She was in a dark place. No taper pierced the darkness; no glow of a lamp drove back the gloom. It was just as well, for the darkness in her heart could not be assuaged.

Desmond was dead. She had no reason to live.

She closed her eyes. It mattered not where she was, or who had brought her to this place of silence and darkness. All that mattered was that her beloved Desmond was dead.

Beloved.

Why had she not told him? It did not signify that he did not or could not love her. She did love him—had loved him from the first word he spoke to her. Her mind cast back to that moment, the brief magic moment when they had met unexpectedly under the stars. Her distraught mind conjured the smells and the sights of the maze. Each breath brought the attar of night-blooming flowers.

She opened her eyes again. The first star pierced the black covering of night above her.

"I am in the maze. But how? Only Desmond and I know of the maze."

She sat up, finding herself upon the bench—their bench. Her heart beat hard and painfully in her breast. Though she knew it was foolish and impossible, she searched the dark corners of the garden. And then, like dawn breaking after a devastating storm, she saw the gilt of his hair.

"Desmond?" she whispered. "Desmond, is it truly you, my love? Are you a spirit come to haunt me?"

"Ah, so you will say you love a ghost but not a man?" a deep, smooth masculine voice asked from the shadows.

"I do love you. Though I know it will be my undoing, I cannot help but love you."

"How long I have waited to hear you say those words." He stepped from the shelter of the vine-covered wall. His arms were strong and real as he embraced her.

"But how?" she asked as he sipped her flesh and kissed her eyes, her nose, her lips.

"The wise women showed me all manner of ways to deliver poison. But only one allows each victim to die in a different way, at different intervals of time. There were only two things constant about the four men's deaths: you, and the presence of Giles, the good abbot of Tunbridge Wells."

She looked into his face, so dark and obscure in the night. The moon was just rising. By tomorrow night it would be full and ripe in the sky.

"And I knew you could never do murder, so it needs must be Giles. But he did not do it with food or drink; of that I was certain. It left only a handful of possibilities. The wise women and I examined every one."

"Why did you not tell me?" She was suddenly gripped by a burst of anger. Her heart had broken when she thought he'd died. "Coy knew, and so he played the farce with you, pronouncing you dead in front of all the castle."

"I could not, lest I was wrong."

"I know 'tis done with the saffron gauntlets, I remembered him wearing them at each wedding, but how?"

"A paste of sheep's lanolin and powerful poison coats the palm of the glove. When Giles gives a blessing and touches the head, face, or hands, the ointment begins to soak into the skin. The longer he holds it to the flesh, the quicker the poison begins to do its deadly work."

"But how did you—"

"Beeswax, my love. The wise women melted down a dozen combs and coated my bare flesh with beeswax. Any part of me that was outside my clothing was covered, but we knew not if it would be enough."

"That was why you smelled like honey when you came to the lord's chamber."

"Ah, so you noticed. I wondered if you would. I returned to them and refreshed my magic armor after we caused so much of it to melt with our bed sport." He grinned at her.

She rubbed her hands over his face and hands. "But I do not feel it now."

He grinned. " 'Tis most painful to remove. I trow my skin will be smooth and hairless as a skinned leveret for many a sennight."

She laughed as Desmond pulled back the sleeve of his tunic to show her his new hairless state. With a giggle she rubbed her palm over his arm.

"Mayhap I will take a liking to this, my lord. Perchance you could do it at each full moon as a ritual before our coupling."

"Vixen, you just want to see me tear up and scream in agony as all my hair is yanked from my body."

They kissed. It was a kiss of joining, acceptance, and joy. She was his now, for good or ill. There would be no turning back. He had her: her heart her soul and her undying love.

"As much as I would like to tumble you in the maze, we needs must hurry."

"Why?"

" 'Tis time to catch the killer of Sevenoaks."

Hand in hand they made their way through the secret passage. Desmond had warned Aislinn to make no sound, no matter what she saw or heard. When they reached the portal that split and went either to the lord's solar or her chamber, they went to her chamber. Together they went to her door and opened it just a crack.

The sound of boots on the stone corridor drew Aislinn's eyes. It was Giles. He looked around quickly and slid the heavy cross he wore from his neck. This he inserted into the lock. The secret key opened the door to the lord's chamber.

Desmond stepped back and drew Aislinn with him. Silently he closed her outer chamber door. "Now we shall go and see what he does."

They entered the secret passage and took the branch to the lord's solar.

A light flared inside the chamber. It created a square ring of light around the seam of the secret door.

Desmond pulled her nearer to him. She could smell his manly musk, feel the heat wafting off his body. It was difficult, but she managed to ignore the allure of being so close to him. She squinted through the thin crack at the perimeter of the secret door.

There was Giles, the abbot of Tunbridge Wells, her trusted cousin—murderer. He had a slender bar in his gloved hand. He was trying to prize up a floor stone beside the hearth.

She and Desmond watched him for a long while as he tried one location and then another. His face was contorted by frustrated rage.

Desmond squeezed her hand. Then she felt his warm breath on her earlobe.

"Do not move from the safety of this spot."

And then, like a candle being snuffed, he was gone. She no longer felt the warmth and protection of his nearness. A swish of air around her ankles. Desmond had opened the portal. He was inside the lord's chamber.

With Giles.

* * *

Desmond kept to the deep shadows of the chamber. Giles was holding the candle, the flickering glow illuminating the harsh planes of his face and little else. His features were gaunt, ghoulish in the wavering light. He set the candle aside and picked up the slender rod again. With an oath hardly fitting a churchman, he tried to pry up an edge of the flooring stones.

Whether the treasure was fact or myth, it was apparent Giles believed it. Desmond was fascinated as he watched. There stood a man who had respect, power, and wealth beyond calculation, and yet it was not enough.

It struck Desmond then, like a sharp, painful blow: he was content. He was content with his wife, the enchanting minx who wanted him to love her in return.

He needed to end this ghastly charade with her cousin and keep her safe so he could bask in peace in the joy of being wedded to her.

"Giles," Desmond said softly.

The abbot's head came up and he cocked his head like a hound, listening, focusing—unsure whether he had really heard.

"Giles, Abbot of Tunbridge Wells," Desmond said, only slightly louder.

Giles spun around, his face a study in terror. He raised the slender rod in a gesture of protection.

"Giles, the murderer, the poisoner, the liar," Desmond said louder and stepped from the shelter of deep shadow.

Giles's face contorted. "Nay, you are dead. I touched you. You cannot have survived."

"Aye, you touched me with your poison glove, your weapon of death. But yet I am here."

Giles looked at him hard. His upper lip curled back in a snarl. "I do not know how you escaped—"

"I was more fortunate than the last four, was I not? Tell me, Giles, why?"

"You would not understand." Giles narrowed his eyes. "You are a man content to obey his king no matter how outrageous the command."

"And you, Abbot, what kind of man are you?"

"I have striven to bring down the monarchy. I have funded the Church and Crusades to make them more powerful than the king. He is a dolt, just as his father was. Lackland lost half of France. And his warrior brother spent no more than a small march of days in England as he pursued pretty boys and battles. I want no single man to have power. There are others like me who believe parliament alone will be a better solution, but I need more money."

"But you are wealthy."

"Do you know how much money it takes to overthrow a king?" Giles laughed. "It takes all I have and more. Theron spoke of the treasure. I need only find it and England will be the better for it. Let me search—search with me; you can aid my noble cause."

"Nay, Giles. You went too far when you tried to harm Aislinn," Desmond said softly. "I could overlook much, but I cannot overlook that sin."

"Ah, ever the gallant, eh? But you will not leave this room alive. Aislinn has become too independent-thinking. She must go as well. But fortunately she has deeded Sevenoaks to the Church, and by the time Henry learns of the sad news, I will have found the treasure."

Desmond lunged at the same moment Giles brought the iron bar down. The blow struck between his neck and his shoulder, sending spikes of white-hot pain down his arm. He drove his head into Giles's chest, sending him backward. They crashed into one of the low chests, splintering the wood with the combined weight of their bodies.

Desmond snatched a spare dagger from the pile of armor in the corner. He turned to find Giles gripping a knife.

"You have been nothing but trouble since you came," Giles hissed. "Turning Aislinn away from me, giving her back her courage and her dignity."

" 'Tis time there was a reckoning, Giles."

"Mayhap someday, but not now, and not by the likes of you. Vainglorious popinjay. Do you know what it is to dream? To plan? I have worked for more than six years to find Theron's treasure, and by the Rood, I will have it."

They rushed each other, Giles trying to come in low to pierce Desmond from underneath. They did a lethal dance, thrusting and dodging. Both drew blood; neither gained the advantage.

"Why did you want to hurt Aislinn by telling her she was hated and cursed?" Desmond asked.

Giles smiled coldly. "I did not wish to wound her, but I needed her to be submissive to me. What better way to ensure she would not thwart my attempts to find the treasure than by becoming her only friend? The rumors, the gossip kept her vulnerable and in her solar."

"And those rumors were no more than your own creation, were they, Giles?"

"Ah, so you have divined all the pieces of the puzzle." He lunged quickly, catching Desmond's side. The air left him in a painful rush.

"When she told me of the curse of her hair, I began to suspect. The more I learned, the more suspicious I became. Why did you not simply go to Aislinn and ask her permission to search?"

For a brief moment, Giles's face froze. It was as if he were considering that possibility for the first time. Desmond took the opportunity to lunge at Giles, but his foot slid along the discarded bar. He was off balance. And that was what Giles had been waiting for. The churchman stepped behind him, bringing his arm around, pricking the flesh of his neck with the point of the blade.

"Now you shall die," Giles said.

Aislinn stepped through the open portal into the deep shadows at Giles's back. He never even knew she was there—until she put her eating dagger between his ribs. Desmond slipped from his grasp. Giles turned. His eyes widened as he looked first at Aislinn and then at the portal behind her.

"The secret door—the door to the treasure—you knew all the time." He slumped to the floor with a fount of blood gushing from his twisted lips.

"Is he dead?" Aislinn asked, staring at the man she had loved and trusted since she was a child.

Desmond bent and touched his throat, feeling for the beat of his heart. There was none.

"He is dead."

"Now Theron and the other men he murdered may finally rest," Aislinn said before the room went black around her.

Desmond stood over Aislinn, watching her, protecting her while Coy and some of his men moved Giles's body to the chapel. The three wise women, Coy, and all the Letchworth knights had been in the corridor to hear Giles's confession. There was no question the proof was damning and would be enough for Henry.

Aislinn moaned softly and came awake with a start. She sat up in bed. One glance at the small bloodstain on the stones of the floor and she began to tremble like a leaf in the wind.

"Do not cry, sweeting. Do not weep for Giles. He was a taker of life; you administered justice."

She turned her tear-streaked face to Desmond. The soft light from the candle on the tall iron stand made her hair bright as flame. "I do not cry for Giles; I cry because you came near to dying once again."

Desmond's heart was cloven in twain by her words. This brave, true nymph touched him in a way he never knew was possible. And, he realized, he cared for her, too.

"Oh, Aislinn, what am I to do with you?"

"I know not, my lord husband."

"I guess I will simply have to love you," he said with a chuckle. " 'Twould be foolish for me to deny the truth. I love you; I adore you. I will cherish you and cosset you all the days of my life."

She gazed at him with wide eyes. Then her lips turned up in a small smile. " 'Tis my duty to accept your love. Tell me, husband, do you now wish to take up Giles's quest for the treasure?" Aislinn asked softly.

"The true treasure of Sevenoaks is here in my arms, lady wife. I have always known that. I need no treasure but your true heart and love."

He swept her up and kissed her soundly as dawn broke over the ragged walls of Sevenoaks. And he could have sworn he heard the soughing of laughter in the secret passage.

Epilogue

Desmond walked down the corridor. When he reached the wall, he turned the ring. As the wall swung away, the scent of night-blooming flowers filled his nose. He looked at the sundial and the bench beside it, where his lovely lady waited.

"You must have been anxious to arrive before me." He chuckled and swept her up into his arms. The king had been sent the proof, Giles's body had been returned to Tunbridge Wells for burial, and Lady Margaret was taking food on her own. So the two had vowed to meet each other in the garden when the moon rose fat and round as a pearl plucked fresh from the sea.

"It has all come to rights, Desmond," Aislinn sighed. A cooling wind blew up. It swept down the curtain wall and through the maze, sounding like many voices whispering secrets, rattling branches and leaves together. A cloud passed over the moon, temporarily suspending the world in darkness. It passed quickly, bathing the maze in bright yellow light. Desmond and Aislinn sat down on the bench and held each other's hands.

The moonbeams shone upon the face of the sundial. A pale shaft of light grew and strengthened. Suddenly, reflected off something in the face, it arced toward the wall of the castle. A stone was illuminated with the moonbeam.

Desmond and Aislinn looked at each other. Then, in one voice, they began to recite the lay.

"The time is marked when the moon is ripe. Surrender the stars and carry a light."

"Surrender the stars—it means go inside," Desmond said.

"And carry a light. Do you have a candle with you?"

"No. Fetch one from the secret corridor."

Aislinn dashed to the corridor and grabbed the first candle she saw in the wall. When she returned, Desmond was at the illuminated stone, running his fingers around the mortar.

"Here, a lever of iron." Another doorway, nearly obscured by vines, began to creak open. It did not work as smoothly or as silently as the other.

"Theron did not tell me of this," Aislinn said in wonder.

"The lord and the lady share a door," Desmond repeated another line of the riddle. "Come, let us follow and see where it leads."

Aislinn smiled and took the hand he offered. The corridor wound around and back upon itself. It was dusty, musty, and inhabited by many spiders. She had no notion of where they would emerge. But suddenly they reached the end of the passage.

Desmond ran his hand along the edge of the ceiling and walls, feeling for another lever while Aislinn held the candle.

"There is nothing," he told her.

She held the candle aloft, looking at the stones. "See here, Desmond, at the top, these strange carvings. What do they mean?"

He took the candle from her and held it higher. There was strange writing on both upper corners. And beneath the writing there were shallow carvings of a hand—one large, one small.

"The lord and the lady share a door," he mused. "Come, Aislinn, put your hand on this side. Yes, just like that."

He put his hand in the other indentation. "Now, together. Shove."

It took a moment or two. There was a sprinkling of dust, the grind of long-unmoved gears, and the rasp of stone against stone. And then the stone began to swing upward and away.

Aislinn and Desmond stood there, staring as the heavy block pulled away from their hands. It slowly became part of the ceiling. The single candle glinted on what they found.

"Riches untold beneath the floor." Desmond finished the riddle as he stared at jewels, pearls, gold, and silver. There were finely wrought rings and thick chains, necklaces, and bracelets. The recessed chamber was filled with a sultan's booty.

"Oh, Desmond, you have found the treasure of Sevenoaks."

He pulled her into his arms and kissed her. She tasted of excitement and wonder. It was a powerful aphrodisiac.

"I agree, Aislinn; I have found the treasure, the most precious treasure of all—you, my beloved lady."

Author's Note

Though the Vaudry family is fictional, it is based on the actual family of Robert de Vaux, who laid the first stones of Lanercost Abbey. Most of the locations are real: Sevenoaks, Mereworth, and Tunbridge Wells, to name a few. Many incidents in this book actually took place.

In 1264, King Henry III beheaded 315 archers at Combwell Priory near Fleniwell, Kent, when his favorite cook was accidently shot and killed. It was said that the king had a particular fondness for spiced blackbirds and that accounted for his rage. I think it was the hot blood he inherited from his grandmother, Eleanor of Aquitaine.

In 1269, Henry III did complete most of the rebuilding of Westminster Abbey and rebuilt many of the tombs there as well. Angered by this spending, the ambitious barons, led by de Montfort the younger, did conspire to present a document at Parliament that further limited the king's powers. And there was a poison that could be made into a poultice that could be absorbed into the skin, and which apparently was used with some regularity.

Recently, during an archaeological excavation of Spitalfields in London, the skeleton of a young medieval man with broken knees, who lived his life in pain and on crutches, was unearthed. The character Tom is my tribute to that young man. The rest of the intrigue in *Surrender the Stars* is my own invention.

If you enjoyed *Surrender the Stars,* I hope you will read the next Vaudry book, *Embrace the Sun.* It is the story of Lochlyn Vaudry Armstrong. Born an English lordling but raised as a Scots reiver, he is neither fish nor fowl. Lochlyn hates all things English, even his own parentage. He struggles to find his place in the world and on his journey finds a love so strong it cannot be denied. Look for *Embrace the Sun* in November 2002.